A MILITARY EDUCATION

★ ★ ★

ANTIQUE DRUM

John Ogden

Antique Drum

KENYA SUEZ ADEN

The sequel to *Silken Dalliance*
and the third book in the trilogy
A Military Education

Thorntons
Faringdon

First published in Great Britain in 2019 by

Thorntons

The Old Barn, Walnut Court, Faringdon SN7 7JH

Typeset in Plantin 10.5 on 14 by Jenni Navratil Graphic Art and Design, Oxford
Printed in Great Britain by Biddles Ltd., Norfolk

A catalogue record for this book is available from The British Library.

ISBN 978 0 85455 047 0

We cannot revive old factions
We cannot restore old policies
Or follow an antique drum.

T S Eliot
Little Gidding

Great Britain has lost an empire
and has not yet found a role.

Dean Acheson

For my sons Peregrine and William,
that they may know something of these days

I am not I. You are not she or he.
They are not they.

Nor is a pound sterling a pound.
The 1955 pound would be worth at least £35 today. In Kenya, the
currency was shillings and there were 20 shillings to the pound.

Contents

1

A riddle and an emergency

'Did he jump or was he pushed?' asked Burgo.

'The court of enquiry found that he jumped,' I replied.

'Yes, yes, I know that, Miles, but what do *you* think?'

Indeed, what did I think?

Burgo Howard and I were sitting in my tent in the officers' mess lines in our camp outside Nairobi. It was the mid 1950s and we were in Kenya to fight in the Mau Mau emergency. We were serving with the Second Battalion of the Prince Regent's Light Infantry, which we had both joined some years before. We had been together in Hong Kong, and fought in the Korean War where Burgo had won a Military Cross. More recently, we had served in Germany in the British Army of the Rhine, stationed on the border between West and East Germany as cold war frontiersmen.

Over three months ago we had been at sea in a troopship, steaming south off the east coast of Africa and a day's run from Mombasa in Kenya, all geared up to join the British and colonial forces fighting in the Mau Mau Emergency. We were commanded by Dennis Parker Brown who, in his two years of command, had developed into a manic, obsessive, and unpredictable autocrat, a Jekyll and Hyde character. One minute he was an educated, charming, and understanding commanding officer, the next an hysterical, screaming tyrant.

During our last night in the ship a man had been seen to fall overboard and a lifebelt was thrown to him. We assembled the battalion and roll call after roll call found every man present. Then we realised that the colonel was nowhere to be seen. The ship's captain had already turned the troopship about and was steaming north. As dawn broke, a lifebelt was spotted floating unattended and a boat was lowered to collect it. The lifebelt was brought on board, a severed arm clutching it. On the little finger of the hand was the colonel's signet ring.

'Whatever the court of enquiry found, I think he was pushed,' said Burgo. 'The question is who pushed him?'

We landed at Mombasa in an uncertain state of mind, relieved that the tyrant had gone, yet appalled that we should have lost our commanding officer. George Bulman, the second-in-command of the battalion, was standing on the quay to receive us. He had flown out to Kenya six weeks before with a small advance party. An old friend, George had been my company commander in Korea, where he had been badly wounded in the leg in an early action. He now walked with a slight limp and had his boots and shoes specially made, as one leg was a little shorter than the other.

As soon as George, moustachioed and hair sleeked back, had come on board he assembled the officers, displaying his usual *sprezzatura*. 'We've come here to fight the Mau Mau,' he said. 'What's happened has happened and it mustn't interfere with what we've come to do.' With these words, he had taken command and immediately we all felt grateful and relieved.

'Who do you think,' Burgo asked me, 'are the suspects?'

Like a newsreel, there flitted through my mind everything that had happened since we had landed. First, there was the day's journey by rail up to Nairobi, climbing five thousand feet from sea level across a vast plain. Then followed a month at our tented camp on the old polo ground at Muthaiga at the northern outskirts of the city, as we acclimatised to living at such a height. During this period each company attended battle camp, learning how to fight and live in the forest. We had our first glimpse of Nairobi, half a carefully-architected tropical city with boulevards lined with bougainvillea, half a shanty town. Despite the prevalence of uniforms, it looked an uncannily peaceful place. We savoured our first tastes of colonial life at the Muthaiga Club and in the city's fleshpots, limited but lively.

'Among the officers,' said Burgo, 'I think Jasper is the leading suspect. He has the motives in spades, that is if an officer could be capable of committing such a terrible act, which I think Jasper could in the circumstances.'

Jasper Knox was younger and shorter than me, lightly built, lithe, and a born horseman, with beautiful hands and dark, wavy hair. He spoke with a slight drawl. He was the fourth generation of his family in the regiment. We had been at school together, though he was younger than me, and we had an affinity, as our fathers had served together in the regiment and both had been killed in the Second World War. His grandfather had been killed in the Great War and his great-grandfather, General Sir Charles Knox, had been the colonel in chief of the regiment at the turn of the century.

Jasper had run foul of Dennis Parker Brown. The trouble had been horses and envy, for Jasper had won more races than the colonel. Whenever Jasper committed the slightest misdemeanour the colonel had jumped on him and punished him unjustly. Jasper had taken to drinking rather heavily. On the last night in the ship I'd noticed that he had been quite sober, and since we'd landed he'd hardly drunk at all. He had been one of the most proficient of the younger officers in learning how to fight in the forest, demonstrating this in Operation Hammer, our first action. We had moved up to the Aberdares, the mountain range whose slopes were covered in the forest where the Mau Mau gangs hid and from which they made their sorties. We had learned how hard patrolling could be, and how demanding the forest. It was Jasper who had made our first kill.

During this operation, Lieutenant Colonel Rex Topham, who was next in line for command and had been serving as a staff officer

at general headquarters in Egypt, had taken over from George Bulman, and George had reverted to being second in command. Rex
had commanded a company in Korea, where I had got to know
him. He could be a fiery fellow, and he cultivated a braggadocio
style, but he had a heart and was a fair man. An experienced and
able soldier, he had commanded a battalion in Burma during the
Second World War.

'Among the soldiery I suspect Big Steel and Little Steel,' said
Burgo. 'I once overheard them discuss what they'd do to him if
they had the chance. And both have the guts to have done it.'

Big Steel was my company serjeant major and Little Steel, his
younger brother, was the Vickers machine gun platoon serjeant.
Their surname was Whettingsteel, hence the nicknames. They
were all one could look for in senior NCOs and I doubted either
could ever push any officer overboard, whatever he thought of
him. Only minutes ago I had walked from my company office,
another tent, where I had been talking to them both. Nothing in
their faces or behaviour since leaving the ship suggested that either
might have anything to hide.

'Come on, now, Miles,' said Burgo. 'Surely you can share your
thoughts with me?'

'I would prefer to think,' I said, 'that he jumped. It's perfectly
plausible, as he was clearly out of his mind. No witnesses came
forward to say they saw him pushed. So he jumped. Can't you
accept that?'

'I concede he could have jumped,' Burgo replied. 'But half the
battalion would have liked to have pushed him so I believe he was
pushed. We must get to the bottom of this, we really must, and
not rest until the culprit has been found. We owe it to D.P. Brown
whatever we thought of him. Justice must be seen to be done.'

D.P. Brown was short not only for Dennis Parker Brown but for
Down Penis Brown, a nickname coined by Adam Hare as Brown was
such a puritan and spoilsport. It had caught on immediately. Burgo
and Adam were close, Burgo being fascinated by Adam's wit and
erudition, and Adam amused by Burgo's capacity for mischief.

'Now I come to think of it,' continued Burgo, 'I distinctly remember saying to you, after D. P. Brown had shut down the all
ranks show on the ship, that Jasper was in a murderous mood.'

'And don't I remember, Burgo, you, too, saying more than once
that you could murder D. P. Brown? I'm glad I wasn't called as a
witness at the court of enquiry and cross examined.'

'Merely a figure of speech, old boy. After all, almost everyone
felt like murdering him.'

'Precisely. Which is why no one did,' I said. 'You're being
melodramatic, Burgo, and a tease. Drop it. It'll do you no good.
The case is closed.'

'*You* may think so,' said Burgo. '*I* shall continue to investigate.'

'Well, go and investigate whether Corporal Cheke has opened
the bar. I'm thirsty. And while you're doing that I shall change.
We're due at the Muthaiga Club for dinner, aren't we?'

'You bet,' said Burgo. 'Abyssinia.'

'Bugger off.'

I took my uniform off, wrapped a towel round me, and walked
through the lines to the shower house, where I stood under a
stream of cold water washing my hair and soaping myself. Burgo
was being contentious, as ever, but I had a niggling feeling he
might be right. The court of enquiry into D.P. Brown's death had
been hastily formed. It had called few witnesses beyond the ship's
captain, our doctor, and our adjutant, Francis Bowerman, and
had come to a quick decision. It had been accepted that Parker
Brown had jumped, for his behaviour had been shown to prove
he was not in his right mind. I suspected that general headquarters
in Nairobi had wanted to close the case as soon as possible. No
one had come forward to question the verdict except Burgo, who
was now cavilling at it and wouldn't leave it alone. I decided he
was just playing one of his games. Perhaps, I thought, we'll never
know what really happened.

When we had arrived at Muthaiga the camp had been mostly
tented. One of Colonel Rex's first acts had been to persuade general

headquarters to make it more permanent and he got permission and the resources to build. Wooden buildings were springing up everywhere. The centre of the camp was the old polo ground, a vast green sward now serving as a parade ground and sports field. On three sides were the company lines and battalion headquarters lay on the fourth. Trees lined the entrance and the road along which battalion headquarters lay; there were more trees on the perimeter which was simply fenced. Everything was green, including the tents. The corporals', serjeants', and officers' messes, and the NAAFI, were now housed in wooden buildings giving better protection from the rains. The officers' mess, for example, comprised a large hut serving as the anteroom, with French windows overlooking a garden; a smaller, but still substantial, hut served as the dining room with some outbuildings for the kitchen and mess servants. All of us slept in tents. Colonel Rex was determined we should be comfortable in camp when we were not fighting in the forests.

We had a reputation for making ourselves comfortable, a matter of envy to some and criticism from others. We were not an ancient regiment but had strong traditions. Raised during the Revolutionary and Napoleonic Wars, we had formed part of a brigade of light infantry trained by Sir John Moore — experimental and avant-garde troops — and had earned an enviable reputation in the Peninsula under Wellington. We were jealous of our light infantry standing and felt elitist about this. Our methods and disciplines still reflected Moore's humane and revolutionary training. After Waterloo, the regiment had been adopted by the Prince Regent — hence our name — thereby allowing him to claim a close connection with a regiment that had been in the thick of the fight. He used to say to the Duke of Wellington, 'I was there, wasn't I, Duke?' And the Duke used to reply, 'I have often heard Your Highness so remark. Your regiment certainly was.' Later, when he had become George IV, he stationed the regiment at Brighton to be his bodyguard. The officers of the time frequented the Theatre Royal. On one occasion they found themselves being pelted with eggs and vegetables. They drew their swords and cleared the theatre. The audience had not been pelting them but the King and Mrs Fitzherbert, who had crept into their box after the curtain had gone up. The King, mistaking this for loyalty, knighted the colonel on the spot and absolved the officers from drinking the royal toast when dining. This we still observed. As a royal regiment we wore blue facings; and as light infantry we wore green in full dress, and many aspects of our uniforms were green.

During the Victorian years the regiment produced some great soldiers including General Sir Garnet Wolseley, later Field Marshal Viscount Wolseley. He won so many small wars that 'All Sir Garnet' became a national catch phrase for all being well, a catch-phrase still in use in the regiment. In the Great War the regiment had raised many battalions, and several in the Second World War, distinguishing itself in both. It was still one of the few infantry regiments to have two battalions, probably due to incompetence in the War Office, friends in high places, and the threatening nature of the Cold War. The officers and serjeants lived in some style. We were proud to do so. It was swank, of course, but we felt we had something to swank about.

Showered and dressed, I walked through the officers' lines to the anteroom, where I found Burgo talking to a small group drinking gin and tonic. Jasper was there, as were Adam Hare and Charlie Chance. Adam was tall, well built, red-headed, and florid with a slightly caddish air. He had done his national service in another regiment before going to Oxford. After graduating he had been offered the chance of a fellowship but had failed to write a word of his thesis. For want of anything better to do, he had then joined us as a regular soldier, through the connection of his tutor who had served in the regiment in the war. Adam was ruthless in the pursuit of pleasure. Charlie Chance, on the other hand, was a national serviceman with only a few months left to serve before taking up a place at Cambridge. He was short, very bright, and fun. And he had great curiosity.

'One for the road?' said Adam.

'No,' said Burgo, 'let's go to the Club now. It'll be more fun and we might meet some new faces.'

'New faces, yes please,' said Jasper.

Before we had left England, we had been given some introductions to various people in Kenya but it was a large country and we had not yet been able to get round to see them all.

'Just the five of us?' said Adam. 'Then we can all squeeze into Burgo's jalopy if I sit in the front.'

'Miles should sit in the front.' said Burgo. 'He's the senior.'

'Don't let's worry about that, Burgo,' I said. 'Better Adam sits in the front and keeps his hands off Charlie.'

Burgo had been one of the first to buy a car on our arrival and had found an old Citroen with a front bench seat and a gear stick that came out of the dashboard. It was black, of course.

The Muthaiga Club was an elegant, long, low building, painted pink with white-dressed quoins. Surrounded by the greenery of shrubs, palms, and trees, the building exuded an inviting, confident air. It was dark when we arrived, for dusk falls early in the tropics, and the large and numerous windows threw out long shafts of light over the lawns and gardens as we walked up to the entrance. Inside, we settled into comfortable wicker chairs in a large square room with arcades on all four sides. A tall African servant wearing a red fez and a *kanzu*, a full-length dress buttoned at the throat and falling to the floor, attended us. Most of us asked for gin and tonic. Adam asked for Campari.

'What do you make of this country, Adam?' asked Burgo.

'It's England's wild west. Most of the settlers are cowboys. Look at all those young men in the Kenya Regiment who've been our guides and trackers. Cowboys all, wild cowboys.'

'They're not all like that,' said Burgo. 'Look at this club, for instance.'

'This is not a young man's club,' said Adam. 'It's full of *old* cowboys, looking for a little comfort. Many of them are none too rich any more and are after a way of life that's no longer possible in England.'

'Didn't someone say that this club had so many peers among its members it was called the House of Lords?' said Charlie.

'Exactly,' said Adam.

'You'd have to be a cowboy to survive in this place,' said Burgo. 'What was it Churchill said about Kenya, "a place in the sun for shady people"?'

'Churchill said that in 1920 when he was Colonial Secretary,' I said. 'A lot's changed since then.'

'So you think much has changed?' said Adam.

'Yes,' I said, 'but not the underlying problem.'

'And what is that?'

'Is this a white man's country or an African's country?'

'That's always been the issue.'

Before anyone could follow that up, Jasper broke in.

'I think this is a wonderful country: horses, fishing, shooting — everything one could want. I can see why the white man came. I'd be a white hunter myself if I'd been born here. Maybe I'll settle here one day and become one. I'm going to enjoy this country whatever the problems.'

'Let's have one more drink,' said Adam, 'and then go in to dinner.'

We did.

'Don't expect the Savoy Grill,' said Adam, as we studied the menu in the dining room, 'but I think this is as good as any restaurant we have found in the town.'

He then proposed what we should eat and drink and, not unsurprisingly, we all agreed.

'Jasper,' said Charlie, 'tell us about the first kill. How did it happen?'

'I would like to think it was skilful patrolling and superior forest lore, but I suppose it was just luck.'

He had all our attention.

'We had been in the forest four days, working our way down. We were wet and cold and tired. Suddenly our tracker got excited and set us following a path which looked like an animal track to me. Not a word passed, it was all signs. He clearly thought we were on to something, and the Kenya Regiment serjeant was doubly alert.

'We broke out of the forest into the open and there, in the clearing, about one hundred yards away, was an African running away from us, not very fast but at the double. We were in the prohibited zone, where no African is allowed on pain of death. I got him with my first shot, in the head and he fell immediately. In half a minute we were up with him. He was dead.'

'What did you shoot him with?' asked Charlie.

'My rifle. I always carry a rifle. I find those Patchett submachine-guns unreliable.'

'That was a good shot, Jasper. What did you do then?' I said.

'We all sat down round him and the men asked if they could smoke. So we all had a cigarette.'

'But you're not allowed to smoke in the forest,' said Charlie. 'The Mau Mau can smell a cigarette from miles away.'

'Yes, I realised that after I'd lit up. I suppose it was a sort of unthinking reaction.'

'What did you do with the body?' Charlie asked.

'We couldn't carry it. So I thought we'd better do what we had been told to do, though I didn't particularly like doing it.'

'What was that?'

'We cut off the hands so that the police could identify the fingerprints. Then we buried the body. Then I said a prayer for him.'

For a moment we were silent.

'What did the soldiers think?' I asked.

'They were rather excited. Well, wouldn't you be? They'd done what they'd been trained to do. You know how the Mau Mau have their hair all curled in tiny knots? Well a few of the men cut some of these curls off and put them in their pockets. "Why are you doing that?" I asked one of them. "We're going to send them home to our mums," he said.'

'Good heavens, how peculiar,' said Burgo

'Yes, maybe it was peculiar but it's war. They didn't mutilate the body or anything like that, as the Mau Mau do. We'd been out for four days, it all happened very suddenly and that's how it takes you. We did everything by the book. I've no qualms. That man should not have been there. He was Mau Mau, probably a courier returning from carrying a message or supplies to a forest gang.'

'Well, you're a hero, Jasper,' said Burgo.

'No, not a hero, just doing what I had to do.'

The meal was coming to an end when a tall man with greying hair, dressed in a safari suit, came across to us. I had noticed him and his party in the far corner as, from time to time, they had been looking in our direction.

'Do forgive me for barging in,' he said, addressing me, 'but I wonder if you are officers from the Prince Regent's Light Infantry from Muthaiga Camp?'

'Indeed we are, Sir' I said.

'Welcome to Kenya,' he replied. 'We had heard you had arrived and delighted we are to have another regiment here. The more the better. May I introduce myself? I'm Tony Hay-Smith and I farm near Nanyuki.'

I introduced myself and then the others. We all shook hands.

'I'd be delighted,' said Tony Hay-Smith, 'if you'd all join us for a glass of port when you've finished your dinner. My wife and I are over there with some friends,' he nodded to the far corner. 'We'll be in the sitting room.'

'That's very kind of you, Sir'

'Please call me Tony.'

He nodded again and rejoined his table.

'That's generous of the old settler,' said Burgo.

'The settlers love having soldiers around their farms,' I said. 'They feel safer as our presence keeps the Mau Mau at bay. I bet he asks us to stay before the evening's out.'

'Never,' said Burgo.

'Bet?' I asked

'A fiver.'

'A fiver it is, or rather one hundred shillings now we're in Kenya.'

'That's a good bet,' said Adam. 'I'll take a fiver, too.'

'I'm not betting with you, Adam,' said Burgo, 'until you pay me back the tenner I lent you to bail you out in France.'

'Are you still broke, Adam?' I asked.

'Let's say I'm still recovering from a long-running piece of bad luck at Monte Carlo, when I was there with Burgo and the others before we set sail. And I wasn't able to recoup any money on the ship as we couldn't gamble properly under D.P. Brown's nose.'

The memory of the ship caused a moment's silence.

'When will you learn, Adam,' I said, 'that it's no good playing for high stakes in the mess? It'll backfire on you.'

'I think I've got that message, thank you,' said Adam. 'I'm hoping I might set up some nice games with some of the settlers here. I'm sure there'll be some who are longing to have a punt. Burgo, let's say double or quits.'

'No. I want that tenner back.'

Burgo and Adam went on bickering.

'Not a bad meal,' said Jasper. 'I'd rather like a cigar. Anyone else?'

'Not for me,' said Charlie.

Everyone else asked for one and Jasper left for the bar saying he'd better choose them himself.

'Where's Nanyuki?' asked Burgo

'Just under Mount Kenya,' I said, 'to the west.'

'I'd rather like to climb Mount Kenya.'

'Mount Kilimanjaro is easier.'

'Yes,' said Burgo, 'I'd like to tackle them both, but, from what I hear, Kilimanjaro is one long, hard walk, whereas Mount Kenya is a formidable climb and much more difficult to reach the top. That's something to tilt at.'

Jasper returned with cigars and we all moved to the sitting room. Tony Hay-Smith had arranged the chairs there so that each of us would sit next to one of his party. There were six of them, men and women. With diplomatic skill, he introduced and seated us. I found myself sitting next to him.

'I'm so glad we're going to have a chance to talk,' he said as he handed me a glass of port. 'This Mau Mau business is a complex one. I don't know what you know, or have been told, but have you met many settlers yet?'

'Not many,' I replied, 'the only local people we've really got to know so far are members of the Kenya Regiment. We've just returned from an operation and have been letting off steam.'

'Just the thing to do. I fought in Europe in the Second War and I know all about coming out of action.'

'What were you in?'

'I was a cavalryman, as was my father. He came out here after the First War and I took over the farm after the Second.'

'Did you go to school here?'

'No, I was sent back to England. Many of us were.'

'We find the young men in the Kenya Regiment a little uncouth.'

'They are,' Hay-Smith said. 'They've been brought up in a hard country. *Kenya born, Kenya bred, strong in the arm, weak in the head,* as the old rhyme goes. But they're rather good at what they do, aren't they?'

'They're streets better than us in the forest. We couldn't operate without their guidance. We just find them different, very tough and single minded. Callous, almost.'

'Most will know of some Mau Mau atrocity first hand. That stiffens their attitude. Have you talked about this with any of them?'

'Not really,' I said. 'We've been told about the Mau Mau oaths and, of course, we've read about the atrocities, but I have no first-hand knowledge.'

'Would you like to hear some?'

'Well, yes,' I said.

'About fifteen miles from my farm is one owned by the McNaughtens. He was a retired naval officer who had come out to Kenya in the early 1930s with his wife Sally, a doctor. Their two children, both girls, are grown up and live in England.

'The McNaughtens were enlightened employers. All their staff were Kikuyu, the cleverest and ablest of the African tribes, and it's Kikuyu country. Sally did incredible work in the neighbourhood, giving freely to any who needed her help. The standards of living, hygiene, and childbirth among their employees, and for miles around, including our employees, were among the highest in the country. They were the most respected farmers I know.

'One evening their syce appeared to lure McNaughten out of the house on a pretext and then the syce and a farm worker butchered him with pangas in the darkness. Sally must have run out at the noise, but not before she had given the alarm. She was cut down and butchered, too.

'When the police found them lying there dead they also found a prize heifer with her udder slashed, her intestines strung round her hamstrung legs and an old headman naked, slashed, and his eyes gouged out. I won't go on. This, after all the McNaughtens had done. It was savagery, brute savagery. You see, Miles, the problem is a denial of civilisation. We have to stamp it out. That's why the men in the Kenya Regiment have steel in their eyes.'

I had, of course, read about the massacres, but this was my first account at first-hand.

'The Mau Mau want us out of the country. Anyone who opposes them they cut down.'

'Yes,' I said, 'but do the Mau Mau stand for everyone? Aren't there many loyal Kikuyu?'

'There are. And look at what the Mau Mau do to them. Have you heard about the Lari massacre? No? Well, one night a thousand Mau Mau fell on the Kikuyu loyalist settlement at Lari on the edge of the escarpment. The Kikuyu in the settlement had refused to take the Mau Mau oaths, so the Mau Mau attacked and killed 84 of them, nearly 60 of them women and children. They did it in the most horrible way. I won't describe it but it was stark, staring brutality in its most blatant form. Savagery, pure savagery. That's why it's got to be stamped out.'

Hay-Smith was clearly stirred.

'You know, it's really some time since all this started and we've made little progress in stamping it out. The Mau Mau in the forest are as free to terrorise as they've ever been. With all the troops we've got in the country now you'd expect some progress, but we don't seem to have begun to get the initiative. What amounts to a civil war among the Kikuyu, and a racial war against us, is terrifying everyone. Most settlers go in fear of their lives and worse. The administration and the army haven't got a grip of the situation yet. We can expect worse if they don't do so soon. I really don't know where it's going to end.'

He was silent for a bit and was clearly very moved. He seemed lost in his memory and I couldn't help being moved myself. For the first time, I realised how serious the situation was.

'Enough of this,' he said. 'You can see why we're delighted to have you here. Stamp it out we must. Your glass is empty. We can't have that.'

He called for port.

'Now, you must tell me what you've been doing since you arrived.'

So we drank port and I recounted what we'd done so far. The others seemed to have hit it off with his wife and their friends and the conversation widened and became more general. When the evening came to a close we parted as if we were already old friends. As we said goodbye Tony Hay-Smith took me aside.

'You must come and stay with us at Nanyuki soon. And we must introduce you to some girls.'

2

Colonel Rex is a man of action.

The following morning, after the mid morning break, Colonel Rex bugled for me. He had been our commanding officer for a month or two and, apart from his mania for building, had made few changes. What now, I wondered.

Rex was sitting behind a trestle table covered in a khaki blanket, which I could hardly see for the trays and files piled high on it. He leaned forward in his chair and looked intently at me, his head framed by two blocks of files. His almost black hair was plastered down either side of a centre parting.

'At present we're organised for a war in Europe,' he said, 'not for fighting in the forest.'

A clerk came in with an armful of files which he placed on the left of the table. Then he collected a larger pile from the right of the table and carried them out.

'I'm going through all this,' Rex said, waving a hand over the files, 'to find out about everything and everyone. I now know every member of the battalion by rank, name, and age. I've read all the officers' confidential reports, and everything else of any matter. And I know all about you, Miles.'

'Not everything, Colonel, surely?'

'Enough. I've been watching you ever since Guy Surtees made you intelligence officer in Korea. I didn't agree with everything

Guy did, but that was a shrewd appointment. And that ass Parker Brown, who should never have been given command, can't have been completely off his rocker the day he made you a company commander, however junior you were.'

'He said he was short of senior officers and was giving me a chance.'

'About the only time he gave anyone a chance, I should think. Of course, he was short of senior officers. None of us would serve under him. But we're not here to talk about *him*. George Bulman speaks well of you, as does Francis Bowerman. And neither of them is out of his mind.'

What *is* Colonel Rex leading up to, I wondered.

'Now, re-organisation,' he said. 'I'm planning to enable us to win in the forest. Some of the other battalions here have done it. We only got a pass mark from GHQ for Operation Hammer. Par for the course, they said, for a battalion fresh from Europe. They were right, from what I saw. That's not good enough. We're fighting an insurrection and we need new tactics. I'm forming a forest company that will be trained to fight in small groups in the forest in order to eliminate the Mau Mau. The other companies will support them by operating on the outskirts of the forest. In doing this, Miles, I'm going to make some changes...'

Why on earth is he telling *me* all this, I wondered. Surely all the company commanders should be here when he announces such changes?

'...and I'm appointing you my adjutant.'

Adjutant, I thought. It had hardly occurred to me. The adjutancy was the prize job in the battalion for someone of my rank and seniority.

'What about Francis Bowerman, Colonel? He hasn't been adjutant that long.'

'Francis is to command Forest Company. I want you to take over immediately. It'll be in today's orders.'

'What about my company?'

'I'm disbanding it.'

'*Disbanding* it?' I said in disbelief.

'Well, not exactly. The anti-tank platoon is already mothballed. No role for them here. I'm transferring the rest to Headquarter Company for administration. For operations they will be attached to the companies on the outskirts of the forest. Do you see anything wrong with that?'

We discussed that. I had to admit it was workable.

'I'm also pulling Colour Serjeant Body out of the officers' mess, where he's wasted, and putting him back in charge of the pioneer platoon, as he was in Korea.'

'He'll like that, Colonel.'

'I'm not concerned with what he'll like. It's a better use of his abilities.'

'He was only given the mess serjeant's job to give him a break after all the hard work he did in Korea.'

'Quite so. I'm promoting Corporal Cheke to serjeant to run the mess. Now, your officers. We've been asked to provide a district miltary intelligence officer, a DMIO. I'm thinking of sending Burgo.'

'He's very able. That's a good break for him, Colonel.' I said, thinking of Burgo's current mania for investigating the demise of D. P. Brown. It would get him away from the battalion and stop that nonsense. I refrained from saying he'd like it. He would.

'Good. Now, I don't know Adam Hare. Tell me about him. How did he get into the regiment?'

'He came to us after coming down from Oxford through his tutor, who'd been in the regiment.'

'I'd heard that he was a protégé of Parker Brown.'

'The tutor had served with Colonel Dennis. That's how it happened.'

'Does he play any games?'

Delicate ground, I said to myself.

'Cricket. He's a rather good batsman.'

'I enjoy a game of cricket myself. Good. Anything else?'

'He enjoys playing cards.'

'What, bridge? He's got a brain, hasn't he?'

'Yes. And picquet. He likes a game of backgammon, too.'

'Does he now? Sounds interesting. I must have a game with him. Did we bring the backgammon table with us to Kenya? I always enjoy a game of backgammon.'

'We brought the backgammon board with us. We left the large backgammon table with all the mess furniture at the depot.'

'Well, I'm going to make him second-in-command to Tony Henderson in Y Company. What do you think about that?'

'Adam's in a rut. He needs a change.'

'I'm glad you said that. How do you rate him as a soldier?'

'The men like him and he's very knowledgeable.'

'That's a good start. He looks an asset.'

'Are you leaving the platoons without officers, Colonel?'

'For a time. You've got good serjeants, haven't you?'

'None better in the battalion. What about Serjeant-Major Whettingsteel?'

'Francis wants him as his company serjeant-major in his forest company.'

That would be a good move for Big Steel, I thought. He hadn't been stretched as my serjeant-major. And Burgo would revel in being a military intelligence officer. The one I was concerned about was Adam. He was congenitally idle. Of course, the Prussians thought that the best officers were the clever and idle ones; I thought being second-in-command of a company would make Adam even more idle and fail to use his intellect.

We discussed my role as adjutant for a bit, then Colonel Rex let me go.

I stood outside his tent for a moment wondering what to do next. On my left were the adjutant's tent and the orderly room, on my right was the second-in-command's tent. I turned right, walked in and saluted.

'Stap me, it's the new adjutant,' said George Bulman. 'I was expecting you. Congratulations.' George was sitting behind an almost empty table reading a report, the table having only a few paperback novels on it.

'This is an enormous break for me, George,' I said. 'Why me?'

'Rex knows you, and Francis is raring to get into the forest.'

'I must say that I think all the changes are good. My only concern is my old company. The platoons need officers.'

'There's not much of a role for the mortars or machine guns in this game, but we'll train replacements immediately. That's my concern, not yours any longer.'

'Any tips for the new adjutant?'

'Just be yourself,' said George. 'Adjutants who strut around are bores and make enemies. Look after Rex: he's very experienced but he can have some madcap ideas. If you get into deep water come and see me. And get a love life. I know you're still pining for Kitty. All that's over. Now, it's time for a celebratory drink in the mess. After that you can go and see Francis.'

It was midday, and George and I were the first to arrive in the anteroom, a basic wooden hut with bare walls, about twenty by thirty feet, only just built. It was furnished with leather chairs and small tables placed in groups, functional not elegant. Corporal Cheke was moving bottles around in his bar, a long alcove built to the right of the door as you entered the anteroom. I asked him to open a bottle of Bollinger.

'Don't you rather like the way this room is so under-furnished?' George said. 'I sometimes feel oppressed by all the regimental furniture and pictures. Thank God no one thought to bring them here.'

'Were we right to bring the silver?' I asked.

'No, it'll be stolen or damaged. But, if we're to be here for any length of time, we'll need something to remind us of civilisation. We mustn't become savages.'

'I rather miss the pictures.'

'Where on earth would you hang them?'

We had some wonderful pictures that we had left at the depot in England, largely battle scenes and portraits by Victorian artists

— Winterhalter, Tissot, Etty, and Lady Butler. The one I missed most was a huge portrait of Garnet Wolseley, Field Marshal Viscount Wolseley, our colonel-in-chief at the end of the 19th century. There was no place for so large a picture here.

'Don't you think the sparseness of the room adds to the sense of action and active service?' asked George.

'Yes, it does,' said Colonel Rex who had just come into the room, 'and we don't want a sense of action or active service in the anteroom. Quite the opposite. We must make this mess, this camp, a refuge for the officers when they're out of the forest. I want it to be a beacon of civilisation, a haven of comfort and elegance in a heathen world. Ah, champagne! Good.'

Cheke brought us all silver goblets of champagne. We always drank champagne in silver goblets. Silver kept the champagne cold. They drank my health. Of course, I was paying for the champagne.

'You can't say it's *not* civilised, Rex,' said George. 'How would you make it more so? It is, after all, no more than a wooden hut.'

'We should have some pictures. Don't we have lots of prints in Hogarth frames? Where are they? They'd look good massed on a wall.'

'I understand they were left behind, stored at the depot,' said George.

'Then I'll write today and ask for them. The next batch of reinforcements can bring them. What about some rugs?'

'Won't they get torn to pieces by our boots?'

'Did they in Germany, Miles?'

'Not that I recall.'

'Well then,' said Colonel Rex, 'rugs. We could buy some here. Let's walk round the mess and see what else we could do to make it more civilised.'

'Wouldn't it be a good idea to have the PMC with us, Colonel?' I said. The PMC was the president of the mess committee responsible for running the mess.

'What, Ben Wildbore? You tell him what we've decided.'

'Rex,' said George, 'the mess is the home of all the officers. Don't you think they should be consulted? I understand the decisions about furnishing the mess were taken by the officers in England. Isn't that so, Miles?'

'Colonel Dennis put some proposals to the officers at a mess meeting which were agreed.'

'Well, let's do that when we've decided on some proposals. You probably thought you were going to have a tent or two and now we've got these lovely buildings. We've got to be civilised.'

With that Rex started to walk out of the room. Then he stopped and turned.

'Where's the backgammon board?'

'Cheke keeps it in the bar.'

'I'm looking forward to a game of backgammon with Adam.'

He then walked across to the dining room. We followed him, George darted me a puzzled look and said, 'Farouk me for a chocolate soldier,' an expression he would occasionally use when nonplussed.

'You'll pick the job up very quickly, Miles,' said Francis as I sat next to him in the adjutant's tent after lunch. 'Kettle knows everything and he's a wonderful prop. You can leave most of it to him. Don't get bogged down in the paperwork, and don't be one of those adjutants who's in the office until the dinner call is sounded.'

Unlike that of Colonel Rex, Francis' table was clear of any files or papers. There was just the covering of an army blanket on which were three empty trays.

'As you can see, I've cleared my desk. It's all yours now. I must go and get to grips with Forest Company. Kettle will look after you. Good luck!' With that, Francis picked up his cap and left.

Kettle was the chief clerk. He ruled the orderly room, and had done so for some years. Good as he was at his job, he was unlikely to go any further, which he knew. This made him slightly dissatisfied and, to a young officer, he could appear supercilious.

I sat in the chair, looking out of the door of the tent straight in front of me, watching the world go by. Perhaps the first thing I do, I thought, is move this table and chair to one side of the tent so no one can see in. Then, I thought, if Francis can keep a clear table perhaps there isn't that much paperwork, quite the opposite of what Big Steel had suggested when, earlier, I told him about the changes, about which, of course, he already knew. The serjeants always seemed to know everything before the officers did.

'All paperwork now, sir,' Big Steel had said, 'sitting on your arse in the adjutant's tent. Kettle'll keep you busy. Do you know what his nickname is, what they call him in the serjeants' mess? "Teapot". Here comes "Old Teapot" they say when he comes in. Not to his face, mind you, but he knows. He thinks his teapot is the cure for everything.'

'I'm pleased you're going to Forest Company with Major Bowerman, Serjeant-Major,' I said. 'I hope you are.'

'Chuffed no end, Sir. It'll be very different. I know Major Bowerman. No rest for idle hands under him.'

'We've had some fun, haven't we?'

'Best company in the battalion it was, Sir. Pity it's being divided up, but I can see the point. I'd better cut along and find Major Bowerman and get Forest Company "All Sir Garnet".'

'You do that, Serjeant-Major, and thanks for all you've done.'

'It's been a grand time, Sir,' and we shook hands in parting.

It was a sad moment but all that was in the past. I stood up in my new tent to see how I could rearrange the furniture, such as it was, when in came Kettle followed by two clerks carrying files.

'Welcome to the orderly room, Captain Player, Sir. I thought I'd bring in a few files to get you started. And these,' he said, introducing the two clerks, 'are Corporal Norman and Private Tudor'.

He proceeded to take the files from Corporal Norman and place them in the pending tray.

'These are the files Major Bowerman was unable to attend to. The ones at the top are the most urgent. They all need your attention, Sir, though I have pencilled suggestions about how to deal with them. If you would like to discuss them I'd be happy to. The other files,' he said, taking them from Private Tudor and placing them in the in-tray, 'are the day's mail. I can deal with much of it, but I thought you would like to see it all before deciding what I should deal with and what you feel you should tackle.'

The table was now loaded rather lopsidedly with more files than I could count. This, of course, was Kettle testing me, seeing how I would react. He could probably have dealt with most of them himself, but he wanted to see how I would respond.

'First, ORQMS, I would like to move this table to the side so that I don't have to look out of the opening all the time and can concentrate on the papers.'

'Sound idea, Sir. Come on you two, move the table as the adjutant asks.'

So they moved the table and the chairs and I sat down behind the table with no view except the walls of the tent.

'Much better, Sir,' said Kettle. 'Now you can work without disruption.' Then, dismissing the two clerks, he said, 'Shall we look at the mail, Sir?'

My heart sank. Quickly, though, we went through the files agreeing what should be done and Kettle left within ten minutes, bearing away all the mail, leaving me to look at the files in the pending tray. As I picked up the first, Peter Quartermain walked in.

'Must be the first,' he said, 'to pay my respects to the new adjutant. Ah, there you are, hiding round the corner. More changes, I see.'

'Pete, you rogue, what do you want?'

When I was first commissioned Peter Quartermain had been the Regimental Quartermaster Serjeant. During the traditional visit of the officers to the serjeants' mess, on my first Christmas Day in the regiment, Peter had made me drunk by giving me cocktails of liqueurs in pints of beer. He had been RQMS in Korea, where he had made a small fortune trading with the Americans. He once offered me a jeep for nothing. Now he was a captain and the battalion quartermaster.

'This Forest Company. How am I to provide all the kit Francis Bowerman is asking for? It's quite irregular. There are no official scales for what he wants. Where does he expect me to get it from?' he asked, waving a piece of paper in the air.

'Don't you have it in your stores?'

'Course I don't. He's asking for seven light machine guns, seven Patchett sub-machine guns, seven compasses, seven everything under the sun.'

'What's all this about?' asked Colonel Rex, who must have been attracted by the high-pitched wailing of the Quartermaster.

'Major Bowerman has sent his colour serjeant to me demanding all this. It's a scandal,' said Peter, handing the piece of paper to the colonel, who read it.

'I think you'll find, Peter, that all this has been authorised by GHQ. If they haven't told you I suggest you nip over with a truck, see your friends there, and bring the stuff back with you. There can be no delay. Francis needs these now.'

'But, Sir...'

'No buts, Peter. Be a good quartermaster and do it now.'

Peter left rather grudgingly, but he did salute.

'Let's go and see how Francis is getting on,' said Colonel Rex. 'He seems to be moving double fast. He can't have been with his company for more than an hour.'

Within five minutes we were standing in Forest Company's lines. Forest Company was, in fact, Z Company. The companies in the second battalion were named W, X, Y, and Z to distinguish them from A, B, C, and D companies in the First Battalion. In the army's phonetic alphabet Z stood for Zulu, a name which Francis's company would later use to distinguish it from the forest companies of other battalions, for there were several British battalions in the country. Now everyone was calling the new company Forest Company. It was a new idea, explicit in its role. Everyone liked it, especially those in the company itself. It already suggested an elite.

'Ah, there you are,' said Colonel Rex, as we found Francis and

Big Steel in their company lines. 'We've come to find out how
you're getting on and whether you've everything you need.'

'We've just sorted the men. We're turning the three platoons into
ten patrols, each of eight men. Each patrol is to be commanded by
a subaltern or a serjeant, with two corporals. I've enough corporals
but not enough subalterns or serjeants. I need four more, and I
need good ones. I've sent the colour serjeant to the QM for arms
and stores, so if you can give me the patrol leaders then I'm all set.
I understand I'm to get a tracker and a serjeant from the Kenya
Regiment for each patrol when we move up country to train. I'd
like to move to a training camp in the forest as soon as possible.
Can all that be arranged?'

'Miles can do that for you, can't you, Miles?'

I hadn't been in the job for more than three hours, but now I
realised what it meant being adjutant.

3

Getting to see more of the country

When Francis and his Forest Company had been up-country training for a week, Colonel Rex decided it was time to visit them. We
motored up to their camp near Naivasha, as they were training in
the forest in the Aberdares under Mount Kinangop. The drive was
spectacular. Near Limuru, the road crosses the escarpment and,
as you start the tortuous descent, the Rift Valley opens up before
you, an exceptional natural fault in the earth's crust stretching
north until it disappears in the shimmering heat of the far horizon.
In Africa you can sense the greatness of the Earth more than you
can in any other continent. You can feel its grandeur, you can
see its lushness, and you can get closer to its nature than you can
anywhere else I've ever been. It is physically overwhelming. And
you feel it acutely as you motor down the Kikuyu escarpment.

The road was metalled, made by Italian prisoners of war in
the Second World War, who cannot have been given adequate
materials or instructions. Only ten years later, it was beginning to
crack and the surface was none too even. We travelled by Land
Rover, and Corporal Bates, the colonel's driver, skilfully avoided
most of the potholes.

Some way before Naivasha we turned off the main road onto a
murram track and started to climb into the foothills of the Aberdares. There, Francis had pitched a small camp on the edge of a

farm and we met those of his company who were not training in the forest at that moment. Colonel Rex went to talk to Francis in his tent and I found Jasper, who had just returned from a patrol.

'Jasper, you're soaking wet, unshaven and you stink,' I said.

'Of course I stink. I've just come off a three-day patrol and I haven't cleaned up. We all stink.'

'It's rather animal.'

'It has to be. You know the Mau Mau can smell a European a mile away. So, when we go on patrol we don't wash. No soap, shampoo, or toothpaste. Trumpers and Eau de Cologne *verboten*. Trouble is, we still smell of meat.'

'Cigarette?' I said, offering him my cigarette case.

'Satan, don't you dare. My patrol has given up smoking. That's been the most difficult thing of all.'

'What've you done with your cigarette case?'

'I keep it here,' he said, tapping his breast, 'in the left hand pocket of my shirt. It's my talisman'

He took it out of his pocket. It was gold and heavy, and it glinted richly in the sun. He opened it to show a picture of his mother and father, his military identity card and some toothpicks. On the inside lid was the presentation inscription to his great-grandfather, for the case had been given to him by a grateful regiment when he had stepped down from being colonel-in-chief before the Great War.

'It's my good luck charm,' Jasper said. 'I always have it with me,' he said, looking up and smiling broadly. 'I've given up drinking, too. Well, not completely but not stupidly as I used to. On the ship I said to myself I'm going to start again. I want to be a good soldier. D.P. Brown falling off that boat was a godsend. I've got my chance and I'm taking it.'

'I haven't seen you so happy since Kitty died,' I said, thinking how could he have said what he did about D.P.Brown if he had pushed him. If he had pushed him wouldn't he have said nothing? I must tell Burgo when I next see him to make him see sense.

'I am,' Jasper said. 'Francis is so good. The best company commander I've ever had. I'm so pleased you asked me if I'd like to be one of his subalterns. Thank you, Miles. It's wonderful here.'

He threw an arm out at the view and I turned and gazed at the soft greenery of the farm in its vast landscape. Below us were farm buildings and, set to one side, a small house, five bays and two stories, approached along a drive of trees, as one might have found in any English county.

I don't know why I mentioned Kitty, but I now became very conscious of her. In Germany she had trained the racehorse on which Jasper had won his races. It was her horse; they made a team and had become very close, like brother and sister. Jasper was nearly as devastated as I had been when Kitty had died after a motor accident. Kitty and I were lovers, had known each other since childhood, and we were to have married and come to Kenya together. Perhaps we might even have lived in a place like this, I thought, as we gazed at the view.

'The settler', said Jasper, 'lets me ride his horses. It's paradise. When all this is over and I've become a general, I think I shall leave the army and settle here.'

He put the cigarette case back in his pocket, saying, 'I must go and change.'

'No, not yet. I'm sure the colonel would like to talk to you as you are.'

We walked across to where Colonel Rex and Francis were talking to Big Steel, and the colonel saw Jasper and turned to talk to him, which I could see they both enjoyed.

'Jasper seems very happy,' I said to Francis. 'I hope you are.'

'It's all going well. Jasper's a star. He's a born irregular and he's in his element.'

'And the men?'

'Most have taken to it well, though we've got some problems and I need to talk to you about them.'

We discussed his problems for the next few minutes and then he said, 'You must come and see Big Steel's ops tent. Where's the Colonel got to? Ah, I see Big Steel is taking him across to it.

Let's join them.'

We went into a large tent inside which was a display of boards at eye height. Some had large scale maps of the area, others had clusters of photographs. On close inspection, the photographs were all named; they were the leaders, and some of the members, of the Mau Mau gangs in this part of the Aberdares.

'How do you know all this?' asked Colonel Rex.

'We've put it together with members of the Special Branch and the Field Intelligence Officers. There are some gaps, but we find it's vital for the men to know who they're hunting.'

'Very impressive,' said the Colonel. 'In the next op every company must have an ops tent like this, Miles.'

'You must come and meet the settler here,' said Francis. 'He's been very good to us. He came out in the 1930s and knows the place intimately. They're called Littlejohn.'

Francis led us down to the house and we went to the front door, where Francis called 'Fred' and 'Anna' in a loud voice. A beautiful woman with greying hair, dressed in shirt and jodhpurs, appeared in the hall and welcomed us in.

'Fred's out on the farm,' she said, 'but do come in and let me give you some refreshments.' She led us into her drawing room, clapped her hands, and a boy, dressed rather like the servants at the Muthaiga Club, came in and she gave him instructions in Swahili.

While the house itself could have been set in England the drawing room definitely was. Polished Georgian mahogany, chintz curtains, Persian rugs, comfortable sofas, and Bergere chairs made one feel one had just stepped into an English country house. And there were paintings on the walls.

Drinks came, followed by Fred, who had clearly been fetched by the African boy from the farm. He was tall, too, rather grizzled by the sun, and dressed similarly to his wife in shirt and jodhpurs.

'Colonel,' he said, 'we're so happy to have Francis and his men here.'

'And we, Sir, are so grateful to you for allowing us to train here.'

'You must understand, Colonel, that they give us almost perfect security. No gang is going to come out of the forest with them here. But, look, do stay for lunch. We have the DC coming and he'd love to meet you, I know, and I expect you might like to meet him.'

'That's very kind. We'd love to.'

'I'm afraid you must forgive me, Anna,' said Francis. 'I must get back to my men.'

'Of course.'

So Colonel Rex and I stayed and, shortly afterwards, a well fed, bespectacled man arrived. He was dressed in khaki drill bush jacket and shorts, with long fawn stockings, and well polished brown shoes. He was driving himself in a Land Rover.

'Here's Jeremy Watts,' said Anna, and she went out and brought him in to introduce us. We had more drinks and then Anna led us into a dining room full of more beautiful English furniture. We all helped ourselves to a cold lunch from the sideboard.

'What do you make of our country, Colonel?' asked Jeremy Watts, the District Commissioner.

'Wouldn't know there was an emergency.'

'That's interesting. Of course, it's different to Malaya, where the terrorists were fully armed and backed by a foreign power. Mau Mau is a religion, home grown, and only the Kikuyu, Embu and Meru tribes are in it. No subversive communist power is involved. It was proscribed in 1950 and, when the emergency was declared in October fifty-two, they were taken by surprise, they weren't prepared. We arrested the leaders, about eighty of them, and it took some time for the rest to get going. We now think about 18,000 went into the forest and formed gangs which are very elusive. They rarely, almost never, stand and fight. They can't, as they haven't the weapons. The standard weapons are the simi, a short sword, and pangas, also called the machete, which is an agricultural tool and cannot be banned. Only half the Mau Mau have firearms, and many of those will be home made. They're past masters at living in the forest and they've had the initiative. The situation is still frightening, as you never know when and where a gang is going to appear. Most of the atrocities have been against their own people who've refused to fall in with them and take the oaths to drive us out of the country and worse. There have been some terrible atrocities against Europeans.'

'How do you rate what the army is doing?'Colonel Rex asked.

'The army is essential. Without the British battalions we just wouldn't have the resources to combat the insurgents. It's your presence that's important. The King's African Rifles battalions are better in the forest, as you'd expect them to be. On a European battlefield you wouldn't expect the KAR to perform like British soldiers, would you? The Kenya Regiment and the police general service unit are the ones who can really track and face the Mau Mau in the forest.'

I wondered if Colonel Rex would challenge this as he was training a forest company.

'The cordon and search operation,' the commissioner went on, 'the army did in Nairobi just before you arrived — Op Anvil — we have high hopes of that. We think we may have given the passive wing of Mau Mau a severe blow. You see, the Mau Mau gangs in the forest are maintained mainly from Nairobi with funds, recruits, supplies — including medical supplies — food, weapons and ammo. If we can cut off their supplies we'll weaken the groups severely.'

'Tell me,' said Colonel Rex, 'about the Mau Mau in the forest.'

'The Kenya Liberation Army, or KLA,' replied the DC, 'is divided into two, one being based on the Aberdares and the other on Mount Kenya. The latter was commanded by Waruhiu Itote, known as General China, who had served with the KAR in Burma in the last war as a mess corporal. They say he was an excellent one. He was captured a year ago and was very co-operative in trying to arrange surrender terms with the gangs. Unfortunately, this came to nothing and there are still gangs on Mount Kenya. In the Aberdares, Dedan Kimathi commands. He styles himself as Field Marshal, Knight Commander of the African Empire, and Prime Minister. He is formidable and he runs a so-called Kenya parliament in the forest. Among his generals are Stanley Math-enge and General Tanganyika, and there's now a lot of in-fighting between the generals and the gangs. The gangs are anything from 40 to 300 strong, including women. In all, we estimate there are still 6,000 to 8,000 active insurgents in the forest.'

'I'm amazed by the intelligence you have,' said Colonel Rex.

'We have discovered that a captured Mau Mau can be de-oathed and turned. We've learned most of what we know through inter-rogation.'

'Torture?'

'No. As you know there are the strictest orders on that. It's psychological. They believe that they're going to be tortured and put to a slow death because that's what their leaders have told them. Once away from their gang leaders they seem to shed their fervour. After a few days of humane treatment they realise how badly they are armed and fed, compared to us, that so much of what they have been told is gobbledegook, that we are so much stronger than they are, and that their cause looks hopeless. Then they are fairly easily turned. What is not generally known is that the police, the Kenya Regiment, and the military intelligence of-ficers are building pseudo gangs of ex-Mau Mau, under European leaders, who go into the forest disguised as Mau Mau. They're beginning to have some success.'

'Why did all this happen, this insurrection?' Colonel Rex asked.

'Well, this is where Fred and I probably part company, and I'm also rather out of line saying this. Most of the settlers and the administration think that Mau Mau is pure evil, a regression to savagery that must be stamped out. So it is, on the surface. Un-derneath, there's a definite grievance over land and participation in government that the settlers and the administration have never faced up to.'

'But, Jeremy,' said Fred, 'we know all that and we know that the Kikuyu are divided. This started as a civil war among the Kikuyu, and that's what it still is. The elders were happy to go along with the proposals for development. The young were impatient. So they came to blows, and particularly bloody and savage the blows were.'

'True,' said Jeremy, 'but the majority of the Kikuyu are sympathetic to Mau Mau.'

'Only because of the dreadful oathing. And when you get gangsters let loose everyone is fearful for his life.'

'Yes, maybe, but I'm only trying to say that killing and rounding up the Mau Mau will not solve the underlying problem. There is a genuine grievance about land and self-government which the settlers, the administration, and the colonial office in London have never faced up to.'

'That's a political issue,' said Colonel Rex. 'I'm only a simple soldier, here to do what I'm told. We'll help you get rid of Mau Mau. The C-in-C has briefed us that it's not a war, it's the repression of a disorder. We are here,' he said, 'not to kill the maximum number of Mau Mau. We're here to win over the Kikuyu to help them destroy Mau Mau. As to the politics, you'll have to sort that out yourselves.'

'And that', said Anna, 'is another conversation, and please not now. Coffee?'

After coffee, Colonel Rex and I made our thanks and left. On the way back to Nairobi he said, 'When I arrived, I thought quelling the insurrection was the problem. Now I can see that that will be fairly straightforward, though it may take a little time. The problem is what happens afterwards. Anyhow, it's Friday. What are you doing this weekend?'

'I'm going to stay with the Hay-Smiths at Nanyuki. We met them at the Muthaiga Club. Charlie Chance and Ben Wildbore are coming with me. And you, Colonel?'

'I'm going to play polo. What about you, Corporal? How are you going to spend the weekend?'

'Polishing the bleeding staff car, I expect, trying to get all this fucking murram off it.'

'Oh, I hope not all weekend,' said the colonel.

The hundred mile drive to Nanyuki took nearly four hours, on a road made of murram for most of the way. I drove Burgo's Citroen, which he'd lent me. He had the use of a military Land Rover in his role of Field Intelligence Officer, in which he found himself based on the farm of a charming widow near Thika, about twenty miles north east of Nairobi.

Of the others who had met the Hay-Smiths at the Muthaiga Club, Jasper was training with Forest Company, and Adam had declined to come. He found up-country not to his taste, and felt that his pleasures were more likely to be found in Nairobi than in places like Nanyuki. He was also settling into his new job as second-in-command of Y company and ingratiating himself with Tony Henderson, his new company commander. So our party was Ben Wildbore, Charlie Chance, and me.

Ben Wildbore and I had served together in, and since, Korea. He had inherited a small fortune from an aunt, which included a five storey house in Harrington Gardens in London where he let me stay. He had ordered a new 3-litre Rover for Kenya but it had yet to arrive. Charlie was an engaging National Serviceman with a few months to go, and had an uncanny ability to pop up when an opportunity like this arose.

We had left camp while it was still light on Friday and arrived at the Hay-Smiths in the dark. Their house was built on colonial lines, a long, low building with verandahs and guest annexes, in one of which the three of us were staying.

'How lovely to see you again, at last,' said Elizabeth Hay-Smith. 'It's so good of you to come. Tonight we're going to have a quiet evening after that beastly long drive. Tomorrow we'll go riding first thing, and then we're going to spend the day at the club so you can play tennis and croquet. There's a dance in the evening. The girls have arrived and they're changing in the other annexe. Don't dress for dinner, but do have a drink to take to your rooms. And drinks before dinner as soon as you're ready.'

There were three girls. Mary Hay-Smith, the only daughter, worked at Government House in Nairobi. She was dark and foxy.

Becky Summerson was tall and elegant; her parents were settlers and neighbours, if you could call someone living fifteen miles away a neighbour. She was an air hostess with East African Airways. And Juno White, a redhead with a slender figure and a beckoning smile, was the daughter of a senior colonial official in Nairobi, where the three of them shared a flat.

They were more Charlie's age, and they were all fun. It was a lively weekend but nothing too intimate happened; at the end it was clear that we would all meet up in Nairobi. Charlie teamed up with Mary. He told me later he was curious to explore what was behind her mask. Ben and Becky had got together. Ben liked girls who were as tall as him; they danced well together and clearly enjoyed it. That left Juno and me. She was more sophisticated than the others, probably because she had been educated in England. She interested me.

We left immediately after lunch on Sunday, for I had arranged that we should visit Burgo on our way back, as he was only a few miles off our route to Nairobi. With some difficulty, we found the estate where Burgo was quartered; then we found Burgo's quarters, a small, brick building, where his soldier servant told us that we were expected at the main house of the estate, which belonged to Nancy Bergman, whom everyone called Ingrid for obvious reasons. This was a large and well-proportioned bungalow, painted white and standing on a low hill with fine all round views. Burgo and Ingrid were standing at the door and, after greeting us warmly, said they'd been watching us circling the estate with some amusement. Ingrid led us into her sitting room and seated us.

'My husband built this just before the war,' she said. 'He never lived in it as, when war broke out, he was called up as a reservist. He was killed in Burma, and I've lived here alone now for twelve years. Not all the year, as I travel. I have a manager to run the farm. I wouldn't want to do that alone.'

She was in her forties, a handsome, soignée woman, and blonde. I detected a slight accent.

'I was born in Sweden,' she said, 'and I met Jim in South Africa, when I was staying with a cousin who was the Swedish consul in Johannesburg. We fell in love and decided to make our lives in Kenya. I've never regretted it. Just look at the views.'

With the sun setting gloriously in the west, it was close to paradise.

'Burgo, darling, it's time for sundowners. Would you look after the drinks?'

So we sat in her sitting room with the magnificent views and talked and drank. I told them how Jasper was getting on, a born irregular. And then I reported what he had said about D.P. Brown falling off the ship.

'What exactly were his words?' asked Burgo.

'His exact words were "D.P.Brown falling off that boat was a godsend".'

'He didn't say "pushed" or "jumped"?'

'No, he said "falling".'

'That's very careful of him. I think you should report that to the authorities.'

'Did you realise, Ingrid,' I said, 'that Burgo is the regimental tease? We sent him here specially to have a respite. I hope he isn't being a nuisance. If he is, we could recall him immediately.'

'He's a darling. Don't you dare. It's lovely to have a man pouring out the drinks, and he amuses me.'

Ben then asked Ingrid about her farm, and I turned to Burgo and asked him what it was like being a Field Intelligence Officer.

'Cerebral.'

'Can you talk about it?'

'I couldn't possibly. It's all top secret.'

'You're just trying to make it sound more important than it is. Anyhow, you owe me a hundred shillings. Have you got your tenner back from Adam yet?'

'I had hoped you had come to see me out of friendship and not to collect. As a matter of fact, Adam has paid up. He wrote to me saying his mother had taken pity on him and his finances were repaired.'

He handed me five twenty shilling notes.

'Well, I've got some news to tell you,' he said. 'Guess who *I've* seen?'

This stopped all conversation.

'D.P.Brown?' said Charlie.

'No, I think he's well and truly in Davy Jones's locker. Think again.'

'Give us a clue,' said Ben.

'Not sure I can. Well, he's a member of the regiment, or was.'

'That could be anybody.'

'No, not anybody, a very special body.'

Who could he mean, I thought. Typical Burgo, raising another hare.

'OK, then I'll tell you. Jack Trench.'

'Jack Trench!' we exclaimed.

'Yes, Jack Trench. He's alive and well and a company commander in the KAR stationed here. I saw him in Nairobi yesterday with Julia.'

'Who's Jack Trench?' asked Nancy.

'Jack Trench,' I said, 'is the regimental bête noire. He commanded a company in Korea, where he behaved very badly when Hugh Jermy, one of our ablest and most loved officers, was killed. In Germany he toadied up to the colonel and deliberately caused a lot of misery among the young officers. Eventually, even the Colonel got fed up with him and he left to re-join the Parachute Regiment, whence he'd come. Jack Trench is an arriviste, bent on winning medals and promotion and wreaking mayhem in the process. His wife, Julia, is a sweet woman, much younger than him, and she was being driven to distraction when we last saw them. He must be here chasing another medal.'

'I think I'm rather looking forward to meeting him,' said Ingrid. 'It sounds as if there's one more cad in Kenya.'

'No good comes of having Jack Trench around,' said Ben. 'I smell trouble.'

4

The Forest calls

For the next month Colonel Rex had the battalion training hard. Not just Forest Company, every company was put through its paces. He had three obsessions: getting fitter, shooting at close range, and practising fieldcraft. Even the orderly room was mustered every morning to exercise under me, followed by a run. We also took our turn on a simulated forest range where we walked along a bendy track and figure targets of Mau Mau sprung up or swung out at us. We still missed most of the targets. We were spared practising forest lore and fieldcraft.

On arrival in the country we had been told we had to learn Swahili, the main language of the country. Tribes, like the Kikuyu, had their own languages, which were more difficult to master, but almost all the Africans we were likely to encounter spoke Swahili. Colonel Rex made this a priority, too. Now and again you'd hear soldiers using Swahili words like *bunduki,* for a rifle, and *chakula* for food, though more often you'd hear 'what's yer *posho* like?' which was the crushed maize eaten by most Africans.

As we were training for the forest it's time I described it.

The Aberdares is a giant upland in the shape of a fishbone, running north and south with two small peaks, Mount Satima in the north and Mount Kinankop in the middle. The bones are steep ridges that run east and west, falling dramatically; and in the valleys between them fast flowing streams tumble down, anything from a foot to twenty feet wide, teeming with trout.

Whereas the Aberdares is a range of very high ground with forested slopes, about 11,000 feet at its highest, Mount Kenya is a snow clad mountain rising to 17,000 feet. Lying to the east of the Aberdares, and separated by about fifty miles, it's a round mass and its ridges are like the spokes of a wheel. At the hub at the top it has three peaks; ridges and streams flow down on all sides, and all the slopes are forested. .

The forest starts at 7,000 feet. Cedar, wild fig, and coniferous podocarp (a native of east Africa) grow to 70 and 80 foot with no lower branches, so that sound carries easily and far. It's a cold, gloomy place which the sun never penetrates. You can only move by cutting a path through impenetrable undergrowth or finding a game track to follow, which is the only way to travel at any pace. If you have to cut a path, you can't move more than 500 yards in an hour; if it's raining it'll take you twice that time. After climbing about 2,000 feet, in which you will have travelled about two miles, you reach bamboo, giant bamboo too big to get your hand round, about 20 to 30 foot high, mixed with young bamboo, and the ground clothed with rotting bamboo — all a formidable barrier. At this height you're beginning to find yourself short of breath and climbing hurts. But you've got to climb for about four miles to reach 10,000 feet, when you scramble out of the bamboo into the cold daylight and open moorland of springy turf, heather, and giant lobelia, where it freezes at night. In the Aberdares you've reached the top. On Mount Kenya you're looking at rock, ice, and snow towering above you.

In the forest you have two enemies. At any time wild game could be a few yards away and a rampant buffalo, or an angry elephant, could be more dangerous than a Mau Mau gang. As you have to use the tracks animals have made, you always have to be on the *qui vive* for them, too.

Charlie Chance had been seeing something of Mary Hay-Smith

and he suggested that I might like to join up with them one evening, and why didn't I bring Juno and ask Ben if he would like to bring Becky. The idea had crossed my mind and I readily agreed. I knew George Bulman was right in saying I should stop pining for Kitty and 'get myself a love life', as he had put it. Juno and I had got on well. So, one evening we all met in the bar at the Norfolk Hotel, went on to the Swiss Grill, and ended at the Equator Club, where Ben and Becky gave a terrific display of bebop and everyone stopped dancing to watch and clapped loudly when the music stopped.

'Ben's quite a card,' Mary said to me, for we had been dancing together.

'He enjoys life and he has the wherewithal to do it,' I said.

'What do you mean?'

'He's quite comfortably off.'

'Aren't you all?'

'By no means.'

'We thought you all were. We understood you were a rich regiment, one of those you have to have £500 a year to get into.'

'It's an expensive regiment but not everyone has that sort of money. Is that why your father asked us to Naivasha?'

'No. He's keen for us to meet Englishmen. He's also very concerned about the Mau Mau and wanted you to learn how he and others settlers feel about it.'

'He made that clear. What do you feel about it?'

'The atrocities are fewer and fewer now. I cannot understand how it could have happened. What went wrong? It all seemed so peaceful on the farm when it broke out. Why do you ask?'

'I'm interested in knowing more about it.'

'You are being serious.'

'You were here when the emergency started?'

'I was at school here, in my last year. Then I was packed off to London for a year. I enjoyed that but I'm much happier here. I grew up here. It's my country.'

'And you liked school here?'

'Oh, yes. It was fun. All sorts of things happened.'

'Such as?'

'Well, the headmistress fell in love with one of the girls and they ran off together.'

'Good heavens! In Kenya?'

'Oh yes. All sorts of things happen here.'

'What happened to them?'

'We were never told but I know that the girl was hauled home by her parents. She was seventeen. We heard that the headmistress left the colony. Come on, don't let's be so serious. Why don't we dance?'

So we danced. And then I danced with Juno.

'You were having a cosy chat with Mary,' she said.

'Not at all. We were talking about the Mau Mau.'

'Is that all?'

'Well, we were talking about growing up in Kenya. You didn't, did you?'

'We came here when my father was posted here. He's in the colonial office. I love it. Of course, there's not much sophistication but it's such a beautiful country, breathtakingly beautiful. I could live here forever quite happily.'

'Don't you worry about the emergency?'

'Not in Nairobi, not any longer. Daddy says it will be all over soon.'

'Not too sure about that. Will you stay here?'

'Depends who I meet,' she said and squeezed my hand.

'You're flirting!'

'Not yet,' she said. 'But I do like you.'

We danced closer for a bit.

'Why on earth did you come here in the middle of the emergency?' I said. 'Many of the girls here, like Mary, were sent away.'

'My parents thought I'd like a break from London. Look,' she said, 'I was engaged to a boy in the Brigade and it didn't work out. It was a good idea to come here. Understand?'

'I'm sorry. I shouldn't have asked'

'I'm over it. I was unhappy at the time but I'm fine now. I think

I'd like a drink. Dancing is thirst making.'

We sat down and each had a John Collins.

It was after midnight, the club was emptying and the girls said they'd like to go home. Ben said he'd take them — his new Rover had arrived — and Charlie and I saw them off. Becky, who'd drunk quite a lot, rather obviously sat in the front seat with Ben. Charlie and I got a taxi back to camp.

'I'm rather keen on Mary,' said Charlie, 'but she doesn't do it. Her mother told her that men like to marry virgins and she's sticking with that. Do you think Juno does it?'

'I really haven't thought about it,' I said.

'Mary says Becky does. Do you think they're at it at this moment?'

I was thinking how unobservant I had been when we arrived at the camp and the guard opened the gates for us. Juno had said she liked me. I liked her. I wondered where all this was leading us. Does one ever know?

'The colonel's been called to see the Brigadier,' said Kettle when I arrived in my office tent after our early morning exercises. He was putting some files in my in tray. 'He left a message for you to call an O Group for 1400 hours.'

'Would you write a message to that effect and I'll sign it. It had better go out as soon as possible.'

'Here it is, Sir,' he said as he passed me a message pad with the message already written. I signed it.

'Anything interesting in the mail?' I asked.

'More requests from GHQ for vital information.' He lifted the top file. 'This one is of particular interest.'

'What's it about?'

'Circumcision, sir.'

'Circumcision?'

'GHQ wants to know how many of the battalion are circumcised?'

'Why on earth?'

'Apparently, in this climate, uncircumcised men can fall prey to a phallic condition so serious that it could render them unfit for duty. GHQ needs to estimate the possible incidence of this condition. I'll ask the companies for a return.'

'What on earth will you ask them?'

'Quite simple. How many of their men are circumcised.'

'How will they know that?'

'They can ask them on a muster parade. You know, all those men who have not been circumcised, two steps forward march.'

'Good, we don't want to have a phallic inspection.'

'No. Would you like a cuppa char, Sir? I always find it helps after a night on the tiles.'

How *does* he know that? The guard commander at the gate must have reported my early arrival.

'We're going to be here for some weeks so let's make ourselves comfortable,' said Colonel Rex.

We were watching the RSM and the Bugle Platoon erect the tents for our tactical headquarters; the Bugle Platoon provided our defence. We were in the native reserve, a little to the west of Fort Hall and about 50 miles north of Nairobi.

'And I mean everyone.'

Colonel Rex was good at ensuring every member of the battalion was looked after.

We had left a small rear party at Muthaiga camp and I had instructed Kettle to stay with it to look after the orderly room there and handle all the routine, which seemed a natural arrangement to me. He'd taken this rather badly and spoken to the colonel, who told me that Kettle had always stayed with tactical headquarters. In the Second World War he had been in the thick of it at Anzio when the battalion had been almost cut off. He had been ordered back but he had refused to go. So he was with us now, having left Corporal Norman behind in his place and was busy building a fire on which to make his tea.

'We can leave the RSM to finish this now,' Colonel Rex said.

'Let's go and see how the companies are getting on.'

Three of the four companies were strung out along the edge of the forest. Corporal Bates drove us in his Land Rover. The staff car had been left in camp, spotlessly clean with strict instructions from Corporal Bates that no one might use it. We motored along a new murram track just made by the Royal Engineers. They were busy everywhere, cutting and laying roads into the forest to facilitate the re-supply of the companies. After a mile we found signs for W company and almost the first person we saw was Percy Smythe, as elegant as ever, even in the forest, who commanded the company. He was a tall and very relaxed officer with a slight lisp who had been adjutant in Korea. He was talking to a strange officer in the uniform of another regiment.

'You're just in time to talk to the Field Intelligence Officer. He has reported news of a Mau Mau gang nearby.'

Percy introduced the Field Intelligence Officer as Captain Mellor and then led us into a large tent, which Percy described as his ops room. He had arrived in his position earlier than we had and had nearly completed setting up his camp. We stood in front of a large-scale map of the area and Mellor told us he had good information that there was a Mau Mau gang operating from a hide about two miles away in the forest.

'How do you know?'

'We've got a tame courier who's told us.'

'Torture him?'

'We don't torture, Sir. After he'd been with us for a few days he realised he was on the losing side and he readily came over. It's quite a process, and he had to be de-oathed, but once started it works. We're finding that a lot now.'

'How do you know he's telling the truth?'

'Once they turn they always tell the truth.'

Mellor was truculent and superior in his manner, probably because he had been in Kenya far longer than we had and knew much more than we did.

'What do you suggest we do?'

'Send a well briefed and experienced patrol in to find them. I'd like to capture the lot.'

'Capture them?'

'You might kill some but I want as many as possible captured. Then we can interrogate them and they will lead us to other gangs.'

'Oh, will they? Well, let's see exactly where they are,' said Colonel Rex, as he examined the map carefully.

'These maps are rather basic, Sir,' Mellor said, 'but the position is about here. I have a tracker and the surrendered Mau Mau who can lead you there. We really need to act on this as soon as possible. The info will get stale. The gang might move at any time. A KAR battalion would know what to do. '

'Now let me see, the spot you identify as this gang's position is outside Major Smythe's area. So, Major Smythe cannot send a patrol.'

All the companies had been given specific areas in which to operate and on no condition were they to wander into another company's area for fear of casualties from friendly fire.

'Surely he can send a patrol?' said Mellor.

'I don't know whether you realise that we're here to take part in a major operation. We can do nothing that would conflict with our orders. We'll have to wait for the operation to flush this gang out.'

'But that will take time, days maybe, and we know that this gang is here, now.'

'Nothing I can do,' said Colonel Rex. 'And that's my decision. It's my responsibility to ensure we have no accidents, and asking Major Smythe to send out patrols into another company's area is courting disaster. Now, if you leave us we can get on with our job.'

I took the FIO's arm and led him away before he said something he'd later regret. 'That's foolish inflexibility,' he said. 'This gang is a sitting duck. Can't he see that?'

'The colonel knows what he's doing. He commanded a battalion in Burma. Besides, he's got his orders and the brigadier was very insistent on everyone keeping to his area.'

'It beggars belief. Here I am, working my arse off getting good info, and when I get it no one takes any notice.'

'I suggest you get yourself briefed on this operation.'

'These large operations are no good. The only way forward is to act on info, good info like this,' he said as he left.

I re-joined Colonel Rex chatting to some soldiers. Then he turned to me and said, 'Time we moved on, Miles, or it'll be dark before we've seen all the companies.'

Corporal Bates was standing by his Land Rover and, once seated in it, Colonel Rex said to me, 'What would you have said to that FIO?'

'I can see he had a point, Colonel, but I can't see how what he wanted could fit into our operation.'

'That's the point. Percy was perfectly capable of mounting a fighting patrol but we would have had to halt everything else, and you know how counter orders lead to disorder, and we couldn't fit it into the Brigade timetable for tomorrow. The FIO has probably put in a lot of time and effort getting that information, so he was naturally disappointed.'

'When I led him away he said that these large operations didn't work and that the way forward was to work on exact information.'

'He's probably right.'

Within a few minutes we found X Company. The company commander had an ops tent, too, in which he'd posted many photographs of gang leaders and members, as well as maps. He also had an enlarged copy of the C-in-C's order about 'The Honour of the Security Forces' and the absolute need for discipline and humane behaviour.

'That's a good point, Miles,' Colonel Rex said, 'I want every company to be reminded of that order. We don't want any slips in behaviour, whatever the circumstances.' He then made a point of talking to some of the soldiers before we went on to find Y Company, commanded by Tony Henderson, to whom Adam Hare was second-in-command. While Colonel Rex was questioning Tony in his ops tent about his stop lines and ambushes, as he did with the other company commanders, Adam took me aside and, when we were out of earshot, he said, 'I hear from Burgo that he's lodging with a handsome widow and that you've been to see them. What's the exact relationship there?'

'Platonic, I'd say. She clearly likes having him around and calls him darling but I suspect she'd call you darling once she got to know you.'

'More importantly, he tells me Julia Trench is living here, too, somewhere near Nairobi, and that Jack is in the forest with the KAR. I must find an opportunity of seeing her. She can be very accommodating and I expect she needs cheering up.'

'I'm a little worried about Jack being here. You know what a brute and a sneak he is.'

'What's he got to sneak about us? He's a poltroon and a coward and, with any luck, one of his men will shoot him in the back.'

Finally, Corporal Bates drove us to see Forest Company, whose camp was placed in the forest and the engineers had cut a road up to it. There the patrols were preparing themselves to go into the forest for several days. They were to climb to the top of the Aberdares and then start patrolling into the bamboo forest, searching for gangs, following any tell tale signs of gang movement, attacking any hides or gangs they found, capturing rather than killing Mau Mau, if they could, and forcing the gangs down the forest onto the ambushes. Each patrol had its own area in which it could move freely, but it was not to move outside it. Each would be in the forest for several days and had to carry rations on which to live.

'All Sir Garnet?' Colonel Rex asked Francis Bowerman when we found him in his ops tent poring over a large scale map with Big Steel.

'Nearly there,' he replied. 'You know, Colonel, these maps leave a lot to be desired. In fact, in the forest they're not maps at all. Not surprising, for how or why would anyone have mapped the forest? Once in the forest, the patrols have to move by compass, the lie of the ground, and instinct. My only real concern about this operation is the ability of a patrol to know where it is and to keep to its area.'

'How well did they do in training?'

'No real problems as the trackers and the Kenya Regiment serjeants with each patrol were familiar with the area in which we trained. Here, it's virgin forest to everyone except Mau Mau.'

'I'm more concerned that your patrols don't run into our ambushes.'

'Everyone knows that they're not to reach the ambush line until the fourth day at the earliest. That doesn't worry me, as we're patrolling in the bamboo and the ambush line is below the bamboo. Anyhow, we've been through it all with them and it's now up to them. They're all as keen as mustard.'

'Let me talk to them.'

Francis led the way out of the tent followed by the colonel, me, and Big Steel.

'Enjoying the front line?' I asked Big Steel.

'I've got less control here than I had in Support Company. It's a lot of private armies, all competing with each other.'

'Well, you've some experience of that.'

'Yes, but not of the Kenya Regiment boys. They're fucking good in the forest but they don't know their arse from their tits as serjeants.'

'They're hunters not soldiers.'

'Too right, but the major is good with them and the men admire them.'

'How's Mr Knox?'

'He's taken to the forest like a missionary to sex.'

We were now in Jasper's lines and the colonel was talking to him. Jasper had his men lined up, including his Kenya Regiment serjeant and trackers with their dogs, and he introduced them. When the colonel moved on, Jasper introduced me to his serjeant.

'Miles, I want you to meet Reggie Ferndale. He's terrific in the forest and speaks Kikuyu as well as Swahili.'

'Hello, Reggie,' I said. 'You've got some interesting days ahead of you.'

'Morning, Captain. As long as the lads remember we're in the forest hunting Mau Mau and not chasing cunt down in Nairobi we might have some success.'

'How come you speak Kikuyu? I understand that not many settlers do.'

'We had Kikuyu on the farm and I grew up with them, so I can speak it as well as they can.'

'Well, good hunting, to you both,' I said and left to catch up the colonel, who was saying goodbye to Francis.

'Good luck, Francis,' Colonel Rex said. 'You've done all you can to prepare for this. I'm impressed.'

The sun was sinking fast.

'Time to return to Battalion Headquarters, Bates,' Colonel Rex said as he climbed back into his Land Rover. 'Nothing more we can do now.'

'Time for my fucking tea, if you ask me,' said Bates.

5

Between forest patrols and ambushes life goes on.

The operation was to start at dawn, with some old Lincoln bombers from the Second World War dropping bombs on the forest. This was meant to terrorise the terrorists there and help to drive them down into the ambushes or out of the forest into the native reserves, where they could more easily be dealt with. We learnt later that bombing did more harm to the wild animals than it did to the Mau Mau. A wounded elephant could cause havoc and be very dangerous to patrols. It also alerted the terrorists that something big was up and put them on the *qui vive*. In some operations the artillery and mortars would open up, too, but not on this occasion as the nature of the ground made it too difficult.

A little before dawn, we heard the drone of the aircraft followed by the sound of the bombs exploding and then the noise of the bombers receding. The ambushes had already been posted and the patrols into the forest would now start. For the next few days Colonel Rex and I would have little to do, for the operation would take a week or more. George Bulman and ORQMS Kettle were with us, as was the RSM. With Kettle present we would never be short of a cup of tea. Also joining us, they had not yet arrived, were the local police officer and district officer, who had key roles to play with the local Kikuyu. We'd brought Serjeant Cheke, now the officers' mess serjeant, with us and left Corporal Chisholm, the new barman, back at our camp at Muthaiga outside Nairobi. Cheke had brought a comprehensive bar with him and been inspired to include the backgammon board, packs of cards and a copy of Hoyle. As soon as Colonel Rex saw the backgammon board he challenged George Bulman to a game. I could see time would not lie idly for them. There is a tide in the affairs of war that sometimes moves swiftly and sometimes hardly at all: long periods where nothing seems to happen. This was likely to be one. It was important to have a proper mess set up, and not just for ourselves. We would have guests to look after and entertain.

Rex and George spent the morning visiting all the company headquarters to see that everything was 'All Sir Garnet'. It was. We had a late lunch and then they settled down to a game of backgammon.

'What are we playing for?' asked Colonel Rex. 'It's not much of a game if we don't play for something.'

'A shilling a point with a five pound limit. That's the mess rule.' George had brought sanity to the betting that had got out of hand in Germany. 'And doubling of course.'

'That's not in Hoyle.'

'We always double.'

'Good. I'll take you to the cleaners. Just you watch me, Miles.'

The colonel and George were sitting opposite each other in the officers' mess tent in canvas arm chairs. They laid out the pieces on the board and began to play. I settled down to watch them, as I was interested to see how they both played. As they started to play I was called to the telephone. It was Adam Hare.

'There's a welcome lull in whatever battle is about to be fought so I thought I'd ring you to give you some info and get some advice,' Adam said.

'Where are you, Adam?'

'I'm back in my company headquarters tent. I've just been to see Julia Trench, and very accommodating she was. She's quite near here and is in a bit of a fix. Her dear husband, Trench Foot, is commanding a company of the King's African Rifles and has been behaving as if he's a member of the Gestapo. Not out of character, of course, but now he seems to have been found out by the proper authorities and no one is going to shield him. He's been charged with murder. Poor Julia is understandably upset so I shall have to pay a lot of attention to her, if you see what I mean.'

'Murder? Who's he murdered?'

'Apparently, when his African riflemen capture a Mau Mau they take him to Trench and he tortures the prisoner. Things with cigarettes, cutting off their ears, you won't want to hear it all, too barbaric. Need I say more? Well, recently one of his Mau Mau prisoners died from being tortured a little too hard. Rather careless don't you think?'

'Completely against the rules. Thank goodness Trench has got his come-uppance, but I wouldn't have wished for it to be like this.'

'Yes. Nice for me too. Julia really needs me.'

'You're a cad, Adam.'

'No, just a kind adventurer. That's the info. Now for the advice. When the lads come out of the forest there'll be no stopping them, so I'm thinking of setting up a company brothel. I was wondering if there're any guidelines in Army Orders or somewhere about how to go about all this? I mean how many tarts per platoon, that sort of thing.'

'Does Tony know anything about this?'

'He leaves this sort of thing to me.'

'You're playing with fire, Adam. Don't do any such thing.'

'Isn't it rather unfair that the men shouldn't have their oats now that I'm being so fortunate with Julia? Besides, by running a company whore house with a generous supply of condoms the medical orderly can check all the girls regularly and I'll see none of my boys will catch VD, which they almost certainly will otherwise.'

'Good tease, Adam. Tease Michael next.'

'You're not being very helpful, Miles. I shall have to settle on the ratios myself, what you might call the company tart scales. Goodbye.'

Was Adam being serious, I wondered. Quite possibly. What should I do about it? Well, it was Tony Henderson's problem, not mine, though I might mention it to the colonel when there was a good moment. Then Kettle told me that the district officer and the police officer had arrived.

This was not the first time we'd had any contact with the local administration or police, but it was the first time we were going to spend so much time in each other's company and, clearly, Colonel Rex was going to make the most of the arrangement. As this was an introductory meeting Colonel Rex decided to hold it in the mess tent. The newcomers were given drinks — the policeman was called Mark Black and the district officer Jim Fairford — and we all sat down.

'Now tell me,' said Colonel Rex, 'was Kenyatta really the master mind behind all this?'

Jim Fairford looked at Mark and then at Rex and said, 'That's a very good question.'

'Undoubtedly,' said Mark Black. 'He had been inciting the Kikuyu for some time, going round the reserves, and holding mass meetings. We should have arrested him and the others much earlier. He's rotting now at Lodwar, drinking a bottle of whisky a day, so we hear.'

'I can't quite agree with that,' said Jim Fairford. 'Kenyatta was undoubtedly the leader of the Kenya African Union, the KAU, the predominately Kikuyu quasi political party. And officials of the KAU certainly used it for Mau Mau purposes. And it's true Kenyatta had been holding mass meetings. Some of those that witnessed those meetings thought that he had been to trying to cool things down, lower the temperature. He did not believe in violence. He thought there were peaceful ways of getting constitutional change. Trouble is, he always speaks in proverbs and he can be interpreted in several ways to suit one's beliefs. There are some who think that if we had not put him inside when we did then the Mau Mau would have murdered him, too, along with the other loyal chiefs they murdered. He was certainly the leader of the KAU, but I'm not sure he was the leader of the Mau Mau. You know that the Mau Mau murdered some of their own chiefs who were loyal to the colonial government before they killed a single settler?'

'What about Kenyatta's trial then?' said Colonel Rex.

'That's another good question,' said Jim. 'The authorities wanted a clear verdict of guilty, and they only got one because the judge had made up his mind about the case before it started. It was a show trial. It's made Kenyatta an even greater hero among the Mau Mau. It may have been as fair a trial as Kenyatta was going to get, given he had to be convicted, but it was hardly English justice.'

'You surprise me,' said Colonel Rex.

'An overriding principle of colonial administration is that the government must be seen to govern.'

'I know that. Now you talk about the Mau Mau and the Kikuyu as if they're different. I thought they were one and the same.'

'Far from it. This whole affair started as a civil war among the Kikuyu. Very simply, the elders of the tribes, all of whom are well off, were reasonably happy with the steps being made towards advancement and independence. Not so the young, who have little. In the last war some had served abroad, in India and elsewhere, and saw what was happening in the world outside Kenya. They want independence now. It's a generation thing in which the elders are against violence and the young see violence as the only way forward. As I said, the first murders were of chiefs, murdered by their own people before any settler was murdered.'

'I see. So what's the feeling among the Kikuyu now? Haven't ninety per cent of them taken the Mau Mau oaths?'

'Mau Mau is a terrorist organisation whose principal aim is to drive the white man out of Africa. It is also a religion. The oaths are the initiation, a rite well understood in Kikuyu culture which is steeped in superstition and witchcraft. The oaths are successive and mount in degree. The first oath is that of any secret society: "I will not give away the secrets of this society"; and the second "I will not help Government apprehend members of this society".

You are right in saying most have taken the basic oaths. They were bullied to do so. They were told that, if they didn't take them, they would not share in the re-distribution of the land when the white man had been driven out. The further oaths, the ones taken by the men and women who went into the forest, are violent and degrading, and many are counter to Kikuyu culture. We are finding that many in the reserves are beginning to have second thoughts about the Mau Mau. I'm not saying the emergency has turned the corner. But ask yourself who supply the men in the forests with guns and ammo, food, money, and clothes? The reserves do, and they're finding it more and more difficult and not all of them like doing it. At the end of this operation we will muster the local Kikuyu women to sweep the area between the reserves and the forest with their pangas. There'll be about 30,000 of them and they'll do it willingly, as they're getting fed up being bullied by the men in the forest.'

'I thought it was about land?' said George.

'Land is the basis of wealth,' said Jim. 'The Kikuyu are farmers, their economy is agricultural. When the settlers first arrived, at the turn of the century, the Kikuyu had abandoned much of their land as they had been decimated by famine and disease and had withdrawn into their heartland. The settlers thought they had bought the land but, in Kikuyu law, the payments did not count as ownership. When, in the 1920s, the tribes began to grow they wanted their land back. In the early thirties there was a royal commission — the Carter Commission — which resolved a few matters in favour of the Kikuyu, but the Kikuyu so over-claimed their case for land that their claims were set aside. This led to further resentment. Today, with the growth of the population, there is genuine overcrowding and a lack of land on which to live.'

'Sounds a political minefield,' said Colonel Rex. 'So it's not so much about political freedom as about land?'

'It's difficult to divorce the two, now, and, to be frank, the Africans have always come second in the political game. The early governors, like Eliot before the First World War, wanted Kenya to grow into a white dominion and that's what many settlers still want. They saw, and still see, the Kikuyu culture and customs as antediluvian. Then, in 1923, there was the Devonshire Declaration that was meant to clarify everything. The Duke of Devonshire was the Colonial Secretary at the time. Put simply, he said that the African's interest in Kenya was paramount but that the interests of the settlers and other communities here should be observed.'

'How do you reconcile those?' asked Colonel Rex.

'Very difficult. It's a paradox. But few Kikuyu, or members of the other tribes, are yet fit to take part in the government of the country.'

'You have one of the most beautiful countries in the world,' said Colonel Rex, 'and what a mess. We'll help you sort out the Mau Mau in the field, but I don't see that as the real problem. You've been very quiet, Black, listening to all this.'

'Yes, sir, I have. Jim knows much more about the country than I do. I've only been here since the emergency started. I look at everything as a policeman. I find the Kikuyu sullen and uncooperative. They're clever and underhand. I cannot believe that Kenyatta is not behind it all.'

'Whether he is or not, he's out of the way.' said Jim. 'We've got to realise that we're dealing with a tribe whose original culture has been destroyed by contact with the white man and the advance of western civilisation. Fifty years ago they didn't have the wheel, and the role of a young Kikuyu was that of a warrior trained to fight a Masai warrior. We've stopped all that. Within my lifetime, the old tribal ways and disciplines of the Kikuyu have broken down and nothing appropriate has replaced them. Mau Mau is a reversion. There is no clear answer but we have to break it, however valid some of their grievances may be.'

'We've probably talked enough for the moment,' said Colonel Rex, 'about all that. Let's get down to discussing what we're all going to do to make this operation a success.'

At that moment I was called to the telephone again. It was Burgo.

'This is a little out of my remit as a Military Intelligence Officer but something has happened which I think you should know about and I'm not divulging any secrets,' he said.

'Is it about Trench Foot being had up for murder?'

There was silence at the other end of the telephone.

'Are you there, Burgo?'

'How did you know?' he said.

'Adam told me with some glee.'

'Glee? Adam is being very gallant and looking after Julia.'

'Don't be a fool, Burgo. Adam's revelling in it and behaving like the cad he can be.'

'Why've you got a down on Adam?'

'I haven't. I just think his pleasure-seeking is getting out of hand. Someone needs to pull him in before he gets into trouble. Why don't you?'

'I've got an important job here. How can I?'

'Not even advise him as a friend?'

'I don't see him being out of hand. And I find him amusing.'

'Amusing maybe. Do you know he's planning to open a company brothel?'

'What a brilliant idea.'

'Don't you realise it's against every rule in the book? Imagine the brouhaha when a journalist gets to hear about it.'

'Why should one? We're in the middle of nowhere, in a backward country. You can't follow British democratic ideals here.'

'However hard it may seem to you, one of our roles here is to be a civilizing influence.'

'Now you're getting pompous.'

'And you, Burgo, are being irresponsible.'

I put the phone down. Oh dear, was I being pompous? Surely it was Burgo being silly and pompous about his important job and his footling secrets he couldn't divulge, which was beginning to irritate me.

Kettle and I discussed some routine issues and returns that GHQ was fussing about. Then I returned to the mess tent where the others were still talking.

'We've been having some success in the reserve areas,' said Mark Black, 'by bringing the Kikuyu into villages so that they can be protected. We've fortified the villages and raised the Kikuyu Home Guard, whom we've armed. This also makes it more difficult for the gangs in the forest to be supplied as, between the forest and the reserves, we've created a no man's land, an area about a mile wide in which any African is a suspect. If he refuses to stop when challenged he can be shot. It might be a woman, too, acting as a courier or carrier. So we're trying to seal the forest off, protect the loyalists, and put the Mau Mau on the defensive. There are fewer attacks on the settlers and their farms, now, and more skirmishes between the Mau Mau and the villages, which are generally beaten off by the Kikuyu Home Guard. One of the roles for the Britsh battalions is to show force in the reserves so that the Kikuyu can see what the Mau Mau is up against.'

'That's been mentioned to us,' said Colonel Rex. 'After this operation we're going to be allocated an area of the reserves to do this.'

'Well, Sir,' said Jim Fairford, 'I think Mark and I had better leave you now, if you've no other questions. We need to have a look round the reserves to see what's going on and how they're reacting to this operation.'

'Fine,' said Colonel Rex. 'I propose we meet at midday daily to exchange information and make appropriate plans.'

'Very good,' said Jim.

I escorted them to their transport. Jim got into his Land Rover and drove off. Mark, the policeman, waited until Jim had gone. Then, as he got into his Land Rover, he turned to me and said, 'You want to take what Jim said with a pinch of salt, he's well known to be a Kikuyu lover.' I returned to the colonel.

'Any news?' said Colonel Rex.

'Nothing important from the companies, Colonel. GHQ is making a fuss about some administrative returns. Nothing serious, but Kettle and I need to return to Muthaiga camp to sort them out.

While so little is going on, I propose we go tomorrow. We'll be away for one night.'

'Do as you think fit. There's nothing to do here except play George at backgammon at which he's being rather too clever.'

'There is one other thing I should mention, Colonel,' I said, 'I heard it originally on the grapevine and I've checked it with GHQ and they say it's true. You know Jack Trench is serving as a company commander with the KAR?'

'I recall someone telling me.'

'He's been arrested and arraigned for murder.'

'Great Scott! I wonder how we keep the regiment out of this? Keep me closely informed. I'd better tell the Colonel of the Regiment.'

In the morning, Kettle and I rose early and motored to Muthaiga, which we reached in time for breakfast. I found Ben and Charlie digging into pawpaw, eggs and bacon, toast, and Cooper's Oxford marmalade. Ben, as headquarter company commander, had been left behind in charge of the camp and the rear party. Charlie had been transferred to Ben's company to help with the administration. As a national service officer, he was due to be demobbed shortly.

'What on earth are you doing here?' said Ben. 'I thought there was a battle going on in the Aberdares.'

'There is. It's in full swing and there's little for me to do. I've come back with Kettle to sort out some absurd admin questions raised by GHQ. You remember they asked how many men hadn't been circumcised?'

'Do I!'

'Now they want it broken down by age, national service or regular, date of enrolment and discharge, etcetera, etcetera.'

'I would have thought Kettle could have done all that.'

'He could. The request, though, was made to the lieutenant colonel commanding so only I, not Kettle, can deputise for him and sign the reply.'

'The mind boggles.'

'You would think they don't realise there's a war,' I said, as a plate of bacon and eggs was placed in front of me.

'It isn't a war,' said Charlie. 'It's an emergency.'

'True enough, Charlie', said Ben. 'Remember what the General said to us when we arrived. It isn't a war, it's the repression of disorder. It is not our object to kill the maximum number of Kikuyu. Our object is to win the Kikuyu over to help destroy the Mau Mau. Our best help comes from the Kikuyu, many of whom have been forced to take the Mau Mau oaths.'

'I stand corrected', I said.

'Well', said Ben. 'It may be it's against terrorists, but it's active service. Why do you think you've got that pretty ribbon to wear on your breast? Miles, are you staying the night?'

'I thought I would. We might go out?'

'Good idea. Charlie can't come as he can't leave camp. He's orderly officer tonight. He's asked Mary to come for a drink here and Mary said she wouldn't come without Juno so they're both coming.'

'What about Becky?'

'Becky's in South Africa and won't be back until the end of the week.'

'So, you've got Mary and Juno coming for a drink here this evening?'

'Yes. Why don't you and I take them out to dinner afterwards?'

'Do you think they'll come out?'

'Of course, this is Nairobi. Girls are game for nearly anything. Charlie,' Ben said, 'would you ring Mary and tell her that Miles has come down especially to see Juno, and for them to be prepared to go out to dinner after drinks here.'

'Charlie,' I said, 'don't you dare say any such thing. But go ahead.'

The previous afternoon Kettle had rung Corporal Norman, his clerk at Muthaiga, and briefed him to start work on the return for GHQ. By mid morning the reply had been written for me to sign.

'That was quick work, Mr Kettle,' I said. 'Now we can have a relaxing day, as I told the colonel that we wouldn't be back until tomorrow.'

'Wait until you see this, Sir,' he said handing me another letter from GHQ which I read.

'Oh, no. He can't do that. What a bugger!'

'I thought you'd say that, Sir.'

'Just what we didn't want to do. Why can't the KAR do it?'

'An officer in his situation is allowed to ask for this.'

'Yes, but do we have to do it? You know what everyone feels about him.'

'Only too well. But he's entitled to ask, Sir'

At that moment Ben walked in. 'Everything's fixed for this evening,' he said. 'The girls are delighted. And pray, who is this that's entitled to ask?'

I must have sighed for Ben took his cap off, ran a hand through his hair, sat down and looked at me with curiosity. 'Well?' he said.

'I don't know whether you know, but Trench Foot has been arrested and charged with murder.'

'I had heard,' said Ben. 'That sort of news travels fast.'

'He's asked for Adam to be his defending officer.'

'That's rather clever of him. I wonder how Adam will react. He could do it brilliantly if he wants to. What an interesting situation.'

He began to chortle until I gave him such a look he shut up.

'Mr Kettle,' I said, 'I fear we'll have to return to the battalion now. I shall have to talk to the colonel about this, and it had better not wait.'

'What about this evening?' said Ben.

'You're going to have a load of fun taking both girls out.'

'Lucky me.'

'I see,' said Colonel Rex. 'I doubt that I've got any option but to
ask Adam if he'll do it. Can you see if I have any alternative? I was
so hoping to keep the battalion out of this'

Colonel Rex, George Bulman, and I were sitting in the colonel's
command tent.

'Adam is very clever. He's about the only person in the battalion
who could put up a plausible defence,' said George.

'Is there a plausible defence?' said the colonel. 'Do we want to
get him off?'

'Not for us to decide. Anyhow, we don't know the circumstances
or the evidence. Trench may be a chateau-bottled shit but that
doesn't make him guilty.'

'Why doesn't he ask for a qualified barrister?'

'Put yourself in his position,' said George. 'Getting a QC or
someone like that wouldn't be that clever because the court martial board would immediately be suspicious and it would put their
backs up. Getting a brother officer from his parent regiment who
knows him might give him a better chance to get an unprejudiced
hearing.'

'Where does that get us?'

'I was merely trying to explain the advantage to Trench that
Adam might give him.'

'I have no alternative to asking Adam have I?'

'No.'

'What if Adam says no?'

'He can't. Not if he's asked.'

'Colonel,' I said, 'there is one thing you may not know. In Germany, Adam had an affair with Julia Trench. Julia Trench is now
out here and Adam has resumed his liaison with her.'

'Well, well. Does Trench know?'

'Hard to say. He must have had an inkling in Germany. It was
such a close knit society.'

'I suspect he does which is why he's asked for Adam. Make
him feel guilt.'

'No,' said George, 'he realises that Adam is very clever and he may find a way of getting him off.'

'Miles,' the colonel said, 'ask Adam to come and see me.'

The following morning, Adam came to see the colonel. The operation was still in full swing but very little information had come out of the forests to tell us how it was going.

'Is this good news or bad?' Adam asked me on his arrival.

'The colonel will tell you,' I said and I took him into the colonel's tent.

'Adam, do sit down. You too, Miles,' the colonel said. 'You've heard that Jack Trench has been arrested and arraigned for murder?'

'Yes, Colonel.'

'He is to be court martialled in Nairobi in three weeks time. He's asked for you to defend him.'

'I would be delighted, Colonel.'

'You would?'

'I've no idea what the evidence is, and I suspect that the general wants to make an example of him, as he's very keen on good behaviour. Murder is a very strong charge and I would have thought that it might be reduced to manslaughter. I doubt if there'll be much chance of moving the board emotionally, but there might be something on technical grounds. When I went on my promotion course in Germany I found the most fascinating bit was military law. This could be an interesting intellectual exercise.'

'I believe you might have a relationship with Mrs Trench?'

'When I heard about Jack's arrest I went to see Mrs Trench to commiserate and she just fell into my arms she was so unhappy. I am a man, Colonel, and compassionate.'

'We have an unwritten rule in the regiment that we don't do that sort of thing with a brother officer's wife.'

'I did think about that, Colonel. Major Trench is serving in the KAR and I understood that he was no longer a member of the regiment.'

'Miles, tell GHQ, Adam accepts.'

'Colonel,' said Adam, 'I really should start working on this straight away. May I have your permission to return to Muthaiga?'

'You're not in that much of a hurry, are you? Won't you stay for lunch and have a game of backgammon?'

The colonel had no more luck playing backgammon with Adam Hare than he had playing with George. Adam took a fiver off him. As he left I followed him.

'What are you up to, Adam?' I said.

'I'm doing my duty. A brother officer asks for help and I give it to him.'

'Don't play the fool with me.'

'This will keep me in touch with Julia and regularise my seeing her. But I don't want Julia hanging round my neck for the rest of my life. If we can reduce Jack's charge to manslaughter that would be better. Otherwise a noose will be hanging round his neck.'

We were in touch with the ambush companies by telephone line and radio, and with forest company by radio. There had been little encouraging in the regular reports. We had heard the odd distant shot but nothing that sounded like a confrontation. Then Francis came on the air. One of his patrols had hit a gang and was returning to company headquarters with some Mau Mau prisoners. I called for Bates to take us up to forest company. It took over an hour and night was falling when we arrived. We were met by Big Steel.

'Major Bowerman,' he said,' is debriefing Mr Knox's patrol, Sir. Could you come this way and watch? It's nearly over.' We followed until we could see what was going on and stopped. There were several groups sitting on the ground being addressed by Francis. They did not notice our arrival. There were a few Tilley lamps lighting the scene.

I hardly recognised Jasper. He had six days growth of beard, his hair was matted and filthy, and his clothes had little semblance of uniform. He was sitting cross legged on the ground holding his rifle across his knees. Next to him was Reggie Ferndale, his Kenya

Regiment serjeant, looking much like him. Also his tracker. Then I noticed the Mau Mau, unmistakeable by their hair. There were three of them, looking forlorn and dejected, sitting apart with two men guarding them. They were dressed in tattered European clothing and were barefoot. A further group was headed by another of Francis' officers, with a small squad round him, looking fresh and alert, all armed and with another Kenya Regiment serjeant and a tracker. I then realised that while Francis was debriefing Jasper and his patrol, he was simultaneously briefing a fresh patrol. I couldn't follow this very clearly and it came to an end.

'Well, Peter,' I heard Francis say to the new patrol commander, 'I propose you leave just before dawn and follow this up. Have you got all the info you need?'

Peter looked round him at his patrol, who nodded, and he said, 'Yes, Francis.'

'I could go with Peter, Francis. Reggie and me,' said Jasper.

'No, Jasper, you've done your bit. Let someone who's fresh follow this up. I want you all to have a good rest before you go out again. Besides, we need Reggie to interrogate your prisoners when the police arrive. Has anyone got anything else to say? No? Then well done, every single one of you,' Francis said, looking at Jasper's patrol, 'that was magnificent work.'

The groups dispersed. Jasper stayed on talking to Francis and we walked towards them.

'Good evening, Francis,' the colonel said.

'Colonel,' said Francis, 'I didn't see you there.'

'I don't know exactly what you've done, Jasper,' said the colonel, 'but it sounds good. Well done. I'm sure you'll be wanting to go and look after your men. Be sure you get something to eat and have a good rest. We'll return tomorrow morning, Francis, with the DO and Mark the policeman, and discuss this at greater length. Now, don't you think it's time for a whisky?'

6

Jasper makes his patrol report

The following morning Bates took the colonel and me back to Francis's company headquarters. Jasper was clean shaven and neat but there was still an air about him of the forest demon of the night before. His beautiful hands were not very clean and his nails were chipped and black. We sat down in Francis' tent — the colonel, Francis, Jasper, Jim the DO, Mark the policeman, and I — and listened to Jasper.

'Reggie, my Kenya Regiment serjeant,' Jasper said, 'and I had a long discussion on how we would go about the patrol. On my earlier patrols we had behaved as if we were on a rough shoot in England, walking up game, always on the move, hoping to flush a Mau Mau. No wonder, Reggie said, you didn't catch anyone. Mau Mau can hear you moving miles away. They can also smell you: your cigarettes, soap, toothpaste, even the meat we eat. So the first rule I made for my patrol was no smoking, no washing, no cleaning teeth, even. Then Reggie and I decided we'd concentrate on a small area of the forest and cover every inch of it. We would make a camp for ourselves and then patrol daily from it. So we went into the forest with a clear plan.

'The forest is an impenetrable hell. Well, not really, but it seems so. It's wet and dark and cold all the time, day and night, and it's very tiring. We followed animal tracks and soon found a place for our camp about a hundred yards from a stream so we had an easy source of water. Our routine was to split into two groups, one to guard our camp, the other to patrol, covering the ground slowly and as systematically as we could, stopping and looking and listening more than moving. During the day, we ate biscuits only. Once it was dark, we lit a fire at our camp and had a hot meal. For two days we patrolled and found nothing. On the third day our tracker found signs that he said were Mau Mau. We followed these, very carefully and slowly, and saw a man making his way towards a stream. We were in a valley some way from the valley in which we had camped. We watched him, and then our tracker followed him carrying water to what he said must be a Mau Mau camp. We couldn't see, but our tracker was certain. The following day, we very cautiously searched the area and found a number of tell-tale marks that confirmed the view we were next to a Mau Mau camp. So, we planned to attack it at dawn the next day from downwind. The camp turned out to be in a small clearing. We attacked, caught them at their morning assembly, and started shooting at about 15 yards. They were completely surprised and ran in all directions. We killed eight. Well over a dozen got away. They were very quick. We explored and found a cave from which came some noises. I lobbed a grenade in. It exploded and I followed it in with a torch. Two women were lying dead at the opening. The cave was L shaped and at the back were three men, stunned and cowering. These we took prisoner with their weapons and all their things. Then I rolled two more grenades into the cave and the entrance collapsed. We returned to our camp, struck it, and came back to the company. Reggie said that those that got away would hide in the neighbourhood until we'd gone and then return. We thought of hanging around, but then felt rather exposed, and decided to come back to camp and get another patrol to follow the lead that we'd got.'

Colonel Rex broke the silence. 'Did you have any casualties?'

'No.'

'What weapons did they have?'

'Curiously, no one fired at us. They panicked and ran. The prisoners had a revolver and a shot gun. We found some home-made guns, too.'

'Anything else?'

'There were papers that looked like records. I gave them to Francis.'

'Francis?'

'Yes. I handed them to the police for them to analyse. They were well written.'

'They might give us some leads.'

'Anything further you'd like to report, Jasper?' said the colonel.

'We went in with no info. None whatever. We had some luck finding that camp, though we had made a good plan to do so. I know we were meant to flush out the Mau Mau onto the ambushes. I don't think that's possible in the way we'd been doing. They are so good at field craft they will always elude us. It's only by very patient patrolling we had this success. We need info. We couldn't have done this without Reggie and the tracker. The men did well too.'

'You did very well,' said the colonel. 'Have you anything to add, Francis?'

'Jasper and his team did exceptionally well. None of the other patrols had any success. Nothing more than the odd contact which evaporated. What about the ambushes?'

'Nothing to report yet,' said the colonel.

'Jasper did train his patrol to a point they were no longer European troops,' said Francis. 'None of the other patrols went to earth, so to speak, in the same way. I think we need to specialise more. Those who can emulate Jasper and his men in patrolling should. We also need teams that can set up and guard camps. And teams that can pursue opportunities immediately, so all the patrols need radios and company headquarters needs to keep a listening watch all the time. I can see a number of ways we can improve. But we are working blind and, like Jasper, I don't see how we're going to win the emergency very quickly this way.'

'Jasper, another question,' said the colonel. 'Were the maps any help?'

'None at all. We made our own as we went along. The maps are fiction.'

'What about the compasses?'

'Unreliable. There's too much iron in the ground. They swing around. We had to make judgements from the lie of the land.'

'Francis,' said the colonel, 'it would be helpful if you let us have Jasper's written report with your ideas of how we can build on this. Now, Jim and Mark, have you any questions or ideas?'

'The prisoners aren't talking yet,' said Mark. 'The papers Jasper brought out are very interesting. They show that the three in the cave — the prisoners — were quite high in the hierarchy. All officers, which is why they were living in the cave with their women. The Mau Mau officers live much better than the rank and file who are treated as dirt. It also looks as if the gang was bigger than Jasper reported, so many may have been on a patrol, either foraging or fetching supplies.'

At that moment, we heard firing from the direction of the Mau Mau camp.

'Sounds as if Peter has made contact,' said Francis.

At first there was a fusillade of single shots, followed by a mix of automatic and single fire, which got heavier and then dried up. It all stopped within thirty seconds.

'I think we'll stay a little longer and see what Peter reports,' said the colonel. 'This gets more interesting.'

'We sent him out with a radio,' said Francis. 'He'll probably call in soon. The instructions were for him to call us when he feels it safe to talk, strictly one way.'

We waited. The colonel walked round the camp talking to everyone he met. He was good at that. The soldiers had warmed to him. They began, behind his back and among themselves, to refer to him as Rex whereas before it been the CO or the colonel. The officers were saying this, too. It was both a sign of affection and respect. We all had coffee and biscuits. Slowly, the sun rose up the sky and it got a little warmer. Peter came on the air and Francis talked to him. Then Francis told us the news.

'Peter says they were ambushed but gave as good as they got. They approached the old Mau Mau camp from downwind in three groups and were to attack altogether at the same time. The left hand group was rumbled and the gang opened fire. It had two minor casualties. The other two groups moved in immediately and opened fire. So, there was a fire fight and the Mau Mau were overcome and those that weren't killed or badly wounded withdrew. There are seven Mau Mau killed and six seriously wounded. Peter has asked for a patrol to bring stretcher bearers for the wounded. Jasper, would you do that? You know where they are.'

'Thank you, Francis,' said Jasper.

After a few more days, the operation finally ended and we all returned to our camp at Muthaiga. No other company had as much luck. The Mau Mau had scuttled through the ambushes. Maybe we had flushed some gangs out of the forest. It was clear we needed better tactics and better information, and doubtful whether the British soldier could ever match the Mau Mau in the forest.

7

Time for games

Kettle and I were talking in my tent back in Muthaiga camp when the telephone went. He picked it up, listened, and handed it to me saying, 'It's Captain Howard.'

'I hear,' said Burgo, 'that Jasper has been killing Mau Mau when no one else has been able to. He's clearly got a lust for blood since he pushed D. P. Brown overboard.'

'Burgo,' I said, 'I'm not going to listen to any more of your absurd nonsense. What is it you want to talk about?'

'Cricket.'

'Cricket?'

'Yes, they play a lot of cricket here. I'm putting together a team to play the police. I wondered if you'd like to play?'

'I'd love to. Who else have you got?'

'I've got some settlers and box wallahs from Nairobi. I thought I should ask Big Steel and Body.'

'Don't you think you should ask Ben Wildbore before you steal his best players. He's the officer in charge of cricket now.'

'I was wondering who was. Yes, I'll ask Ben. I've already re-cruited Adam.'

'How's he getting on?'

'Adam is making interesting progress in the case of Regina ver-sus Major Trench. A top lawyer has been appointed to Adam's defence team.'

'Burgo, do you spend any time gathering intelligence on the Mau Mau?'

'I'm at it night and day.'

'It seems to me that you're on a very cushy number. And it's not just me that thinks that. The colonel is asking what you're doing, and you'd better give him a better story than you're giving me when he asks you.'

'Does he play cricket?'

'Why don't you ask him?'

Two days later, after first parade, the colonel said to me, 'You play cricket don't you? Yes? Well I'm putting together a team of soldiers and settlers to play the police. It should be good for our relations with both. Bat don't you?'

'Yes, Colonel. When is this to be?'

'Soon. Burgo Howard is helping to manage it and he's arranging the date now. He's calling my side Colonel Rex's XI. Any views who else I might ask?'

'Well, Ben Wildbore is cricket officer. There are some excellent players in the serjeants' mess. Serjeant Major Whettingsteel and Colour Serjeant Body, for instance.'

'Burgo mentioned them. Good idea to include them as they'll mix well with some of the settlers. They're not all upper crust, you know. In fact, far from it. Burgo also mentioned Adam Hare. Didn't you once say he was good with a bat?'

'On his day, none better.'

'Why don't we settle for them and you ask them on my behalf. That's six of us and Burgo will put together six settlers, so we'll be able to field a team if someone has to fall out. I'm sure Kettle will agree to score. I'm rather pleased with Burgo arranging this. Perhaps he's not as idle as I thought.'

Later, in the NAAFI break — military vernacular for the mid morning coffee break, though a cup and a bun for most — Ben Wildbore came up to me and said, 'Do you know anything about a cricket match the colonel is said to be arranging?'

'Oh good, you know about that. He asked me to talk to you about it. He's raising a team of soldiers and settlers to play the police. Good for our relations with both, he says. Burgo is helping him as he knows some cricketing settlers. Don't ask me how.'

'I know how,' said Ben. 'I introduced him to the local cricket club and, while you were on the last operation in the forest and I was looking after the camp here, Burgo was drinking with them and thought up this wheeze of his. I think he's overstepped the mark. Cricket is my responsibility.'

'It's only a friendly match. Colonel Rex is pleased about it. Don't rock the boat.'

'Hmm,' he said and he poured himself a second cup of coffee.

The day came for the match. Slowly, we all assembled at the ground. Colonel Rex was wearing an MCC tie to hold up his white flannels. Adam was wearing a Free Forester's tie in the same way. We were practising in the nets when the six settler members of the team arrived in ones and twos. Burgo introduced us. He seemed to know them all well. Then the police team arrived in a bus. Burgo seemed to know most of them, too. We won the toss and the colonel opted to bat. Adam and one of the settlers opened the batting for us. They were both on form and made runs quickly off the police fast bowlers.

'So, Colonel, you're getting the better of the Mau Mau in the forest?' said a settler called Bill Ambrose, who was padded up ready to bat.

'Well, we haven't really got the hang of it yet in the forest, but we're making progress. They're very elusive.'

'They all ought to be hung, drawn, and quartered.'

'That's rather strong, isn't it?'

'If you'd seen some of the horrendous killings they've done, as I have, you wouldn't show them one second of mercy. They're barbarians.'

'Isn't that over reacting?'

'They've got to be stamped out. We're not tough enough on them. The governor is weak.'

'So what do you propose?'

'We settlers should have more say in the running of the emergency. We'd hunt them down and give them no quarter.'

'Adam's out,' said Burgo. Adam had tried to hit a six, he'd already hit two, but the ball had fallen short of the boundary into the hands of an outfielder, who held the catch safely. 'You're in, Bill,' Burgo said, and Bill Ambrose got up from his chair and strode out to the wicket.

'If we were playing football I'd put him way out on the right wing,' said the colonel.

'True enough,' said another settler, called Christopher Hetherington. 'Underneath he's a very kind man but he's had a hard time from the Mau Mau. They've slashed his cattle, burnt his lines, trashed his shamba. It's a wonder he's alive. He's had a very hard time.'

'Hard time, maybe,' said the colonel, 'but you can't just exterminate the Mau Mau. Haven't you got to look at the underlying grievances and do something about them?'

'Of course, and we are. But there's a strong element among the settlers who see Kenya as a white colony and are not prepared to concede that the Kikuyu have a case for betterment. They see Mau Mau as pure barbaric evil.'

'What do you see, then?'

'I see an ancient world of tribalism exploding under the impact of western economic society. The tribe is already divided into the haves and have-nots. The haves are content with slow progress. The have-nots are desperate. So, all this starts as a civil war within the tribe. Those we call loyalist may be so. But really they're disgusted by the depravity and degradation of Mau Mau. They see the Mau Mau oathing process as contrary to all their beliefs, as oathing is an important part of Kikuyu culture. They see Mau Mau as bringing nothing but disaster to the tribe. We obviously have to stamp out Mau Mau lawfully, but we must address the underlying grievances.'

'And what are the underlying grievances?'

'It's too simple to say it's just about the Kikuyu ownership of land. It's also about the whole process of agriculture, and the economy in the reserves, and having a share in the government of the country. But the underlying problems are poverty, education, and lack of skills.'

Another wicket fell. Ambrose had refused to run a single and the settler batsman who had opened was run out.

'You're in next, Miles,' said Ben. So I walked out to the wicket and missed the rest of the conversation between Colonel Rex and Hetherington.

I made a dozen runs before I was caught behind the wicket. Bill Ambrose went on to make twenty runs not out when our last wicket fell. He had stayed in, playing a very careful defensive game. Most of our other batsmen failed and we only made 145 runs in total. The police team went in to bat and made runs quickly. Their wickets fell more quickly, and their last man came in to bat when their score was 109, so we thought we would have an easy win. Slowly, the last two put on runs until the score was 142. One four was all they needed to win. The batsman swung at the next ball, missed it and was stumped by Big Steel.

While we had been in the field, spectators had gathered and Serjeant Cheke had arrived to set up a bar. There was quite a crowd.

'Hello Miles,' said a woman's voice with a slight foreign accent, and I turned to find Nancy Bergman, Burgo's friend. She was looking very attractive, with a large hat and a loose flowing dress. 'I love watching cricket. It's so elegant. Not that I can understand it. Who won?'

'We did, just,' I said. 'How lovely of you to come and watch.'

'Burgo insisted I came, and I thought it would be fun. He says we're all going out to dinner, and dance afterwards.'

'That I didn't know. Good. So he's organised the evening too.'

'He's very keen it all goes well. I think he feels a little out of things and he wants to impress your colonel. Where is your colonel? I'd like to meet him.'

'He's talking to the captain of the police team. I'll take you across.'

So I took Nancy to Colonel Rex and introduced her. They took to each other immediately.

Bill Ambrose was in a heated discussion with a group of policemen, so I avoided them and, seeing Burgo and Adam in the distance, was making for them when someone tapped me on the shoulder.

'Hello, Miles,' said a familiar voice. 'Remember me?'

It was Juno White looking gorgeous.

'Juno, of course. How lovely to see you.'

We looked at each other.

'I'm so sorry,' I said, 'about the other evening. It's very difficult to make plans when we're in the forest. I hope you had a lovely time with Ben?'

'Oh, we did. He took us to the Equator, and Mary and I had a fine old time. I think Ben's got some plans for this evening. Are you coming?'

At that moment Ben joined us.

'There you are,' he said. 'Juno, I want you to meet our colonel. He's been asking who you are.' He guided her away to Colonel Rex, and I wondered what was going on between them. As I looked after them and pondered I became aware of someone standing next to me.

'Hello Miles,' said a girl's voice, and I turned to find Becky Summerson smiling at me.

'I think you may have missed the boat there. If you must go and play soldiers in the forest you can't expect girls to hang around for you, especially when there're rich predators around. An air hostess like me has to take her chances, too. Come on, you need a drink and so do I.'

She took my arm and steered me to the bar.

Serjeant Cheke had made some Pimms and we both had a glass. We found ourselves in a group of policemen, who were drinking Tusker beer with Big Steel and Colour Serjeant Body.

'That was a great afternoon,' said one of the policemen, 'different to chasing Micks in the forest.'

'We must do it again so you can get your own back,' I said.

'Trouble is, we're just too busy policing the reserves. It was your Captain Howard who fixed it with our superintendent. He's a great chap, Captain Burgo. You should see him with a bottle of whisky.'

They laughed. They clearly had.

They all looked fit and sunburned. But the policemen had a hard look in their eyes, which Big Steel and Body did not have.

Burgo joined us, handing out more beer. We broke up into smaller groups. Burgo and Becky talked to a policeman, and I talked to Body and Big Steel.

'They're a tough lot,' said Body. 'Not a good word to say about the Kikuyu. It's as if they despise them. I wouldn't want to be caught by them.'

'Some of them served in the war as NCOs. Now they're police officers on a bloody good racket,' said Big Steel.

'Attracted?' said Body.

'I like it here in Kenya, but I like the regiment too. They may be fighting in the same emergency but I prefer the way we do it.'

Colonel Rex joined us.

'That was great wicket keeping, Serjeant Major, though none of us batsmen covered ourselves with glory, did we, Body?' The colonel had only made three runs and Body had been bowled first ball.

'I hope we've some more games,' said Body.

'I've asked Major Wildbore to get a fixture list going. Somehow we must find time for more games. It's been a wonderful break from the forest, don't you think?'

'Yes, Sir,' said Body and Big Steel together.

'Quite a rum lot these settlers and policemen,' said Colonel

Rex.

'The police are a bloody tough lot, sir,' said Big Steel, 'So are the settlers, but they are all very kind to us. It hasn't all been a bed of roses for them. I don't just mean the Mau Mau. Beautiful as the country is, they've had to plough a hard furrow to make a living.'

'How do you find it, being here? I don't mean being in the forest, but being here in camp in Muthaiga?'

'The camp's getting better all the time but Nairobi is expensive. My Mrs comes out next month. I wonder if we'll be able to make ends meet. Is your wife joining us?'

'Yes, I'm glad to say, next month, too. It'll make a difference to have our women here now we're getting a feel for the place.'

Becky joined us. Burgo and Nancy followed.

'Hello,' said Colonel Rex, 'I don't think we've met. I'm Rex Topham.'

'I'm Becky Summerson.'

'You're not related to General Summerson, are you?'

'He's my uncle. Do you know him?'

'He was our brigadier in Burma. He never told me he had a beautiful niece.'

'I haven't seen him for years, so he probably still thinks I'm an ugly duckling.'

'Never. Now, what are you all going to do now?'

'We're going out to dinner at the New Stanley Grill,' said Burgo. 'The police have got to leave but some of the settlers are joining us. Then we're going on to the Equator Club.'

'I'll come to dinner but I don't think I'll come dancing.' Then, looking at Nancy he said, 'Too many temptations.'

Becky and I looked at each other and smiled. Then she raised her eyebrows, came across to me, took my hand, and kissed me lightly on the cheek.

We sat down at the New Stanley Grill, a dozen for dinner. Colonel Rex put Nancy on his right and Becky on his left and then invited us all to find places. I sat on Nancy's right. Christopher Hetherington,

the settler, sat on my right and Burgo sat on his right. Bill Ambrose
was there, but he'd already had a skinful and he spent his time playing with his food, knocking back a glassful, and sleeping.

'Have you lived here forever?' I asked Christopher.

'Well, yes, on and off, forever. I was born on the farm just before
the Great War. My father had arrived a year or two earlier with a
young wife and I was the first born. Those were pioneering days.
I was sent home to school when I was old enough, staying with an
aunt and uncle in the holidays. Then I returned to help my father.
Those were difficult years, the thirties. The depression knocked all
the prices. We had to borrow from the bank. But they were glorious
years, too, full of freedom and adventure and the feeling that it
would all come right. There were land problems with the Kikuyu,
but nothing came of them and they certainly didn't affect us.

'Then the second war came. They were boom years. Agricultural
prices were good and we paid off the bank and, for the first time,
we felt secure. We had some good years. Then the emergency
happened and things have got quite tough again, but in a different way. Though I think we'll slowly defeat the Mau Mau, I feel
that the great sense of hope has gone and I can't see the long term
outcome.'

'I suppose,' I said, 'that there're a lot of people in your situation.'

'Yes, most of those who farm. The curious thing is that people
are still coming out to settle here.'

'What are you two talking about' said Nancy.

'Christopher was telling me how he grew up here.'

'Then he probably speaks Kikuyu,' she said.

'Do you, Christopher?'

'I learned it as a child growing up on the farm. I suspect the
Kikuyu I played with and made friends with then have all taken the
Mau Mau oaths and I'm a sitting duck to be picked off at will.'

'Duck!' said Burgo, who was sitting on Christopher's right.
'Duck? Do you have duck to shoot?'

So Christopher and Burgo started to talk about shooting and

I was left to listen to Colonel Rex and Nancy and wonder who Becky was talking to and what about.

'How do you find Burgo?' said Colonel Rex.

'He's a lovely man, fun and very useful to have around the house. He mixes an excellent Martini.'

'Does he spend a lot of time with you?'

'Goodness no. He's not my lover. He's out and about all day working with the police, as far as I can see. He doesn't talk about it. He says it's secret. You're not going to take him away are you?'

'One day he'll have to come back to us, but not at the moment. I'm glad you say what you do about him.'

'Are you going to come on and dance, Rex? Why don't you relax and have some fun?'

'Would you dance with me?'

'I'd love to.'

Burgo was leaning forward over the table in front of Christopher trying to catch my attention.

'Did you hear that, Miles?' he said. 'No, I didn't think you did. Christopher is offering us some shooting. What do you think about that?'

'I think it's a wonderful idea,' I said. 'What might we be shooting?'

'Duck, you fool.'

Not all the party went on to the Equator Club. Bill Ambrose wanted to, but Christopher Hetherington thought it was time to take him back to the Muthaiga Club where they were both staying. Becky came with me and, as soon as we were settled at a table at the Equator, we started dancing. She held me quite close and she danced like a nymph. The warmth of her body made me feel remarkably relaxed and, at the same time, rather excited. When we sat down Colonel Rex, who had been dancing with Nancy, asked Becky to dance and I danced with Nancy. Becky, Nancy and Juno, the three girls, were constantly on the dance floor with someone, and I found myself sitting and talking to Adam, who seemed to have come along with us only to drink.

'How's the tyro barrister coming along?' I said.

'Very nicely, now you ask,' he said. 'In fact, I've cracked the case for the defence. I won't say I didn't have a little help from the lawyers but I did put my finger on it first. We believe we have a foolproof case to get Trench Foot off.'

'So what is it?'

'Do you think I'd tell you? Wait for the case to come to court.'

'You're being as pompous as Burgo.'

'Burgo is playing a game. I'm being professional.'

'How's Julia?'

'Julia is becoming a strain.'

'Not co-operating?'

'Over co-operating, I'd say. She won't let me alone. She says she loves me. Now, I wasn't after love, just sex. She's rather good at that.'

'Who's rather good at what?' said Becky as she returned to sit next to me.

'I'll tell you if you dance with me,' said Adam.

'Yes, please.'

I found myself with Burgo.

'How do you think the day has gone?' he said.

'Rather well, Burgo.'

'Do you think Colonel Rex thinks so?'

'The way he's dancing with Nancy I should think so.'

'I didn't think they'd fall for each other. Do you remember him in Korea? Always so competitive with the other company commanders and, especially, with Colonel Guy. And so full of *braggadocio*.'

'He's changed. Getting command has relaxed him and made him more confident.'

'There's still a bit of *braggadocio*, but, what a relief, don't you think, after D.P. Brown.'

'You're not going to start on him, are you?'

'Well, I've still got Jasper in my sights.'

'Burgo!'

'Alright then.'

Becky came back with Adam and I asked her to dance.

'So, who did he say was rather good at what?'

'Adam asked me if I'd go to bed with him and then he'd show me who was rather good at what.'

'What did you say?'

'I told him I had a lover who was very good at what and I wasn't on the market.'

'You mean Ben?'

'No, silly. That was just a one night stand. He's been after Juno for some time. Haven't you noticed they're becoming as thick as thieves? Look at them now.'

I did. They were clearly close.

'You've been away too long,' she said

'So, who's your lover now?'

'Well I haven't got one but I'm thinking about it.'

'Don't keep me in suspense.'

'Well, think,' she said, and, squeezing my hand, she held me closer.

'You're teasing me.'

'Don't be silly again. Next week I'm in Nairobi. Mary is going to stay with her parents and she's taking Juno with her. We'll see a lot of each other. Alright, darling?'

The following morning Rex called George Bulman and me into his office.

'That,' he said, 'was a very good day that Burgo arranged for me yesterday, and I'm delighted with how it went. It's a pity you weren't there, George. Burgo has clearly made an impression on the settlers and the police and knows how to organise an event. He's doing a good job.'

'Stap me!' said George. 'That's a change of mind.'

'Maybe, but I hadn't seen Burgo in action before, so to speak.

He's a credit to us.'

At that moment, Kettle came into the tent and handed Rex a piece of paper.

'This came in overnight,' Kettle said.

Rex read it. 'Great Dickens!' he said. 'Thank you, Kettle, that will be all.'

Kettle withdrew reluctantly.

'Well, well, well,' said Rex. 'It's from the colonel of the regiment. Let me read it to you. It's cable-ese and this is what he's saying: "Para Regt confirms Major Trench is theirs, attached KAR. Advise withdraw Hare immediately from role of defending officer and distance him and regiment from trial. If necessary post to regimental depot. GHQ East Africa Command informed. Acknowledge."'

'That's pretty clear,' said George.

'What do we need to do, then, to limit the damage?' said Rex.

'It seems dire to send Adam home,' said George. 'Couldn't we just send him back up country somewhere?'

'I suppose the problem is journalists,' said Rex. 'They'll find out that Trench was once in the regiment, wonder why Adam was withdrawn and come sniffing round here.'

'We can say Adam was out of his depth and Trench needed the best possible legal advice.'

The telephone went.

'Answer it, Miles,' Rex said, so I picked it up.

'May I speak to Colonel Topham,' a voice said.

'He's in a conference with his second-in-command and adjutant at the moment. Who is that?'

'The chief of staff.'

'Would you wait a moment, Sir.' I handed the telephone to Rex telling him who it was.

'Good morning, General,' Rex said and listened. There was no conversation. Occasionally Rex said, 'Yes, General'. Finally he said, 'Yes, General. Thank you, General,' and put the telephone down.

George and I looked at Rex.

'He was very decent. They know all about the colonel of the regiment's view and the C-in-C is determined to make an example of Trench. So, anything that might influence the court martial in his favour must be avoided. To be defended by an officer of his former regiment is not to be allowed. They don't think that Adam needs to be got out of the country. Moving him up-country is fine. But any journalists are to be referred to the public relations officers at GHQ. We are to have no dealings with journalists. He accepted that his staff was responsible for getting Adam involved. No skin off our noses. So that's that.'

'Thank God for that,' said George.

'Miles,' said Rex, 'ask Adam to come and see me immediately.'

'Yes, Colonel.'

'And Miles, let me have Nancy Bergman's telephone number. I must ring her and reassure her that Burgo will be staying on as field intelligence officer and she's not to worry about that.'

8

Some surprises

Since I had arrived in Kenya, I had been corresponding regularly with my mother. The mail took time to arrive and we had settled down to exchanging news every two weeks. I had quite a lot to write about. My mother's letters were mainly about local news, the garden, the weather, her neighbours and, frankly, were not very interesting. One day a letter arrived with some disturbing news.

Much of her wealth lay in shares in what we had always regarded as a family company, started by her great grandfather. Over the years the management had changed and we had lost touch with the company but mother, for sentimental reasons, had retained the shares she had inherited. The company went downhill and was taken over. It continued to pay dividends, but not such good ones, as it was clearly not doing so well. My mother explained it in great detail, but had clearly not understood what had been going on. Now it had gone bankrupt.

These shares in what had always been regarded as the family company, and which had once given my mother a very comfort-able income, were now worthless and she was distraught. 'I have lost everything,' she wrote. This was not entirely true, as she did have other capital, but it was clearly a devastating blow.

She explained all this in order to tell me that she would no longer be able to send me the allowance I had been receiving since I was in Germany. This accounted for why my mother had been so close with money and how difficult it had been to get an allowance. It was obviously a blow to me. Now I was a captain I was better off than I had been in Germany but I would have to think carefully whether I could afford a car. And I was planning to buy a horse.

I also corresponded with General Fisher, my father's great friend, who lived in a great house not far from my mother. He had been in the regiment, had known me since childhood and was interested to know what we were up to in Kenya, which he had once visited in the 1920s. In his latest letter, which arrived at the same time as my mother's letter, he said he had seen mother and had to tell me that he didn't think she was very well and looked very preoccupied.

This worried me. I was thinking about it and wondering what I could do when Rex called me and George into his tent for a briefing.

'There's to be a change in strategy,' said Rex. 'GHQ has at last decided that the big cordon and sweep operations are out dated. As if we haven't been telling them that. The tide, they say, has turned in our favour, the large gangs have been broken up, and we are now going to operate in smaller groups on better information. They've finally woken up and we're going to redeploy. W, X and Y companies are going to move into the forest, with company areas aligned with the police areas, and we're going to work hand in glove with the police. These companies are to establish base camps alongside the police and the platoons will dominate their areas inside the forest, working on information supplied by the police. We have been given areas in the Fort Hall and Kiambu districts.'

'That,' said George, 'is a much better strategy. What are your plans for our Zulus, the forest company?'

'I'm giving them a dual role as training company and forest reserve. They will be responsible for making the new drafts that come from the depot forest-worthy. And they'll be on call to provide patrols when we get special info to track a gang. They'll be positioned in the Kiambu district. There's an interesting role for the band and bugles. They're to put on a show in the new Kikuyu villages, going round playing and generally showing the flag. Zulu company are to provide weapon training teams to accompany them and display their weapons. They are to show the Kikuyu how well armed we are, compared to the Mau Mau. That'll reassure the loyal Kikuyu.'

'And battalion headquarters?' I asked.

'Good question, Miles. We'll set up a tactical headquarters next to the Zulus. But you, Miles, will have to base yourself here in Muthaiga and come out daily, as necessary. It'll only be an hour or so away. We need someone to be here to control the flow of paper, and that can't be Ben. He's got enough on his plate running the place while we're away on operations. You'll have Kettle with you.'

'I'd prefer to be with you, Colonel.'

'That I understand. Let's say you'll be based in both places, a foot in both camps, as needed.'

'I trust,' said George,' that I'll be with you.'

'Of course. There's an important role for you with the companies, seeing that everyone's up to scratch.'

'And when does this happen?'

'Next week. Now we need to work out the details.'

That evening I had arranged to spend with Becky. We were to meet at the Nairobi Club, which hardly anyone in the regiment used. It had a fine modern building in the middle of Nairobi and its membership was made up of people who lived in and around Nairobi, mainly civil servants and businessmen. It wasn't as lively and old fashioned as the Muthaiga Club, but the food was good, as was the cellar, and it had a good lending library. Becky and I were to meet in the bar on the right of the main entrance.

As I was sitting in the bar with a dry martini, Rex walked in. His surprise was as great as mine.

'Goodness, Miles, what are you doing here?'

'I'm waiting for Becky Summerson. We're having dinner here.'

'Becky Summerson! Charming girl. You're a lucky young man.'

'I'm hoping so, Colonel.'

'What are you drinking? A dry martini? Just the thing. Do they make a good one here? Yes? Barman, I'll have a dry martini.' He was quite nervous, which I'd never seen before.

At that moment Nancy Bergman walked through the door, to which Rex had his back, and looked round the room searching for someone. When she saw me she seemed surprised. Rex, realising he'd lost my attention, looked round and spotted Nancy the moment she spotted him.

'How lovely to see you, Nancy.'

'Lovely to see you, Rex.' She walked up to him and let him kiss her on both cheeks. Then she turned to me and said, 'and lovely to see you, Miles.' She let me kiss her too.

'Do you take Miles everywhere, Rex?'

'He never leaves my side. But this evening he's free. He's meeting the charming Becky Summerson here and then they're going on to dine somewhere. Is it the Norfolk, Miles?'

'Well I've arranged to meet Becky here and I was going to ask her where she'd like to go. I thought we might dine here.'

'Not very romantic,' said Rex.

'Is that why you've asked me here?' said Nancy.

Before Rex could answer that, Becky came into the bar, dark hair flowing and eyes flashing with a look of mischief. She kissed everyone.

'Well,' she said. 'A foursome. I hadn't thought of that.'

'Why not,' said Nancy. 'Let's all dine together here and go on to the Equator. I'm dying for a martini, Rex. I expect Becky is too.'

Later, lying in bed with Becky, she said, 'Do you think Rex and Ingrid went to bed, too?'

'I think we almost ruined his evening.'

'Do you think they're that close yet?'

'I've always thought that Nancy was up to having a little fun but

I can't make Rex out, though I know him quite well. He's changed since he took command of the battalion. Much more assured, and he's enjoying life, almost as if the power he is wielding gives him great pleasure.'

'Don't you think he's met his match in Nancy. She commanded the evening.'

'He was nervous to start, but that was because we were there. His wife is joining him here next month. That'll complicate things.'

'I don't see Ingrid being a passive mistress.'

'Darling Becky, I'll have to go soon.'

'Not quite yet, darling.'

When I explained to Kettle that he and I were to be based mainly in Muthaiga he was incensed.

'I've never, Sir, in all my days, Sir, heard of such an arrangement in this regiment, Sir,' he said. 'It doesn't make any sense, Sir. You and I need to be with the commanding officer. You'll never know what he'll get up to without us. You've got to talk to him again, Sir.'

'I'm not sure talking to him will have much effect.'

'You've got to, Sir,'

'I think we'll just set up at Tac HQ, make it a *fait accompli*. He's not going to order us back to camp. If he questions it we'll say it's the only way we can do our jobs.'

'That's better, Sir. You never want to let a commanding officer off his lead. They can get all kinds of odd ideas and do a lot of damage. We'll leave Corporal Norman and Tudor here. They're competent.'

'They're very competent. You've trained them well. Don't you think it's time for them both to be promoted?'

'Not yet, Sir.'

'I'm thinking that if Norman was a serjeant he would be a clear deputy. It would give you more stature.'

'I don't need more stature, Sir. I need to be near the colonel.'

He walked out.

Not a minute later, Peter Quartermain walked in.

'What's all this about each company now having a semi permanent base camp on the edge of the forest,' he said, thrusting a paper under my nose. 'Where do they expect me to get all this kit from?'

'It's all been authorised by GHQ. It's their idea.'

'It's all so irregular. I've got to account for all this kit. There're going to be some hefty bills if we lose anything. You'd think there was a war on, the way you're all behaving.'

'There is, in a way. I don't think we'll have any problem, Pete. What's really troubling you?'

'That took you in, didn't it? I've got it all arranged. You really thought I was upset.' We both laughed.

'Pete, I know you well enough to realise you've something on your mind. You don't just come here to play practical jokes and pass the time of day.'

'It's the contractors. They're ripping us off, I know. But I'm buggered if I can see how.'

'Why don't you talk to George about it? He's got immense experience.'

'Good idea,' said Peter and he left.

Quarter of an hour later, George came into my tent and sat down.

'Thank you for sending Pete to see me.'

'I thought you'd be able to help him.'

'He can't stop thinking everyone is diddling him.'

'That's because he's spent most of his life diddling everyone. Do you remember how he made a fortune in Korea?'

'After my time. Anyhow, he's probably onto something. We're going to set a trap for one of the contractors. He'll enjoy doing that. What I really came to say is how delighted I am that you've got a girl friend, and a charming one at that.'

'Who've you been talking to?

'Rex told me.'

'Did he tell you that he's got a girl friend?'

'You mean Nancy Bergman, Burgo's landlady? Hardly. He said he was dining with her, as he wants her to talk on life in Kenya to the wives when they arrive next month. A rather good idea, don't you think?'

He looked at me. Then he raised his eyebrows, got up and left.

Later Kettle came in with the mail. He seemed to have calmed down.

'Mr Kettle, you're the source of all our knowledge here in this theatre. On what basis can we allow a man compassionate leave to see a close relative in England who may be ill?'

'I'll have to look it up, Sir. I suspect they have to be dying or dead. Any one in mind?'

'Have we faced this since we've been here?'

'No, Sir.'

'Do you think the man is flown home for nothing?'

'Almost certainly by the air force.'

'That could take some time?'

'Slower than the commercial airlines but no charge. Do we have a case, Sir?'

'Not that I know of yet.'

The companies took to the new strategy and plans with enthusiasm. It gave them much more independence, especially the platoons. Once the company headquarters were in position, the platoons moved into the forest and the engineers cut roads to them so that they could be re-supplied easily. The platoons built strongholds as their bases.

These bases were real forts, from which the platoons sent out patrols during the day and withdrew into them at night. In this way they began to dominate their areas and restrict Mau Mau movements. No fort was ever attacked. From time to time, the police would pass us information they had gleaned from a captured or surrendered Mau Mau who had turned and told them where a gang was hiding. Then a patrol would immediately go out from a platoon or from Zulu company. More often than not the patrol would make contact. It would rarely destroy a whole gang, but it would generally kill some of its members and take a few captive. All this activity increased the pressure on the gangs, harassing them and keeping them on the move. Life became much harder for them. It also became harder for them to be resupplied from the reserves, because the Kikuyu in the reserves had begun to cut off their support. Many gangs were reduced to hunting animals and searching for edible grasses and flora to keep themselves alive.

Kettle and my ploy to establish ourselves at Tac HQ worked, and we heard no more from the colonel on that. Kettle loved being in the field and making do. He excelled at always being able to have tea ready in an instant. I was getting rather tired of drinking tea all the time. I was able to visit the companies with the colonel. One day we went to see Tony Henderson and his Y company. The colonel had a long discussion with Tony, and I was able to talk to Adam.

'How's life?' I said.

'Rather mixed, I'd say,' said Adam. 'I don't much care being here on the edge of the dark, dank forest. It's really exceptionally uncivilized and it's scuppered my plans for a company brothel that the lads are longing for.'

'How so?'

'Not enough men. With all the platoons in the forest there aren't enough men here to run a whorehouse efficiently and economically.'

'Why not?'

'Look at the mathematics. Take 100 men in one place, allow them an average of three copulations a week, and you get 300 copulations. Divide that by seven days and you have an average of about 40 copulations an evening. Given that a tart can service ten men an evening that means four tarts. Add two for illness and days off makes six tarts. At half a crown a time — half the price in Nairobi — the headman who provides the girls gets his cut, the girls make a good nest egg and are inspected regularly by the medical orderly, there's no VD, the lads are assuaged and the company makes a small profit. "All Sir Garnet" I'd say. But with no more than ten men here it doesn't work and it wouldn't be equitable for company headquarters to have a whorehouse denied to the platoons in the forest. Anyhow, Tony was chary of the idea.'

'Oh dear, you are being thwarted.'

'Not completely. This place is a good meeting place for settlers. They like coming by for a drink. So, I'm running a bar which is a nice little earner for company funds. And I'm planning a roulette afternoon for the settlers, which could be a nice big earner for me.'

'What does Tony think about that?'

'Loves the bar. Have yet to disclose the roulette idea. I think I'll wait until he's out with the platoons which, luckily, he is every day.'

'Any news of your former client Trench Foot?'

'I'm very interested in that. He comes to trial next week and I can't wait for the result. Julia is being particularly exacting. That's the one advantage of being here, away from her. Now, what news have you got? How's Burgo?'

'Burgo's the soldier in the sun and Rex is very pleased with him.'

'I'd rather like to be a soldier in the sun and I must think something up.'

'I doubt running a roulette wheel for settlers will endear you to him.'

It was at this time that the pseudo gangs became more active and were beginning to have success. They were not a new idea. They had been used in Palestine, during the Arab and Jewish troubles in that country, and in Malaya against the Chinese communists. They achieved their greatest success in Kenya. The police had found that Mau Mau warriors, once captured, could be easily turned. It only took a few days of good treatment for them to realise that everything they had been told about how they would be treated once captured was nonsense. The Kikuyu had an ability to change allegiance overnight. They came to realise that they could live a far better life out of the forest. Quite willingly, they agreed to go back into the forest in a pseudo gang and confront the real gangs. These pseudo gangs were led by young Europeans, most of whom had been born in Kenya. One or two were regular army officers. Dressed in rags or animal skins, like Mau Mau, and with faces, and sometimes their bodies, blackened by boot black or burnt cork, these incredibly courageous young men accounted for many gangs. In addition, terrorists, despairing of the helplessness of their situation, were surrendering of their own accord. Some were killed in Mau Mau arguments, many being strangled to death by their leaders for infringing minor rules. Their morale was increasingly shattered by the hardship of the forest and the shortage of ammunition and supplies. It was the preudo gangs that broke Mau Mau. To defeat Mau Mau, they had to find Dedan Kimathi, the last of the Mau Mau generals.

As Rex had told me to have a foot in both camps, I was able to return to Muthaiga occasionally and stay the night if there was a good reason. In that way I saw Becky from time to time. Being an air hostess, she wasn't always there as her work took her north to Kampala, in Uganda, and as far south as Johannesburg and Cape Town, in South Africa, when she could be away for several nights. We saw enough of each other to get to know one another better, and her liveliness and enthusiasm lifted a wistful pall that had been hovering over me since Kitty died.

Becky was fascinated by Ben and Juno.

'He's so old,' she said.

'Only 33,' I said.

'Only! Why that's more than ten years older than Juno. What does she see in him?'

'You should know.'

'What does that mean?'

'Didn't you go to bed with him?'

'I'd forgotten all about it. I was pissed and was carried away by his dancing. You don't hold that against me do you, darling?'

'I suppose it rankles a tiny bit, if I think about it.'

'You weren't showing any interest in me at all. In fact, I had to seduce you.'

'Thank you, darling. Anyhow, I think they make a fine couple. It's time Ben got married and I doubt he'll find a better girl that Juno.'

'What about what Juno wants?'

'It's up to her. She'll find it hard to do better. Ben will be able to keep her in some style.'

'What about love?'

'He loves her alright. And he'll look after her. Ben is very constant.'

'That's probably because Juno doesn't do it and that makes Ben love her all the more and pile on more treats.'

'They just seem to me to be very well suited. Darling, I shall have to leave you soon.'

'Not before you give me a kiss and show me how well suited we are.'

The following morning I was in my tent, going through the mail with Kettle. When the telephone rang he answered it, as he liked to do, because he always wanted to know who it was.

'Captain Howard for you, Sir.'

I took the telephone.

'Have you heard?' said Burgo. 'Trench Foot got off.'

'How on earth did that happen?'

'A technical error on the part of the legal boys drawing up the charge. They arraigned him on a charge of murder but failed to identify who he'd murdered. Gross carelessness, don't you think?'

'How could that have happened?'

'Well, it did, and do you know who the clever bunny was who

spotted it?'

'I suppose it was Adam.'

'You knew?'

'No, I just guessed. He's been dropping hints about it. What happens now?'

'They say that the C-in-C is out of his mind with fury, as he was so determined to make an example of Trench Foot. He's ordered him to be re-tried on causing gross bodily harm. Unfortunately, he's been interrogating the legal boys on how it happened and he's been told that it was clever Adam who spotted the loophole. Adam told me he wanted to be a soldier in the sun like me. I fear he's heading for the shadows. Have you heard about the roulette parties he's been having?'

'He told me he was going to hold one.'

'One? He's held several and has made a tidy sum for himself, though he says he's seen that some of the settlers have benefitted too. He did nearly have a disaster when he was badly down and he had to take extraordinary steps to keep the game going to give him time to re-coup.'

'What happened?'

'A policeman called in and told Adam that there was a Mau Mau gang in the neighbourhood, gave clear instructions where, and asked him to send a patrol. Adam pressed one hundred shillings in his hand and asked him to take his info on to the next unit. And he did, quite happily.'

'I can't believe it. Well, I suppose I can. Adam's living very dangerously, walking on a tightrope. I wish you hadn't told me.'

'Luckily, the next unit caught the gang.'

'I hope no one else knows about this.'

He rang off.

Kettle, who had left while I was talking on the telephone, walked back into my tent.

'The colonel would like you to join him and Major Bulman for a meeting,' he said. So I joined them, and Rex beckoned me to sit down. George was already there.

'We've got to find,' Rex said, 'an officer to command the training company at the depot. The fellow who's doing it now has chosen to go to Cambridge to learn Russian. Any ideas?'

This was news to me. It was a rather good job.

'What about Miles?' said George.

'I don't want to lose you, Miles. Sorry, you're too important to us here.'

'What about Burgo?' said George.

'He's doing very well and I'd like to keep him here. Besides I've promised Nancy Bergman not to move him.'

'Well, there's Adam.'

'That's a rather good idea. Do we think Adam could do it?'

'He always despatches his duties competently,' said George. 'Nothing ever seems to go wrong when he's in charge. The serjeants clearly like him. He's clever and sophisticated. I looked at his file recently. His report from the small arms school, when he trained on the Vickers Machine Gun, was outstanding. They wanted him to stay and be an instructor. I don't think you could go wrong.'

'What do you think, Miles?'

I was dreading the question. What did I think? I swallowed and said, 'Yes, Colonel, he could certainly do it.'

'He could,' Rex said. 'He's idle and he's clever. It'll test him, though. I'm concerned whether he has the making of a real soldier. He's louche and he's out for his own pleasures. So are a lot of people, but I wonder if he has the application for the job. It could, though, get him and us out of a bit of a fix. I was talking to the chief of staff who said that the C-in-C is furious that Trench got off. He recognised we hadn't put a foot wrong and that Adam had done what was asked of him, but he hinted that maybe Adam would be better off outside the theatre, and so would we if he was. Perhaps we should take that advice. Miles, would you ask Adam to come and see me?'

The next day Adam saw the colonel and then came and saw me.

'Wonderful news, Miles,' he said, 'Guess who's the soldier in the sun now. I don't know whether you know but the colonel has asked me to go to England to command the training company at the depot. Couldn't be better, and I can't wait to leave. And rather convenient in getting away from Julia. Sad he didn't ask you or Burgo. I shall give a little celebration dinner at the New Stanley Grill. You must come. I think we'll start with *Escargots Bourguignons*.'

9

The Battle of the Swamp

'Telephone, Sir,' said Kettle handing me the instrument. At Tac HQ we shared a tent and he, naturally, answered my telephone so that he knew what was going on.

'Is it Captain Howard?' I said. It was generally about this time in the early afternoon that Burgo rang me if he was going to gossip or had got a good tease.

'No, the police.'

I took the instrument and said, 'Player'.

'Who am I talking to?'

'Captain Player, adjutant 2 PRLI.'

'Captain, this is the police from Kiambu. We've had a tip off. There's a gang of Mau Mau in the swamp north of Kiambu. Do you know it?'

'I know where it is. How large is the gang?'

'We don't know. I think it would need a platoon. Can you cope?'

'I'll meet you there with a platoon within the hour.'

I handed the telephone back to Kettle and asked him to get me the Forest Company. Both Rex and George were in the forest and were not expected back for hours. I had to act immediately. A moment later I was talking to Big Steel.

'Is Major Bowerman there, Serjeant Major?'

'He's in the forest.'

'Who *is* there?'

'Mr Knox. He's just back from a patrol.'

'Anyone else?'

'No. All the other officers and platoons are out at present. Just Mr Knox.'

'We need a platoon to go to the swamp just south of Kiambu. Would you alert Mr Knox and I'll come round and brief him.'

I found Jasper in his tent with Big Steel. He was naked, had clearly just washed and shaved and he looked tired. He was about to put on a clean shirt.

'What's all this about, Miles?' he said.

'There's a gang of Mau Mau in the swamp south of Kiambu. I want you to take a platoon and capture them. You'll need your Kenya Regiment serjeant. I'll take you there.'

'My men are dead beat. So am I. We've just returned from a three day patrol.'

'Sorry, Jasper. You're the only officer around and we've got to move fast or the gang will evaporate.'

'Serjeant Major, get my platoon back on parade. Tell them there's a gang of Mau Mau nearby that's a sitting duck. They'll like that. Miles, we'll be ready to go in twenty minutes.'

'And Serjeant Major,' I said, 'we'll want a good signaller.'

An hour later we were at the swamp to be met by the police officer, who immediately took Jasper and me aside as the men were debussing and led us to a slight rise beside the swamp.

'Do you see the spreading thorn tree?' he said. 'Got it? That looks like the centre of the gang. They seem to be in small groups. You can see that they've cut avenues in the papyrus and there's a network of paths. It looks like a regular Mau Mau camp. I wonder we haven't found it before. I can't tell how well they're armed and there're more of them than I expected. What are your ideas?'

'Let me walk round,' I said. 'We'll need more than a platoon. It's a big area and we'll be hard pushed to cordon it. What sort of gang do you think it is?'

'It's probably a courier gang, composed of a few hardcore Mau

Mau, that has been in Nairobi, recruiting and raising supplies, and is now returning to the forest, so I doubt it will be that well armed.'

'Jasper, as a start, post your men round the swamp in a cordon. Then we'll walk round ourselves and make an appreciation. The cordon mustn't get too close, but it should make itself known.'

'OK, Miles.'

Turning back to the policeman, I said, 'We'll need many more to cordon it off properly.'

'What about the Kikuyu Home Guard?'

'Perfect,' I said, 'we'll need at least a hundred to make a strong cordon.'

Jasper, Reggie Ferndale his Kenya Regiment serjeant, and I then walked the circuit of the swamp. In the confluence of two rivers flowing from east to west, it formed a triangle. The sides were about 150 yards and the base was about 75 yards. The apex was where the two rivers met. It did not appear to be deep, it was clearly uneven and it seemed as if one could easily walk around in it without getting too wet. The rivers were slightly banked and provided some growth in which to hide. The inner part of the triangle was all papyrus, zig zagged with paths, and provided good cover.

'What do you think, Jasper?' I said, when we had returned to our original spot.

'When it gets dark they might try to escape. Our cordon isn't very strong but it still might deter them. I think we should tell them they are surrounded and that they should surrender. If they don't we'll have to attack them.'

'Why attack? We want to capture as many as we can,' I said.

'Don't you think,' said Reggie Ferndale, 'there's a fair chance they will try and slink away under cover of night. You know their ability to disappear.'

'I don't like the idea of attacking,' I said. 'We don't know exactly where they are or how heavily armed they are. Besides, if you attack you'll need covering fire.'

'Can I have the mortars?' said Jasper.

'I'll get them up. And we'll need more troops.'

'I don't think we should do anything before the Kikuyu Home Guard arrives and we have a stronger cordon,' said Reggie. 'But I think we should do something before night falls. Why don't I tell them they're surrounded and call on them to surrender? If they do, well and good. If they don't, then we'll attack. We'll learn pretty quickly if they'll fight. Remember, we've never known a gang to stand and fight back.'

'Are you happy with that, Jasper?' I asked.

'Yes.'

'OK,' I said, 'we'll do that once the Kikuyu Home Guard arrive and are in place. Jasper, work out how you'll do your attack. I'm afraid we won't have the mortars in time for this.'

It was an hour or so later when the Kikuyu Home Guard had taken over the cordon from Jasper's platoon, but there was still an hour before nightfall. Jasper was going to attack starting from the base of the triangle with one section, followed by a section to mop up, with his third section in reserve.

'Are you ready, Jasper?' I said.

'As ready as we'll ever be.'

'Then, Reggie, tell them to surrender.'

Reggie had arranged to stand on the shoulders of two of the Kikuyu Home Guard, so he commanded a view of the swamp and the Mau Mau would have been able to see him. His voice was loud and clear and it carried across the swamp. I didn't understand what he said in Kikuyu but it was short and had authority. It immediately drew loud and rebarbative retorts from the swamp, but not that many.

'What are they saying, Reggie?' I said.

'Insults, mainly, and vile ones.'

'Tell them to surrender or we attack.'

Reggie did and was met by similar retorts.

'Alright, Jasper, all yours,' I said.

Jasper gave the order to advance and the first section moved towards the swamp. As it reached the edge of the swamp the Mau Mau opened furious fire with a ferocity that astonished us. Every

kind of firearm opened up on the section which immediately hit
the ground. Bullets from rifles and an automatic weapon, and
shot from shotguns, whistled out from the swamp, whizzing over
our heads, followed by arrows and missiles. I hit the ground and,
looking round, I saw everyone else had too.

'More of them and better armed than we thought,' said Reggie.
'For once, they're going to put up a proper fight.'

'About time too,' said Jasper. 'We'll have to wait for the mortars
and reinforcements.'

Miraculously, no one was hurt.

As dusk fell Rex and Francis arrived.

'What's happening, Miles?' said Rex, and I told him.

'I wouldn't have done anything different,' he said. 'Now, let's
discuss what we do next. Reggie, what do you think they'll do
now?'

'The bastards will know they're surrounded. There are probably
about a hundred of them, not a few dozen as we thought. If it's a
courier group making its way back to the forest, as the police and I
think it is, then most will be recruits, many of them reluctant ones.
They'll be very scared and unarmed, not know what to do, and I
doubt many of them will try and escape during the night. The hard
core who recruited them will have to stay and fight. Escaping isn't
really open to them. If they do, and make their way back to their
gang in the forest without recruits or supplies, they'll be punished
by their gang leader, probably strangled. They know this. They've
got to fight. We've got a fight on our hands.'

'I don't disagree with your appreciation,' said Rex. 'We'll attack tomorrow at dawn, not in the dark. And we'll soften them
up with the mortars at first light when we can begin to see what
we're doing. When it's light and we can really see what we're
doing, we'll attack. Francis, get another platoon to be here to be
on standby all night, in case we need them. Jasper and his men
can stand down and get some sleep to be ready for the morning.
They'll need blankets. I think we'll have two sections of mortars,
just to be sure. Now, where are the police? Are you satisfied with

the Kikuyu Home Guard and the cordon?'

He went on discussing the plan with the police. By this time the commanding officer of the Kenya Regiment had appeared from nowhere and Rex went over the plan with him.

'All set,' he said. 'Now, Miles, well done for setting all this in motion. You hand it over to Francis, it's his company. I want you to go back to Tac HQ to hold the fort there.'

Reluctantly, I went back to Tac HQ, leaving them to it.

The next morning, I settled down in my office tent doing the hundred and one things an adjutant has to do. Kettle had some issues he wanted to discuss. The Bandmaster wanted to have a word. The Bugle Platoon, for whom I was directly responsible, had to be inspected. There were some new cases of VD, which would irritate Rex. A signal arrived from London saying the colonel of the regiment was going to visit us. Becky had left a message asking if we could meet at the weekend. The difficulty about that was in the forest there were no weekends. The padre would go round the companies holding short communion services, which were not as well attended as they were in Korea, which says something about the lack of danger the men felt they were in. I was expecting Pete Quartermain, but then I was told I was wanted on the radio. The signals platoon had established a radio link with those at the swamp as I had asked. I imagined someone was going to tell me how the battle was going. It should have been over by then. The operator gave me the headphones and microphone and said that Major Bulman wanted to talk to me. I followed the radio procedure, announced myself, and he came on air. Reception was not good.

'Is that you, Miles? Over.'

'Yes. Over.'

We didn't follow correct voice procedure and spoke in clear, as on the telephone. What did it matter if the Russians were listening? The Mau Mau weren't.

'Jasper has been shot. He's asking for you. Get here as soon as you can. Over'

'Badly shot? Over.'

I couldn't hear his reply and he went off air. Jasper shot, I said to myself. How? We'd had hardly any casualties so far during the emergency. How could Jasper have been shot? I found Kettle and told him. He handed me a cup of tea and said, 'Drink that. It'll make you feel better.' I must have looked how I felt, a little shaken.

'I must go. Is there a jeep handy?'

'There's a motor bike. Can you ride one?'

'We were taught at Sandhurst but I've hardly ridden one since.'

'Better ride pillion. Safer. And finish your tea first.'

So I rode pillion on one of the signallers' motor bikes and got to the swamp in under half an hour. I found Jasper propped up on the ground with Reggie beside him. Reggie didn't say anything, just beckoned me down.

'What's happened, Jasper?'

He looked strained. His face was grey and his cheeks were pinched. His eyes were wandering and seemed far away.

'Miles?' he whispered.

'Yes, Jasper, it's me, Miles,' I said and I took his hand. It was bloody. He was breathing heavily and blood was seeping from his mouth.

'I got him,' he said.

He was silent for a bit.

'I got him,' he said again and he tried to smile. His eyes wrinkled and he looked up at me.

'Yes, I got him. Tell Mummy I got him.'

'You'll be able to tell her,' I said.

'No, you tell her.'

'I'll tell her, then.'

He smiled. Then he choked a little and sighed. He breathed out and his head fell slowly on its side.

Oh, no, I thought. Not Jasper. How could this have happened? I felt numb and looked at Reggie. His face was implacable.

'Jasper,' he said.

I couldn't believe this possible. Jasper was lying there absolutely still; the life had gone out of him. He was just an inert body. I waved my hand over his eyes. They didn't blink. I closed them. He was dead.

'What on earth happened, Reggie?'

'I didn't see. I was with your colonel and someone came and said Jasper had been shot. I ran to him. Two of his men were carrying him out of the swamp. They laid him on the ground here. The medical corporal came and gave him morphine. He said Jasper had been shot in the lungs, that it was very serious, and that he should be got to hospital as soon as possible. He sent for an ambulance but that had to come from Nairobi. Jasper sank slowly. He was jabbering away to begin with, but he slowly got quieter. Your colonel came, with George the 2IC and told him how well he'd done. I hope he heard. He liked to be praised. He told me once that no one had ever praised him before he came to Kenya. He was a bloody good soldier. The men loved him. I'd follow him anywhere.'

'I'd better go and tell the colonel,' I said, and got up. I could see him in a group with George and Francis talking to the police, and walked over to them. Rex looked at me and raised his eyebrows. I shook my head and said, 'He died two minutes ago. He seemed to be content with what he'd done, almost proud.'

'So he should be, but he overdid it. He didn't need to go into the swamp at the end but he was determined to see it through. He was exhausted. It was selfless of him. What a terrific operation, and we have to lose Jasper of all people. I asked him if he was able to go on and he said he must. "I can't ask my men," he said, "to do things I'm not prepared to." Bloody brave, he was. A born soldier. What a loss. He had a genius for fighting. I'm sorry, Miles. I know you were old friends.'

'I dread telling his mother,' I said.

'I'll do that. That's my job. There's a lot for you to catch up with here. George, tell Miles what's been happening.'

George took me aside.

'I'm sorry, Miles. He's a dreadful loss. How did he die?'

I told him.

'Yes, I can see him saying that. Typical Jasper. I'll tell you what happened. When there was enough light for us to see, we got Reggie to tell the gang to surrender or we would bombard them. Vitriol was thrown back at him. He told them again only to receive more vitriol. Rex gave the orders for the mortars to range. We had two sections. So four mortars ranged on the swamp in turn. When they'd all got the range Reggie once more told them to surrender. They were silent, and we could hear some screams, but no one came out of the swamp to surrender. So Rex gave the order to fire and the mortars started their bombardment, hammering away into the swamp. It was a fearful scene. As they were landing in a swamp, the bombs can't have done as much damage as they might. The explosions were mixed with screams. Some Mau Mau began running out with their hands up. Some escaped down the river, eluding the Kikuyu Home Guard who, I expect, must have been pretty tired by then and rather indisciplined. After ten minutes Rex called it off and then a lot of Mau Mau came out. Clearly not all, as there was some sniping going on. So Jasper led his men in. It was really tough, clearing the swamp. It had to be done area by area. It took a lot of time, as we found the really hard core were not surrendering. It was then that Jasper went to the help of one of his sections which was having problems in particularly thick papyrus. He was pushing into a big clump when a Mau Mau lying there shot him in the chest. As Jasper fell he shot the man in the head. Francis saw it happen, told Rex and me, and we went to Jasper immediately. Rex told him how well he'd done. Then the medical corporal told us how critical Jasper was and we realised we could do little for him. This is a very unusual operation and we didn't have proper medical back up, but even if we'd had an ambulance here, I doubt it would have got him to hospital in time. He wouldn't have been in much pain as he'd been given morphine. Rex and I talked to him for a bit but he wasn't making sense. He said your name once or twice and I sent for you.'

The ambulance had now arrived and I helped move Jasper's body to it. He looked serene and untroubled.

As I watched the ambulance drive off, I thought of a night four years earlier in a valley in Korea. I had had to rescue my great friend Hugh Jermy. He was returning from a patrol in which he had captured a prisoner. He had been wounded, and was returning to our lines and had sent his serjeant and the patrol on with the prisoner while two men had stayed with him, to help him back. In the dark they had wandered into one of our minefields. Trench Foot, his company commander, had refused to go and rescue him. He was euphoric about the prisoner that Hugh had captured and was very drunk. You would have thought that Trench had caught the prisoner himself. So, I went and found Hugh. I could see it all clearly: the darkness, the lights being sent up to help us see our way, the tape we laid through the minefield to mark our path getting to Hugh, the occasional stutter of machine guns. When we reached Hugh and I talked to him he thought we were sailing in a race and that he'd capsized and was drowning. We talked for a few minutes and he died as I held his hand. I could see it all so clearly. And now Jasper had died as I held his hand. I stared after the ambulance, not believing this could have happened again.

Someone tapped me on the shoulder. It was the policeman who had briefed me the previous afternoon.

'Captain,' he said, 'that was a bad thing to happen, but let me tell you how successful we've been thanks to you getting it going yesterday. We clearly surprised them when we put a cordon round the swamp. Let's walk over and you can see the haul we've made.'

The prisoners were assembled in groups some way from the swamp, guarded by the Kikuyu Home Guard with a few of Jasper's men and some police. There was also a long line of dead bodies, almost all in states of disfigurement and with injuries suffered from the mortaring.

'We found thirty dead in the swamp and there are fifty prisoners, some seriously wounded, who we've sent off to be attended to. We know a few escaped. But we captured the leader, the one over there with a captain's pips sewn on the shoulders of his shirt. He's there with the hard core. He's been forthcoming about what they were doing here. We've learned a lot.'

I saw a small group of Mau Mau sitting round a man clearly their superior and looking arrogant. They all looked thin and undernourished. Tatters of police and military uniform hung loosely round them. Their hair was matted. All these were signs of their having been in the forest for some time. Then there was another small group of men, again in tattered clothes.

'Who are they?' I said.

'They are ones who have escaped from prison. They have no pass papers, no labour documents, no certificates of release. They're fugitives. The only place they can go is the forest. They're doomed.'

'And the rest?'

We were looking now at a motley assembly of all ages, all in civilian clothing somewhat worse for wear. There were women and children among them.

'They're the recruits that they were bringing from Nairobi to the forest. I doubt if any joined willingly. Most would have been taken by force, or just arrested, and then made to take the oaths and go with the gang.'

'They look pitiful,' I said. 'Poor buggers.'

'All the men will hang.'

'What do you mean they'll all hang?'

'They'll all go to trial. The women and children will be released. The rest will hang.'

'How could the recruits hang if they were forced to take the oaths and join?'

'Consorting and aiding the Mau Mau. That's enough for the gallows.'

'All of them?'

'It's the law.'

10

Time out and more surprises

The day after Jasper died, Trench Foot went to stand trial by court martial again, this time charged with causing grievous bodily harm. The prosecution had prepared its case more thoroughly and the case was quickly dealt with. Trench was found guilty, given five years imprisonment, and cashiered. He was to serve his sentence in England, which some of us felt was lenient. I suppose it was against the custom at that time to have sent him to a prison full of black people in Kenya.

'Thank God that's closed,' said Rex.

'He'll crop up again somewhere,' said George. 'Five years sounds a long time, but he'll only be 43 when he comes out.'

'He'll be a broken man, good for nothing.'

'He's managed to survive in the army for 20 years and he managed to be acquitted on a murder charge. Loathsome as he is, he seems to have a little luck on his side. He'll turn up somewhere.'

'What about his wife? What's happening to her? Do you know, Miles?'

'You once told me it wasn't strictly our business, Colonel, but I understand that the army will send her home by sea.'

'True enough, Miles, but she was once one of us. What was the word Adam used? Compassion? Is there any future for her in that relationship?'

'Knowing Adam, I doubt it, Colonel.'

We were sitting in Rex's tent at Muthaiga Camp, taking stock after coming out of action in the Kikuyu reserves and adjacent Aberdare forests. The new tactics had paid off, we'd had some luck and we had helped disperse the gangs and make life increasingly uncomfortable for them. We were now in for a period of re-training, and assimilating fresh drafts of national servicemen to replace those who had served their two years and were returning to England. This was a routine process, which we had mastered and for which George was responsible. The new recruits had also to spend their first month acclimatising, as we did when we first arrived.

Rex was more interested in spending the time at Muthaiga in engaging in activities that would liven up all our lives. There were to be brigade competitions in athletics, boxing, and football and Rex had appointed officers to train teams in these three sports; the officers were well aware that Rex expected them to win, not come second, and certainly not third. As important was preparation for the visit of the colonel of the regiment, for whom we would parade as a battalion, be inspected, double march past — a spectacular movement which we did to the 'Keel Row' — before the final march past to the great regimental march of Berlioz's 'The Trojans'. All this would need preparation. And the colonel of the regiment would need entertaining: visits to the forest and a safari for him. Further, Rex planned for the officers to give a party, which would probably take more planning than anything else in the programme, and in which Rex was taking a keen personal interest.

'Where do we stand on the arrangements for the party?' said Rex.

George and I looked at each other.

'Don't you think that we'd better get Ben here? He's in charge of the party,' said George.

'Quite right. Get him please, Miles.'

As I went to do it, he said, 'Actually, it would be a better idea to talk about the party in the mess, so let's go there now.'

Ben was, fortunately, at the officer's mess, so I was able to get a message to tell him to wait for us.

The mess was looking more comfortable and better decorated than it had when we last went into the forest. The Hogarth prints of regimental battles had been brought from the depot by the last draft of recruits, and were massed on the walls looking colourful. There was also, over the fireplace, a good small portrait of Field Marshal Lord Wolseley 'Our Only General'. Adding to the furnished look were several Persian rugs and kelims on the floor, which had been bought from an Arab dealer in Malindi for a not unreasonable sum. These improvements had met general approval and had pleased Rex, who had proposed them.

'It won't rain on the day, will it?' said Rex.

'The rainy season is some way away,' I said.

'Fine. So, Ben, what's the plan for the party?'

'We've drawn up a guest list of about seventy five.'

'Seventy five! I want a party. Double it. Make it one hundred and fifty. We don't just have official guests. Every officer who has been receiving hospitality from settlers must ask them. Damn rude not to and not our style. One hundred and fifty.'

'Where will we put 150, Colonel?'

'Open the French windows and we can use the garden as well.'

'A party is best in one room, Colonel'

'Not this party. Make it two hundred. I want it to be the best party of the year in Kenya. What about drinks?'

'I thought champagne. We generally give champagne.'

'Champagne? This is Kenya. They drink the hard stuff here. Whisky. Gin. Cocktails, if you like. Not a glass of champagne. They'll think we're a lot of nancy boys. What about food?'

'We can do a range of small eats.'

'See to that. They'll need something to fill their stomachs or we'll have them drunker than they normally are. Now, parking and reception? Miles?'

'We'll have a double guard on the gate. On arrival, the guests will be asked their names by the orderly officers, there'll be two, who'll have an alphabetical list of guests. Then they'll be guided to park on the old polo ground and then here. The VIP cars will be directed here.'

'That sounds right. Good, Miles. What about the end?'

'The end, Colonel?' said Ben.

'Yes, how are we going to end the party? They'll stay here until midnight if we don't watch out.'

'Well,' said Ben, 'we'll have the band playing, so we could play "God Save the Queen" '

'The band!' said Rex. 'What about the band and bugles sounding retreat on the old polo ground first? Then we hold the party afterwards. That way the serjeants' mess can have a party too. And all the men can watch. We've got time to organise this. This'll be a bumper party. Ben, let me have your revised guest list tomorrow, with your detailed plans. It's going to be a great party.'

'How do we pay for it, Colonel?' said Ben.

'The officers pay. They're having a bloody good time here.'

Back in Rex's tent, George said, 'Hadn't we better talk about Jasper's funeral?'

'I've signalled and written to Mrs Knox,' said Rex. 'Poor woman. First her husband, then her son. End of that line of Knoxes. They've done the regiment proud. Father killed at Dunkirk. Grandfather killed in the Great War. Great Grandfather a full general and colonel of the regiment. We need to pack up his things and the next officer returning to England must take them to his mother. Where's his cigarette case, the gold one?'

'I've put it in my safe, Colonel,' I said. 'It's bent. It must have deflected the bullet from his heart to his lungs. He always used to say he'd either become a general or would die in battle. More recently he said he'd like to be a white hunter in Kenya when all this was over.'

'I can see that. This country does have a pull on one. Now to the funeral. Full military honours. Band and bugles and a company guard of honour, the Zulus, and smart as the guard at Buckingham Palace. We're not just honouring Jasper, we're honouring a great regimental family. Many will come. The brigadier will be there, I know, and probably the chief of staff. Maybe the C-in-C. I've recommended Jasper for a posthumous Military Cross. He did wonders in the forest. Let's see.'

We moved on to discuss more plans and then broke for lunch.

Sitting in my office tent after lunch, the telephone went and I knew who it was.

'I'm sorry about Jasper, Miles,' said Burgo.

'So am I, Burgo. He's a terrible loss.'

'I gather you were with him when he died?'

'I got there just in time. He wasn't in much pain as the medical corporal had given him morphine.'

'Did he say anything?'

'Yes. A little.'

'Can you tell me?'

'He looked at me as if he had accomplished something satisfactorily and he said "I got him." '

'What do you think he meant?'

'The terrorist had shot at him from the ground shooting upwards. Jasper was very quick and as he fell he shot the terrorist in the head. Not easy. So I think he was proud and satisfied about killing his adversary, so he said, "I got him" '

'Anything else?'

'Yes. He said, "Tell Mummy." '

'Did he now! Don't you think, as he was dying, he might have been thinking about someone else?'

'What do you mean?'

'About another, and former, adversary.'

'Burgo?'

'D.P. Brown. He was talking about pushing D. P. Brown over the side of the troop ship.'

'For God's sake, Burgo. Be sane. He was talking about what he had just done.'

'I'm not so sure.'

'Let Jasper die in peace.'

'We'll have to. We'll never know, now, for sure, but I think, and I'll go on thinking, that Jasper was talking about D. P. Brown.'

'I trust you'll keep these thoughts to yourself. You won't be popular if you voice them again now.'

'He's a hero, either way.'

We gave Jasper a grand funeral. The C-in-C had approved an immediate MC for him. This recognised his daring and ability, and pleased the regiment. Very few military crosses were awarded during the emergency. I had a letter from Verity Knox, Jasper's mother, in reply to mine. She asked me to make a point of going to see her when I was next in England, so that we could talk about Jasper and she could learn more about what he had done in Kenya. She said she had been sorry to learn that my mother was not well and she hoped everything went well for me. That she should know that my mother was unwell surprised me. She must have learned this on the regimental grapevine, and it worried me. I would be the last person to whom my mother would tell any real news. So, I wrote to cousin Sonia to ask if she knew anything about how my mother was. She was my mother's second cousin and had always been good to me, more like an aunt or a godmother, and I had been her husband's aide-de-camp when he had been governor of Hong Kong. My mother and Sonia were not close, but they saw each other from time to time and if anyone could find out what was wrong with my mother, Sonia would.

At this time, Rex was getting very worked up about the various competitions in which the battalion was to compete. Unsatisfied in the progress being made, he had placed senior officers over those originally appointed to prepare the teams: George to be in charge of boxing, Francis Bowerman of football, and Percy Smythe of athletics. The only training now being done in camp was sports training and this was started all over again. Inter-platoon competitions were held, then inter-company competitions, to find the best athletes, boxers, and footballers. The men had entered these competitions willingly, as this was an easier way of spending their national service than in the forests. Some able talent was identified in addition to the known talent; squads were formed for the three sports, to train full time for the competitions, and they were relieved of all other duties. This was not popular with the rest of the battalion, as the squads had become an enviable elite that observed a different time table, sometimes ate at different times, and were believed to get special, and better, food. The rest of the battalion were now engaged on fatigues and camp duties and little could be more boring. Both George and I remonstrated with Rex about this, but all he would say was, 'We are going to win these competitions'.

The boxing and football competitions would take place over three weeks. The athletics would take one day and this was the first to be held. The old polo ground at Muthaiga made a fine athletics field on which to hold the competition and was selected as the venue. Competing teams came from the other two battalions in the brigade, from the engineer and signal squadrons, from the ordnance, and the REME. It was a walkover for us. We had been the only battalion to take it seriously and some of the other entrants had come straight from the forest. We won five out of six of the track events and four out of six of the field events.

Rex was well pleased, and the battalion conceded it might have been worthwhile after all. We then fought our way into the finals of the football and won it convincingly. Finally came the afternoon for the boxing final. This was also held on the old polo field. A boxing ring was placed in the centre and chairs from the men's dining room and the NAAFI had been arranged around it. A large crowd had formed; there were many visitors, as well as our own men. There were to be seven bouts and we were to fight a lowland Scots regiment which recruited in Glasgow. It had reached the final quite easily.

We, though, had a reputation for boxing. We had fought an Australian regiment in Korea, some years back, and had won every round. Serjeant Foxton had been our outstanding boxer and trainer. He was now a training serjeant at the training company at the depot and George did not have anyone of his ability in the battalion to help him.

The colonel of the lowland regiment had come, as had the brigadier. The match started and Rex sat back, looking confident he would make a clean sweep of all the bouts.

We won the first two. The Scots then won the next two. It wasn't going to be a walkover. Rex remained confident and bet the colonel of the Scots battalion a fiver that we would win. We won the next bout. The sixth bout was close and the Scots won it. So it was now three bouts all and everything turned on the last bout. The Scots colonel bet Rex another fiver and Rex had to take it. This was like betting on the toss of a coin. It was a heavyweight bout and our boxer was a corporal in the assault pioneer platoon, a big man, well known in the battalion. He stepped into the ring to a loud cheer. Then the Scots heavyweight stepped into the ring to cheers from his supporters. They looked well matched. As they fought through the first two rounds I couldn't see much difference in them. Both landed good punches. Neither looked pressed. This was going to be a tough decision for the judges. The last round started. The Scot suddenly got in a left to the body and our man staggered and fell. He quickly scrambled up and fought on but not as strongly. That was it. We lost.

'Damn glad you won something,' said Rex to the Scots colonel as he handed over two new one hundred shilling notes and led him and the brigadier off to the officers' mess for drinks.

'What happened?' I said to George.

'They were too good, much better than I expected. Our boys fought well. We only lost narrowly. But we lost. Rex is going to be desperately disappointed. I dread to think what he'll say tomorrow morning.'

He went off to congratulate his boxers.

The next morning Rex called George and me in to discuss plans.

'Well, George,' he said, 'your boxers did well. They only lost narrowly. We won overall and we showed the brigade what we could do. The brigadier was impressed. He said there was no better battalion in Kenya. We're no longer just another battalion here, what with our achievements in the forest and on the sporting field. You know, I never thought we could win all three. We just had to try and we did very well. Now, let's review where we stand with the party. Miles, ask Ben to join us.'

The party was a great success. It started with the band and bugles sounding retreat on the old polo ground. The officers and their guests took the side next to the saluting stand, where seats had been placed. The serjeants and their guests took the opposite side, where seats had also been placed. On the two open sides most of the battalion came and sat on the ground. Few of the guests were familiar with light infantry drill, and the band and bugles showed off with skill, and a little swank, while they gave a lively mix of old and new band music. When it came to sound the last post and reveille, everyone stood up unhesitatingly. It was a moving performance. After the band and bugles marched off to 'The Trojans' there was loud applause and we moved to the mess.

We had invited officers from the two other battalions and units in the brigade, from GHQ, from the Kenya Regiment, the ordnance depot, and every military outfit we wanted to know or had been helpful to us. Some who had wives in Kenya brought them, so it wasn't just all men. And we had invited all the settlers whom we had met. Among the first to enter the anteroom was Bill Ambrose with Christopher Hetherington, who had played cricket for Rex's XI. Bill Ambrose was also the first to get drunk and Christopher led him away, but not before Bill had confided in several people that he could run the emergency better than the governor. Rex was not the only person to be relieved when they left.

Fred and Anna Littlejohn had come from the Kinankop. They were very sad about Jasper and said how much they had admired him. They hoped we would come and camp with them again.

Later, talking with George, they agreed we could set up a permanent training camp with them. This was to be a great boon for us.
Jeremy Watts, the District Commissioner we had met with them,
had come too. Once again, I was impressed with the clarity of his
insights about the emergency. He also said it was time we formed
a polo team or two and came and played at Naivasha. Jim Fairford,
the district officer, came up to us and congratulated me on the
successes we had had in our operations, which surprised me as I
didn't think we'd had that many.

The Hay-Smiths had come from Nanyuki. He was pleased with
the way the emergency was going and felt that the tide had turned
in our favour. They asked us to go and stay with them again. Mary
was with them. I hadn't seen her recently, though I knew that she
had taken up with one of the new national service subalterns after
Charlie Chance had left. Nancy arrived with Burgo. She seemed
to know most of the settlers there. I am sure she had been invited
by Rex. He had recently announced that he was not to be joined
by his wife, who had decided to stay in England to look after their
children.

Juno brought her parents. Her father was a senior colonial official, who was very interesting about what was happening in the
upper echelons of government and some of the almost insuperable
issues they were facing. Becky arrived late, gave me a kiss, and
disappeared into the crowd.

The party became noisier and noisier and hardly a soul left. At
nine o'clock Rex gave the signal to Ben, who told Serjeant Cheke
to stop serving drinks and then talked to the bandmaster, who was
conducting a small string band. Now he conducted 'God save the
Queen'. Slowly the guests left, protesting what a good party it had
been. It certainly had.

I found Becky. Together we found Ben and Juno. It wasn't until
nearly ten that we were able to leave for the Equator Club. Shortly
after we arrived Rex and Nancy walked in.

The battalion returned to its former posting near Kiambu and the companies resumed their positions. This had the great advantage of our knowing the ground and the forest, as well as being on good terms with the local administration, police, and Kikuyu Home Guard. While we were gaining the upper hand against the Mau Mau, we had fallen in love with the country and felt part of it. We were cocooned there and took little notice of what was happening in the outside world. We were cut off from everyday life in England which, though it was now recovering well from the second world war and its aftermath, still remained spellbound by it and its memories.

George and I were sitting in the colonel's tent and had almost finished discussing plans with him when Kettle appeared at the entrance.

'I am sorry to interrupt you, gentlemen,' he said, 'but I thought you'd like to know that the radio had just announced that Nasser has nationalised the Suez Canal.'

'Great Gatsby,' said Rex.

'Did the radio say why?' said George.

'No, Sir.'

'Have one of the clerks listen in and let us have any further news bulletins and comment, Mr Kettle.'

'Very good, Sir,' he said.

'Suez is our lifeline here,' said George. 'So, Nasser controls our lifeline.'

'And he controls the passage for Middle East oil,' said Rex. 'That's more serious.'

'Why did he do it?' I said.

'He wants to build a dam at Aswan,' said George, 'to irrigate the desert to produce food for his rapidly increasing millions. The United States said it would fund it and then changed its mind. I presume Nasser proposes the Suez Canal will fund it for him. All rather precipitate.'

'What will we do?'

'We'll have to mount an operation,' said Rex, 'to take it back. Can't have a Wog like that dictating to us.'

'How do we do that?' I said.

'We'll send in an airborne division or two, immediately, to re-occupy the canal.'

'We don't have one airborne division, Rex,' said George. 'This will be interesting for us to observe.'

I returned to my tent where, almost immediately, Kettle came in with a long face and handed me a personal signal. It read, 'Mother seriously ill. Advise immediate return. Sonia.'

11

Return to an England in crisis

The plane took three days to get home. We stopped at Entebbe to spend the night, Khartoum to refuel, Tripoli for another night, and, finally, at Malta to refuel. We landed at Blackbushe — a military trooping aerodrome on the A30 near Hartley Wintney — in the evening. It was still light and warm, being August. Before I left Kenya, I had sent a telegram to Sonia to tell her where and when I was arriving and Phyllida met me. We kissed each other on the cheek, once and rather shyly.

'Mummy's with your mother. I'm afraid she's dying. I'm sorry to say that.' She took my hand and squeezed it. 'Chang will drive us straight there. It won't take long.'

Chang was the Cathay's Chinese servant and driver. He carried my bags and put them into the boot of a Humber Snipe, a large and long, black saloon car. He then ushered us into the back of the car and we motored away.

'How was the journey?'

'Noisy and rather tiring. I came back with some soldiers who are to be demobbed. They were rather cheerful. I hope, in view of this crisis over Suez, that they won't be disappointed and have to stay on. What's the latest news?'

'Everyone's excited about it. The general reaction was we must have it back, we can't let Nasser get away with it. Now people are beginning to tread water and are asking how are we going to do it and why isn't something happening. Mummy and Daddy talk about it endlessly. Daddy seems to know what's happening and won't tell Mummy, which infuriates her. You'll have to see if he'll tell you anything.'

Phyllida's father, Ivan Blessington, was married to my mother's cousin, Sonia. He had been ennobled as Viscount Cathay when he finished his term as governor of Hong Kong and was active in the House of Lords on the Conservative benches and, therefore, for the government.

'What's Kenya like?' she asked.

'Very beautiful. Quite different from here,' I said, as I looked out of the window. We were motoring through Basingstoke.

'I meant the fighting.'

'We're winning slowly, but not easily,' I said, and I thought about Jasper.

'Are you wearing what you wear when you fight in the jungle? I've never seen you in uniform. You look very smart.'

'The forest, Phyllida, not jungle. Forest.'

I was travelling in a tropical service dress, which I'd had made in Nairobi, and I was wearing a Sam Browne belt and a green fore and aft cap.

'No, I put this on to travel. We wear an olive green uniform in the forest. Not half as smart but more practical.'

'And have you won all those medals?'

'No, they're only campaign medals.'

'What are they?'

'The first two are for Korea and the third is for Kenya. It's called the Africa General-Service-Medal and was first issued in 1902.'

'How romantic. You're quite the soldier, aren't you?'

'If you say so.'

'You're not being very friendly, Miles.'

'I'm sorry, but I was thinking about my mother and I'm not looking forward to all this.'

'Oh, I'm being so insensitive. Sorry.'

We sat in silence for the rest of the journey, which wasn't that long as we were just passing Sherborne Court, where General Fisher lived, and our house was only a few miles on. We drove into our drive, past the gardener's cottage, and stopped in front of the house, which had been built at the turn of the century. My parents had bought it when they came back from India in the 1930s. It was very comfortable, but far too large for my mother now. She had wanted to move to something smaller but hadn't found anything she liked in the neighbourhood, which she didn't want to leave.

Sonia must have heard the car, for the front door opened almost immediately and she walked out and flung her arms around me as I got out of the car.

'Oh, Miles darling, I'm so glad to see you,' she said.

She hugged me. I could see she had been crying and I feared the worst.

'Oh, Miles,' she said.

We looked at each other and I knew.

'It was only an hour ago.'

I nodded.

'Let's go in, cousin Sonia, and you tell me all about it.'

We went into the house and sat in the drawing room.

'I think it's wonderful of you to have been with her and to have done everything you have,' I said. 'When did you come down?'

'She has a nurse who was keeping me up to date. Two days ago she alerted me that your mother was going downhill, getting worse, and she feared the end. I came down immediately. Then Phyllida got your telegram and rang me and we agreed she would meet you and bring you straight here. Convenient you came to Blackbushe.'

'Sweet of Phyllida. I came as quick as I could.'

'I know you did. I suppose I should have telegraphed you earlier but I didn't want to alarm you.'

We sat in silence for a while.

'Would you like a drink?' she said.

'That would be lovely,'

Sonia mixed whisky and soda for both of us, and then we sat

on in silence.

'Do you want to see her?' said Sonia.

'In a moment. Was she still *compos mentis*? I haven't had a letter from her for four weeks, though I've written to her. We exchanged letters once a fortnight. She never said anything was wrong, only that life was getting difficult. She's been saying that for a long time.'

'She was talking a bit, making a little sense.'

'Did she say anything you think I should know?'

'You mustn't be upset, Miles, and it was rather jumbled. She was saying what a mess she had left for you, what a mess she had made of things. There was a lot about your father and how it was all his fault. And then she said how she loved him and how she loved you. Then she would start all over again and say what a mess she'd left for you.'

'What do you think she meant?'

'Well, money, I presume. I can't really understand what she meant, for she was left a small fortune. I can't believe your father, who *was* a big spender, can have spent that much, and he was killed thirteen years ago.'

'I'll have to see the solicitors and talk to the bank. There is a will, I know.'

'There was a lot in trust for you, I know. Oh well, we'll soon know. But it was on your mother's mind.'

We sat there in silence again.

Phyllida put her head round the door and said, 'I'm putting together something for us to eat. You must be starving, Miles, after that terrible journey. It'll be ready in quarter of an hour.' She left.

'I think I'd like to see my mother.'

Sonia led me out of the big drawing room and up the staircase to my mother's room. I entered it alone.

I was very conscious of coming to see not just my mother, but another dead person. How many had I seen? Not that many, but too many close friends in battle: Hugh Jermy in Korea, the night I tried to save him; Jasper in Kenya, only a few weeks ago; and now my mother. She was lying on her back, pale, eyes closed, her flesh almost marble, all spirit gone. But she was in repose. It had been relatively peaceful for her, unlike the others. I knelt at the side of her bed and said a prayer, I can't remember what, and thought about her. We hadn't really been cosy with each other. She had, I think, been afraid I would be too like my father, and had tried to hold me on a rein. This I had resented and felt she was trying to clip my wings. She had loved me, though, and I'd loved her. I'd have loved her more if she'd been easier with me. I kissed her lightly on the forehead and rejoined Sonia.

Then Sonia, Phyllida, the nurse and I went into the dining room and ate a delicious omelette Phyllida had cooked, followed by a salad, and some strawberries she had just picked in the garden. We were a little sombre to say the least.

'Darling,' said Sonia, 'your bed is made up in your room. Phyllida and I are staying the night and we have to go in the morning. I've rung the doctor and he'll be round sometime soon. You must be tired, and if you want to go to bed, we'll look after everything.'

So I went upstairs, had a much needed bath, found a clean pair of pyjamas in a drawer, slipped into my own bed, and slept.

The next morning, shortly after I'd finished breakfast, the nurse told me that General Fisher wanted to speak to me on the telephone.

'Hello, my boy,' he said, 'your cousin Sonia rang me last night and I wanted to tell you how very sorry I am and if I could do anything I'd be very happy to. Now, I'd like to see you. What are you doing for lunch?'

I thanked him and said I had no plans.

'Well that's settled then. See you at one o'clock.'

Sonia and Phyllida were getting ready to leave. The nurse was going to stay until the funeral directors had been. I had to fix that. The doctor, Sonia told me, had been the night before, while I slept, and written the death certificate. We talked about the funeral and agreed a tentative date. I would have to discuss it with the vicar. Then there was a notice for *The Times* and *The Daily Telegraph*. There was plenty to keep me busy.

'Darling,' said Sonia, 'I'm sorry to leave you so soon but we must get back for Ivan, and I have to go to Paris. There're all your mother's things. Don't worry, we'll be back in a day or two and help you sort all those out. I'll ring you tonight.'

With that, they left and I was alone with the nurse. When I had fixed with the funeral director to come that day, and done a few other things, it was time for me to go to Sherborne Court and I rang for a taxi. Mother had a car in the garage but I didn't want to use it as I had no idea how road worthy it was. I could leave that till later.

Sherborne Court had been built in the 17th century, on an older site, and added to a century later. A great Palladian portico set it off, dominating a short drive from the road. There was no grander house in the county. The Fishers had lived in it for three centuries, since General Fisher's ancestor had been made one of the first baronets. The general had been in the regiment and my father had been his protégé. They had been great friends, which is why we had come to live nearby. Bradley, the general's old man servant, who looked after the house and the general with Mrs Bradley, opened the door.

'Good morning, Captain Miles. Mrs Bradley and I are very sad to hear your news and give you our deep condolences.'

'Thank you, Bradley. It's good to see you, though it is a very sad time. How's the general?'

'The general's fine, Sir, and he's waiting for you in the morning room. He's got a fire there, though it is August. He likes a fire.'

He led me to the morning room.

'There you are my boy,' said the general, 'It's wonderful to see you, though the occasion is a sad one. I've missed you. Sherry?'

He handed me a dark looking glass of sherry and noticed my expression.

'Oloroso,' he said. 'Keeps me warm in these cold summers.

Would you prefer something lighter?'

'No, General. I'm happy with this.'

'So, tell me about Kenya. How many polo teams have you? There was always good polo to be had in Kenya.'

'We do play a little, but we're rather occupied with the Mau Mau in the forests.'

'So you are. How's that going?'

'We're just getting the better of them.'

'Glad to hear that. Sounds a nasty business. Tell me about it.'

We talked about Kenya until we went into lunch. The meal was simple and delicious: vichyssoise, then cold salmon trout with a bottle of Batard-Montrachet 47, followed by a bowl of strawberries.

'Lot of nonsense,' he said as we started the meal, 'about gentlemen not eating soup at luncheon. Edwardian twaddle. I always have, and always shall. Now, tell me, what do you think about this new fracas we've landed ourselves in?'

'You mean Suez?'

'Of course.'

'I'm rather ill informed. I've been in an aeroplane these last three days and I haven't seen a newspaper since leaving Kenya, and that wasn't exactly up to date or comprehensive.'

'Well, it's a farce. We go and withdraw from the Canal Zone without taking any precautions about safeguarding our interests there. When Nasser nationalises the canal — rather clever of him — there are no plans, let alone troops, with which to get it back. Eden should have gone in immediately. Do you know there are parachute battalions in Cyprus, but I'm told they've had no parachute training for a year and there're no planes available to drop them? There're marine commandos there too chasing EOKA terrorists, but there are no landing craft to carry them. It's pathetic. He should have gone in immediately but he hasn't any troops available. The longer he leaves it, the more he'll lose the sympathy of the world. Same old problem. No strategic reserve. It's just like France in 1940, when the Germans broke through. The French had no strategic reserve. Unbelievable. Or, now I think about it, all too believable.'

'Are the French interested in this?'

'So I hear. They want Nasser's scalp, too, as they say he's behind all the problems they're having in Algeria. But their troops aren't ready either. You'd better ask that cousin of yours, Cathay, isn't it? He'll know more than me. I'm planning to go up to London soon. I'll stay at Brooks's and dine at the Senior and see what I can pick up. Have you got a club yet?'

By the 'Senior' he meant the United Service Club, the senior of the military clubs.

'I'm a member of the Army & Navy, like most of the regiment,' I said.

'Makes sense. You're probably too young to get into the Senior. Time you joined Brooks's. The younger you're put up, the better.'

'I'd like that very much.'

'Count it as done. Now, you must say if I can do anything else for you. Do you want to stay here? Do you need any help?'

'That's very kind. I think it's best if I stay at home. It'll be a little empty but there's a lot to do. '

'Well, if you change your mind let me know. Now, Bradley will drive you home. I'm going to have a rest. Wonderful to have seen you. That Montrachet was good, wasn't it?'

When I got home, the nurse told me that the funeral directors had been and taken my mother away, and that she was packed and ready to leave. I rang for a taxi to take her to the station. Once she'd gone, I was alone in the house. Then the vicar rang.

One of my tasks was to take Jasper's things, especially the gold cigarette case, to Verity Knox, his mother, who lived in London. I also needed to see the solicitors and the bank, both in London. I didn't think I could stay in the house until the funeral, which was now planned for a date two weeks ahead. I decided that after Sonia had returned to help me sort out mother's things, I would go to London for a few days. Before I left Kenya, I had arranged with Ben to use his flat in Harrington Gardens and all I had to do was to ring his housekeeper, Mrs Pooley, whom I knew, to say when I was arriving. I could stay with the Cathays, but it would be easier to stay at Ben's.

I sent a telegram to Colonel Rex explaining the situation and he replied, telling me to take my time. He didn't mention the crisis and I wondered if the battalion would be affected or involved in any way. Then I forgot about it.

Sonia and Phyllida returned and we started to sort out mother's clothes and belongings. She clearly hadn't thrown away much since she moved in. Not just clothes, but bags, luggage, hats, letters, notes recording appointments, wrapping paper neatly folded to use again with string rolled up in little balls. Her desk was overflowing with papers. I found my letters going back to school days. I also found the letters she had written to my father and his replies. I burnt these without looking at them and then regretted it. I should have left them for posterity. While going through the house, sorting things out, I noticed that some of the furniture was missing and several pictures had been removed from the walls. I mentioned this to Sonia but she didn't think it odd. She thought my mother had got bored with them and put them in an outhouse. Then I forgot about it. We were kept busy for two days when Sonia said she had to leave to go to Paris and that Phyllida would stay on which she did. She didn't seem to think there was anything improper in Phyllida and me being alone in the house together. By this time Phyllida and I had broken the barrier between us, which I had probably put up on our way from the airport when she met me, and we had become more relaxed together.

She was younger than me. For years I had treated her as my little cousin. Now, she was grown up, a young and beautiful woman. As we worked together, I had to admit to myself that I found her attractive. Two years before she had come out to Germany to ski and she had proposed that I deflower her. She said she wanted to get it over with. I refused. I couldn't take her seriously and I thought it inappropriate. She was cross. Later, when we were in

London, before the regiment left for Kenya, I had seen a bit of
her and fancied her and she knew it. She had scolded me as an
opportunist. Now we were together and I was enjoying being with
her a lot.

'What,' she said as she packed another suitcase full of clothes,
'are the girls like in Kenya? All tanned and long legs, I expect.'

'Tanned all over and the longest legs you ever saw,' I said.

'Don't tease. I'm serious. We very rarely see any girls from
Kenya in London, though London girls go out there.'

'Some girls went out with their parents when they emigrated,
some were born there, the daughters of settlers. Most of the girls,
especially the daughters of settlers, have been educated there and
see no point in leaving. It's their country and they love it.'

'Have you made a friend?'

'Oh, Phyllida, why do you want to know?'

'So you have!'

'There's one girl I see a bit of, but there's nothing agreed between us.'

'That's what I wanted to know. You made a pass at me at that
party mummy gave for you and your friends before you left. I
just wondered where we stood. I like you, Miles. You know that.
But I wasn't doing anything as a last minute fling. That suitcase
is full. I need another.'

'What are you going to do with all those clothes?'

'Mummy's selected the best which she thinks could be sold. Not
many but some good, like the furs. The rest are going to one of
mummy's charities and they'll sort them. Now find me another
suitcase.'

When we'd finished for the day, Phyllida made another delicious
omelette, with ham this time. Then we watched Robin Day on the
television set assessing the crisis and then, rather tired, we crept to
our own beds. I would have to think carefully about Phyllida.

At breakfast the next morning I asked her why Sonia had had to
go to Paris.

'Ostensibly,' she said, 'to buy clothes, but hardly in August. She's staying at the embassy. In fact, I believe she's gone to see if she can find out what's going on. The French are so indiscreet, she says, she thinks she will find out more than even Daddy knows.'

That day we finished everything we could do together. It was now left to me to sort through my mother's papers. Chang arrived with the large black motor car, into which we put all the suitcases and hat boxes.

'Thank you, Phyllida,' I said, 'so much for all you've done. I shall be coming to London tomorrow. Would you like to have dinner with me the day after?'

'I'd love to,' she said, and kissed me on the cheek with not a sign of shyness.

The next day I saw Jasper's mother. She was in her late fifties, and a very chic and lovely woman. At one time she had been my father's mistress, much to my mother's chagrin. Jasper and I had been to the same schools, Jasper following me. We had all known each other well. She now looked tired and older than when I had last seen her, before we went to Kenya.

'Oh, Miles,' she said, 'how kind of you to come and see me. I want to know everything you can tell me about Jasper. I really miss that darling scamp.'

I told her how he had died, how the colonel had recommended him for an immediate Military Cross, how the general had agreed and how she would be invited to Buckingham Palace for the presentation to receive it.

'I've done that before,' she said.

I remembered how her husband had been killed at Dunkirk and won a posthumous MC. Then I gave her Jasper's things such as they were, including the gold cigarette case damaged as it was by the bullet that had hit it and been deflected into his lungs. She held it in her hands for a while saying nothing.

'How Jasper,' she finally said, 'how Jasper loved that case. It must go to the regimental museum with the MC. That's where they belong. Would you see to it?'

Then she said what a lovely letter she had had from Colonel Rex and she thought that the letter should go with the cigarette case and the medal, but she didn't want to part with it.

'All the men I've loved, Miles,' she said, 'have been killed. First Jasper's father at Dunkirk, then your father in that dreadful plane crash in the war, now my darling Jasper. What have I done to deserve this? Life is so cruel.'

'You've loved some very brave and courageous men who ran out of luck.'

'Ah, luck. Yes, I've had a run of bad luck. Let's hope it's over now. At least I have the knowledge that they were all brave, as you say. Foolishly brave, I think.'

She took my hand as she said this and tears trickled down her lovely cheeks.

'Come on now,' she said as she dabbed at her tears, 'I'm taking you out to lunch. We're going to the Aperitif Grill in Jermyn Street.'

That evening I collected Phyllida from her parents' house in Eaton Terrace. Her mother and father were there, and he made Martinis for us all. Sonia was just back from Paris.

'I don't know whether you know, Miles,' he said, 'but Sonia's been to Paris to buy some dresses. For once she returned empty handed. Well, it was August.'

'They were so busy at the embassy with this crisis that there wasn't much time for shopping.'

'Did you learn anything?'

'I learned the names of the generals to command the expedition. Hughie Stockwell and General Andre Beaufre. You could have told me that.'

'You know perfectly well that I'm bound by the Official Secrets Act and can't say anything.'

'This was general knowledge at Paris.'

'The frogs have a different view about secrets.'

'If you continue to deny me any knowledge I'll have to go back to Paris.'

'Don't forget to bring some dresses back next time,' he said and, turning to me, said, 'where are you off to tonight?'

'I was going to take Phyllida to the Aperitif, but I was taken there for lunch, so I think we'll go to L'Ecu de France, if she'd like that.'

'That's a good choice and a favourite of the French embassy. Phyllida might hear some secrets she could pass on to her mother.'

'Stop teasing, Ivan, and make us some Martinis,' said Sonia. 'I'm dry.'

Phyllida and I went to the L'Ecu de France. There were some French diplomats there at a table far from us, deep in conversation. We couldn't hear a word. Afterwards we danced at Hatchetts. I told her about how beautiful Kenya was and she said she'd like to see it. We tentatively agreed she should come out when the emergency was over.

The next day I went to see my mother's solicitor, who showed me her will.

'You'll see,' he said, 'that everything comes to you after one or two minor bequests. I'm sorry to say that I don't think there'll be much left after the debts have been paid.'

'What debts?' I said.

'You know the house and land is mortgaged?'

'Mortgaged? I had no idea.'

'She was so shaken by losing the money in what she used to call the family business. You know about that? Apparently, she wanted to make it back, the money I mean, and she felt guilty about your inheritance. You see, the money was in trust for you. A neighbour of hers, a rather questionable stockbroker — I must be careful what I say — told her he could make a lot of money for her. She started to buy and sell shares regularly. She lost money but she went on, as the stockbroker told her she had to be prepared to lose money as well as make it. The first I knew about this was when she came to me and told me she wanted to mortgage the house. I advised her strongly against it. She insisted. I managed to raise a fifty per cent mortgage on all the property. That went, too. At the end, she was living off a small army pension and an annuity. I suspect that's what made her ill. I can see that this has come as quite a shock to you.'

'Will there be any money?'

'Maybe a little, but nothing like the money it was intended you should have. That's after selling the house. We'll have to do that.'

So that, I thought, explained the missing pictures and furniture. Mother had been selling things from the house. Yes, she had left a mess for me. And I thought I knew who the questionable stockbroker was.

Two weeks later, just as the First London Conference on Suez started, we buried my mother. There were family there, and I was surprised at how many friends came. The village turned out in force. I didn't see the questionable stockbroker in the congregation.

Colonel Rex sent me a telegram. He said that, due to the crisis over Suez, the movement of the drafts of trained national service-men from the regimental depot to Kenya had had to be halted. He wanted me to report to the depot, take charge of the drafts, get them fit and train them to fight in the forests until trooping was resumed, when I could bring them out to Kenya. I packed my things.

12

A Britain divided

Rain lashed the windows of the train as I peered out at the countryside. It was as opaque as the situation about the Suez Canal. I was on my way to the regimental depot, in response to Colonel Rex's orders, and I was travelling in a service dress uniform which had been hanging in my room in my mother's house.

'Will you be involved?'

Sitting in the far corner, opposite me, was a man in his early thirties wearing a business suit. There was no one else in the compartment. I looked at him.

'Do you think you'll be involved?' he said.

'I've just returned from Kenya,' I said, 'and I'm on my way to my regimental depot. I've had no briefing, yet, and I'm not at all clear about what's going on.'

'I wonder if anyone is. Why didn't he go straight in?'

'I'm told he didn't have the troops ready to do it.'

'That doesn't make sense. We've nearly three quarters of a million men under arms. At his last Defence Review, the Defence Secretary said we'd never been more prepared in peacetime.'

'Almost all the troops are committed somewhere. Malaya, Kenya, Cyprus, Germany. I'm told we have no reserves.'

'Extraordinary. I think Eden may have lost his chance. If he'd gone straight in the country, probably the world, would have backed him. But now? The country's becoming divided and there's this Suez Conference sitting in London. What do you think will be the outcome of that?'

'I really don't know.'

'Nor do I,' he said. 'It'll depend on what line the Americans take. It's up to them now.'

I looked out of the window. It was raining cats and dogs.

It was still raining when I arrived at my destination. I was hoping that I might be met, as I had telegraphed ahead to say when my train was arriving. There was no one to greet me. I realised I would have to take a taxi so I beckoned the only one on the rank. The taxi driver jumped out of his cab, bundled me into the back, threw my luggage into the boot, got back into the cab as fast as he could, and said, 'Good afternoon, Captain Player. You couldn't have chosen a wetter day to arrive. Lucky I was here.'

It was Doughty, who had been my driver in Korea.

'Goodness, Doughty. Where did you spring from?'

'I've been doing this caper ever since I was demobbed. My dad's had this taxi business for years. That's how I could drive when I joined the army. Have you been in Kenya, Sir?'

'Yes, I came back because my mother died.'

'I'm sorry to hear that, Sir. I thought you'd returned to sort out this muddle about the Suez Canal.'

'Good joke, Doughty. I doubt we'll be involved. The paras and the commandos are generally thrown in on these occasions.'

'The last time we were alone together was at the cemetery at Pusan, when we held that service for the lads killed in Korea. You were lost in thought standing in front of Mr Jermy's grave. If I hadn't pulled you away I think you'd still be there.'

He chuckled.

' If you're going to be here for the pheasant shooting, the barracks has these shoots, same as we had in Korea. I see you haven't got your gun with you. There'll be some spare ones at the barracks. We had a lot of fun in Korea didn't we? Those were the days.'

He sighed.

'There're a lot of new officers at the depot. Captain Hare's one I've got to know. I take him to the races. He likes his horses, he does. When he wins — he does more often than not — he gives me a good tip.'

We drove into the barracks, through the gates and past the great metal eagle the Second Battalion had removed from the German barracks at Cologne, where it had been stationed in the occupation of the Rhine after the Great War, on past the guard room, turned to the right beside the parade ground, and stopped outside the main entrance to the officers' mess. Doughty and his taxi were clearly well known as the guard at the gate had waived him through with a nod. Doughty placed my cases in the hall of the mess. As I paid him, and I gave him a good tip, he said, 'Some of the lads from Korea have get togethers. Would you come to our next one?'

'Please invite me,' I said. 'It was good to see you again, Doughty. See more of you, I hope.'

'I hope so too, Sir. I can't wait to tell the lads. What is it you do now in the battalion?'

'I'm adjutant.'

'Well done, Sir. You'll be colonel next.'

He hopped into his cab and drove away. It was still raining.

I looked about me. The mess sounded empty. I took off my cap and Sam Browne belt, hung them up on a row of hooks, and went into the anteroom. Sitting in armchairs in various states of dress, a mix of plain clothes and uniform, were three people eating tea. There was a fine spread on a table: boiled eggs, crumpets spread with anchovy paste, toast, butter and jam, fruit cake, and a pot of tea. Adam Hare looked up from his boiled egg and said, 'Welcome Miles. I saw Doughty bring you in. He's a good driver. I use him a lot.'

'He told me. He was my driver in Korea.'

'Was he now? I'm sure we'd have sent someone to meet you if we knew when you were coming.'

'I sent a telegram.'

'Ah, but to whom?'

He got up, chose another egg, cracked it and started to peel it.

'If you want some fresh tea, press the bell and one of the mess staff will come.'

This I did, ordered myself some tea and asked for my luggage to be taken to my room. At least the mess staff were expecting me.

'We've had a tiresome day on the range. Too exhausting in that rain,' said Adam.

This accounted for their dress and their wet hair. They must have got soaked, had baths, and changed.

'Are you going to introduce me?' I said.

'Don't you know them? Algy Poppleton on the left and Peter Petitpierre on the right.'

They stood up and shook hands with greasy fingers. They were both subalterns and I recalled they had both been with the 1st Battalion.

'That's better', said Adam as he finished the last egg, 'I needed that. What are you doing here, Miles?'

'I'm here for a few weeks. I have to discuss it with Tom Warburton tomorrow. '

Adam stood up. 'I hope you brought a black tie with you. We shall be sitting down to a decent dinner tonight, none of that Muthaiga Camp muck, and we dress. Drinks at seven forty five, dine at eight. I've found it's best not to have too many pre-prandials. They wreck the meal and the gut. Don't be late. I'm off to study for the staff college now.'

When I arrived for drinks before dinner, Poppleton, Petitpierre, and Adam were all there in black ties with another officer, a second lieutenant, in uniform. He came up to me and we shook hands.

'I'm Edward Dering,' he said. 'I'm a national serviceman and my grandfather and father were in the regiment. I must apologise for not having you met at the station. I'm orderly officer and I'm afraid the rain rather disrupted everything today. I had to go on the range and I didn't get your telegram until after you had arrived.'

'Luckily my old driver from Korea was in the cab rank and he brought me up.'

'Oh good. What are you drinking? Adam is drinking a mixture of Punt e Mes and Fernet Branca topped up with soda water. He says it's good for the gut.'

'So it is, but don't I see a decanter of sherry on the table there? I think I'll have a sherry. How long have you been here?'

'Six weeks and I should be in Kenya by now but they've stopped sending drafts so I'm looking after the drafts here.'

'Well, I think we'll get to see a bit of each other.'

'I'm really looking forward to going to Kenya. You know it's quite difficult to get into the regiment now the second battalion is in Kenya. It's very popular. I shall miss being here, though. We live very well.'

The door opened and in walked David Vane, whom I knew. He was the adjutant here at the depot.

'Hello, David,' I said.

'Miles, it's good to have you here. I'm late because there's an unholy mess about reservists being recalled for the 1st Battalion. As you probably know, the battalion is in 3 Div and it's been earmarked for Suez and is being brought up to strength. I expect you may well end up with it.'

'I never thought of that. You know I'm still under Colonel Rex's command?'

'That may have to change. The 1st Battalion is short of experienced officers. I see dinner is about to be announced. Sit next to me.'

The mess serjeant had come into the anteroom and he announced dinner. When we went into the dining room I saw that the large Victorian dining table had been moved to the window, with most of its leaves removed and the Regency rosewood round table, which used to sit in the window, was now in the middle of the room with six chairs placed round it.

'Much cosier like this,' said Adam as he beckoned me to sit on his right. David Vane sat on my right and the others seated themselves.

'Life is very agreeable here, Miles,' Adam said. 'Very occasion-ally we have a bad day, like today, which is only to be expected, but I really couldn't be more fortunate to have been posted here to this job. Beautiful cathedral city which caters for all tastes, not too far from London, several good race courses within easy mo-toring, a fine mess with well trained servants, an excellent cellar which has a lot of old claret that no one's been drinking, and the serjeant major and the subalterns do all the work. Once a week we play in the evening cricket league here. And, best of all, it's far from that heathen country you all love so much. I can't think why. I couldn't be happier here.'

'You've fallen on your feet, alright. I hope you don't do any-thing silly.'

'Like what?'

'You're clever and idle, Adam, and you get into financial scrapes.'

'I'm doing quite nicely here, thank you, and the horses are being kind to me.'

'That won't necessarily go on forever and this seems to be an expensive mess.'

'I've changed things a little. I'm president of the mess committee and the regiment must be seen to do things properly. I suppose I should ask you about the battalion in Kenya. Is the Swiss Grill still any good?'

I brought him up to date with people and places but he wasn't really interested, so I turned to David Vane.

'You don't really think,' I said, 'that there's a chance of my going to the 1st Battalion, do you?'

'It's quite possible. Aren't you rather excited about the idea?'

'Yes, but what about the 2nd Battalion and Kenya?'

'It would only be temporary. Taking the canal back couldn't take long.'

'Do you know anything about what's being planned?'

'We understand, though we learn everything on the grapevine, that the landing will be made by the paras and the commandos and

3 Div will follow them up and take over. It's one hell of a palaver getting it organised. Our job is helping to get the 1ˢᵗ Battalion up to strength. It's woefully low, as you've had all the recent drafts to keep you up to strength in Kenya. There are drafts waiting here now for you but my guess is that they'll be switched to the 1ˢᵗ Battalion.'

'We need them in Kenya.'

'Priorities, Miles. There's about to be a war.'

I cannot remember what we were eating and drinking — it was very good and certainly far better than I remember having before at the barracks — as I was thinking about the chance of going to the 1ˢᵗ Battalion and all that meant. Exciting as it sounded to be part of the expeditionary force, I still felt very much engaged in Kenya.

'After dinner, which I hope you are enjoying, Miles,' said Adam, 'we're going to have a game of cards, chemmy tonight. You'll enjoy it.'

'Count me out, Adam. The last few weeks haven't been easy and I don't feel like that tonight.'

'We'll miss you. There'll be plenty of opportunities for you to join in. We play once or twice a week.'

So I went to my room and thought about what might happen to me in this crisis over Suez. It made a change from thinking about my mother and then about Phyllida. Then it struck me that I'd hardly thought about Becky since I'd been back in England and wondered what she might be up to. And it didn't worry me at all.

The office of Tom Warburton, the commandant of the depot, was on the first floor of the depot headquarters building. The block looked as though it might have been designed for the Indian sub-continent as it had a veranda the length of the first floor. You could either enter the commandant's office via the veranda or through the office of the adjutant in the building. Out of courtesy to David Vane I went through his office and David announced me.

When I was last in the commandant's office it had been provided with War Department furniture. Tom had changed this. He sat behind a Victorian campaign desk made of mahogany and edged in brass. It was in three pieces. The top part rested on two sections of drawers, so that it could be easily assembled and unassembled and transported. It was a handsome and practical piece and clearly Tom's. And he was sitting in a large Victorian Windsor chair. On the wall behind him was an oar almost the length of the room. It was embellished in gold with the names of the college eight with whom he had had rowed, and on the walls were mounted photographs of Tom and his fellow oarsmen in various stages of rowing. I had forgotten that Tom had been at Oxford before the war, and had never known that he had been an oarsman. He had made the room sporting and stylish. It was a surprise. Tom had commanded a company in Korea and was a friend. One night, towards the end of our tour, he was sitting in his stationary jeep with his driver and wireless operator, on a corner by the side of an icy road when a lorry skidded into it. His wireless operator was killed, his driver lost a leg and Tom lost an arm. His arm was amputated. As he sat there in uniform you wouldn't realise that it wasn't his own arm, though he did wear a leather glove on his right hand. When he had recovered from the amputation he had had a job on the staff which didn't require any physical competence. Now he was commanding the depot. The room was a statement of his former sporting life.

'What a lovely room, Tom,' I said after I had saluted.

'I'm glad you think so, Miles. It was all rather drab when I arrived so I brightened it up. I'm so glad you've come to spend some time with us. I do hope you'll be here for the shooting. Do you remember old General Lord Albury, the colonel of the regiment before General Flaxman? You probably don't. He had been in the regiment, was Lord Lieutenant, and had thousands of acres. Well, his nephew, the new peer, has gone to live in South Africa and has leased us the shooting rights for virtually nothing. Not quite as many acres but fantastic. You must stay for the shooting.'

'It all depends on what's happening about the Suez Canal. Has Colonel Rex told you why he's sent me here?'

'He signalled us to expect you and to look after you, as you couldn't return to Kenya at the moment.'

'He's asked me to take over the drafts here waiting to go to Kenya, and to train them for fighting in the forest.'

'There won't be any need for that. The drafts have to go to strengthen the 1st Battalion.'

'Do you think I should go to the 1st Battalion?'

'I wouldn't do that. The commandos and the paras will be the first to go in and get all the credit. The 1st Battalion, with the rest of 3 Div when they get there, will take over and be exposed to all the sniping and booby traps of the bloody minded gyppos. Don't I remember! I was in Egypt before we handed the Suez base over. Decidedly unpleasant it was. And it'll be damn hot. Besides, will anything happen? The whole thing is a shambles, at the moment. And you'd miss the shooting here.'

'I'll have to ask Colonel Rex.'

'He won't let you go.'

'Why on earth not?'

'He won't want to lose you. Once you're posted you're lost to him as then the 1st Battalion won't let you go. Battalion rivalry. Besides, he's your patron now. Don't lose him.'

'What do I do then?'

'Take it easy here and wait for events.'

'How long is this going to last?'

'Who knows? Well into the autumn is my guess. They haven't got an expeditionary force together yet. You could assist Adam here.'

'I'm senior to him. I was his company commander.'

'Yes, delicate. Leave it with me. Have you had any leave yet?'

'I've just been on compassionate leave to bury my mother.'

'I'm sorry about that. I should have said that earlier. I remember your mother in India, before the war. Your parents were very decent to me and to all the subalterns. They gave wonderful parties.

You were a child. I remember you well with your ayah, and your beloved pony. How long ago all that was. Another world. Your mother lived near General Fisher in Hampshire, didn't she? What are you going to do about the house?'

'I'm going to have to sell it.'

'Take two weeks leave. Organise the sale and anything else you have to do. And have a good time. I'll work something out. I wouldn't volunteer for the 1st Battalion yet. When you come back we'll have a game of tennis.'

I put my name in the leave book, sent a telegram to Mrs Pooley to say that I would be arriving in Harrington Gardens that afternoon, and sent another to Phyllida asking her to have dinner with me. Then I packed and sent for Doughty to take me to the station.

When I arrived at Harrington Gardens, Mrs Pooley told me that Phyllida had rung to say that she and her mother were going to the opera, that her father Lord Cathay would like me to have dinner with him at Brooks's, and we'd all meet up later in the evening. He would see me there at 8 P.M., if he didn't hear to the contrary. So at eight o'clock I walked into Brooks's in St James' Street, was met by Ivan Cathay, and we went straight into dinner. Ivan ordered champagne for us.

'How is it you've got more leave, Miles? I would have thought the army would be crying out for your services.'

'Flights to Kenya have been halted, so I'm stuck here. Tom Warburton, the depot commandant, has told me to go on leave to sort my affairs out while they decide what I should do. So I'm on my way home to arrange the sale of the house.'

'Sonia has explained all that to me and selling the house is a wise move. Clear the debts from the estate. I'm sure there'll be something left over.'

'I hope so,' I said. 'Now I'm torn between wanting to return to Kenya and taking part in the Suez expedition.'

'How do you know there's a Suez expedition?'

'The priority at the depot when I left it this morning was to build up the strength of our 1ˢᵗ Battalion which, you may not know, is in the 3ʳᵈ Division assigned to the expeditionary force. We understand that the division will take over from the commandos and the paras when they've re-taken the canal.'

'Goodness, how do you know that?'

'Everyone seems to know, and it makes sense militarily if we are going to invade. Are we?'

'We want to find a peaceful solution. The problem is Nasser and oil. We can't sit back and let Nasser consolidate his position and gradually gain control of the oil-producing countries in the Middle East. Our information is that Nasser is out to wreck us. That's why Eden wants to unseat him. So, it's bigger, much bigger than just the Suez Canal. If Middle East oil is denied to us for a year or two, our gold reserves will disappear. If this happens, the sterling area will disintegrate. We won't have any reserves, we'll not be able to maintain our forces in Germany or anywhere else, or pay the bare minimum for our defence. If we can't provide for our defence we're finished. Getting the canal back will unseat Nasser. Menzies, the Australian Prime Minister, has been negotiating with Nasser and got nowhere. Now Dulles, who earlier seemed to support us and the French, has come up with the idea of a Suez Canal Users Association and I doubt Nasser will accept it. Nasser's playing to win. We're playing to win. Deadlock so far. We may have to invade. Would you like some claret with your grouse?'

'Yes, please.'

Ivan ordered a pint of claret for me and a pint of champagne for himself.

'What about the United Nations and the Security Council?' I said.

'Good question. We have to work with them and we need to be very careful how we do it. We need the United States on our side in the Security Council and they're not completely with us at the moment.'

'Aren't there two different issues? The issue of taking the canal back under international control and the issue of getting rid of Nasser.'

'They're indivisible. Nasser is the leader of Arab nationalism. He's turning everyone there against us, weakening our influence. Eden puts it to Eisenhower that Nasser's operating like Hitler in the 1930s, when we never stood up to him, and look what happened. Nasser nationalises the canal. What next? In Libya there's a plot to kill King Idris, in Saudi Arabia King Saud is threatened, Syria is virtually under Egyptian control, in Iraq the prime Minister Nuri es Said faces the disaffection of the younger officers. The Kremlin is laughing. As to the canal, the Egyptians can't operate it. They haven't the skills. We must take it back.'

'What does Eisenhower say?'

'He's told Eden he's for negotiation and against force. But he doesn't understand. The canal and the Middle East is not his frontier. It's ours. And it's our oil.'

'I see.'

'Let's turn to more personal things. General Fisher tells me that he is putting you up for Brooks's and has asked me to second you. I'm very happy to do that. I told Sonia and she's delighted. One of the reasons for bringing you here to dinner tonight is so you can meet some members. So, let's go and have coffee with some.'

'That was a delicious dinner.'

'There'll be many more.'

We went upstairs to the Great Subscription Room.

'Port or brandy?'

'Port, please.'

'A lot of port is drunk here. Let's join my friends in the corner.'

He introduced me as Fred Player's boy and Sonia's cousin.

'Your father's death was tragic,' said one of the members, whose name I didn't catch. 'Tragic, he was going to the top of the army. What are you doing?'

'I followed my father into his regiment and I'm on leave from Kenya.'

'I hope you'll say that things are now under control there at last? Are they? Good! Has Ivan been priming you on the case for re-taking the canal?'

'He's been very clear about the need to do that.'

'I doubt we can do that. Partly because we can't do anything important without American support, partly because as a founder member of the United Nations we must work through it. Anything that looks like threatening to invade Egypt if Nasser doesn't hand it over isn't very subtle diplomacy.'

'We're not threatening,' said Ivan. 'We're working through all the correct channels.'

'Why, then, are we assembling an expeditionary force?'

'In case we do have to go in.'

'I see that as threatening. I agree Nasser is a thug, but I don't see how we have an excuse to use force. An invasion would turn world opinion against Britain and would be violently unpopular at home.'

'We're only proposing an invasion if diplomacy fails, so we have to get an expeditionary force ready.'

'What we need is to marshal world support. The surest way to do this is to offer Nasser terms that it would be unreasonable and provocative for him to reject.'

'That's what we're trying to do.'

'I'm glad you say that. From all I hear, Eden has a strong leaning towards the use of force. If so, he's living in a world long gone.'

A hall porter bent over Ivan and gave him a message.

'Miles,' he said, 'it's time to go. Sonia and Phyllida are outside and offering us a lift home.'

We left the clubhouse and found Chang waiting to open the car door for us. Sonia and Phyllida were sitting in the back of the car. Ivan and I got in and sat in the bucket seats.

'Lovely boys' evening, was it?' said Sonia.

'Ivan gave me a wonderful time,' I said. 'How was the Opera House?'

'It wasn't the Opera House. We went to the Aldwych to see *The*

Threepenny Opera. It was crazy. Phyllida wants to see it again.'

'I'll take you, Phyllida.' I said. 'I was wondering if you would all like to come up the road to Hatchetts. We'll be in time for the cabaret and we could dance.'

'You go, darlings,' said Sonia. 'Go and enjoy yourselves. Ivan and I won't come tonight, will we darling?'

'No, not tonight,' said Ivan.

I thanked Ivan for the evening. Phyllida and I got out of the car and, as we walked up the street to Hatchetts, she put her arm through mine and said, 'Miles, you're a darling. I couldn't think of anything nicer.'

13

What's happening?

'It's a good idea to sell the house,' said General Fisher. We were dining at Sherborne Court. 'You're not ready for a house like that. I wonder your mother kept on there for so long. Who's going to live there while you're away in the army? It'll be an expense to look after. You'll be well rid of it. You know, I'm thinking of getting rid of this house, well the ownership of it.'

'You've talked about that before.'

'Have I? The National Trust are finally interested. A tall, thin fellow comes round and we've now got to the point of how much land I'm prepared to give with the house. This fellow impresses me, as he knows his stuff and he likes the house. Of course, I'll go on living here with the Bradleys, tenure for life. That cousin of mine in Rhodesia, who will inherit the baronetcy, is perfectly happy about it. Doesn't want to live in England, though the way the colonies are going I wonder how long he'll want to live in Rhodesia.'

'Rhodesia looks settled to me, and it's got a larger European population than Kenya.'

'Is it large enough? The problem with all these settlers in Africa is that they can't count. They're no good at maths. How many settlers are there in Kenya?'

'All told about 60,000 Europeans.'

'And how many native Africans?'

'Over six million.'

'And in Southern Rhodesia?'

'About a hundred and thirty thousand settlers and two million Africans.'

'Let's work this out. In Kenya there's one settler to every 100 Africans, and in Rhodesia one settler to every 15 Africans, and they think these countries can go on being white colonies, or even white dominions, in a democratic age? They're out of their minds. That's their affair. Well, it's not. Kenya is very much our affair, and Rhodesia will become so. Too many problems. I can see that *my* immediate affair is to tie up this house and estate for the National Trust so it does not become a problem for anyone.'

Neither of us talked for a bit. What he had said seemed so final.

'Why don't you come and live here? I'll have your company from time to time and you'll have a base. I'll get Bradley to prepare a room for you. You'll need a base. We all do. I'll write that into the deeds of transfer. You may live here for my lifetime. That's settled. So what are you doing now?'

'That's immensely generous of you, General George. I very much appreciate it.'

'Say nothing of it. The least I can do for your father and mother. We'll put aside a suite of rooms so you will be independent. The house is large enough. Of course, we'll eat together. So what are you up to now?'

'Tom Warburton, you know him I think, he's the commandant at the depot...'

'Chap with an amputated arm? Amazing what he can do with that arm. Still a dead shot. And he plays a hard game of tennis, I'm told.'

'He's given me another two weeks to sort out the house and my affairs. They're building up the strength of the 1st Battalion, which is part of the expeditionary force, and there's a possibility I might join it.'

'The operation is called *Musketeer*. I learned something about it when I went up to London. It's a joint operation with the French though we're in charge. It was called *Hamilcar* until Paris pointed out that in French it's *Amilcar*. Not a good start to Anglo French co-operation. I gather there's trouble with the objectives. Do they take the canal or do they take Egypt? You could take the canal with a division or two. To take Egypt you'd need an army of two or three corps, six or more divisions. They don't exist. Even if they did, they'd have one hell of a job holding the country against a hostile population. Of course, Eden wants to topple Nasser. I think taking the canal would be enough to do that. Have you any news?'

'Not from the barracks. Ivan Cathay took me to dinner at Brooks's — I must thank you for putting me up — and we talked with some members after dinner. There was a clear division of opinion whether force was possible or even right. I got the impression that Eden may be working the diplomatic channels, but he's in favour of force.'

'What's his excuse to invade? I *cannot* see how he can. He was doing a good job till this Suez crisis. Now I think he's floundering, out of his depth. Keep your ear to the ground, Miles, and let me know what you hear.'

A London and Basingstoke agent was going to handle the sale of the house, which they said should be straightforward as the house and land — there were paddocks and fields, that were let for grazing, and woods, in all about 30 acres — were in good condition. My mother had seen to that, however pushed for income she must have been. Next I had to sort out the furniture. I kept some of the pieces that I knew my parents had inherited, including some pictures and the Regency dining room chairs. General Fisher had said that I could store them in one of his outhouses, where I found furniture already stored. I included a lot of linen and blankets, and good things that the auctioneers told me had little secondhand value and would be expensive to buy. Then I picked some pieces that I thought would be useful when I did finally settle down, and sent the rest to the auction rooms. I came to regret this later, but *force majeure* made me. It was a difficult and emotional two weeks and

I broke them by going to London for a long weekend to see Phyllida. I would have liked to have had Phyllida with me to help sort
everything out, but she had been offered a job at a charity which
she had long wanted and didn't feel she could turn down. So, on
Friday I took the train to London and went straight to Harrington
Gardens. I had hardly got there when Phyllida arrived with a basket
full of food, out of which she made us dinner. Then for the first
time, we made love. We had crossed the Rubicon.

'Sit down, Miles,' said Tom Warburton. 'I hope you've managed
to sort out your affairs?'

'I have, as far as I can. Everything's in train. Thank you for
giving me the time to do this.'

'Good. Now, I've discussed what you should do with the colonel
of the regiment. As VCIGS, I expect he knows more than almost
anyone about what's going on militarily. Diplomatically I wonder
if anyone knows what's happening. He thinks this situation, you
might call it stalemate, is likely to go on for some time. He does not
want you to join the 1st Battalion, where there's no obvious position
for someone of your rank and experience. They seem to have filled
up all the officer appointments now. Trooping to and from Kenya
will probably start again soon, by using a route through West Africa
via Kano in Nigeria, thus avoiding the Middle East. But he's got
a job for you here in England. His MA, Military Assistant, is seriously ill. He wants you to go to him, as his temporary MA, until
the MA recovers or the general has to find a replacement. It's a
job normally held by a Major who's passed out of the Staff College
near the top. It's one hell of an opportunity for you.'

'Does that mean I'll be in London until I can return to
Kenya?'

'Yes.'

'What does Rex say about this? Does he know?'

'I've told Rex and he has had to agree, of course. He's appointed
Burgo temporary adjutant.'

'Has he! That's odd. He promised he'd leave Burgo as Military

Intelligence Officer on a farm where he was based.'

'Exigencies of the service. Burgo is standing in for you.'

'So, back to London I go?'

'Not before we've had a game of tennis. Get the tailor to put some crowns on your shoulder straps. You're a major now, however temporary.'

I had often walked past the War Office building in Whitehall but had never entered it. Five stories high and ten bays wide, with a circular turret at all four corners, it had been built in the first decade of the 20th century in the Edwardian baroque style. It was an imposing building, with giant Ionic columns in between the windows on the front, and each turret had a stone dome. I learned later that the ground on which it had been built had been unstable, so the foundations were massive and the basement was a warren of rooms. I walked up the main steps to be confronted by a tall frock-coated head porter in a gold-banded top hat standing in front of an immense and grand staircase. I explained who I was, and a messenger was summoned to take me to a room on the second floor where the members of the Army Council had their offices. I felt as if I was entering a palace.

On the second floor, we entered a large room with five desks round it, at four of which someone was sitting. All were wearing plain clothes. I was in uniform. One of them stood up and came across to greet me.

'You must be Player,' he said, 'we've been expecting you. I'll take you in to meet the VCIGS.'

Lieutenant General Sir James Browne was sitting in an armchair in the middle of a large room. By the window there was a desk with a few papers on it. On one side of the room was a large table with chairs round it, clearly a conference table. In between were some armchairs and side tables, in one of which the general was sitting, reading *The Economist*. He rose out of his chair with a spring.

'Ah, Player! Miles, isn't it? I knew your father. I had the privilege of being on his staff in North Africa. He was a wonderful man and very kind to me. Welcome to the War Office. It's very lucky for me that you happen to be in England, though I'm sorry for the reason. Your colonel has told me all about you. Now you're here you will be very useful. Tom Warburton explained everything, didn't he? I'm glad you've put your crowns up. That will give you more authority and the extra pay will help, you being in London. Do sit down.'

He indicated a chair next to his.

'You are, essentially, my personal staff. You keep my diary and make all my arrangements, as I have no ADC. More important, you accompany me in my duties, take notes, advise on courses of action, and liaise with the general staff, especially those of the CIGS in the room you sit in. You'll catch on, and the other MAs will help you. You're one of a team.'

When we left England for Kenya, the general had come to see us off on our troopship and my memory of him was of a sleek man with a quick eye, a lively step, and a word for everyone. His black hair was still sleeked back but now I noticed he had a definite air of authority and a kindliness and warmth that had missed me earlier. I had thought he might be one of those Montgomery generals, full of dash and military epigrams, but I saw he was a more rounded man and warmed to him.

'At the moment,' he said, 'we are putting together an expeditionary force to take back the Suez Canal. There's a joint expeditionary headquarters — joint in that it's the French and us — in the basement here, working it all out. We have to keep a helping eye and hand, so you'll be liaising with them and keeping me informed of what's going on. We may have to visit some of the troops involved. It's quite an undertaking, but we're getting there. At the moment it looks as though the plans may have to be revised. That's the broad picture. I need to know how things are going and what the problems are. It'll take a day or two for you to find your feet. The other MAs will help you, I'm sure. The fellow who brought you in, Tom Nugent, a light infantryman like us, is the MA to the CIGS and very able. Treat him as your mentor.'

'I'm going to have potted shrimps and lamb cutlets,' said Tom Nugent, as he wrote out the order form for lunch.

'That sounds good,' I said.

We were in the coffee room of the United Services Club, another palatial building, and designed by Nash, at the top of the Duke of York's steps in Pall Mall. It was a short walk from the War Office.

We sat down at a table in a corner. Portraits of generals covered the walls.

'I thought it easier to talk over lunch as we're always being disturbed in the CIGS's office,' he said. 'Your master has asked me to bring you up to date. There's a lot of ground to cover. What you read in the newspaper is misleading, inevitably. Not necessarily the diplomatic aspects, though I suspect much of that is inaccurate, but the military. Originally, when this crisis broke out we were directed by the Egypt Committee — that's the inner group of the cabinet looking after the crisis — that, while the ultimate purpose was to place the canal under international control, our immediate purpose was to bring about the downfall of the Egyptian government. For Egyptian government, read Nasser. The planners decided that an attack on Port Said and the quick capture of the canal, would bring down Nasser. So the first plan was for a landing at Port Said.'

The potted shrimps arrived.

'General Stockwell was then appointed commander of the expeditionary force. He preferred to land at Alexandria, attacking from the sea, and from Libya with the armoured division there, and advancing to take the canal on a broad front. He didn't like the idea of attacking down the canal on a very narrow front. Whether we took Cairo or not was still to be decided. This is the second plan that has been made with the French and is called Musketeer. The Prime Minister has approved the plan. The expeditionary headquarters making these plans is in the basement of the War Office, in totally inadequate accommodation with no daylight. I'm glad I'm not part of it. You don't know whether it's night or day down there. Everything, of course, has to be planned with the French though, as far as I can see, we take little notice of them and they spend their time in the better restaurants of London. They don't like the plan to attack Alexandria and propose that they land at Port Said. I think they have a point.'

The lamb cutlets arrived with a decanter of claret.

'Now, the politicians are getting cold feet about worldwide opinion if we land at Alexandria. We are anticipating that the expeditionary headquarters staff will have to revise the plan back to a landing at Port Said. They've also discovered that we cannot use our armoured division in Libya, as the Libyans would object. It was never a real possibility as the division has only one weak armoured brigade and is only a division in name. Besides, it has no tank transporters so it would never have got to Egypt! That, coupled with finding the shipping let alone the troops to mount all this, has provided quite a challenge, not just to us at the War Office but the Admiralty and the Air Ministry. Then there's the inter service rivalry about what's possible. The Chief of the Air Staff wants to bomb Egypt for a month before we go ashore. That is certainly not politically practical. So, you can see that any plan has to be thought through politically and that makes it all doubly difficult. Nothing is straight forward with this operation. All the plans will have to be re-written, and you know what happens when one changes plans. The other issue is no dates have been set. The original plan said we would be ready by 15th September. We couldn't put an expeditionary force together before that. This date will now slip. The aim is to be ready as soon as possible to await the starter's orders. Let's go and have coffee in the anteroom.'

We moved to a long room at the back of the club that overlooked gardens.

'May I ask a question?' I said.

'You may, but I may not be able to give you an answer.'

'Why didn't we go in immediately Nasser nationalised the canal?'

'The armed forces of the crown are organised for two roles, for all-out war with Russia or for counter-insurgency operations in the colonies. We little thought we might have a limited conventional war against a third party, like Egypt sprung on us. There were not enough forces, airfields, transport aircraft, or shipping in the Med. We were taken unawares. The nearest base with a proper port is Malta, which is six to seven days by sea from Port Said. So an airborne invasion couldn't have been supported under seven days. Besides, we had no airborne troops ready and trained. This is a mini Normandy landing, and D Day took two years to plan at the height of the Second World War, when the nation was geared for war. I think we're doing rather well to have got this far.'

'Can we do it? I mean, is it possible for us to take back the canal?'

'Militarily it's perfectly possible. It won't be difficult. Not at all. There just needs to be a good reason to justify it.'

We'd drunk our coffee.

'Now,' he said, 'let's get back to the office and discuss exactly what it is you have to do for the VCIGS.'

'Mummy is so excited that you're at the War Office and in the office of the CIGS,' said Phyllida. 'She can't believe her luck.'

We were lying in bed before dinner.

'She's telling all her friends that she now has a cousin at the centre of things and she'll learn everything about what's happening.'

'Please tell your mother that I'm not in the headquarters of the expeditionary force, which is making the plans, but in the office of the CIGS, well VCIGS precisely, which has to direct the army worldwide. Besides, like your father, I'm subject to the official secrets act.'

'I don't think *I* will tell her that, and I wouldn't advise *you* to say it quite like that. She's hardly talking to Daddy.'

'If that's so, she's being unreasonable.'

'When was mummy ever reasonable? She's a bucketful of emotion and love and she wants to know everything that's going on. Anyhow, she's told me to bring you to dinner as soon as possible so you can both have a deep discussion about what *is* going on.'

'I can come, would love to come, but you know I can't have the deep conversation that your mother wants.'

'That's your problem, but you'd better come to dinner soon. She's beginning to wonder what we get up to. "The time you come home," she says, "surely you can't go out dancing every night?"'

'What about tonight? Are we eating in or out?'

'I've planned that we eat in. Didn't you see my basket? I've got figs and Parma ham.'

'You don't want to eat yet do you?'

'Oh, darling.'

'So you're working for Jimmy Browne?' said General Fisher. I was staying the weekend at Sherborne Court.

'He's able and idle. And he's very clever. But he's probably too lazy to get the very top job. Interesting he asked for you to stand in for his MA. I recall he had a lucky break, at one stage, and your father gave it him. It was when your father was commanding a brigade in North Africa and Jimmy was his brigade major. Then your father got a division and he recommended Jimmy got command of a battalion. It wasn't Jimmy's turn, but he commanded well, got a DSO, and never looked back. You need breaks like that, and it looks as though you've got one now. I know it's only temporary but it'll go on your record and you'll be exposed to a lot of people. You've got a new patron. You need a patron to get on.'

'It's fascinating work. I'm having to learn very fast.'

'I don't suppose you can tell me anything and I won't ask.'

'I really don't know that much. All the major decisions are made way above me. I see the reports but I'm not in the meetings.'

'Well, it's very good of you to come and see me.'

'General, I'm seeing a lot of my cousin Phyllida Blessington, the Cathay's daughter. I wondered if I could bring her down here one weekend. She knows I'm with you and she'd love to see the house.'

'Of course, my boy, bring whom you want. It'll liven up the

place. I'll tell Bradley and we'll have a party. I'll expect you both next weekend.'

Phyllida and I dined with her parents. There was no one else there.

'So, what's happening?' said Sonia.

'The trouble with Dulles, and his Suez Canal Users Association, is he's not getting anywhere,' said Ivan. 'And now he's scuppered himself by saying that the idea has no teeth.'

'I know that,' said Sonia. 'And he's also said he's not taking sides with the colonial powers. Call the Americans allies? I can read all that. When I ask what's happening, I mean what's happening behind the scenes? Whose lipstick is on which cup? You know what I mean. I want some good gossip.'

'We can't discuss this as if it's the peace conference at Versailles. We're in a very difficult position. Eden and Selwyn Lloyd are still pursuing the case through diplomatic channels.'

'Oh, darling, I know all that. Isn't there anything to know that isn't in the newspapers? Miles?'

'I can't tell you whose lipstick is on which cup, as I don't go to the meetings. I may be in the office of the CIGS but I'm not party to the planning. There's a lot going on and everyone is very confident, but I know no more than that.'

'Not a word, Miles? Not one piece of good gossip? Everyone knows I have a husband in the Lords and a cousin in the office of the CIGS, and everyone expects me to say something, however trivial. Have you no gossip, nothing at all?'

'Miles can't tell you anything more than I can,' said Ivan. 'Not only because of the official secrets act, but because everyone will know who's told you and it will ruin his career. I really think you need to be more careful and responsible.'

'You're both as bad as each other. You're both traitors to me, traitors to your family.'

With that she got up and flounced out.

That weekend at Sherborne Court, where General Fisher gave us a wonderful weekend, Phyllida told me that her mother had gone to Paris saying she'd find out something there. She added that her mother had forbidden her to see me. We laughed. We went to my mother's house to collect the mail and check the house was safe. And we made love.

There were some letters for me, including one from George Bulman in Nairobi. I'd already heard from him when my mother had died, as well as from Rex, Ben, and Burgo. Now George wrote again.

My dear Miles,

We hear you are in the CIGS's office at the War Office. Everyone here is v. impressed. How do you do it? You mustn't be persuaded to stay there. You are needed here.

Rex hauled Burgo back from that farm to do your job. There was no real job there for him any longer, and the passion Rex felt for the blonde Swedish lady had abated, so he no longer felt bound by his promise not to move him. Burgo's cricketing organisational skills had made such an impression on Rex that there was no question that anyone but Burgo should fill the gap you had created. I'm not sure he holds Burgo in such awe now. You know Burgo better than most. As acting adjutant he has cultivated his stare to the nth degree and uses it on all and sundry, including the colonel. I've advised him against this, but he doesn't take advice easily. Not from me. Not from the colonel. Nor from the ORQMS. The subalterns are terrified of him. The view is that Burgo has developed this stare after that for which Dedan Kimathi is apparently famous. There is a major police operation in place to catch Kimathi. They're not having much luck yet. When they do I think we may be taken out of the forest.

Try and come back soon.

Yours ever, George.

P.S. Some of the Mau Mau have apparently heard that Nasser has nationalised the canal and are delighted that the white man will have to leave Kenya to fight Nasser. You must be the repre-sentative white man!

For a moment I wanted to be back in Kenya. Then Phyllida put her hand on my arm and I realised I was caught in England.

As Tom Nugent had foretold, the date planned for the expedition to be ready had slipped. D-Day was put back three times. Operation Musketeer was re-written for a landing at Port Said, and was then re-written again to satisfy the politicians and the French, and was now known as Operation Musketeer Revise. This was the fourth plan in four weeks. Even then, some of the details of the operation, such as the preparatory bombing and timings, were still open. I could tell that the CIGS himself was getting frustrated with all the changes and restrictions that Eden, in particular, was imposing. Selwyn Lloyd, the foreign secretary, was now in New York with the French foreign minister, Pineau, making the case at the United Nations.

But everything was dragging. The CIGS's office was now concerned over keeping the expeditionary force at a high pitch of readiness. Repeated postponements were creating problems. The reservists who had been recalled were increasingly worried about their families, jobs, or businesses. The morale of those who had been assembled, whether in England, Germany, or Malta, was declining. Those in Malta were living in squalid conditions, and the *Daily Mail* ran a story to say some Guardsmen had mutinied. The paras and commandos in Cyprus had gone back to chasing EOKA. All this worried us. One weekend I went down to the regimental depot for a shoot and everyone asked, 'What's going on?'

The planners then had to introduce two new factors. The ships had to be reloaded, as the batteries in the vehicles were running down. This created a further postponement. Then they introduced a winter plan. It was a date beyond which a seaborne landing could not be made. They said launching an operation in the Mediterranean in November would be too risky.

'Mummy's back from Paris and is cock-a-hoop, darling,' said Phyllida. 'She wants you to come to dinner tomorrow, just the four of
us. She's brought home some foie gras, has some interesting news,
and wants to have a really deep discussion.'

'I wonder what that could be,' I said.

'She's not telling.'

'Has she recovered her sangfroid?'

'Very much so. She's her old self.'

'I couldn't go through another dinner like the last.'

'Nothing to fear, darling. Eight o'clock tomorrow at Eaton
Terrace.'

That night I was dining with General Fisher at Brooks's. He was
staying the night as he found coming up just for the day tiring.
He also wanted to be around for longer to pick up any news that
might be in the air. By staying the night, he was able to have two
lunches and a dinner.

'You must bring Phyllida again,' he said. 'What a lovely girl.
She reminds me of Kitty. What a pity it was about Kitty and you.
Why did she marry that dreadful bore Horace? Horses, I suppose.
You'd have been well matched and you would have had Sherborne.
Now it's going to the National Trust. Could be worse, I suppose.
I think you've chosen well in Phyllida.'

'I like Phyllida very much, but nothing's agreed.'

'A girl like that will be snapped up. I'd move quickly, if I were
you.'

There was a silence as I didn't know what to say.

'Have you heard the latest news?' he said. 'Selwyn Lloyd is
back in London from New York. Called back, I understand, and
I can't understand why. The indications were that he and Pineau
were making headway with Fawzi, the Egyptian foreign minister,
and that Fawzi had virtually accepted their six principles for the
future running of the canal. Of course, we don't know if Nasser
would have accepted them, probably not. But I don't understand
why Selwyn Lloyd should have been brought home just as he was

about to bring off an agreement.'

'I think we're running out of time. You know about the winter plan, don't you?'

'The date after which an invasion cannot go ahead? Yes, I suppose that's getting close?'

'It is. What happens then?'

'Eden has always argued that the expeditionary force is only a contingency plan, one to use as a last resort. Did you read his speech at the Conservative Party Conference at Llandudno the other day? He said that international disputes must be settled by peaceful means and that we had given an example of restraint and respect for international undertakings. And he argued that the military precautions we were taking were not excessive. Better be safe than sorry, he said. Contingency plans, you know, may be plans you only use in the last resort, but they develop an impetus of their own. I think Eden is looking for a *casus belli* and I still cannot see one.'

'The expeditionary force is ready and poised to act. Everyone knows that.'

'That's what worries me. Let's go up to the Great Subscription Room and see what's going on there.'

We went upstairs, had coffee, drank port, and talked to some members. No one knew what Eden was up to.

'Darlings, I do apologise,' said Sonia, 'for my rather heated behaviour when we all last had dinner together. I was getting so frustrated. Now I've been to Paris, I realise that both of you, Ivan and Miles, must have been harbouring such secrets that you couldn't possibly have mentioned anything at all. And I realise you probably still can't. I do now understand why.'

She smiled sincerely and lovingly at us both and placed her hands on ours and squeezed them.

'I do admire you for being so close,' she said. 'I don't know how you managed it.'

'I have no idea what you're talking about, darling,' said Ivan, 'but

I'm grateful that you think we are justified to have said nothing.'

'Justified, of course. Now, without you having to give anything away, let me tell you what I found out.'

Both Ivan and I were sitting there wondering what could be coming.

'First,' she said, 'there's some jealousy about Britain dictating the strategy, and a lot of criticisms about the strategy. They think it's a second rate copy of the Normandy landings applied in a nineteenth century colonial manner. They say there's no elan, no panache. They might be right, and you'll know best. I have to admit, they didn't distinguish themselves in Indo China, so maybe you get the benefit of the doubt there.'

She stopped to eat her last piece of foie gras and take a sip from her glass of wine.

'Isn't this foie gras wonderful? Well, I went out and about a bit and, do you know, I kept running into Israelis, not just ordinary Israelis but politicians and generals? Don't look surprised. I know I'm telling you nothing you don't know, and you don't have to say anything. I just want you to know that I know, too, so we can all share the secret. I didn't find out exactly what the French and the Israelis are plotting, but they're up to something. I could tell. I wonder what? I'll tell you what I think. I think the French and the Israelis are cooking up something to do together. All this inaction is pushing the French, and I was told this on two occasions, towards going it alone if we get cold feet. Naturally, they want an ally. If not us, who better than Israel? But you know all this, don't you?'

'Sonia darling,' said Ivan, 'I know nothing of all this. On my honour.'

'Miles?' said Sonia.

'This is completely new to me. I mean, Israel being in some way involved. I know all about the differences of opinion about the landings. I've never heard or read anything about Israel.'

'I think I believe you,' said Sonia. 'You both look so genuinely surprised.'

The foie gras had been followed by escalopes de veau and crème brulee.

'What, then, is going on?' said Sonia. 'Are we alone in all this? Dumped by the United States and at loggerheads with France?'

'It's time for the nine thirty news,' said Ivan. 'Let's have coffee in the drawing room and listen.'

We moved. Ivan turned on the wireless. A concert was coming to an end. Then the familiar voice of Raymond Baxter came on the air. There were riots against the Russians at Budapest, more troubles with the unions, and Princess Margaret was returning from Nairobi after a successful tour of East Africa — something I had missed. Then he said, 'Reports are emanating from Tel Aviv that the Israeli government has announced it is mobilising its armed forces due to the heightened tensions in the Middle East. Commentators believe this action might have been taken to protect itself against Jordan.'

'There you are,' said Sonia, 'something's up.'

'Yes, but,' said Ivan, 'that doesn't look as if it's all part of a larger plan about Suez. If Israel attacks Jordan then we have to go to Jordan's aid.'

'But,' said Sonia, 'we don't *know* they've mobilised against *Jordan*. Can't you see further than that?'

14

Non scire fas est omnia*

What I had not told Sonia, or Ivan, or even Phyllida, was that there had been a just perceptible increase in tension in the office in the last few days. As I sat in the outer office of the CIGS with his staff, I could sense it coming from the CIGS himself. He was continually being summoned by the Prime Minister and, from the little I saw of him, I could tell that he was being pressurised. He was a man of great character and charm, with enormous presence. When he was in the room he dominated it. He liked barking at one but he always had. He still had his great sense of humour, and his heart was as warm as ever, but I could see he was being put under some pressure. I sensed something must be coming to a head.

When I got to the office the next day, there was still a sense of tension, though when I went in to see my general to go through his diary he was as relaxed as he always was.

'I see the Israelis are mobilising,' I said.

'Yes,' he said. 'I'm more concerned with the fighting in Budapest. Heaven knows what the Russians will do, but I can't see them withdrawing from Hungary. It's more likely they'll move in and put the riots down. Now I'd like to have a meeting this afternoon with our intelligence people.'

We discussed this and the arrangements for the following week.

*It is not permitted to know all things

Years later he told me that he had been excluded from most of the final arrangements and discussions, as the Prime Minister wanted to talk direct to the CIGS, and there was only a tiny inner circle who knew what was really going on. The CIGS had had to sideline most of the staff.

'Miles,' he said, 'you've been doing a wonderful job. That's not just me saying it, but Tom Nugent agrees. I've been fortunate to have had you with me these last few weeks. My MA is now fit for duty and will be returning on Monday week. So next week will be your last week. You will then have to return to the regimental depot. I'm sure you'll be able to take out a draft to the Second Battalion very soon now.'

'I shall be sorry to leave you, General, but I've always known this would only be temporary. It's been a great experience for me.'

'Good, Miles. You've done it splendidly.'

I took this news with some ambivalence. Much as I wanted to return to my job as adjutant of the Second Battalion, and to the beauty of Kenya, I now had the problem of Phyllida, and I did not want to leave her. I say problem as our relationship had developed in a way I had not anticipated or necessarily wished. Phyllida and I had developed a very strong attachment. I didn't want to lose her. On the other hand, where was this going? Marriage? Was I ready to get married? Did I want to get married? Did Phyllida want to get married? Sonia seemed relaxed about our relationship but Ivan had said nothing. We were second cousins. Did that matter? More important to me was the fact that I was now a comparative pauper compared to Phyllida, who was a rich young heiress; not that she would inherit Ivan's title but she would get everything else. That had been niggling me for some time. Did I want to be married to a rich woman?

We were both going to stay the weekend at Sherborne, as General Fisher was having a shoot there on the Saturday. He had specifically asked Phyllida and then, surprisingly, he had asked Sonia and Ivan. I motored down in my mother's little car, which was proving very useful, and Ivan drove Sonia and Phyllida down. I had been very pleased that the general had asked the Cathays but now I was a little disconcerted for it was going to make it more difficult to talk to Phyllida, as it might not be easy to get her away from her mother. Certainly, being able to make love would be tricky.

We all arrived in time for dinner on the Friday evening. The general was most hospitable, showing everyone to his or her room. He had put the Cathays in the far wing from me, and Phyllida was between us. Also staying were Tom Warburton and his wife, Cecily, and there were some neighbours for dinner. It wasn't until after dinner that I was able to take Phyllida to one side.

'Darling,' I said, 'Next week is to be my last week at the War Office. Then I'm to go to the regimental depot to wait until I can take a draft out to the battalion in Kenya, and General Jimmy seemed to think that would be soon.'

'I knew something was up. You've been looking puzzled all evening and you've hardly entered into the conversation. Quite unlike you. I'll come to you later.'

'Do be careful.'

'Don't be silly. I'll come to you.'

Everyone retired early but it was not until midnight that Phyllida came to me and slipped into my bed. .

'Sorry, darling. Mummy came to my room and wanted to talk. I had to tell her about you going back to Kenya. I hope you don't mind. She could see I was upset and she wanted to know why. Oh darling, yes darling, don't stop darling. Oh darling.'

After we had made love, we talked. I told her all my fears. She said she loved me very much and she had always had her eye on me. She would like to marry me, though it didn't have to be immediately. She had an allowance, but nothing much, though it was understood that when she got married she would get a settlement, enough to buy a house and more. She was not that keen I was a soldier, as she knew that being a soldier's wife was all 'pay, pack, and follow'. Sonia had told her that she should follow me out to

Kenya. Sonia had friends there with whom Phyllida could stay. Seeing me in Kenya with the battalion would help her make up her mind, though she said she thought she had made up her mind and asked me if I'd made up mine. I said I thought I had. Well that's settled then, she said, and we made love again. Then she said that Sonia said that, as happy as she was about it, we should have an understanding and shouldn't get formally engaged until we had set a date for the wedding, and that could wait until after she'd been to Kenya. Then Phyllida left me, but not before saying I needed to sort out my girl friend in Kenya before she arrived. I didn't sleep that well, and I ruminated that I seemed to have lost control of my life.

During the shoot the next day I found myself standing next to Tom Warburton.

'The colonel of the regiment,' he said, 'is very pleased with what you've done for him. He told me he's sorry to see you go. He would have liked to have kept you, but it's too soon for you to do that job permanently, and you have to go to Staff College before you can. When are you going to take the exam?'

'Next year is the first time I can sit it.'

'As long as you prepare for it, you'll pass it.'

'I doubt Africa will be an easy place to study.'

'There'll be some courses there and there're postal courses.'

'I've never taken to them.'

'Well, find someone at GHQ to tutor you.'

A covey of pheasants flew over, quite high. Tom brought two down with a left and a right. I got one.

'How long do you think I'll be with you at the depot? General Jimmy said I would be taking out a draft fairly soon.'

'He must know something I don't.'

'I sense something is going to happen quite soon.'

'What do you sense, Miles?' said Sonia.

As we had been talking, Sonia and Phyllida had come up behind us unheard.

'I sense more birds are on their way.'

'Oh? I thought you meant something was going to happen about Suez quite soon.'

'You know I'm not in the know about that.'

'So you say. I think you pretend not to be and I admire your discretion.'

'Oh Mummy, don't always jump to conclusions,' said Phyllida.

'I have to, as no one tells me anything,' said Sonia. 'Any how, I, too, know something's going to happen very soon. I just don't know exactly what.'

'Here we go again,' said Tom.

Another covey flew over us. Tom got two. I missed.

We stopped for lunch. It was a fine autumn day and we ate in the open by a gazebo next to the lake. I sat next to Cecily, Tom Warburton's wife.

'What a lovely day this is,' she said, 'and what a lovely house. We've been asked before for the shooting and I'm always stunned by the beauty of the place. What's going to happen to it?'

'It's generally known that the general is negotiating with the National Trust.'

'Has he no heir?'

'He lives in Rhodesia and doesn't want Sherborne.'

'I can see that I might prefer that, too. I was born in Rhodesia. It's a glorious country, the bread basket of Africa. My father grew tobacco. It has a wonderful future. As I think you have, Miles. I do like Phyllida. She's so lovely. I think you've made an excellent choice.'

'We may be very good friends, you know, but we're not engaged.'

'Oh? I rather understood from Sonia that you were, or almost were.'

'We'll have to see. Are you enjoying the day? Tom's shooting as accurately as ever.'

'It's one of the two things he loves. Shooting in the winter. Tennis in the summer. I come third.'

There was a respectable bag: one hundred and nine pheasants, eighty three partridge, and one hare. General Fisher was pleased, especially with Tom Warburton, who had shown great marksmanship. We were having tea at the gazebo, this time inside. There were sandwiches and cake and whisky and cherry brandy for those who wanted it. Then the general said, 'That's a fine bag, Miles, don't you think? By the way, come and have a drink with me when we get back to the house and before you change for dinner. There's something I'd like to talk to you about.'

He turned to talk to Sonia. Ivan came up to me.

'Miles,' he said, 'I hear you're to leave the War Office. Tom Warburton tells me that you'll be with him at your depot until you return to Kenya. I just want to say how happy I am about you and Phyllida. You may be concerned about being cousins but I don't think being second cousins counts, first cousins maybe. And rest assured, Phyllida will be well looked after whenever she gets married.'

'Thank you, cousin Ivan,' I said. What else could I say?

'A little whisky won't hurt either of us,' said General Fisher. He poured two large ones and added a little soda from a siphon.

'I want to bring you up to date over the house and the National Trust. We've reached heads of agreement and the final papers are being drawn up by the lawyers. It's all gone well and I'm sure it's the right thing to do, to tie it all up in my lifetime. I don't want any loose ends, or there to be any problems after I die. They've agreed you can live here during my lifetime. There's no problem about that, that's my decision and they'll recognise it. I couldn't persuade them to extend that to your being married and living here. There're all sorts of legal problems of tenure and rights, things like rights of third parties, of a wife, of children, and my lawyers say that's understandable and no one would agree to that. I'm sorry. I presume you are going to marry Phyllida? She's a lovely girl. When's it to be?'

'We're very good friends but we've decided nothing definite yet. I'll be going back to Kenya very soon and we thought she might come out there soon, so we can get to know each other better. I'm only twenty seven.'

'In my day no one in the regiment got married before he was thirty. Now you all seem to marry younger. I shouldn't worry too much about that. You mentioned before that you had plans for her to go out to Kenya, but you'll never get to know each other better until you're married. I wouldn't miss her if I were you. She's very beautiful and desirable — and an heiress too.'

There were partridge for dinner, washed down with Chateau Mouton Rothschild 1934 which, the general said, was the best vintage of the 1930s. It was glorious. I felt it was some recompense for the day that I felt had been getting out of control. Later, when Phyllida came to my room, she remarked how quiet I had been and realised how unhappy I must be, knowing we were to part, but I should cheer up as Ivan and Sonia had agreed that she should come to Kenya and they were both very happy about the arrangement. We made love but we didn't talk much. We'd done enough talking.

The following Monday was normal in the office. The tension was still there, but that didn't stop us talking about our weekends. Most had been shooting. In the afternoon, the CIGS was called to see the Prime Minister. At five thirty I left the office, had a drink with a friend from the regiment, who was in London for a few days, and then returned to Harrington Gardens, intending to have a quiet evening by myself. When I got back Mrs Pooley was standing in the hall.

'The Israelis,' she said, 'have invaded Sinai. It's on the wireless. What does that mean, Major Miles?'

'The what, Mrs Pooley?'

'It said the Israelis have invaded Sinai. Where's that?'

'Sinai is the desert to the east of the Suez canal. It's part of Egypt.'

'Well, the Israelis have invaded it. Do you think it's something to do with the Suez Canal?'

'Not necessarily but possibly.'

'About time, and a good thing, too. Oh, there's a message from Miss Phyllida. Would you ring her? What a lovely young lady Miss Phyllida is.'

Well, I thought, Sonia is going to be unstoppable, and went into Ben's flat and rang Phyllida. She answered immediately.

'Oh darling, have you heard the news?'

'I can't believe it.'

'Mummy can.'

'I don't understand it.'

'We're going to have supper in front of the TV. Robin Day will almost certainly be covering it. Mummy says you must come round and hear what's happening. Do come.'

'I'll be round.'

'Do hurry.'

When I arrived at Eaton Terrace, I found that the television set had been moved to the dining room and Sonia, Ivan and Phyllida were waiting for me.

'So,' said Sonia, 'I was right.'

'I've already told Sonia, Miles,' said Ivan, 'that I know nothing about this, and it will be as much a surprise to you as it was to me.'

'It is a complete surprise to me,' I said.

'I'm inclined to believe that,' said Sonia. 'Let's try and work out what's going on.'

Chang came in with a dish of kedgeree and put it on the sideboard. We helped ourselves.

'So,' said Sonia, 'the Israelis attack Sinai. Can the Egyptians stand up to them, can they stop them, Miles?'

'The Israelis won't have much of a problem. The Egyptians will run away under any sustained attack.'

'The Israelis must know that. What are they attacking for?'

'They must primarily be interested in ridding themselves of all the terrorist attacks they've been suffering along their frontiers from the *Fedayeen*.'

'Nothing else?'

'Strategically, they could be interested in opening up the Gulf of Aqaba, which the Egyptians closed to them a few years ago. It's an important waterway for them. Do you remember the United Nations told Egypt to open it up and Egypt refused?'

'And the canal?'

'I can't see that the Israelis are that interested in the canal, except that it's Egyptian. They hate the Egyptians and vice versa. Can you, Ivan?'

'No, I can't.'

'So you don't think the Israelis are making for the canal?'

'Why should they, and alone?'

'What if someone put them up to it? Don't you think that the French could have put them up to it? Why did they give them all those aircraft, the Mysteres? What are they for?'

'They're for defence as well as attack. Israel is geared for war. It has to be.'

'When I was in Paris, I heard all the rumours and I saw the Israeli generals. I think the French have got the Israelis to start a war. And, as the French are our allies, we're in this too in some way.'

'Oh, Sonia,' said Ivan, 'I can't believe that. The Israelis are being constantly provoked by their neighbours. They're just getting their own back. It's a local skirmish, not an all out war.'

'I think different,' said Sonia. 'I think there's a master plan somewhere, and that the Israelis have been persuaded to start a war, and that the French and we are the persuaders and sponsors.'

'I cannot believe,' said Ivan, 'that Eden would start a war or be party to what you're suggesting. For months he's been saying that he's looking for a peaceful solution.'

'What do you think, Miles?'

'I agree there's something funny going on, but I don't know what.'

We ate our kedgeree and then watched Robin Day. We were none the wiser.

'Well, it's all very exciting,' said Sonia.

'It's all rather dangerous,' said Ivan.

On Tuesday there was a noticeable increase in tension in the office. Perhaps tension is the wrong word. There was an alertness in the air that suggested great events were about to happen. We didn't discuss it. We just got on with the day's business. Eden was to make an announcement in the House of Commons. We waited for this to be reported on the ticker tape. Shortly after 4.30, Eden rose in the Commons and made his statement, which we read on the ticker tape. He said that on Sunday night Israel had responded to the Egyptian incursions and that the UK had urged restraint on Israel and had held tripartite talks in Washington. Now, Israel had penetrated deep into Egyptian territory and there were reports that Israeli paratroops had been dropped near the Suez Canal. The urgent thing to do was to stop hostilities and safeguard the canal. France and Britain had, therefore, instructed their representatives at the United Nations to seek an immediate meeting of the Security Council; and urgent communications had been sent to the Egyptian and Israeli governments that, unless they both withdrew from the canal within 12 hours, France and Britain would intervene.

'So,' said Tom Nugent, 'we've issued an ultimatum. Something's happening at last.'

After work I went to Eaton Terrace, where Phyllida reported that her mother and father were in the strangers' gallery at the House of Commons. The evening news confirmed all the above, added that Eisenhower had sent formal messages to Eden and Mollet, the French Premier, dissociating himself from their actions, and then reported there was still street fighting in Budapest. We ate, and then played backgammon, which Phyllida won, while we waited for Ivan and Sonia to return, which they did about ten thirty.

'What an exciting day,' said Sonia. 'I need a drink and I'm starving.'

'Me too,' said Ivan.

Phyllida mixed them whiskies and soda and went and made bacon and eggs for them. We had already eaten.

'I don't think Eden's in his right mind,' said Sonia. 'He spoke in such a feverish manner. I think he's ill.'

'I thought him calm, statesmanlike, and consensual,' said Ivan.

'No, darling. He wasn't himself.'

'What happened when the debate resumed later?' I asked.

'Eden added little,' said Ivan. 'Gaitskell began to question Eden's logic saying there was nothing in the UN charter that justified a nation appointing itself as a world policeman. If Britain could, he said, then anyone could. When the house divided, the government won by 270 votes to 218. But, I'm sorry to say, the house is divided and it will make Britain look disunited.'

'Were there any good bits, Mummy?' asked Phyllida.

'Selwyn Lloyd had one of his jammed machine gun moments. When challenged whether the Israelis really were near the canal, he said something like, "Israeli forces are within a very few miles of Suez. They are moving towards Suez. They have been moving towards Suez, they are moving towards Suez, and they are within a very close distance of Suez." How does he know where they are? Have the Israelis told him? It's clear to me there is a master plan and we and the French are all part of it.'

'I'm not convinced of that,' said Ivan. 'Eden struck me as being very statesmanlike.'

'You've said that before,' said Sonia. 'We'll see very soon.'

On Wednesday, by the time I went into the office, it had been announced that Israel had accepted the ceasefire but there was no word from Egypt. It had also been announced that, at the Security Council, Britain had used its veto for the first time against a US resolution condemning Israel's aggression and demanding an immediate ceasefire. France had used its veto too. Russia had voted with the United States.

It was a day of uncertainty, in which everyone was asking what's happening and what's going to happen next. The predominant mood had changed from tension and alertness to one of mild exhilaration that something was happening at last. The main news was the mounting opposition from round the world, especially from the United States, to what we were doing. The CIGS was called to a meeting with the Prime Minister. He returned looking frustrated and, as he walked through our office, I heard him muttering to Tom Nugent, 'He keeps on trying to muzzle us.'

On Thursday evening I was at Eaton Terrace again, with Phyllida, waiting for the Cathays to return from watching the debate in the Commons. We ate and then played backgammon. Phyllida won again and suggested I might prefer to play gin rummy. I declined, as I was determined to get my own back at backgammon. The Cathays returned about 10.30. Phyllida had organised a proper supper for them.

'I didn't know grown men could behave like that,' Sonia said. 'The shouting and the calculated rudeness. Women would never behave like that.'

'The uproar in the house was worse than at Munich,' said Ivan, 'and that's saying something. I have to admit that Gaitskell spoke extremely well, some said it was the most brilliant speech from the opposition benches for some years. He accused the government of abandoning, at one blow, the three principles governing British foreign policy since the war: solidarity with the Commonwealth, the Anglo-American alliance, and adherence to the United Nations Charter. He finished by adding that the opposition would oppose the government action by every constitutional means.'

'And guess what he also said?' Sonia said. 'He said that there was a strong story going round that the whole business was a matter of collusion between the French, the British, and Israel. Collusion! So that's that!'

'He only said it was a story and Selwyn Lloyd denied it. He said it was quite wrong to say that Israel was incited to this action by us and there was no prior agreement.'

'I just don't believe him.'

'What then stirred the house was an MP coming into the chamber and interrupting another to announce that the ticker tape in the Commons library was reporting that, at that moment, British bombers were bombing Egyptian territory. There was uproar.'

Friday was my last day at the War Office. It was lively and there was a genuine sense of excitement. The bombing of Egyptian territory had been the bombing of Egyptian airfields, and it was reported to have been successful and was carrying on. That made sense, for the Egyptian air force would need to be put out of action before any landing took place. The Egyptians had over one hundred Russian Ilyushin bombers, which were capable of doing a lot of damage. We also learned that Nasser had sunk blockships in the canal at Port Said, thus closing the canal to navigation.

I went in to see my general.

'At last, Miles,' he said, 'events are beginning to unfold.'

'Are we and the French going to invade Egypt?' I asked.

'There are plans to intercede between the Egyptians and the Israelis, in accordance with the ultimatum to which Egypt has not responded.'

I realised he was not going to say more than that and I was surprised when he went on.

'It's unfortunate,' he said, 'that this is happening when the Russians are having trouble in Hungary, where street fighting is still going on. I don't think, as some do, that the Hungarian rebellion will last for long as the Russians will crush it. Nor do I think it will lead to a wider conflagration, but it's a pity the eyes of the world are being diverted from it by what's happening at Suez. The danger is that the fighting at Suez could set the Middle East alight, so we are taking some precautionary action. Today the 2nd Battalion at Nairobi was given a warning order to move to Aden and, by now, Colonel Rex should have left with his advance party. The battalion needs to be positioned to move anywhere in the Middle

East where tensions might break out. I think you'll be re-joining the battalion very soon, but not in Kenya.'

As a soldier, I welcomed this news. As a man, it confused me more than I already was about what I should do about Phyllida.

15

Whither?

I now had to ready myself to fly to somewhere in the Middle East, so this would be my last day or two in London. I would have to go to Sherborne to leave some of my clothes there, and to collect some belongings. I had long cleared my mother's house, which was hanging on the market. The agent had said it was too large to sell quickly. Phyllida and I had managed to arrange to miss the nightly Cathay family news gathering, and we were to meet at Harrington Gardens and go out to a bistro round the corner, as we had known this might be the last we might see of each other for some time. Now this appeared definite. When she arrived, I poured us both a drink and we sat on the sofa together and I told her what General Jimmy had told me. She was adorable and came into my arms and said she would miss me terribly but that we were all but engaged and she would wait for me whatever happened.

'Darling,' I said, 'I may be going to a war and who knows what will happen. There's a chance I may not come back. I must absolve you of any commitment. It just isn't fair.'

'Don't be silly. I'm here and yours.'

'Well, let's go out now and talk about it over dinner.'

We went to the bistro, ate Chicken Kiev, drank Chianti, and talked about the latest news. I told her what I knew.

Then she said, 'Don't you want to make a commitment?'

'In the circumstances in which I'm leaving, I don't think it's fair on you.'

'Piffle. It's not that. You don't really love me.'

'I love you more than anything.'

'So what's happened? I've rushed you into it? It's all happened too quickly?'

'Possibly. I'm confused. I have my life as a soldier and then there's you. I want you badly but I don't see how you can fit into what I'm going into. Everyone's taking it for granted that we're getting married and I find that some way off. I can't quite see it. How? When? Where?'

'Oh my darling, you are being a muggins. Go off and fight in whatever war you must. I can wait. We are made for each other. I adore you. I love the way you make love to me. Let's go back and make love. Now.'

She took my hand and lifted it to her lips and kissed it. I was completely captured.

On Saturday evening I was with General Fisher at Sherborne, my last night there. Eden was broadcasting to the nation on radio and TV. We listened.

'All my life,' he said, 'I've been a man of peace, working for peace, negotiating for peace. I've been a League of Nations man, a United Nations man, and I'm still the same man with the same convictions, the same devotion to peace. I couldn't be otherwise, even if I wished. But I'm *utterly* convinced that the action we have taken is right.'

'Hmm,' said General Fisher, 'that's what he says. Trouble is, he's got a thing about Nasser, wants him out at any price, and I think he has colluded with the Israelis and the French to create this war. He'll have to go on but I doubt he'll come out of it smelling of roses.'

The next day, Sunday, I travelled to the regimental depot. Everyone there seemed very relaxed and there was no atmosphere of war. Adam Hare welcomed me warmly, and there was a great air of gaiety. After a relatively light supper for the depot mess — it was a Sunday evening, after all — someone said Gaitskell, the leader of the opposition, was going to speak to the nation. We all moved into the room reserved for television viewing. Gaitskell started by examining the language that was being used to justify the action — police action, fire brigade, separating the combatants — and then he said, 'make no mistake about it. This is war. The bombing, the softening up, the attacks on radio stations, telephone exchanges, railway stations, to be followed very, very soon now by the landings and fighting between ground forces. We are doing all this alone, except for France, opposed by the world, in defiance of the world. It is not a police action, there is no law behind it — we have taken the law into our own hands. I undertake to support a *new* Prime Minister in halting the invasion of Egypt, in ordering a ceasefire, and complying with the decisions and recommendations of the United Nations.'

'Well,' said Adam Hare, 'that's a stab in the back if ever there was one.'

'What a traitor.'

'Sheer treachery.'

'There's Eden standing for everything that has made England great and Gaitskell scuppers him for naked political motives.'

I was in a group that was deeply patriotic and believed in 'my country right or wrong'. This was unsurprising in a group of young officers. What of the country as a whole? The Sunday newspapers I had read on the train clearly indicated a deep split. This was exemplified by *The Observer*, a newspaper that had recently overtaken *The Sunday Times* in circulation. Its leader writer that day wrote that, 'we had not realised our government was capable of such folly and such crookedness. Britain and France have acted not as policemen but as gangsters.' This issue was convulsing the country tearing apart every party, every class, and every family in a civil rift that was rare in Britain. What of me? As a soldier,

I thought the whole thing a mess but I had to do my duty. As a citizen I was perplexed.

'Some days ago the 1st Battalion sailed for Suez with the 3rd Division,' said Tom Warburton. We were sitting in his office on the following day, Monday. 'They've had the last two drafts. Another will be ready to move this week and the orders are for it to go to the 2nd Battalion, wherever that may be. The last I heard they were heading for Aden and they'll probably all arrive there today.'

'As long as this crisis has taken to come to a head, it all seems to be falling into place very neatly, now. General Jimmy told me that the battalion was being positioned at Aden to go anywhere in the Middle East where tension might erupt. Where do you think that might be?'

'I'm not an Arabist. It could be anywhere. We'll know soon enough. You need to be ready to take a draft of about fifty men from the end of the week, and you'd better take command of them now. Edward Dering is looking after them.'

'I'll find him and take over. I presume he's part of the draft?'

'Yes.'

'How can the 2nd Battalion be spared from Kenya?'

'Haven't you heard? The British Army has been withdrawn from the emergency. Dedan Kimathi was captured at the end of last month. The 2nd Battalion is now strategic reserve East Africa and, in view of Suez, available for the Middle East too.'

'What do you make of all this, Tom?'

'Do you mean as a soldier or as an Englishman?'

'Both.'

'Come and have dinner tonight,' he said, looking at his watch. 'Cecily is longing to see you and we can discuss it then. I've got an inspection in a few minutes and must get ready,'

After tea in the mess, Adam Hare appeared in the anteroom with the evening paper and asked me to check the racing results for him.

'I think,' he said, 'I've pulled off a Yankee.'

We checked the racing results carefully together. It looked as though he had won such a bet.

'Before you celebrate,' I said, 'don't you think it would be a good idea to ring the bookie and see if he agrees?'

Adam went to the telephone while I read the racing pages. He returned looking relieved.

'He says I've won.'

'Congratulations. How much?'

'Four thousand pounds.'

'Did you say four thousand *pounds*?'

'Yes.'

'That'll come in handy. What will you do with it?'

'One thou will pay off my most pressing debts and I'll have three in hand. I think I'll buy a Bentley to take me to the races.'

'Do you often win sums like that?'

'This is the best yet. We'll have Krug tonight.'

'Sorry, I won't be able to be with you. I'm dining with the Commandant.'

Adam strode out of the room. I sat down and turned the newspaper to the front page. The headline screamed, 'Paras drop at Port Said'.

Cecily Warburton had made the Commandant's quarters very comfortable. It was a house with three reception rooms and five bedrooms, attached to the far end of the officers' mess. Much of the furniture was official property but she had clearly arranged some of their own things, including some bric-a-brac, chair covers, rugs, and lamps so that it was cosy and didn't look like an army quarter. Tom poured us whiskies and we talked regimental gossip until we went into dinner.

'You asked what I felt about the Suez affair,' Tom said, 'and I've been thinking about that. I've never known anything like it before. We seem to be at odds with the United States, and most of the world, and I can't see how it could have happened. When Nasser nationalised the canal world opinion was largely with us.

The Americans were not, and Dulles was particularly officious. They want to liquidate all empires and ours is the major empire they want to go. They don't understand we are freeing our empire slowly. You cannot do it overnight. They see our stand on Suez as blatant colonialism. We see it as trying to contain the Middle East from communism and extremism.'

'Do you think if we had acted at once we could have toppled Nasser, which seems to be the main objective?'

'All we could do immediately was drop an untrained parachute brigade with no troops to follow up. It was considered at the time and thought far too risky.'

'What do you think will happen now?'

'With the Russians and the States against us, we don't have much chance. Militarily, it should be a walk over, if the politicians keep their nerve. We need not more than 60 hours to take the whole canal. Of course, it's really all about oil.'

'Is it?' said Cecily. 'I thought it was all about national pride, and Eden has more pride than most.'

'True,' said Tom, 'but the Middle East provides over half our oil. Where will we be without that?'

We moved back to Cecily's cosy drawing room, where Tom left us, called away for urgent business.

'Why, Miles, are you so elusive about your intentions over Phyllida?' said Cecily. 'I think I know you well enough to ask. She is one of the loveliest young girls I know, if not the loveliest, and she clearly adores you. The suitors must be at her like bees round a honey pot.'

'We have an understanding. Sonia has told her not to set a date for the wedding before we announce our engagement formally. We can't do that in the current circumstances.'

'It's deeper than that, isn't it? There's something holding you back?'

I sat and I thought and I felt very uncomfortable.

'Is it Kitty?' she said. 'Kitty is dead. Kitty's gone. You've got to move on.'

'No, it's not Kitty. Of course, she's still there and always will be. But I have moved on. I had a girl friend in Kenya. It wasn't that serious but it was fun.'

'What is it then? Is it that you're a soldier and you can't see yourself married in the army?'

'Phyllida isn't that keen on being married to a soldier, and it must be difficult being married to a soldier.'

'It is but, if you love someone, it's possible.'

'I think it's because, as much as I love Phyllida, I do not want to get married.'

'Whyever not?'

'I saw my mother and father at such cross purposes. I saw my mother's exasperation and desperation. I saw my father's unkindness and blatant behaviour. I admired my father and I respected my mother but there was no great love shown. General Fisher held us all together, and then there was the war. My father may have been a great soldier, much admired by all, but I've come to the conclusion he was a bit of a shit. Why? I don't want to be like that. I'm frightened of marriage and what it does to people. As much as I love Phyllida, and long to be with her, I don't want to get married.'

'Just because that happened to your parents doesn't mean that it's going to happen to you and Phyllida. As I understand what happened to your parents is that after your mother's miscarriage she couldn't have any more children. Your father, and what a charming man he was though I only met him once, wanted sex and your mother couldn't give it him. So he looked elsewhere. It can't have been easy for either of them or for you. But I don't think that should be an excuse for denying you the pleasures of matrimony, which are very considerable. I think you'll find that you'll be much happier married to Phyllida. Tom thinks that too.'

'I'm not unhappy.'

'You have been ever since Kitty died. Everyone commented on it. I thanked God when I saw what was happening between you and Phyllida.'

At that moment Tom returned.

'News from the front,' he said. 'Colonel Rex and his advance party have left Aden and no one knows where they've gone.'

On Tuesday morning the newspapers were full of parachute landings at Port Said. There were not many details. Some of the press were elated with the news, others against it. The Times was circumspect, and also reported that Russia had bombed Budapest. There didn't seem much chance of helping the Hungarians.

That day everyone was interested in the news. Everyone wanted to know how the expeditionary force was doing. There was little detailed news but what came across was encouraging. It was clear that the Anglo-French troops were making good progress. We awaited more news. Everyone in the barracks was excited by this.

Adam, following his great coup, had remained calm, and we had spent much of the day discussing the situation. That evening we assembled in the anteroom before dinner and Edward Dering came in and said, 'Did you know? Eden's announced a ceasefire?'

We were all stunned.

'Could you,' said Adam, 'please enlighten us, Edward?'

'I thought you would all know. Eden's announced in Parliament that he's gained the objective in parting the Egyptian and Israeli forces, has announced a ceasefire at midnight tonight, and will hand over the canal to an international force being prepared by the United Nations.'

'But we haven't taken the canal yet,' said Adam. 'This action becomes rummer and rummer.'

It was a very dispirited and puzzled group that entered the dining room.

Tom Warburton walked in.

'Forgive me, gentlemen, for interrupting your dinner. I have more news from the front. I thought you would like to know that the 2nd Battalion has landed in Bahrain.'

'Where's that, Commandant?' said Adam.

'It's a small island, off Saudi Arabia, in the Persian Gulf and a vital entrepot for oil.'

   'Why there?'

   'They've gone to quell the riots.'

   'But it's all over. There's a ceasefire at midnight.'

   'Not at Bahrain. It's ablaze.'

   'So,' I said, 'Edward and I will go to Bahrain?'

   'Very probably.'

   'It all,' said Adam, 'gets more bizarre every minute.'

16

Oriental Interlude

'Thank God you're back,' said Burgo.

He was standing at the bottom of the gangway as I descended from the plane at Muhurraq, the airport at Bahrain.

'Why did you have to stay away for so long?'

It was early evening and the day was darkening. Not warm, I thought to myself, nor cold as I breathed in the dry, slightly spicy scent of the east. The draft descended from the aeroplane and I introduced Ed Dering to Burgo.

'Welcome, Dering,' said Burgo. 'Check your draft and its gear and then get them into the three tonners. They'll take you to the old palace. Be sure you've got all your men and kit. Serjeant Jones will guide you.'

Burgo walked me to a Land Rover. For a minute I thought he was going to invite me to sit in the back. He hesitated and then climbed into the back himself.

'Old Palace?' I said.

'Yes, Godibiya Palace. It's antique. As soon as the Sheik got his oil money flowing in the thirties he builds himself a glorious new palace. His old palace lies empty and crumbling, so when we drop in, it's ready for us to take over. Only the best for the Prince Regent's.'

'So, what brought us here?'

'Rioting, or so they say. They were rioting in the streets, loot-

ing and burning. If you talk to Zulu Company they'll tell you how
they went straight into action as they got out of the plane. They
said they could see the smoke from the air while they circled the
airport. A load of nonsense. There wasn't any rioting.'

'What was happening?'

'There were suspicions there might be trouble. Quite believable. Most of the Arabs are hostile because of Suez. As soon as
the would-be demonstrators realised we were here to stay they lost
their fervour and all became quiet. We had a curfew, but no longer,
and we don't patrol. The head policeman was in the regiment,
Colonel Banon. And the chief justice, Colonel Battiscombe, was
in the regiment, too. All very useful. You'll meet them.'

We were travelling across a causeway and entered a town.

'Manama,' said Burgo, 'the capital, such as it is, and where the
rioting was supposed to be. The natives aren't that friendly, but
the Sheik and his family are pleased that we're here.'

'What are you going to do now that I'm back?'

'The colonel has made me his liaison officer. I'm to look after
relations with the Navy and RAF, the local authorities, the police,
and the oil company BAPCO, that sort of thing. Important role,
reporting to the colonel, of course.'

We had travelled round the town not through it, and now we
were motoring beside a high wall and came to some gates.

'Here we are,' said Burgo, and I returned the salute of the sentry
on guard, who waved us through. 'Godibya Palace, with all the
luxury of the Orient.'

An imposing building stood before us in a large forecourt in
which were a few vehicles and some soldiers attending them. In
the distance I could see tents. The building had two floors and a
central core with two wings. Both floors had verandas all the way
round the building.

'George will be in his office. He wants to see you. I'll show you,'
said Burgo. 'Colonel Rex has gone to see the Brigadier. He'll be
back for dinner. That's something to look forward to. The dinner, that is. I'll have your bags taken up to your bit of the veranda.

We all sleep on the veranda except the colonel and George, who have rooms.'

We entered an office in the middle of the building. It was sparse and the walls were peeling. On one hung a large map of Bahrain, on another one of the Persian Gulf. George was sitting at a trestle table covered with an army blanket that held nothing but a small pile of paperbacks. He was reading one.

'Here,' said Burgo, 'is the prodigal adjutant, looking a little fatter than when he left us, don't you think?'

'Stap me, it's Miles. How lovely to see you. Thank goodness you're back. Come and sit down and tell me all about your adventures.'

Burgo made a fuss of finding a chair and unfolding it for me. Then he said, 'I'll be off now for a last stint in the adjutant's office. Join me when you've finished.'

'Yes, do that, Burgo,' said George, 'and close the door.'

Then, turning to me, he said, 'You do look as though you've put on a pound or two. Good living in London? Have you found a new girl friend?'

I brought him up to date with what had happened to me since I'd been away. We had written to each other but there are things you can't say in a letter. I did mention Phyllida, but I didn't tell him the whole story. I didn't tell him about Adam's win which, looking back, I wish I had.

'What's happening here?' I asked.

'Let me show you on the map,' he said, indicating that on the wall.

'The island is tiny, about thirty miles north and south, and ten miles wide, smaller than the Isle of Wight, bigger than the Isle of Man. It's the largest island in an archipelago and is ruled by the Sheik and his family, who've been here since the 18th century. It's a British Protectorate and the Sheik, or The Ruler as he's called, has a resident British adviser who's been running the place for him and his father, dead some time ago now, for years. There's also a British Resident who is responsible for looking after our British interests in the Persian Gulf. It's a very colonial set-up. You'll see. The ruling family is Sunni and the population, a little under 200,000, is evenly divided between Sunni and Shia. The Battalion came here because of so-called riots but, in fact, we're positioned strategically to go anywhere in the Persian Gulf where we might have to protect British interests.

'We could only muster three full companies to come here. Z Company — still under Francis Bowerman — is on the west coast at Budaiya, which is a charming government farm, the only place with fresh water springs. They're in tents. Y Company — Tony Henderson — is at Awali, the headquarters of BAPCO. They're in air conditioned buildings, not that that's much of an advantage at this time of year, but they're very comfortable. W company — Percy Smythe — is here with us in the old palace which, as you can see, is run down and the worst of our camps. And Ben is back at Muthaiga looking after our base and our families and,' he said, looking straight at me, 'the girl friends.'

'What's Burgo going to do?'

'Ah, Burgo. Do you remember that cricket match?'

'It seems years ago.'

'Six months, in fact, but it does seem years. Burgo could do no wrong. Rex didn't think twice about getting him to stand in for you. No question, no discussion. Burgo picked up the reins immediately. So much so he was running the battalion by himself. He'd take executive decisions on his own account that even I couldn't, or wouldn't, have taken. He jumped into deep water and I had to dive in and rescue him from Rex, who was rather put out, to put it mildly. It's running fairly smoothly now, but I'm glad you're back and so will Rex be.'

The door opened and in walked Rex.

'Miles, it's excellent you're back,' he said, shaking me by the hand and patting me on the shoulder. I thought he was going to embrace me. He pulled up a chair and we three sat round the table.

'You did very well with General Jimmy. He wrote you an excellent report. I'm so glad that it happened and it went so well as it reflects on the battalion and on me, well, on all of us. So we're riding high. You look well. Good time in London? Found a new girl friend?'

He winked at George.

'You'll probably want to sort yourself out a little before dinner, after your journey. We can catch up with the detail tomorrow but let me tell you what we're doing here. The position on this island has stabilised and the next hot spot looks like being Kuwait, at the top of the gulf, and we have to be prepared to go in there. That will be a seaborne landing which we'll have to practise — yes, George, the brigadier briefed me this afternoon — and next week we have to exercise with the Navy and RAF to do this. We'll need to plan this tomorrow.'

'Am I to re-occupy the adjutant's chair?'

'Immediately.'

'What is Burgo to do?'

'Ah, Burgo. You know, Miles, you need to put people into jobs for which they show ability, not square pegs into round holes. I'm not sure that Burgo was really suited to being adjutant. Looking back at the cricket match — do you remember the cricket match? — what Burgo was clearly very good at was getting on with the outside world, external relations is the word, I think. I'm making him Liaison Officer with the government administration and the oil company. There's a role for him there.'

'Just the government administration and the oil company?'

'Yes, that'll keep him occupied and it's important.'

'What about liaison with the other services?'

'What services?'

'The Navy, and the RAF, and the police.'

'Oh no, George and I will do that.'

'Will you tell him, Colonel?'

'No, I've spoken to him already about it. You confirm it. He will report to you. Now it's time to let you wash and brush up. Then a drink and dinner. You'll enjoy it here. We're having a lot of fun.'

I found Burgo in the adjutant's office, similar to George's and as run down. It was neat and there were few papers on the table. He led me up a vast staircase to the first floor, where he showed me the veranda which was to be my quarters. It was open to the elements. I had a bed, on which he'd put my kit, and a small space on either side in a line of beds, the beds all being collapsible military camp beds and very low. Some had sleeping bags, others had blankets. On my bed were some blankets.

'Where do I put my clothes?'

'You don't,' said Burgo. 'Everything has to be folded. You're lucky to have a bed. The soldiers sleep on the ground. The ablutions are round the corner where I sleep. I think they're working today. Settle in and wash and then join me in the anteroom, the large room at the top of the stairs. Whisky?'

'Yes, please.'

When I joined him in the anteroom he had a whisky and soda waiting for me. With ice.

'Ice but no sheets,' I said.

'Not always. Depends on the electricity, which isn't that reliable. You'll see.'

Percy Smythe came up to me. 'I was sorry to hear about your mother, Miles.'

'Thank you, Percy.'

We had been quite close in Korea, where he had been adjutant and I was intelligence officer.

'This place, Miles, is the bottom. I mean the palace not the island, which has its charm. You should have stayed in England a little longer. What a bugger's muddle Suez was. Surely you didn't have anything to do with that?'

'I think we military did rather well in the circumstances. It was the politicians who were in a muddle, as you put it.'

'No shop in the mess,' said Colonel Rex. 'At sometime, Miles, we'll all want to know what exactly went on. Come and eat and I'll tell you how we got here.'

We sat down at a long table at the end of the anteroom. The

room had clearly been the main reception room of the palace it was so large. We ate 'compo rations', the composite tinned food that the army ate in the field, as we had in Korea. It was cooked in the battalion cookhouse and brought to the mess none too hot.

'So, how did you get here, Colonel?'

'I was fishing in the Aberdares and getting a good catch. Suddenly a man comes wading up the stream, ruining everything. "What the hell are you doing?" I yell. "Are you Colonel Topham?" he asks. I nod. "There's an urgent message for you to report to the Chief of Staff immediately." That's the end of a dream day. We hurry back to Nairobi. I have the sense to change into uniform before I go to see the Chief of Staff. "Your battalion has been put at 48 hours notice to move. We don't know where or why. I'll tell you when we learn more." "The whole battalion?" I say. "As strong as you can make it, but you're to leave a rear party to look after your interests here. Something is blowing up somewhere. Probably something to do with Suez. *I* didn't *say* that did I?"'

'Were you expecting anything like this, Colonel?'

'We'd talked about being drawn in, hadn't we, George, but not suddenly, like this. It didn't sound like a carefully planned move. The Mau Mau was almost over and we'd been pretty well withdrawn from the forest. Kimathi had been captured. We were looking forward to a much easier time. This started a rumpus. You can imagine the re-organisation going on. We ended up with three fairly strong rifle companies and a rear party big enough to look after our interests, especially the ponies and the pigs. We also had to practise everyone in 'aid to the civil power' drills, as I could see that was what we would probably end up doing. It had to be connected with Suez, but not the main action at Suez.'

'You'll be amused,' said George, 'at the briefing. We were told that officers should take greatcoats and battledress — neither of which we had — and we should put into a small tin trunk, to follow by sea, a white mess jacket and a suit. That made us wonder where on earth we could be going and what we might be asked to do. We ignored it.'

'I go ahead with the advance party to Aden,' continues Colonel Rex, 'where no one is expecting us. Then someone says, "Ah, yes, you're to go to Bahrain." When I ask them why Bahrain, they say they don't know but they think there are riots there and I'll get orders when I get there. We get into another plane and set off. I decide to go and talk to the pilot to see if he knows anything. "Where are you going?" I say. "Kuwait," he says. "Kuwait? I was told you were going to take me to Bahrain." "Oh," he says, "do you want to go there?" So he changed course. You can imagine the international incident if we'd landed at Kuwait.'

It was not the last time Rex would tell that story.

'Colonel,' said George, 'are we really going to go on eating this food from the men's cookhouse. We eat at different times to the men, it's hard on the cookhouse and we're not in action.'

'We didn't have much choice when we first arrived, did we?' said Rex. 'We could well afford to set up our own messing, now.'

'Tomorrow,' said George, 'I'll ask our new Liaison Officer to find us a civilian contractor.'

'Yes, that's something Burgo could well do.'

'I wasn't sure when I was going to see you again, Sir.'

Mr Kettle, the orderly room quarter master serjeant, was standing at the side of my trestle table in the office. It was eight o'clock the following morning.

'I wondered, too,' I said. 'All well with you, I hope?'

'All Sir Garnet.'

'I haven't heard that recently, and I now know I really am back with the battalion.'

'I shall miss Captain Howard. He had a good sense of humour and he let me get on with things. It was a pity he didn't hit it off with the colonel. Do you know what he's going to do now?'

'He's going to be Liaison Officer with the government administration and the oil company.'

'He'll like that. He likes to be out and about. He wasn't desk driven.'

'Is there much paper work here?'

'Nothing I cannot deal with, Sir. There's no command head-quarters breathing down our necks, asking for ridiculous returns for the sake of it. It's really rather relaxing here. You know I like being in the field.'

'Who did you leave behind at Muthaiga to look after things there?'

'I brought Tudor with me and left Norman. When we came here I asked Captain Howard to promote them both to give each of them more status: Norman to Serjeant and Tudor to Corporal.'

'I'm glad to hear that. Didn't we talk about doing that some time ago? Gives you more status, too.'

'Did we, Sir?'

Oh dear, I thought to myself, Burgo has clearly been putty in Kettle's hands and given him his head.

'Well,' I said, 'if there's so little paper work, I'd like to see everything that comes in for a few days to get back in the swing of things.'

'If that's your wish, Sir.'

'For the moment, it is. Here comes Captain Howard. Thank you, Mr Kettle, that will be all.'

Kettle made a rather formal exit. A minute later Burgo entered.

'I hope you like the chair?' Burgo said.

'It's fine,' I said. 'Burgo, I've decided that, as Liaison Officer, you can have a table and chair in the office, over by that wall I think. That'll mean that we can work together.'

'*You've* decided?'

'Yes, you are to report to me. Colonel Rex has briefed me.'

'But I am to report to the colonel.'

'No, he was absolutely clear about this. You are to report to me.'

'I don't understand.'

'I think I do. Let's walk around the palace and its grounds, and you can show me everything. And we can discuss all this.'

He followed me a little reluctantly.

'What did you get up to as adjutant?' I said. 'Colonel Rex doesn't want you reporting to him. Kettle seems to have been running the orderly room independently, with little reference to you. George tells me he had to pull you out of deep water.'

He was silent. We walked around the palace buildings and were approaching company lines.

'Say something, Burgo.'

He stopped and said, 'Do you want me to show you the camp or do you want to interrogate me?'

'Both.'

'Let me finish showing you the compound then we'll go and sit in a corner of the mess, where we cannot be overheard, and I'll tell you what happened.'

After ten minutes walking round the compound talking to several people, we climbed the stairs to the anteroom and sat down in two comfortable armchairs — about the only good things in the anteroom — and he started to talk.

'As soon as you had left, Colonel Rex bugled for me and said it was important for me to come and be his adjutant. I reminded him he had promised Nancy he would leave me with her. Do you remember that? Well, he had, though I'll admit it was a convenience. He said my days as a FIO were coming to an end, and I would have to return to the battalion sooner or later, and he would explain that to Nancy. After all, the Mau Mau were no longer the threat they were. And here was a real opportunity for me to be adjutant. I got the impression the job was mine even if you did return, which seemed unlikely as everyone believed you would join the 1st Battalion and go to Suez. Lucky you, we thought. What really had happened was that he had fallen for Nancy and she was flattered. I was in the way. I didn't realise at first. Nancy was *my* friend. Admittedly, there was nothing physical between us, but we were the greatest friends. Now she began to ignore me — that's not too strong a word — as Rex captured her attentions. I was put out. I think he moved me so that I wouldn't be in the way with Nancy.'

'Understandable, maybe. I happen to know that he gained a high regard for you over the way you handled the cricket match, and that when I left there was no question in his mind that you were the right man for adjutant. So I think you were being paranoid. But why did you have to behave so independently when you became adjutant?'

'I was pissed off with Rex pinching Nancy. I decided to trip them up and played the odd trick on him, and on others. I suppose I overdid it. I was angry.'

'What happened then?'

'George rescued me. He pulled me out of the fire of Rex's wrath. Trouble was, Nancy dropped me, then she and Rex got bored with each other and she went to South Africa for a holiday, and she was still away when we left to come here.'

'And Kettle? What did you do with him?'

'I left it to him. He seemed very competent and I'm not interested in paperwork.'

'He's had a field day running the orderly room and he's made it clear to me that he regrets your departure and my return. He's going to be difficult.'

'I'm sorry, Miles.'

'You're clearly on probation, Burgo. That's why Rex has made you report to me. That's nothing new. You did this before, when I commanded Support Company in Germany. We get on well, or we used to. You've got to pull in your horns and kowtow. You've been too mischievous.'

'Yes, Miles.'

'First of all, your duties as Liaison Officer are with the government administration and the oil company. Our sister services and the police are not included. Second, George wants to talk to you. He wants you to find a contractor to run the messing for the officers. Third, you report to me. Of course, you'll see Colonel Rex and George, but I'm responsible for you. Don't let me down or, rather, yourself down. You've had your fun.'

The following week was taken up by Exercise 'D-Day', the practice seaborne landing to prepare us for going into Kuwait, if we were ordered to. We boarded a cruiser and two frigates that took us to sea. This was a new experience for most of the battalion and not everyone found they had sea legs. This was compensated for some by the food and civilized living conditions, even if they were a little crowded, that were missing on the island for all not fortunate enough to be with the oil company.

We were instructed on how to make a landing. Then we transhipped into landing craft which steamed — a word the Navy still used though it had long been propelled by oil — for a deserted island in the archipelago. There was a breeze and the sea was not flat. Many had to wade through choppy waves getting ashore, while the battleships let off a salvo or two for realism and RAF Venom fighters buzzed above us to create more reality. The exercise also tested our communications with the ships and the planes. It was a new experience for almost all of us, though Tony Henderson and a few members of the serjeants' mess claimed to have done it before, and a damn sight better, on 6th June 1944. A soldier dropped a Bren light machine gun in the heavy seas as he was getting off his landing craft, and was lucky not to be drowned as he went after it without success. When we checked the weapons after the exercise, we found it was the only loss. Once we were back on board the ship's spirits were high, enlivened by a tot of rum.

'Makes a change from playing fuckin' football every afternoon,' said a soldier.

'If you want to get your bollocks drowned in fuckin' salt water, too fuckin' true,' said another.

'Anything for a tot of fuckin' rum,' said a third.

Burgo had been left out of battle — as the saying goes — to get on with his new job, especially to find a contractor, and when we arrived back he was all smiles.

'McTavish, who runs the public works department here, has fixed me up with an Arab who he says will do us a good job.

He's asking 15 rupees a day and he'll feed us like kings.'

'What's 15 rupees a day?' said George.

'One and sixpence' *

'That's less than we spend in Kenya.'

'A bargain. I took the decision to employ him immediately, so there'll be a good dinner for your return tonight.'

'Have you tried him out?'

'McTavish says he'll be good.'

'But have you tried him?'

'There'll be curried lamb tonight followed by fresh fruit.'

'Have *you* tried him, Burgo?'

'No need and I didn't have time. How am I, alone, able to try his skills for fifteen or more people? We're lucky to find him. There aren't many like him on this island.'

When it came to dinner, the lamb was tough and the curry too hot. Luckily, the fruit was good and plentiful and it assuaged and soothed everyone.

'Not good enough, Burgo,' said George.

'We must give him time to settle down to our tastes and ways.'

'Yes, but how long?'

'I'm sure he will improve. There'll be bacon and eggs for breakfast.'

The following morning there were, indeed, bacon and eggs for breakfast. They ran out. Fortunately Rex had eaten his breakfast before George and I arrived to be faced with bread and jam.

'Really, Burgo,' said George, 'this is worse than before.'

'That's unfair,' said Burgo. 'There was a run on the bacon and eggs. Colonel Rex had two helpings. And he wasn't the only one. How can you cater for that?'

'Everyone's hungry.'

'We're having a lovely Persian dish for lunch, *Frezenjam*. It's

---

* *One and sixpence is 7.5 pence: in today's money about £3.*

a speciality, old as the hills, and always served at Persian wed-
dings.'

That morning Rex was holding a de-briefing conference on the 'D-
Day' exercise. There were a few lessons to be learned and shared.
On the whole, the battalion had performed creditably, established
close and cordial relations with the Navy and Air Force, and the
brigadier had approved.

'Well,' said Colonel Rex, 'that's it. Well done, everybody.' And
he dismissed the meeting. Turning to George and me, he said, 'I
say, Burgo's already changed things for the better. I had bacon and
eggs for breakfast, first time since we got here. There was rather
too much oil floating around the eggs but what a change. There
we are. We've put him in the right job.'

'You didn't dine in last night.'

'No, I had an excellent dinner with the Ruler's Adviser and his
wife. How did you fare here?'

'None too well,'

'Early days. I'm looking forward to lunch.'

By this time I had met some of the permanent residents in Bahrain
and began to realise how well the officers had been looked after,
and how easily they had been able to put up with the hardships
of the old palace. The serjeants, too, had been able to tap into the
naval and air force messes. The soldiers at Awali were well looked
after by the oil company, too well, some thought. Budaiya was
an oasis and the company there was able to enjoy a pleasant life.
The old palace, positioned as it was on the outskirts of Manama,
presented no such amenities. It was a wired camp and there were
no outlets for the soldiers. Colonel Rex realised this.

'Christmas is coming and we must give the men here at the old
palace a good Christmas, Miles. Any ideas?'

'We could have a pantomime, and the traditional hockey match
between the officers and the serjeants. And a football knock-out competition, but that's nothing special as they play that every day.'

'It'll be easier for the companies at Awali and Budaiya, but we have over 200 here in this crumbling palace and we must entertain them.'

'What about Christmas dinner?'

'That's it. I'll have turkeys and Christmas puddings flown in. We'll give them one hell of a Christmas dinner. Ask Peter Quartermain to join us.'

Peter, our quartermaster, could be tricky. On this occasion he was co-operation itself and thought it an excellent idea. He undertook to get turkeys and everything necessary to make a fine Christmas dinner for the men, and Colonel Rex gave him a generous allowance from regimental funds to do this.

'And,' said Colonel Rex, 'we'll have plenty of beer. Really spoil them.'

'The men will like that, though not too much, Colonel. We don't want to repeat the farce of that Christmas in Korea when the cookhouse caught fire.'

'Not in my company it didn't. That was at battalion headquarters.'

'Exactly, Colonel.'

There was little to do in the run up to Christmas, our orders being to stay put in Bahrain in case of emergencies elsewhere. None happened. Try as we could to keep the men in the old palace occupied, one night some of the looser and more adventurous went marauding. They broke out of the camp and tried to break into some of the houses nearby, looking, of course, for women who had been too easy to come by in Kenya. Luckily, the regimental police were alerted by the local police and brought the vagrants back into camp under arrest, and an international incident was only averted by the chief of police, Colonel Banon, hushing it up for the regiment's sake. The next morning, Colonel Rex got everyone on parade.

'We are here,' he said, 'as guests of the Ruler of Bahrain. He is our friend and we are here to protect his interests and ours. We are here to make good and friendly relations with his people. We are *not* here to go marauding around his island looking for bint. This has got to stop, and it's got to stop now. You fellows seem to want to put your pricks where I wouldn't put the tip of my cane.'

There was a titter through the ranks, which the Regimental Serjeant Major pounced on.

While the preparations for Christmas were going on, Burgo was still struggling with the messing arrangements for the officers' mess. The food continued to present grave problems.

'What now, Burgo?' said George.

'The contractor says he could do much better for 30 rupees a day.'

'Do you believe that?'

'Three shillings a day is really not very much.'

'That's not the point. Do you really think it would improve the scoff?'

'It might.'

'Sack him, Burgo.'

'What, now?'

'Give him 24 hours notice and pay him off.'

'What then?'

'Go and find out what the Navy and Air Force do, where they get their food, and do likewise.'

'But I'm not to liaise with the RAF or the Navy. I was explicitly told I was not to.'

'Don't be so silly. This isn't liaison. You're hooking into their supply system. Stop arguing.'

'Very good, George.'

Burgo went off smiling.

'Do you think,' I said, 'that this farce with the contractor was Burgo being mischievous again?'

'Very likely. Let's see what happens now.'

The RAF and the Navy, Burgo said later, were only too happy to help. Burgo became the contractor himself, so to speak, and the food improved dramatically. 'If only,' he said later, 'I had been allowed to liaise with them earlier, this would never have happened.'

'What's all this about Adam winning a small fortune on the horses, Miles?' said Colonel Rex. Rex, George, and I were in his office.

'Yes, he did,' I said. 'It happened just before I left the Depot to come here. How did you hear, Colonel?'

'One of the new subalterns, Edward Dering, told Francis Bowerman, and Francis mentioned it to me when I saw him this morning. So I talked to Dering and he told me all about it. He also said there were some high stake chemmy and baccarat games being played, and quite sizeable sums were being won and lost. He said you were there. Did you know about it?'

'Adam won £4,000 on a Yankee at Wolverhampton. As to the gambling at cards, I knew about it as I was asked to join in but declined. I didn't know what stakes they were playing for but, knowing Adam, I imagined quite high. I did talk to him about it, and warned him that his luck would turn against him. He wasn't listening.'

'He's a damned fool. I trusted him and I sent him. Do you think Tom Warburton knows about it?'

'I couldn't say. We didn't discuss it. We were all so caught up in the Suez Crisis we talked about little else.'

'I'll write to Tom.'

'I wouldn't do that, Rex,' said George. 'If Adam is going to ruin himself, let him. I doubt anyone can control him.'

'You backed me sending him to the Depot.'

'I did. I thought, as you did, he needed to be tested. It looks as though he is being. Besides, Tom won't want to hear of this from you.'

'I'm thinking how he is corrupting these young officers. If he goes broke that's his look out. But I don't want any young officers to be led astray. Of course we gamble in the mess, but only for shillings. High stakes always lead to unhappiness and disasters.'

'I really do think it's up to Tom and it might backfire if you wrote to him.'

'All right then. You do it.'

Christmas Day came. First I opened the present Phyllida had sent me, some wonderful books. We had been writing to each other regularly, and I'd been able to arrange for her to be sent some Chanel No 5, which was then thought to be a rather sophisticated scent. Then I changed into clothes in which to take part in the traditional hockey match between the officers and the serjeants. The officers won the game. Most of those in the old palace watched it, and cheered on the sides noisily. When a goal was scored there was a roar of approval, whichever side had scored.

Meanwhile, the cooks were busy cooking the Christmas feast on their field burners. This presented a problem that no one had really thought about. They didn't have ovens or hobs, just burners and they were finding it a challenge to cook the meal. The turkeys had to be boiled, as roasting was beyond them, so no roast potatoes. The Brussels sprouts, chipolatas, puddings, and mince pies, all flown in, presented less of a problem, but it all took time. Colonel Rex had provided the promised free beer. Somehow, the men started on the beer when the hockey match had finished and they began to queue for the dinner, though it wasn't going to be ready until 1230 at the earliest. Of course, the time slipped. The officers and serjeants had retired to the serjeants' mess, where the serjeants traditionally entertained the officers on Christmas morning. Colonel Rex, who was almost feverish in his excitement about the dinner, didn't leave the mess until well after one o'clock, as we had been warned the meal was running late. When we arrived we found chaos and an unprecedented scene.

Some of the soldiers were still standing in line waiting for their food. Many were lying around the compound surrounded by plates of half eaten and half cooked food and tins of beer, mostly empties. A few were staggering around carrying tins of beer. Some were throwing food at each other. The cooks looked exhausted from the heat and the pressure. The cook serjeant was in tears. It was a shambles.

'What's happened?' asked Rex.

'It's all rather sad,' said the orderly officer.

'Sad?' said Rex. 'It's disgraceful.'

'Well, you see, Colonel, the cooks had great difficulty cooking everything. The men started to drink the free beer and went on drinking until the food was ready, but the cooks started to serve it before much of it was cooked, they were under so much pressure, and by that time some of the men had had so much beer that they were incapable of eating. There are some men still waiting for their food who haven't drunk that much, but many are blotto. But they all seem to be having a good time and they're quite peaceful. I've talked to some and they say it's all fucking great, if you don't mind me saying that, Colonel.'

'It's a tragedy,' said Rex. 'After all I tried to do. What a tragedy.'

A soldier staggering past us carrying a plate full of turkey in one hand, a can of beer in the other, said, 'Fuckin' marvellous', hiccoughed, and followed his plate to the ground still clutching his beer.

'It would be best, Sir,' said the Regimental Serjeant Major, who was with us, 'to let them be.'

We walked away.

'Oh well,' said the colonel, 'there's still the pantomime.'

When it came time for the pantomime, there were so few soldiers standing that it was thought wise to cancel it for fear of it turning into a drunken brawl.

'It does seem,' said Colonel Rex, 'that there's a curse on regimental Christmases. First Korea, now here and wasn't I told there was an unfortunate Christmas in Germany? The sooner we get away from here and back to Kenya the better.'

After Christmas, Rex moved the rifle companies round to make a change for everyone and give them all a fresh start. This was welcomed by the company at the old palace, but not by the company that replaced it. The members of Headquarter Company, that was stationed there permanently, became stoical and dreamed of returning to Kenya. In the New Year, we were beginning to think we were forgotten when we were told we were no longer needed in the Persian Gulf and were to return to Kenya; not immediately, as it would take time to assemble the number of planes needed for a routine move. The officers had a great party, to which we asked everyone we had met on the island, for we had enjoyed wonderful hospitality. They were sad to see us go. I suppose we had made a change for them. And the serjeants had a similar party for their friends, mainly from the other services and the oil company, but there was little for the soldiers and everyone was glad to be return-ing to Kenya. Now, I thought, I can arrange for Phyllida to come out so that we could be together again. It was clear from her letters that she was missing me. I was missing her. Then I began to wonder about Becky and seeing her again. We had not corresponded but she had sent messages to me.

17

African Dream

We landed at Nairobi with a bump.

As the doors of the aeroplane opened the scent of Africa invaded the plane: that rich, warm earthiness which, once or twice in the last few months, I had wondered if I would ever smell again. A great sense of happiness and anticipation filled me as I thought of what Kenya now had in store for us. George, who had left Bahrain earlier, was waiting on the ground to greet us with Corporal Bates, looking rather shamefaced, and the colonel's staff car. Ben was also there with his Rover.

'Good flight, I hope, Colonel?' said George.

'Good as it could be,' said Colonel Rex. 'All well here?'

' "All Sir Garnet",' said George, and they both got into the staff car and drove off.

Kettle assembled the orderly room staff and reported they were all present. Then he said, 'Much as I enjoyed our excursion to the Gulf, I think we will all be happy to be back at Muthaiga Camp.' Then he took them to a waiting three ton truck to take them to camp.

'How's the Rover?' I said to Ben as we got into it.

'Marvellous. I'm really pleased with it.'

'Is everything really "All Sir Garnet"? I sense something's up.'

'That's one of the reasons why I came to collect you. "Something is up", as you say, and you should know about it before we get to camp.'

'Then I can't wait to hear about it.'

'Yesterday morning a very formal letter arrived from the Secretary of the Muthaiga Club addressed to the commanding officer. I opened it. It was vitriolic. He accused Colonel Rex of being in the club last week and behaving in an outrageous manner not expected of an officer and a gentleman and a member of the club. He intended to report him to the management of the club and advise the committee to suspend the membership of all the officers of the regiment. There was also a matter of reparations for damage caused.'

'Impossible.'

'Exactly. I showed the letter to George, who had just returned. He was amused by it all and suggested I do some sleuthing. So, I went round to see the Secretary and, after a little investigation talking to members of the staff, it transpired that it could only have been Corporal Bates impersonating Colonel Rex. I had Bates up and he denied all knowledge. Then I said we would have an identification parade at the club and he immediately confessed. He'd even been sick.'

'Nothing new there.'

'No, but he finally admitted to being drunk and rowdy, so I discussed it with George again and we decided to wait for Colonel Rex to return and deal with him. I had him up in front of me formally and remanded him for the commanding officer. You know how Colonel Rex is and how he dotes on Bates as a pet. He wouldn't have wanted us to deal with him. So, one of the first things you must deal with is the charge against Bates.'

'He had been getting very cheeky. It'll be interesting to see what Rex will do. What else has been happening? I've been away for a long time.'

'We've had the usual goings on among the wives, with the men away, but nothing too serious. Becky has been asking for news of you.'

At that moment we drove through the gates of Muthaiga Camp.

We had not been in the camp an hour when the RSM marched Corporal Bates in before Colonel Rex and I read out the charge sheet.

'What's all this about, Bates?' said Rex.

'Well, you see, Sir, with you away in the Gulf, there wasn't much to do except polish the car and, after a bit, I took to having a beer and I don't know what got into me and I can't remember a thing.'

'Are you guilty or not guilty?'

'I don't rightly know, Sir, but Major Wildbore thinks I'm guilty.'

'I'm not interested in what Major Wildbore thinks yet, I'm interested in what you think. Are you guilty or not guilty? Did you, or did you not, do the things you are accused of?'

'I can't rightly remember, Sir.'

'Don't be an ass, Bates. Of course you can remember.'

'Perhaps it's coming back to me.'

'Did you do what you are accused of?'

'Perhaps I did.'

'Then you're pleading guilty?'

'I suppose so.'

'Call the commanding officer "Sir"!' shouted the RSM.

'Sir,' said Bates.

'You're a bloody fool, Bates. This isn't the first time you've been up for drinking and bad behaviour. You, the commanding officer's driver. You've put me in a very embarrassing position. Major Wildbore, as his company commander, have you anything to say about Corporal Bates?'

'He's an excellent driver, Sir, and has been an exemplary soldier since we came to Kenya.'

'You're fortunate, Bates, in having an officer to stand up for you, but I cannot forgive you for what you have done. Will you accept my decision?'

'Yes, Sir,'

'You're reduced to the ranks. May that teach you a lesson.'

'Yes, Sir. Am I still your driver, Sir?'

'Of course you're my bloody driver. But you won't be if you ever do anything like this again. March out.'

'Private Bates,' shouted the RSM, 'about turn. Quick march. Left, right, left, right. Pick your feet up.'

Bates was propelled out of the tent and Colonel Rex rolled his eyes to heaven.

'What do we have to do, now, about the Muthaiga Club?' he said.

'We'd better write them a diplomatic letter,' Ben said, 'and I'll take it to the Secretary now and acknowledge the damage. Some of the officers who returned today may want to go round tonight.'

'Humble pie. All right. Draft me something and I'll sign and pay up. I suppose it's my fault and I've over indulged him. No, I'll write it now myself. Ask Kettle to come in and I'll dictate it with you.'

The following day the colonel went to see the chief of staff. On his return he called George and me into his tent.

'The pursuit of the Mau Mau is now the business of the police. There are still quite a lot in the forest, but with no leadership and the gangs are small and scattered. The police will continue to track them with their pseudo gangs, which have been so successful. Our new role is to be the strategic reserve for East Africa, and be able to go anywhere at the drop of a hat. The Chief of Staff confirmed that we would be the only British battalion in Kenya and that we would be here for another year. We need to train for conventional warfare and be able to carry out duties in aid of the civil power.'

'We're adept at that from our time in the gulf,' said George.

'Exactly, so we'll concentrate on the first role, conventional warfare. We'll have a battalion exercise to test everyone. Advance to contact, attack, defence, withdrawal — the lot. '

'It'll probably be a shambles but it'll wake everyone up.'

'That's my intention. Then we'll hand everything over to the companies to go through the rigmarole of section, platoon, and company training, working up to another battalion exercise. And we'd better learn to shoot again. Our shooting has been appalling. Job for you there, Miles.'

'Are you going to tell everyone this?' I said.

'Call an officers' meeting for tomorrow and I'll tell them about our new role. I'm really pleased with the way things went in Bahrain, and I shall tell them that too.'

'What about congratulating those that stayed behind? They've done well keeping everything going here.'

'Yes, of course.'

'Have you seen how they've built a building for the NAAFI?'

'No. Let's walk round the camp now, unannounced, and see everything. Miles, ask the RSM to join us.'

The four of us walked round the camp. There was an air of activity everywhere. We visited all the companies, admired the new NAAFI building, looked in at the cookhouse, looked over such transport as had already returned from the Gulf, inspected the ponies and the pigs, and ended up at the officers' mess.

'I thought the spirits everywhere were high,' said Rex.

'Everyone is chuffed to be back, Sir,' said the RSM.

'We must keep them so. After the officers' meeting tomorrow, Miles, we'll have a meeting for all officers in charge of sports. We must get the sports going again and make some priorities. RSM, you must be there, too.'

'Very good, Sir. What about the men?' said the RSM.

'What about them, RSM?'

'They haven't seen a piece of skirt for months. After pay day this Friday, Sir, there'll be quite a few swarming into Nairobi looking for it.'

'Yes, I see what you mean. What's the VD rate, Miles?'

'Lowest ever.'

'No opportunities in the Gulf, I suppose. Well, we're not going to be able to keep it that way but we must do our best. RSM do

you think you could arrange for the guard house to be kept supplied with contraceptives, which could be handed to the men as
they sign out of camp? And don't tell the doctor.'

'Very good, Sir.'

That evening, a number of us went to the Muthaiga Club. Ben had
done a thorough job in placating the Secretary and had handed over
a sum of money, to cover the damages and give a *bonne bouche* to
the staff. Colonel Rex had been generous. We were well received
and settled down to drinks before dinner. Burgo was there, as was
Edward Dering, making his first visit. Two more new National
Service officers, Jeremy Veny and Harry Unton, were there, too.
They were both going to Oxford after their service. They had
flown out from England a week or so earlier and had already been
to the club with Ben before the Bates fracas. Ben was not with
us. He said he had arranged to see Juno White, and Burgo and I
wondered what was going on there.

'It's wonderful to be here,' said Jeremy Veny. 'It's all so relaxed
after all the training we've been through.'

'I was sorry to miss Bahrain,' said Harry Unton.

'You were fortunate to miss Bahrain,' said Burgo. 'Interesting
as it may have been there for some, Kenya is a paradise with a
wonderful climate.'

'Except when the rains come,' I said.

'But the rains will be warm,' said Burgo.

'I would like to get a licence to shoot an elephant while I'm
here,' said Harry.

'Perfectly possible,' said Burgo.

'I would like to climb Mount Kilimanjaro,' said Jeremy Veny.

'Perfectly possible,' I said. 'You could take your platoon. They'd
enjoy that.'

'I'd like to go to Malindi and swim in the ocean,' said Edward
Dering.

'All possible, once you've earned your leave,' I said.

We went into dinner and continued to discuss the wonders of

Kenya and all one could do there.

At breakfast the next morning I sat next to Ben.

'I saw Becky last night, when I was with Lucy,' he said. 'She asked if you were back and I told her. She said she'd ring you. Why don't you ring her first?'

My first parade was with the Bugle Platoon and, when I got to my office tent, Kettle was waiting for me with some files. He said, 'A lady called for you, Sir. A Miss Summerson. She asked if you could call her. I've written her number down for you.' He handed me a piece of paper with the number. 'You've just got time before the commanding officer's conference. I'll bring you a cup of tea.'

I had time but I decided not to. I had been thinking what I'd do when this happened, for I knew it would, and I still had not made up my mind exactly what to do or say.

'Thank you, Mr Kettle', I said, and purposely sat down and started looking at the files and I then went to the colonel's meetings, which didn't finish until noon. Then I picked up the telephone and rang Becky.

'Hello,' I said.

'Darling,' she said, 'I heard you were back. How wonderful. Do you remember me? Such a long silence. I suppose you've been making love to dozens of girls and you've forgotten all about me?'

'Not at all, Becky, I've been thinking about you a lot.'

'Oh you liar. Are we going to meet?'

'Let's have lunch on Saturday. Can you do that?'

'Of course. Where shall we meet?'

'Let's meet at the Nairobi Club at one.'

'That's not very romantic.'

'We'll get a good lunch and I've bags to tell you.'

'Alright and you'll keep the rest of the day free won't you?'

'I'll try to, but there's a lot going on here, now we're back.'

'Oh I do want to see you, darling.'

'See you on Saturday.'

The next few days were very busy, catching up and adapting to a new routine or, rather, an old one. George went off to recce the Ngong Hills, where we were to hold the battalion exercise the following week. I was responsible for hockey and shooting and had to get both going. There were problems in the Bugle platoon. And, now we were back at Nairobi, Command Headquarters were taking an interest in us again and asking for a lot of useless information, or so it seemed to Kettle and me.

Saturday came.

I arrived at the Nairobi Club in good time and sat in the bar, sipping a gin and tonic. Becky arrived. She was looking gorgeous in a floral dress, which showed her bare arms and shoulders, a hint of décolletage, and a luscious tan.

'Darling,' she said. She held my hands and kissed me on both cheeks.

'Gin and tonic?' I said.

'Oh, yes please.'

She looked at me.

'You look older and you've lost your tan,' she said. 'Not at all what I was expecting. But it's you, at last. What a long silence. I suppose you're going to say you were so busy you didn't have time to write.'

'You didn't write, either.'

'I was too shy to say everything I wanted to in a letter. But I did miss you so.'

'I expect you were able to find a lover or two?'

'Yes, but it wasn't the same. What about you then?'

'Well, I met someone or, rather, I caught up with someone I knew.'

'I knew there was someone but let's start from where we left off. I was so sorry about your mother, darling. Start there.'

'Let's go and have lunch and I'll tell you everything that happened.'

We walked to the dining room, where I had booked a table in a corner, ordered food and wine, and talked. I told her about my mother, how Sonia and Phyllida had helped me, and how I had gone to the regimental depot. Then Suez had intervened and I had gone to the War Office.

'It was while I was in London,' I said, 'that I saw a lot of Phyllida and it happened. She's a wonderful person and we are thinking of getting married.'

'You can't marry a cousin.'

'She's a second cousin.'

'What difference does that make? I knew something had happened, damn it. Of course propinquity is all. If your mother hadn't died, and you hadn't gone home, we'd still be together. I don't know if I'd marry you, but I probably would if you asked me. You're such a wonderful lover. Alright, I've had a boy or two but, as I said, it's not the same. But you haven't seen her since October and it's now four months. Do you still feel the same about her?'

'Yes.'

'And you write to her and she writes to you?'

'We do.'

'Oh damn and blast. You never wrote to me.'

'You'll meet her. I hope she's coming out to Kenya soon.'

'I don't want to meet her. I want you. You'll come back and have coffee with me at the flat, won't you?'

'Of course. I'd love to see Juno and Mary. How are they?'

'Juno is inseparable from Ben. Mary is hoping to find someone, now you're all back.'

We finished lunch and took a taxi to her flat. Once inside she said, 'We're alone. Mary's gone to Nanyuki for the weekend and Juno's gone to watch the polo with Ben. Kiss me.'

We didn't have coffee. We went to bed.

Afterwards she said, 'You've changed your technique. It wasn't the same.'

I saw her sometimes after that, at parties, in the street, in night clubs, generally with a different man, and she would say, 'Hello, darling. How's Phyllida? Are you married yet?'

Colonel Rex decided he would be the chief umpire for the battalion exercise, and that George would command the battalion. George thought he should be chief umpire and that Rex should command the battalion, but there was no way Rex would agree to that. Ben was to command the enemy, which was to consist of a platoon put together from members of Ben's Headquarter Company and a unit provided by the RAF. In such exercises, those who were playing the enemy have the most fun and the RAF were keen to take part. They also provided some of the umpires.

George reported that the Ngong Hills were not quite like Salisbury Plain, the army training ground in England that most of us knew, but it would do. They were a row of hills to the west of Nairobi covered in scrub and completely different to the forest. We were told that they represented a small country in the Middle East where an opposition party — the Reds, of course — had taken over and we — the Blues — had been sent to take the country back.

The exercise started well, with Percy Smythe's W Company advancing to find the enemy, then Francis Bowerman's Zulu Company making a successful attack, and Tony Henderson's Y Company following up so that, by the end of the second day, all three companies had taken up a defensive position on three hills for the night. Burgo, now the company commander in charge of the Vickers machine guns and the three-inch mortars, went round the companies to inspect the positions of the battalion's heavy weapons. He recounted this to me later.

'You cannot,' he said to Francis, 'place the machine guns as you have. You've used them to protect your front. The machine guns should be placed to fire across Percy Smythe's front, on the hill to your right. The machine guns in Percy's position have been sited to fire across your front to protect you.'

'I've no intention,' said Francis, 'of *my* machine guns firing across Percy's front, or anyone else's front. They're *my* machine guns and I'll use them to cover my own front.'

'They're not *your* machine guns, Francis,' said Burgo.

'Yes they are, and don't tell me how to use them.'

'No, they're not, they're *mine*. They are battalion weapons and I'm responsible for placing them and deciding their field of fire.'

'Absolute nonsense. Go away. I'm trying to recce my routes for withdrawing and you're wasting my time.'

'Why are you thinking about withdrawing? You've only just arrived in this position.'

'We're obviously going to have to retire, probably tonight.'

'It's very bad for morale to start talking about withdrawing as soon as you've arrived on your position. You may be asked to defend this position to the last man.'

'Don't be a fool, Burgo. This is an exercise. We're going to have to withdraw and I want my company to be able to do it in the dark, if necessary, without losing a man or any weapons or equipment.'

'If you cannot use the Vickers machine guns properly then I shall have to advise George to withdraw them from your company area, and I'll find a position where they can fire across Percy's front to protect him, in the way his Vickers machine guns are firing across your front to protect you.'

'Go and advise George anything you like. They're *my* guns and they're staying here.'

Burgo walked to Battalion Headquarters, where he found me, and told me his sorry tale. George had already gone forward to visit the companies.

'Francis is a lunatic,' he said. 'He doesn't know the first thing about machine guns. And he's spending his time preparing to withdraw.'

'I know you're right, but there's nothing I can do about it,' I said. 'You'd better wait till George gets back. He'll want your fire plans for the mortars and machine guns, so be a good fellow and mark them up on the map.'

This Burgo did, and then he said, 'I must go and see how the mortars are settling in. Thank goodness George kept them as a platoon under his command.'

George returned to Battalion Headquarters to say all the companies seemed fine. Then he asked to see Burgo's fire plan.

'What's this?' he said. 'The machine guns in Francis' company position are pointing the wrong way.'

I told him what Burgo had told me.

'Oh dear,' he said. 'Do you think Burgo is playing games again?'

'Far from it. He was rather agitated. When he plays games he plays them very coolly.'

'What got into Francis? It's against all the rules of interlocking fire and weakens the battalion position. Didn't he see that? It's too late to re-direct the machine guns now it's dark. We'll have to leave it until morning. I think we'll alter the fire plan to what it really should be in case Colonel Rex comes to inspect them, which I'm sure he will.'

I re-wrote the fire plan to show that the machine guns in Francis' position were covering the front of Percy's position. As George had predicted, Colonel Rex, accompanied by some of his RAF umpires, arrived and asked to see the fire plan. They were obviously looking for any weaknesses to guide them in briefing the enemy where to attack. I took Rex through the plan — Burgo, fortunately, had not returned from the mortars so he couldn't gainsay me — and he examined it carefully.

'Very good plan, Miles. Is this all Burgo's work? He's to be con-gratulated. I thought I might find some weaknesses in the position and fire plan, gentlemen,' he said, turning to his fellow umpires. 'There's nothing to exploit here.'

We had a quiet night and the enemy did not attack until dawn, when they were easily beaten off. Then we were told that our position was exposed, as the imaginary battalion to our left had been forced to withdraw. So we had to withdraw, which we did in daylight, and the exercise came to an end.

What interested me about the exercise is that it had exposed a flaw in Francis; and Burgo had shown himself to be very profes-sional. This I would not have expected. George had noted this, too. I am sure he told Colonel Rex.

The rains came. The sky, bright and blue in the morning, darkened towards midday and, with a disciplined regularity, broke at lunch-time and poured down a deluge of hard, cool rain, not as warm as Burgo had predicted. Sometimes the rain stopped quickly; more often it continued through the afternoon and into the night. The camp, once neat and dusty, was soaked. Every road was a stream, most tents sat in a pond, and the old polo ground, which served as a parade ground and sports field, was a swamp. It poured for weeks. Then it stopped as suddenly as it had started, and we started to enjoy the run of the country and all it had to offer.

'The Colonel of the Regiment is coming to see us,' said Colonel Rex.

'That'll please Miles,' said George.

'He's a kind and interesting man,' I said, 'not at all what I had been led to expect.'

'He's making a tour, starting in the Gulf, then Aden, and then down East Africa as far as Mauritius. He'll spend two days with us and he'll be staying with the general here. I expect they'll be going round the command together. He says he'll try and be with us for Waterloo Day.'

Waterloo was one of the two battle honours that were written on the strings of the silver bugle of our cap badge, which was surmounted by the Prince Regent's crown. In 1815, the regiment had arrived back in Europe in time to fight at the battle of Water-loo. We had been fighting in America in the War of 1812–1814, where we had burnt the White House. Washington was the other battle honour. We celebrated these two victories — Waterloo and Washington — annually on the 18th June and 24th August.

General Jimmy duly arrived on Waterloo Day, when the bat-talion paraded for him, four divisions strong, each division over one hundred officers and men, with the band and bugles. We executed the general salute, the march past in quick time to the regimental march 'The Trojans', then in slow time, and, finally, the double past. We were a fit, bronzed, and well drilled battalion.

General Jimmy said he had never seen it better done. Then he walked round the camp talking to everyone. Finally, I was called in to talk to him.

'Colonel Rex and I,' he said, sitting next to Rex in his tent, 'want you to take the staff college exam in November. You're an able young regimental officer, you have shown ability as a staff officer to me, and you need to jump on the ladder now.'

'It'll be the first year that I can sit for the exam,' I said, 'and I'll need to study. Don't you think that will be difficult to do in Kenya?'

'Not at all, Miles. I've had a word with the GOC. He says he has on his staff a lieutenant colonel who was previously an instructor at the staff college and he could coach you and anyone else taking the exam.'

'That would be an enormous help.'

'How's your military history?'

'I've always been interested and have read a lot.'

'That exam shouldn't be difficult, then. What about current affairs?'

'It's rather difficult to keep up with what's going on in Kenya, let alone outside.'

'Every evening before dinner you need to sit down for half an hour with the first leader of The Times and précis it. Within three months you'll know about everything that's going on, and you'll have learnt to write succinctly. You pass the exam, Miles, and I'll ensure you get a place next year. Do you agree, Rex?'

'I think Miles will do it.'

'So do I. By the time you go to Staff College, the battalion will have returned to England and your next station will be in England. Now, Rex, the government is talking about ending National Service and having a smaller, all regular army. We're discussing how many infantry battalions we need. I want to discuss that with you. And one more thing. Over the years we have neglected the regimental chapel in the cathedral. It needs funds. Do you think you could hold an open day or something like that here to raise some money?

I've asked the First Battalion to do the same. Oh, Miles, no need to keep you. It was very good to see you again.'

Burgo was waiting for me in my tent.

'What,' he said, 'did your friend General Jimmy have to say to you?'

'He wants me to take the staff college exam in November.'

'I think I'd like to do that. I need to get out of this regimental rut I'm in.'

'Well, there's a lieutenant colonel at Command Headquarters who will coach anyone who wants to take it, so we could do it together.'

'That'll make a change. Count me in.'

The battalion had made great friends with the Littlejohns. We had met them when we arrived in Kenya and Francis Bowerman had set up a camp at their farm at the Kinankop when he took over Zulu Company. I vividly remember talking to Jasper Knox there the morning he had come out of the forest after a training patrol, elated by his new role. The Littlejohns had allowed us to continue with the camp which was now available for companies to train. They had also befriended me and I used to spend weekends there. Fred played polo and he used to mount me.

One weekend he asked a number of settlers and their wives in for a party, among whom was Michael Bishop, a settler and farmer who was also a prominent politician.

'How are you enjoying your time in Kenya now you've been withdrawn from the forest?' Michael said.

'We're having a wonderful time. You would think that the Mau Mau had never happened. The country is a paradise and it seems truly peaceful and settled.'

'Yes, it does seem to be, but there's a strong feeling among the Africans, and this means most of the tribes, that they want to be more involved in government. We're going to have to widen the franchise. This will have to become a multi-racial society.'

'Oh, Michael,' said Anna Littlejohn, 'don't talk like that. You tell me Mau Mau is defeated and now you're going to invite the Kikuyu into government?'

'Not just the Kikuyu but all the tribes. We've got to move with the times. The Gold Coast has got its independence and is now Ghana, Nigeria next.'

'But they're not ready for it,' said Fred.

'That may be, but it's their country and they want to take part in running it.'

'We've built this country. You're not saying we're going to hand it over to them?'

'Sooner than you think we're going to have to involve them. Westminster has always seen Kenya as a trust, held on behalf of the African population, the object of which has been the protection and advancement of the African races.'

'No, they haven't. What about Amery's 'dual policy' when he said the trust was shared between the settlers and natives? Every Secretary of State for the Colonies comes up with a different policy. Trouble is that Westminster never sticks to one policy and has chopped and changed.'

'That may be but it's not the twenties or thirties any longer. We live in the nineteen fifties. It's a new world.'

'What happens to us, then?'

'There will always be a role for us, but we won't be able to run the country without the Africans.'

'Well, maybe in the long run.'

'No, soon and now. There's pressure from Westminster, pressure from the Africans, pressure, too, from the Indians.'

'We've defeated the Mau Mau and now you're giving in to them.'

'Not at all. Remember, Mau Mau was a civil war among the Kikuyu. Yes the Mau Mau wanted us out. That's over. Whatever we have done, it was the loyal Kikuyu who really won this war. Now we have to advance the form of government for all or we may face unrest again.'

'Why doesn't Westminster station some more battalions here to ensure there is no unrest?'

'Westminster will never do that. Those days are over.'

'The outlook doesn't look very good for us then.'

'It's fine for us, if we realise that the world has changed and we take part in that change.'

'I'm not sure I want to take part in such a change.'

'You'll have to, if you want to stay here.'

'I cannot believe what you are saying or that you're saying it. Next, you'll be telling us that Jomo Kenyatta will be released to run the country.'

'No, never. But Westminster are going to hold talks soon to decide on a new constitution.'

This conversation puzzled me. It seemed so intangible. But it didn't really affect me or the battalion. I continued to think that, even if Africans did take a greater role in government, it wouldn't change things much for us, or for Kenya, for years. The situation in Kenya seemed ideal. The emergency over, everything seemed settled to us. We were having a wonderful time with the run of the country: fishing in the trout streams of the Aberdares, shooting on the lakes and the plains, polo with the settlers, and racing at Nairobi. Not just the officers. Everyone was enjoying the freedom of the country, exploring the game parks on safari, climbing the mountains, taking in all the pleasures that the coast could offer. Companies would spend weeks away, camping on various farms, training in ideal conditions. There were great sporting opportunities, too. The football team won the national competition and you could pursue almost any sport. The battalion was much happier than it had ever been in Germany or England. There were far fewer men coming up in front of their company commanders for petty misbehaviour. It was an outdoors life, of course.

But the conversation between Michael Bishop and the Littlejohns continued to puzzle me. I could see both their points of view but there didn't seem to be a meeting point. Anna and Fred were not right wing, dyed in the wool settlers. They were irreproachable settlers. They ran a most professional farm, looked after their African staff with great consideration and fairness, and had made great progress with both. They had prize herds and grew excellent crops. It was a model farm and the Africans on it prospered. I suppose it was paternal and, looking back on it now, the days for paternalism in Kenya were over, the demand for freedom — whatever that meant — was growing stronger, the experience of other colonies could not be ignored, and the initiative was with the Africans. At the time I did not see it, nor did the other officers. The beauty of the country, and the life it offered, dazzled us.

One evening Ed Dering confided to me that he had been enjoying himself so much that he had been thinking about becoming a regular soldier. He had written to his father to say this and that he wouldn't go to Cambridge after all.

'That's a wonderful idea, Ed,' I said. 'We'd welcome you. What did your father say?'

'He wrote back and asked if I was in love with the army or with Kenya.'

In our new role we were to have an anti-tank gun platoon, which had been put into abeyance when we came to Kenya to fight in the forests in the emergency.

'Ordnance have just rung me,' said Peter Quartermain, 'to say they have four anti-tank guns for us to collect. What's that all about?'

'News to me,' I said. 'Let's ask the colonel.'

We walked into the colonel's tent.

'Pete tells me that Ordnance have four anti-tanks guns for us,' I said.

'Excellent,' said Rex, 'Get Burgo. And George.'

George arrived. Burgo followed.

'Burgo, you are to form an anti-tank gun platoon. Miles, get the ORQMS to search all the records for men who served in the anti-tank platoon in Germany and have them transferred to Burgo's company. I'd like to see the names.'

'There'll be very few, Colonel,' I said.

'There should be some NCOs. Burgo, you'll have to take men from the other platoons in your company. I'll let you have four men from the next draft. No more. We're short everywhere. Peter, (he always called him Peter) we'll need a building for four anti-tank guns. Do you know the specifications? They're called WOMBATs.'

'What's a WOMBAT?'

'I expect,' said George. 'that it stands for War Office Mobile Battalion Anti Tank. It's the new 120mm giant rocket launcher on wheels, and each will need a jeep or Land Rover to trail it.'

'I haven't got any to spare,' said Peter.

'Then Ordnance will have to issue four more,' said Rex. 'There must be a War Office specification or correspondence on this. Miles, get onto Command Headquarters about this.'

'Who's going to command this platoon?' said Burgo.

'Poppleton, Alexander Poppleton,' said Rex. 'He was at the depot and, before that, with the 1st Battalion. He's on an anti-tank gun course at Netheravon, at the moment. He's due here in a month. And the 1st Battalion is sending us a trained serjeant. He'll probably be a rogue they want to get rid of, so keep a close eye on him. I've been planning for this, if Command Headquarters haven't. I suppose the idea of anti-tank guns in Kenya is a bit bizarre.'

'What about training?' said Burgo.

'Poppleton can do that.'

'Yes, but where. We'll need to fire them. We can't do that here at Muthaiga.'

'Send the platoon up to the Littlejohns'. Plenty of space there. They'll enjoy that. So, at last, we've got a proper battalion equipped to go anywhere. Do we know where the guns are, Peter?'

'They're in a siding at Nairobi railway station.'

'Well, we'd better collect them before anyone else does.'

Alex Poppleton arrived and Burgo and I took him to dinner at the Muthaiga Club with some others.

'What's the news from the depot?' said Burgo.

'Morale is low, I'm sorry to say. Adam has slowly been losing the money he won on the horses. No big wins, in fact few wins at all. The Bentley has been sold. The hampers from Fortnum & Mason have stopped coming. No more caviar or foie gras. The card games have dried up as no-one has any money and the expensive chemmy shoe stands idle.'

'That does sound depressing.'

'Peter Petitpierre, the other training subaltern at the depot, is quite close to Adam and I think he's got money problems, too. I kept out of the gambling these last few months as I thought the stakes had become too high for me.'

'This is terrible. We must help Adam out. What do you say, Miles?' said Burgo.

'I'm sorry to say that I've long foreseen this might happen and I warned Adam that his luck would run out.'

'Yes, but we must help him,' said Burgo. 'I'll send him a hundred pounds.'

'He needs more than a hundred. More like a thousand,' said Alex.

'Then we must all send him something,' said Burgo.

'He'll have to appeal to his family, as he has before,' I said. 'It does sound as if he's dug a hole that he might find it difficult to climb out of. What do you think Alex?'

'He's counting on his luck turning. It depends, I suppose, on the bookmakers and how much credit they're prepared to give him.'

'What's he doing for his amusements? He needs amusements.'

'He's playing a lot of cricket and scoring runs.'

'That won't pay the bookmakers.'

Alex assembled his platoon and took them to the Littlejohns' to train. When it came to firing the guns, he set the Kinankop alight and it took two days to put the fire out. The Littlejohns were remarkably understanding. The Battalion named the platoon

Poppleton's pop guns.

'I've told the colonel of the regiment that we'll hold the fete in the week before Christmas,' said Colonel Rex. 'Now I want ideas of what we can do and how to attract the crowds.'

Rex had assembled the company commanders and each, in turn, undertook to run a money-making sideshow or event. Finally it came to Burgo's turn.

'The difficulty with all the support weapons,' he said, 'is we cannot fire them in the camp. We can demonstrate coming in to action, that's interesting to watch, but we cannot actually fire.'

'I can see that with the mortars and machine guns,' said Rex, 'but is there no way of simulating fire from the new anti-tank guns?'

'How, Colonel?'

'Supposing you let off a thunder flash to demonstrate the gun firing?'

'How would you do that?'

'Well, put a thunder flash in the barrel.'

'Mightn't that not damage the barrel?'

'Hardly. I can see a scene where we have a mock tank advancing — the Quartermaster can make one — and the anti-tank gun comes into action, fires, and the tank is knocked out. I think that could be a star attraction and would pull the crowds.'

'It's possible,' said Burgo. 'We'll work something out.'

The day for the fete came. There were sports, endless side shows, demonstrations, ice cream and soft drinks bars. Africans and settlers flocked in from Nairobi for all the fun of the fair. It had been well advertised. The star event was 'The Tank Battle', presented by Alex Poppleton, with Burgo in the background.

The tank rolled slowly on to the field, propelled by four men inside it, and looking predatory and realistic. The Quartermaster's men had done a great job. The anti-tank gun team dashed on to the flank unseen by the tank, came into action, and fired. An enormous flash and explosion came out of the barrel followed by smoke. The tank's turret flew off, the tank crew scrambled out with their hands up, and the tank burst into flames. A team rushed forward to fight the flames and put them out. Everyone clapped and cheered. It was a huge success.

At the end of the fete, which ran for two days, the regimental paymaster announced we had made over twenty thousand shillings, that was over one thousand pounds. Colonel Rex was very pleased.

As well as studying for the staff college every week, I had been writing to Phyllida; in fact, we had been writing to each other most weeks since I had left England. Her letters were full of what was happening in London, plays and films she had seen, what her parents had been doing, dances she had been to, and how she missed me. Mine had told her of our life in Kenya, what an amazing country it was, and how I was longing for her to come out soon for a holiday. The charity she was working for had agreed that she could take four weeks holiday to do this, but only after she had been with them a year. Phyllida liked the job, the charity, and the people she worked with, and felt bound to wait. The year was now up. We arranged that she should come out soon after Christmas and she would stay with some people her mother knew, who had a farm near Nakuru, to the north of Nairobi. How I was looking forward to this.

After the effort put into the fete, Rex encouraged everyone to take advantage of Christmas and take leave to explore Kenya, for it would be our last Christmas there. He was also conscious of avoiding another Christmas farce. Some went to the coast at Malindi, some to climb Mount Kilimajaro, some to stay with settlers, and some to go on safari in the game reserves. Some, of course, had to stay in camp, and Colonel Rex stayed with them.

The Littlejohns invited me to stay and they also invited Burgo. After Alex Poppleton's guns had set the Kinankop alight for two days, Burgo had gone to extraordinary lengths in putting it out and then ordered the choicest food for them from the best grocer in Nairobi. We wondered if Colonel Rex would let us go. He did. He said we'd seen enough regimental Christmases to know how eccentric they could be and urged us to enjoy ourselves more conventionally. So we went. It was very relaxed and they invited some neighbouring settlers in for Christmas dinner. I sat next to a Coldstreamer who had been in the Great War and he told me what Christmas had been like in the trenches. When I told him about our disastrous regimental Christmases in Korea and Bahrain, he felt we'd had a far more exciting and dangerous time.

The highlight of our stay was a duck shoot on Lake Naivasha. One morning we rose at four. There were four of us: Fred Littlejohn, Burgo, myself, and a settler. Just before dawn we waded into the lake, apprehensive of the hippos, who were grunting and snoring, though they probably weren't as near us as they sounded. By first light I was in a hide in the middle of the lake with water up to my knees. The duck started to flight. The sun rose and the hills around us slowly changed colour. Above us flamingoes flew. The hippos continued to grunt. We could only have been in Africa. It was idyllic and the shooting perfect. About nine we came out of the water with a bag of thirty two duck. Fred identified them as Cape Widgeon, Hottentot Teal, Gargany, European Shoveller, and African Pochard.

'Juno has agreed to marry me', said Ben. He had just come into my tent.

'Oh, Ben, how wonderful.' I said. 'Congratulations. She's a lovely girl. You couldn't do better.'

'Thank you. I want you to be my best man.'

'I'd be delighted. When is it to be?'

'Well, with the battalion returning to England soon, the colonel has asked me to be in charge of the rear party, so I'll be the last to leave. He says why don't we get married here in Kenya and he'd let us have enough leave for us to motor down to the Cape and then return here to look after the rear party.'

'Sounds idyllic. Will you include Namibia? I'm told it's amazing.'

'Could do. I think I'm very lucky in Juno and I'm really very happy about it.'

'As lovely as Juno is, I think she's very lucky in you, Ben. Have you fixed a date?'

'One month from today.'

'Could Phyllida come? She'll be here.'

'The more the merrier.'

'Alex has told me,' said Burgo, who had just entered my tent, 'that he thinks the barrel of the anti-tank gun that he used at the fete is irretrievably damaged. He found putting a thunder flash in the barrel didn't really work, the bang was so pathetic. So he used some high explosive, some gun cotton, instead and, as we saw, that did work. He says that weakened the barrel and it will be too dangerous to use live ammunition in it.'

'Does Rex know you used gun cotton?'

'Yes, when we had the rehearsal Rex agreed the bang wasn't loud enough and proposed gun cotton. Alex is waiting outside.'

Burgo, Alex, and I went in to see Rex. Alex explained exactly how the damage had been caused by the gun cotton with technical detail.

'I see,' said Rex.

We were all silent.

'Well, Miles?' Rex said.

'If we hand over the gun to the regiment taking over from us they'll spot it and if we return it to Ordnance they'll want to know how it happened. We're in a jam.'

'Burgo?'

'Well, Colonel, these guns cost a fortune. Either way there'll be a court of enquiry and we'll be asked to explain.'

There was a long silence.

'Perhaps,' I said, 'we could say that that the damage was due to a defect in the ammunition when we were live firing at the Kinankop?'

'Could that be possible, Alex?' said Rex.

'It could be argued,' said Alex. 'As far as I have been able to discover, there's no one in Kenya, apart from me, who knows anything about the technical aspects of these guns. So in any court of enquiry I would have to be called as the expert.'

'Perhaps, then,' said Burgo, 'the platoon should return to the Kinankop, go through the motions of firing the gun again, with the other guns firing, and then find the barrel defective and report it.'

'Good thinking, Burgo. Alex, after that you had better go to England on the advance party to get you out of the country so you can't be asked any questions at a court of enquiry here.'

So Alex went on the advance party to England. George Bulman led it.

I was sitting in my tent, working on some tiresome papers to do with drafts and reinforcements, when Mr Kettle came hurrying in.

'Priority message, Sir,'

'Put it there,' I said, pointing to the side of the table.

'Priority message, Sir,' said Kettle with emphasis.

'Yes, Mr Kettle,' I said, 'can't you see that I'm busy?'

'Then I think I'd better take it into the colonel.'

'Oh, what is it? Give it to me, then.'

He handed me the message. It was from Command Headquarters. It read:

> *Two strong rifle companies to be placed at 48 hours notice for active service Aden Peninsula.*

'Yes, thank you, Mr Kettle. I'd better discuss this with the colonel.'

I took it immediately to Rex.

'Excellent,' he said. 'At last, some real soldiering again. Two companies, eh? I'd better ring the chief of staff. I'm not sending two companies anywhere for someone else to command. I'll take Tony Henderson and Percy Smythe's companies. Francis can stay behind and command, as I don't want to upset Ben's wedding arrangements by leaving him in charge. I've promised him a month off. I'll take a small tactical HQ. And we'll need the Mortars and the Machine Guns. Not Poppleton's pop guns, I think. You'll come of course.'

18

Arabian Skirmish

'Do you think it's always as hot as this, Sir?' said Kettle.

'In Aden, probably, even in winter. It's a furnace, isn't it? Where's the colonel?'

'The colonel is still at the Kremlin.'

'The Kremlin?'

'That, I am told, is what they call the headquarters here. All obscurity and *dictats.*'

This was our second morning in Aden, where we had been put into a tented camp with few amenities. It was very hot, a very wet heat that made you sweat all the time. I had just returned from visiting the companies which were practising their drills in aid of the civil power, in case they were called upon to suppress riots. There was plenty of tension in the air. Aden itself was a colony on the key route from Europe to the East through the Suez Canal, and was the second busiest commercial port in the world after New York. The Aden Protectorate, in the hinterland, was a collection of feudal sheikdoms under the protection of Britain. To the north of the Protectorate was the Yemen, a hostile Muslim state that had become increasingly aggressive since the Suez War. Cairo radio, we learned, had been spreading the anti-colonial and anti-Western message continuously. Aden itself was being de-stabilized by Marxist propaganda and the Protectorate was being infiltrated by the Yemenis, who had Russian advisers and support.

'The colonel's back,' said Kettle.

Bates had driven his Land Rover up to the Battalion Headquarters' tent and Colonel Rex stepped out and walked in.

'The headquarters here is a shambles,' he said to me. 'No one seems to be able to make a decision. They weren't expecting me or you. The chief of staff told me they had asked for two companies and didn't realise I might come too. I told him I might have let one company go, but two companies needed my leadership. And I told him they were fortunate to have such a well-trained and experienced outfit, not some raw troops from England. He muttered about how he didn't know how he was going to fit us all in and would have to talk to the air vice-marshal. The RAF run this command. I'm to go back at five o'clock. He did brief me on the situation. All very interesting.

'Apparently, about 80 miles north of here is a place called Dhala, just short of the Yemen border. A few months ago the Sheik there was still living in the middle ages and cutting hands off as a punishment for theft. He also dealt in Qat, the narcotic substance, that he was importing from the Yemen. It's banned in Aden, so it was an embarrassment. The Governor reprimanded him but the Sheik continued in his medieval ways. Well, one day he cut off one hand too many, so the Governor sacked him and put his cousin in his place. The old Sheik decamped to the Yemen, where he has gathered some of his old followers and got the support of the Yemenis. Last week a group of them crossed the border, captured the local political officer, an Englishman called Aeneas Manners, and locked him and his team up in his fort, on a great mountain called Jebel Jihaf. Someone has got to go and release Manners and send the Yemenis back across the border. That's why they sent for our two companies, but they can't decide who's to command the task force. I'm to go back at five o'clock. Call an O Group for six o'clock, Miles. Now, what's been going on here?'

'I went to see the companies and we've averted what could have been a major embarrassment.'

'Embarrassment? How?'

'All the platoons have had banners made, in case of a riot. You know the one that says in Arabic "Disperse or we fire." '

'Yes, quite straight forward.'

'Well, no. Edward Dering decided to check on what his banner actually said in Arabic, found an Arab speaking British officer of the Levies here who took one look at the banner, laughed, and advised Ed not to use it. It read "Fire or we disperse".'

'Great Scott,' said Rex. 'Were they all like that?'

'They're all being checked.'

'If it wasn't so potentially dangerous it would be hilarious,' said Rex. 'Well done Ed.' Then he burst into laughter.

The O Group met at six and waited for the colonel's return. The group consisted of the two company commanders, Percy Smythe, of W Company, and Tony Henderson, of Y Company, the mortar and machine gun officers, me and Burgo. When I had told Burgo he was to stay at Muthaiga he immediately asked to see the colonel, which I could not deny him. He said that soldiering was his life, that here was an opportunity for action, and pleaded for the chance to go. Rex relented and appointed him general factotum, which covered anything that no one else wanted to do, including being temporary Quartermaster.

Six thirty came, then a quarter to seven. Shortly before seven, Colonel Rex returned with a smile.

'What a shambles,' he said. 'Well, I won. I am to command the task force to lead the operation.'

First of all, Rex briefed everyone on the situation, as he had done for me in the morning. Then he continued.

'We'll be re-inforcing the troops already at Dhala. There are two troops of armoured cars of the XXV Hussars, a company of our old friends The Borderers, and one of the local Aden Protectorate Levies — native troops with British officers — a section of a light battery, and a detachment of a Field Ambulance. We shall also have strong cover from the RAF, and two Air Liaison Officers. So, we have the equivalent of a strong battalion group and excellent air support. The first thing we have to do is get to Dhala. We leave in

convoy at midnight tomorrow. We'll get to the Khureiba Pass at
the foot of the mountains about five. Then you, Percy, will be in
charge of picquetting the road, such as it is. It winds up through
the mountains, and you can be sure that some dissident tribesmen
will be on the look-out for us. Picquetting is straight forward but
hard work. I was on the North West Frontier of India before the
war, where we had to do it all the time.

'Now, you may think that the enemy is the dissident tribesmen
and, when we get to Dhala, the Yemeni. You're going to find
more enemies. First, the heat, though that will get drier as we
climb higher, thank God, but no cooler. There'll be the dust of
these medieval roads, and road is a euphemism. We've been used
to fighting in the forests. Now we'll be fighting in the mountains
and their parched valleys. When you've climbed a peak, you'll
always find there's another peak. Water will be scarce, so water
discipline will be vital. Re-supply of everything will be difficult.
And remember, there's the heat, always the heat. You've got to
ensure your soldiers all understand this.'

He covered some administrative points, answered questions, and
then said, 'Time for a drink. What's everyone drinking, Percy?'

'Shandy, Colonel.'

'Shandy?'

'Yes, lemonade shandy. Beer by itself is too strong. In this heat
it will send you to sleep.'

The convoy left the following day at midnight. As predicted, we
reached the Khureiba Pass, at the foot of the mountains at 5 A.M.,
where the platoons of W company took it in turns to picquet the
mountains on either side of the road. The platoon commanders
had wrapped a length of white cloth round their chests so that
any aircraft in support could recognise them. They felt rather
conspicuous to the dissident tribesmen. As they picquetted the
mountain sides, the convoy moved in bounds, with the armoured
cars leading and bringing up the rear. Suddenly we were fired on
from about 1,000 yards, and the driver of the Scammell Recovery

vehicle was hit in the arm. Immediately, our Air Liaison Officer called in two Venom fighters, which rocketed the rebels' position. Then a helicopter arrived and evacuated the wounded driver. We were impressed, and relieved, by such support. We moved on in bounds slowly, as the last few miles wound up a tortuous and seemingly endless climb. At last, at 5,150 feet, we reached Dhala. It had taken sixteen hours.

Two tented camps were laid out on the rocky plateau above the town. Both were fortified by a six foot high sangar — a wall made of stones — topped by sand bags. At each corner were gun emplacements, sited with machine guns and mortars. The Borderers were in one camp, the Levies in the other. We joined the Borderers. Overlooking the camp at a distance was the immense Jebel Jihaf, from the craggy slopes of which the dissidents would fire at us at night. We found the tents had been dug down into the ground by a foot or two. Lying in my tent at night, I would wake to the sound of bullets ripping through the top of the tent. Then the machine gunners and mortar men would run to their weapons and return fire at the distant flashes. One night a mortar bomb scored a direct hit, for the fire stopped instantly and the dissidents didn't fire at us again for two nights.

The fort where Aeneas Manners was imprisoned with his men, at As Sarir, was on a peak of the Jebel Jihaf, which boasted several peaks, many of which would have to be captured for they all provided cover for the dissidents. After a reconnaissance of the area Rex called an O Group of the commanders of the various units involved.

'The Jebel is a hard nut to crack,' Rex said, 'but crack it we will. We'll start by W Company, you Percy, making a diversionary attack, with one troop of armoured cars, by advancing up the old Turkish Road as if we are going to assault from the south. Once you've engaged the attention of the rebels, then the Levies will make the main attack from the east. I want the Levies to make the main assault and release Manners at As Sarir for political reasons. The company of the Borderers will support the Levies. Y Company, you Tony, will protect the airstrip, act as porters for the forward companies, and be the reserve. The second troop of armoured cars will give supporting fire from the base of the mountain, and cut off the rebels' line of retreat from the north. You will have the support of the Venom fighters, which will be on call in a taxi rank out of sight and sound. That's the plan of attack. The rebels will make themselves a nuisance, but I do not believe they will stand and fight.'

He then went into the details and the timing and many administrative points.

Looking back now, it all seemed to go to plan. At the time it didn't look as if it was, and there were many troubling moments and events. Colonel Rex and I watched the attack from the edge of the airstrip with Tim, our Air Liaison Officer. Most of the action was out of sight. Fortunately, the main wireless network linking us with the company commanders worked well; not so the smaller wirelesses, that proved useless in the mountains.

Percy Smythe led the diversionary attack up the Old Turkish Road. Moving out of camp before dawn he picked up a camel train carrying his equipment and mortars, and advanced up the road, or rather the track. Shortly after dawn, we heard firing from Percy's direction.

'Good,' said Colonel Rex, 'Percy's got some attention. It's the most direct route to As Sarir. Let's hope he draws the dissidents away.'

Throughout the morning the firing continued. It was mainly rifle fire, and Percy reported from time to time that he was continuing to advance. Once or twice we heard the heavy machine guns of the scout cars, and mortar fire, which must have been Percy's as the dissidents were only armed with rifles. We had little idea of what was actually happening.

'We'll keep on letting Percy distract them,' said Rex. 'Tell him we can hear he's doing a good job, just what he was asked to do.'

I talked to Percy on the wireless, but he wasn't very forthcoming.

Meanwhile, the main attack had started at 0800. First, Shackleton bombers from Aden were to drop bombs on the two villages on the Jebel that the Levies had to capture before being able to get to the fort at As Sarir and release Aeneas Manners. We watched three Shackletons arrive and start to drop their bombs.

'What's that bomber doing?' said Rex.

One of the bombers had deviated from the path of the two others and was veering towards us. Suddenly, it released some bombs on the lower slopes of the Jebel, far from the villages and not far from us. There were terrific explosions. Then, the Shackleton rejoined the other two planes. We could feel the shock of the bombs and were all stunned.

'He's way off target, Tim,' said Rex. 'And who's that sprinting towards us?'

'Harry Unton,' I said.

Harry had been positioned, with his platoon, on the lower slopes of the Jebel to protect the airfield, where we were. I could see that he had put out huge cloth fluorescent recognition panels to indicate his position to the air. The Shackleton must have misread them. Harry arrived very puffed.

'Do you think,' he said, 'that the Shackletons,' he paused for breath, 'could be asked,' another pause, 'not to bomb,' another pause, 'my platoon?'

Tim had already seen it all, though rather late, and had directed the Shackleton onto its proper target.

'Sorry, old chap,' he said.

Blasts of machine gun and mortar fire were now coming from the Old Turkish Road.

'Sounds as if Percy's having fun,' Rex said. 'I hope he's not overdoing it. I don't want him to have any casualties. Ah, look, there go the Levies.'

The Levies had started to climb the mountain in front of us, and made good progress as we watched them through our field glasses.

'It'll be a piece of cake,' said Rex, 'Look how fast they're scaling the Jebel.'

He'd hardly spoken when the sound of rifle firing on the mountain broke the air and the Levies, who had looked like swarming ants, stopped in their tracks, and the rattle of machine guns started.

'They're calling for air support,' said Tim. 'I'll bring down two Venoms from the taxi rank.'

Sure enough, within a minute two Venoms appeared from nowhere. Tim talked them in to the mountain above the Levies, and they rocketed the area. Explosion after explosion rolled off the mountain. Then, as suddenly as it had started, it stopped and the Venoms disappeared. The Levies started to move up the mountain again. Then we lost sight of them as they climbed over the brow of a hill.

'Tea, Sir?' said Kettle.

Task Force HQ was a three-ton truck, which had been stripped of its awning and was completely open. Colonel Rex was sitting on it, just behind the top of the cab, so he had an elevated view of the mountain. Tim, the Air Liaison Officer, was standing by the side of the truck, with his Land Rover next to him with its wireless communications to the planes. I was also standing by the side of the truck with a wireless set, and was responsible for controlling the signals network on the ground. I could hear all the transmissions and everything that was going on. Kettle was sitting at the back of the truck with his typewriter and various stores, including his tea brewing equipment. Kettle liked to be at the heart of the action, and he had become the colonel's personal assistant as much as ORQMS. Much as I found Kettle difficult at times, he was very useful, especially in looking after Rex as a sort of major-domo.

'Tea, Sir?'

We all had mugs of tea, which were surprisingly invigorating in the heat.

Now the fog of war descended. Occasional sounds of firing came from the area of the Old Turkish Road, and bouts of heavy fighting came from the Levies on the mountains. From time to time, Tim answered calls for air support and Venoms would sweep in with their rockets. By the time the explosions had rolled off the mountain, the Venoms had disappeared. From time to time the gunners, who hadn't been much employed to date and had their mountain howitzers ready for action on the side of the airstrip not far from us, would answer calls for fire support and fire salvoes onto the mountain, but we couldn't see what was actually happening on the mountain. Colonel Rex resisted calling for constant reports. 'They've got their orders,' he said, 'they know what to do. They do seem to be making rather slow progress. But we must let them get on with the job. They'll call us when they need us.'

The morning turned to afternoon. It was becoming a long drawn out day.

There was silence from the area of the Old Turkish Road. Percy had reported that the dissidents who had been firing at them had withdrawn and he was continuing to advance up the Old Turkish Road.

'Sounds to me,' said Rex, 'that Percy's done as much as he can, especially if the dissidents there have withdrawn. I suppose by now they've realised the main attack is coming from the Levies. Let me talk to Percy.' They talked on the wireless and Rex ordered Percy to withdraw, return to camp, and form the reserve.

At last, the Levies reported they had captured the village of Dar al Karn, and asked for the Borderers to take it over quickly so that they could attack Shimar, the next village and their next objective. The Borderers had been waiting half way up the mountain. We watched them scurry over the top and out of sight. We also watched Tony's company, with their green berets, follow them up, carrying ammo and supplies and disappear out of sight too.

'At last,' said Rex. 'I feel more comfortable about it now. I hope they haven't had too many casualties.'

Shooting broke out again, from the Old Turkish Road, but not as heavy as in the morning. It went on sporadically for an hour or two and then died out.

'I wonder,' said Rex, 'what's happening there. Oh well, we'll know soon enough. I wish we could see what's holding the Levies up.'

The Levies called for an air strike on Shima. Two Venoms dived out of the sky and disappeared behind the mountain. Explosions followed. The Venoms reappeared and flew back up into the sky. After an hour the Levies reported they had captured Shima, and then I heard them on the wireless talking to the Borderers, asking them to take over Shima so that they could go on to As Sarir. They were also talking to Tony, asking him to come up with the ammo and supplies. There was a sense of urgency about these conversations. We looked at our watches. There was only about an hour left before nightfall.

Colonel Rex finally decided to talk to the Levies commander.

'Congratulations,' he said. 'You've done a great job. Do you think you can get to As Sarir before dark?'

'Advancing now.'

As dusk fell, the Levies commander reported they had freed Aeneas Manners. He had been a prisoner of the Yemeni for eighteen days. That evening, Rex sent a long message to the Kremlin at Aden. Kettle typed it and took great pleasure in marking the message 'Operation Immediate'.

That evening, back at the camp, Percy joined Rex and me and told us all about his day.

'Had we had a brass band,' he said, 'we could not have caused greater interest, which was, of course, exactly what we wanted. Hardly had we passed Dhala town, when we were fired upon by some enthusiasts. They made remarkably good rifle practice at long range — over 1,000 yards — and the bullets struck the ground all around us. There was plenty of cover and we had no casualties, except one man had his rifle butt shattered by a bullet. Then the armoured cars started blasting away with their Browning machine guns and I sent one of the platoons up on to the ridge. The mortars got into action, and the rest of us got up onto the ridge and pushed on, advancing north west. The rebels clearly thought that we were being unsportsmanlike, not walking up the road, and withdrew.

We continued advancing until you recalled us at about 1400 hours. Then the snipers came back and had a go at us again.'

'That,' said Rex, 'explains all the firing we heard. Well done, Percy. You carried out your orders perfectly.'

At about 5 A.M. the next day, Colonel Rex and I climbed up the Jebel Jihaf, taking the rest of Tony's Y Company that wasn't already on the mountain with us to strengthen the position there. We met Aeneas Manners.

'I'm delighted to meet you,' said Rex. 'How are you?'

'Relieved, in more senses than one,' Aeneas said. 'We were reasonably well looked after and I haven't any complaints about that.'

'I thought they might spirit you away when they left.'

'It crossed my mind, too. Once you began to attack yesterday, the Yemenis became increasingly apprehensive. They were terrified you would turn the Venoms onto them. As soon as they saw the Levies advancing on the fort they diplomatically withdrew, taking the dissidents with them and leaving me and my men. I suspect they didn't really know what to do with us.'

We talked on, and then Rex talked to the Levies commander.

'That was excellent work you did yesterday. I'm sorry to hear about your casualties but you did it all very well. It looked much harder than we anticipated. I think we underestimated their strength.'

'Yes, Sir, we did. I didn't think we were going to have any serious opposition.'

'Tell me what happened.'

'We got up the foot of the mountains easily. The steepness of the climb slowed us down, and then we came under some very accurate sniper fire from above, and rocks were thrown down on us. We had several casualties and we couldn't move until we had the Venom strike. That saved us and we were able to storm the ridge. We continued in this way, calling for Venom attacks and artillery fire, and finally we took the village of Dar al Karn. It was a hot fight, in more ways than one. Then we asked the Borderers to come up and take over our bridgehead, so that we could continue the attack. We also called for ammunition. As we were waiting for the Borderers, three snipers, dressed in the light khaki uniform of the Regular Yemeni Forces, broke cover and raced for the village of Shima. It was like a shooting gallery. None reached the village.'

'Ah,' said Rex, 'then the Yemenis were more involved than we thought.'

'Yes, it was they who stiffened the resistance.'

'Well, you did extremely well carrying the day. Brilliant work.'

Suddenly, Burgo popped up.

'So you're here too, Burgo. I hadn't realised you were part of it.'

'I was leading the donkeys up with ammo and supplies.'

'Can you add to what happened?'

'Well, I can tell you, Colonel, that it wasn't an easy climb. All the men were weary, the Levies had heavy casualties, and the Borderers had men suffering from the heat. We all got mixed up. A man carrying a heavy wireless set passed out with exhaustion, and he wasn't the only one. The heat in the middle of the day was terrible, with no shade anywhere. Then we were held up in a gully by a casualty who had been shot through both legs. We were in no condition to bypass him by scaling the rocks, and there were too many snipers. It took a lot of time to evacuate these casualties but it was being well done.'

'How many were there?'

'I don't know the exact figures, but the Levies were badly hit and the Borderers had a lot of heat stroke.'

'What happened then?'

'Well, after the Levies had stormed Shima, there was less than an hour of daylight left to free Fort As Sarir, the Levies were down to about twenty men, and the company commander wondered if he would make it in time. I went with him, with some of my men carrying ammo. The old donkeys hadn't managed the climb. We found Aeneas and his men happily waiting for us. Shortly after we arrived, RAF Valettas made an air drop of supplies on the far side of As Sarir, too far away for us to rescue them, as there were still snipers around. We watched the rebels carry them away.'

'Good stuff, Burgo. You did well.'

Later that day we watched another drop of supplies by an RAF Valetta from Aden. The first run made a free drop of six foot angle picquets, which broke free from their bundles and fell like a cloud of javelins. The runway party ran for their lives. The second run consisted of rolls of dannert barbed wire, which unravelled as they fell to earth, causing the runway party to retreat even further. The third drop was a large wooden packing case, which miraculously landed intact. When unpacked, we found inside a magnum of champagne for the major commanding the company of the Levies, who had been awarded an immediate DSO for leading his company so ably in the battle the previous day.

The following day we returned to our camp at Dhala and there I was told by Kettle that there was good news for me, and that he was sure the colonel would tell me as soon as he had read his messages and mail. Was I, I thought, possibly going to be given leave to return to Kenya to see my beloved Phyllida? Unlikely, I thought. So, totally bemused, I went to see Colonel Rex and said I understood he might have some good news for me. Colonel Rex beamed. 'Congratulations. You've passed the staff college exam and you've got a place there this autumn,' he said. 'I knew you would. Well done, Miles. I'm very pleased, and so is the Colonel of the Regiment, who has just sent a signal to tell me.'

'What about Burgo?'

'Burgo, I regret to say, did not. He got good marks, but he failed the current affairs paper. I expect he was too outspoken. Pity. He's doing a very good job here.'

The following day I received a letter from Phyllida in Kenya. She had just arrived and was staying with a friend of her mother's, as arranged, on a farm at the Menengai crater outside Nakuru. She thought Kenya was beautiful, hoped to meet some of my brother

officers left behind at Muthaiga Camp, and had been invited to a
dance at Government House. She was clearly upset that I wasn't
there, for her visit had been long planned, and she was very worried
about what was happening to me in Aden. She wondered when
we would see each other. I had, of course, telegraphed her as soon
as we were put on notice to go to Aden, and written to her, but
she had already left England and didn't learn about our leaving
for Aden until she arrived at Nairobi. I had written to her from
Aden and our letters had clearly crossed each other in the post. I
sat down immediately to write to her again, but I was unable to tell
her how, when, or where we might meet again, for there was more
work for us to do in the Protectorate, and I wondered whether we
would return to Kenya or be shipped home from Aden.

The letter had been around for a day or two, as it had been sent
up to me at As Sarir, but I hadn't received it there. Ed Dering
had been responsible for collecting and delivering the post for Y
Company. By a careless error he had sent the incoming post, just
received, back to Aden and returned the outgoing mail, written
by his company's men, back up the Jebel. Tony Henderson was
furious with him and ordered me to have Ed court-martialled, so
important, he said, was the handling of the men's mail. I mentioned
this to Colonel Rex.

'Ed Dering?' he said. 'He's an able subaltern. Lose the papers
in your pending tray, Miles'. He grinned. He knew full well that
I hadn't got one.

Aeneas Manners had agents throughout the area. Once he had been
round them, he reported to Colonel Rex that not all the rebels had
withdrawn from the Jebel. Some had returned across the border,
but he estimated there were still at least three hundred in the area of
the Jebel and between the Jebel and the frontier. He had discussed
this with his masters in Aden and we were now ordered to clear
the area systematically.

Colonel Rex sat down with Aeneas and planned the next operation. They decided that the company of the Borderers and that

of the Levies should concentrate on clearing the Jebel Jihaf of any remaining dissidents. The Levies were the most agile of troops and the Borderers the resident British battalion. They were used to working with each other and they were already established in the bridgehead on the Jebel. The PRLI, with its supporting troops, was to move to the Yemen frontier and ensure that the dissidents were cleared there. We had strict instructions not to cross the border, but if we were fired at from the other side we could return this fire. We were not to engage any civilians. These terms of engagement were to be strictly observed, for Britain still had diplomatic relations with the Yemen.

Colonel Rex took the company commanders, the officers commanding our supporting arms, and Tim, our Air Liaison Officer, on a reconnaissance to the frontier and they planned what to do. The operation was to be called Op Wolseley after Sir Garnet Wolseley, the great Victorian general, who had been Colonel of the Regiment and had made his reputation fighting small wars like the one we were now in.

At last light, Task Force HQ, the two companies, and the supporting arms moved out. It took us two hours to cover the nine miles along a poor track to short of the border, where the two companies dug in one thousand yards apart near Sana. With the help of a three quarter moon, the force took only six hours to dig its position in stony ground, W company on the right, Y on the left, with the Task Force HQ and armoured cars behind Y company. At first light, we found we had a fine view of Jebel Jihaf behind us, and in front of us we could see Kataba, on the far side of the border and the surrounding country clearly. Kataba was an ancient walled town and a mile to its west was a barracks. Lying between them and our position, but on our side of the border, was a long ridge.

At 7 A.M. a troop of armoured cars of the XXV Hussars moved out to reconnoitre the area. They came under fire from rifle and light machine guns on the long ridge. Colonel Rex, Aeneas Manners, the Air Liaison Officer, and I were watching through our field glasses.

'So,' said Rex, 'they have encroached across the border and occupied the long ridge. Cheeky buggers. This means a fight. We can't have them there.'

'Opportunity for an air strike, Colonel?' asked Tim.

'Wait a moment,' Aeneas said. 'Look at Kataba. Hordes of people are running out of it.'

'So they are,' said Rex. 'What an exodus. Goodness, there're hundreds of them. Why?'

'I expect Cairo Radio has told them to expect an attack.'

'That's the last thing we're going to do.'

'I know,' said Aeneas, 'but Cairo Radio exaggerates our tiniest move. They'll be saying that a British army is invading the Yemen. Besides, the inhabitants of Kataba will all know what's been happening on the Jebel Jihaf and will be frightened of reprisals. I'm really not surprised at them abandoning the town.'

'Well,' said Rex, 'I think we'll have an air strike on the ridge, let's call it Sangar Ridge, because I can spot four sangars on it. Can you see them?'

We all said we could.

'Remind the pilots on no account to fire on Kataba.'

'Wilco,' said Tim.

'And Miles, ask the mortars to put down a concentration on those sangars. Those armoured cars need our support before the Venoms come.'

Within a minute the mortars were putting bombs down on the ridge, enabling the armoured cars to withdraw. When they returned to us later in the day, we saw the bullet marks on their vehicles: nothing serious, but accurate shooting.

Tim talked the Venoms in. As they fired their cannons and let go their rockets at the ridge, some anti aircraft heavy machine guns opened up on them. One was sited on Sangar Ridge, another on the roof of the barracks.

'Terms of engagement, Colonel?' said Tim.

'Engage,' said Rex.

Tim instructed the Venoms to re-direct their fire on the HMGs.

We watched.

'Those machine gunners are rather persistent,' said Colonel Rex. 'I wouldn't want to have a Venom pounding me like that.'

'This is very interesting,' said Tim. 'We haven't done this before. I mean engage Yemeni Anti-Aircraft HMGs. This could be dangerous.'

We watched the Venoms circle and re-engage the HMGs with their canon and rockets. We heard the stuttering of the HMGs retaliating. Suddenly there was only one HMG firing.

'We've got one,' said the ALO.

'Well done,' said Rex. 'Tell them, we're impressed and thank them. But they've been distracted from their task to make the Yemeni feel damned uncomfortable on that ridge. I think we'll have another strike.'

More strikes came in. Every time, Yemeni HMGs opened fire at the Venoms from the barracks and various points along the frontier. Every time, the Venoms had to be diverted to attack the HMGs. The barracks took a number of direct hits and crumbled in places. One of the Venoms got a direct hit in its main fuel tank. Another got flack through its fuselage. It took five strikes, each by two Venoms, to subdue the anti-aircraft weapons. At dusk, Sangar Ridge was still occupied by the Yemeni.

The next morning, the armoured cars went out to recce Sangar Ridge. They reported the two left-hand sangars had been abandoned. The other two were still manned, and fired at the armoured cars. They withdrew and we mortared the sangars.

The Venoms were called for. As soon as they started to attack, they came under fire from fresh HMGs across the border. The Venoms switched target and attacked the HMGs. Slowly, the Venoms got the upper hand, but at nightfall the two sangars were still firm on Sangar Ridge.

In the morning, Colonel Rex said to me, 'It's no good relying on the RAF to dispose of those sangars. Air power is not absolute. In the end, the infantry always have to clear the ground. In the twenties the RAF said they could control the Aden Protectorate, which is why this command is still run by them. One can see that aeroplanes have a better chance of covering the ground than we could, but it's not possible for them to control it. We'll have to take those sangars out ourselves.'

The sangars really niggled him.

'I think,' he said to me, 'we'll take them out tonight. Percy can deal with the left hand one, and Tony the right.'

'Tonight?' I said.

'Yes, they can send fighting patrols. I want these sangars destroyed. The patrols will need to be co-ordinated to attack at the same time for surprise.'

Percy briefed Jeremy Veny, and Tony briefed Ed Dering to make the attacks. They were each to take a patrol of ten men, with plenty of grenades, advance on a compass bearing to their objectives, and attack simultaneously at midnight. The men detailed to go on these patrols were very keen and made every preparation for them. Colonel Rex and I visited them in the afternoon, and both patrols reported 'All Sir Garnet'.

As dusk fell, and we were enjoying the relative cool of the evening, Colonel Rex was called to the wireless to speak to the Kremlin. I couldn't hear what was said, but Rex raised his voice more than once. He returned infuriated.

'The patrols are off,' he said. 'The bloody politicos have cancelled them. We're not to take those sangars out. They say that it will be interpreted as British Forces crossing the frontier and invading Yemen. I ask you! I argued, but it's an order. We are to return to camp tomorrow, and concentrate on patrolling the villages on and round the Jebel. Those damn Yemeni have got away with it.'

We returned to the camp outside Dhala. Every day we would go out on punitive patrols to the villages round the Jebel Jihaf, and all the days seemed the same to me now. We called it Op Wolseley Two. After travelling for some time along medieval roads in the mountains, we would arrive outside a village and throw a cordon round it. The Mortars and MMGs would take up defensive positions, in case we met some opposition. Then a small group with two armoured cars would go in, with the political agent and his team, to search the village. Generally, the dissidents had had warning of our arrival and had escaped. If a dissident had been in the village it would soon become known. Then his house would be demolished. We would rarely find any arms or ammunition. The dissidents took them with them. It was exhausting work, and it always took place in the heat of the day. In one village an old Arab came up to Colonel Rex, and said in immaculate English, 'Can you refrain from driving through my village, as we feel compelled to fire at you, but you must understand that most of us don't want to kill anyone'. On the way to a village, or on our return journey to camp, we would invariably be shot at from a distance. The armoured cars would return the fire. We had no casualties but bullets flying around were unnerving.

A letter arrived for me addressed in handwriting I didn't immediately recognise. On opening, I found it was from David Vane, the adjutant at the depot.

Dear Miles,

I am sorry to write to you with this news but I know you are close to Adam and you will want to know. He has resigned his commission and will be out of the army any day now.

He was batting in a cricket match we were playing against the county gentlemen when a telegraph boy walked on the pitch and asked him if he was Captain Hare and being told he was handed him a telegram. Adam put it in his pocket. I asked him — I was batting with him — if he shouldn't open it and he said later. He then went on to make fifty five before he was caught on the boundary trying to hit a six. At tea he handed me the telegram. 'Not good news,' he said. It was from his bookies and read, 'Unsettled account must be paid Monday or will apply your commanding officer'. I asked him what he was going to do and he said that after the match he would go and see Tom, confess and hand him his resignation. He had no alternative. It wasn't only the bookies he owed. Worse. You will remember he was President of the Mess Committee and Peter Petitpierre was mess secretary. They had both being paying their mess bills on time but none of their cheques had been presented. The mess accounts looked healthy but there was no money in the bank to pay the bills. Adam went to Tom, who told him to leave the barracks the next day, hide somewhere with no forwarding address and Tom would talk to friends at the War Office and get his resignation published in the London Gazette within weeks. Tom has written to Adam's father asking him to pay Adam's debts, otherwise we shall have to claim on the mess insurance. Peter Petitpierre's family have paid up for him and he's being sent off to some colonial regiment to sweat it out.

I think Tom has written to Colonel Rex about it but don't know as no one is meant to talk about it here, though we all are. We'll miss Adam and all the fun but he was a bit of a cad. I hope you're flourishing in whatever war you are fighting now.

I talked to Colonel Rex about it. He had heard from Tom. 'What a waste,' he said, and changed the subject. I found Burgo to tell him. He'd already had a letter from Adam and Burgo had sent him £100. We discussed it for a long time, decided that Adam should never have been a soldier, and wished him well.

One morning Kettle said, 'We're going home. Read this signal, Sir.' The gist was that the rear party at Muthaiga camp would soon embark at Mombasa on a troopship destined for England, and it would pick us up at Aden in about ten days. I told Colonel Rex.

'Yes,' he said, 'it's time we went home. There's a lot left to do here, but the politicos are too frightened to be tough. This is another outpost of empire that will fall someday soon. When

Kenya gets its independence, I can see there's a chance of their being able to stand on their own feet, and becoming members of the Commonwealth. There's no chance here. The Yemenis and the Russians will walk in. It'll become another People's Marxist Republic, the worst sort of tyranny, and it will prolong the existing tyranny here. The Governor is trying to enlighten them, but how on earth do you do that under a century or two?'

A letter arrived from Phyllida. She said that my letters had finally caught up with her and she loved them. 'How exciting it must be,' she wrote, 'to be in a world where time has stood still. It must be like serving on the North West frontier of India before the war.' She didn't say which war. 'I wonder,' she continued, 'if I'll recognise you when I see you, whenever that will be. Your regiment leaves here soon by troopship. Major Bowerman, who speaks kindly of you, asked me if I would like to travel with them. I thought it would be all too public for us, and said how kind but no. I'm staying on here until we go to Rhodesia for a trip. Then I'll come home and I do hope we'll both arrive at the same time.' I replied immediately.

Aeneas Manners had become our friend, and he said we must say goodbye to the Emir of Dhala, who wanted to see us. Colonel Rex, Percy, Tony, Burgo, a few others, and I went to lunch in his palace though it didn't resemble any palace I had seen. It looked just like any of the houses in Dhala, bleak, tall, and faceless from the outside. Inside it was an oriental delight: rugs on the walls, rugs on the floor, and a gentle scented breeze wafting through the building. The Emir was most welcoming. He was a jolly fellow with mischievous eyes, and you could see he was delighted to have us with him. We sat on the rugs and a meal of kid and rice was brought in. We drank cinnamon tea and ate with our hands, none too successfully, which caused much laughter. Aeneas sat on the Emir's left and translated throughout the meal. Colonel Rex sat on the right of the Emir, and there was a lot of banter between them. They had much in common. The Emir was amused by our stories of being shot at during the night from the slopes of the Jebel.

He explained that the miscreants were followers of his cousin, the
former Emir, now in the Yemen, and they would regularly visit
their wives for a meal and conjugal rights. On the way back to
their hiding places in the Jebel, they delighted in taking pot shots
at anyone. He said we shouldn't take it too personally. He had
heard about the direct hit we'd had earlier with a mortar bomb,
and confirmed that we'd killed one dissident and wounded two
others. Colonel Rex said that we hoped everything would now be
more peaceful for him. He replied, 'Allah only knows'. He knew
he lived on a volcano. Then he presented Colonel Rex with a fine
Persian rug, thanking him for all our help.

We left Dhala at 0530 hours and arrived back at the lines in Aden
at 1630, picquetting the way down in the way we had on the way
up. We were much more sunburnt. We exchanged the dry heat
of the Protectorate for the sticky heat of Aden. We didn't have to
wait long for the troopship, and in our spare time we went into
Crater to search for duty-free bargains. Burgo bought himself a
Rolex, and I bought a Cartier tank watch for Phyllida. We hadn't
spent any money for weeks. Then the officers went to lunch with
the RAF, and we finally met the pilots face-to-face who had been
the real heroes of our battles. They drank me onto the floor, and
I cannot remember how I got back to my bed.

The troopship docked and we all embarked. Francis Bowerman
was standing at the top of the gangway and said to me, 'What a
load of ragamuffins. Didn't anyone think of seeing the men had
a haircut — and the officers?' Ragamuffins we may have looked.
We were anything but. We were an unusually confident, experienced, and hardened body of men, and we had despatched the
recent operations with great dash. I felt remarkably good about
the way the battalion had performed, and I knew that Colonel
Rex did too. We had been like the battalion had been in Korea. I
liked to think that, given able leadership, we were an exceptional
battalion.

After three days steaming up the Red Sea in unbearable heat, hotter, it seemed to me, than the Protectorate or Aden, Rex called a meeting of the officers. I thought he wanted to pull us all together, those who had been at Aden and those who had been left behind at Muthaiga. There was clearly a rift of experience between us.

Half an hour before the meeting, he told me what it was all about. I was stunned.

We assembled in a hot, airless, and crowded saloon.

'Gentlemen,' he said, 'I have some interesting news for us all. First though, I want to say how pleased I am that we are all back together again. Those of you who went to Aden did well. Both the governor and the air vice-marshal told me how well you had done. Those of you who had to stay at Muthaiga, to pack up, did well too. It was not a thankful job. The chief of staff cabled me when the troopship left Mombasa to say in what an excellent condition we had left Muthaiga camp, and the general cabled me to say how sorry he was to lose us. Good. I should have expected nothing less. I'm prouder than I can say of having commanded this battalion in action, in the forest and in the mountains.

'Now for the interesting news. In the latest Defence Review, to be published in England today, it will be announced that National Service is to finish and we are to have an all regular army. This will take time and will be phased over the next few years. I shall not argue the pros and cons about this. The debate had been going on for some time and, being in Kenya, we may not have taken much notice of it.

'How will this affect this battalion, you will ask?

'Well, the army is to be reduced to 150,000 officers and men. The corps of infantry will, therefore, have to be reduced too. There will be no two battalion regiments, except in the Brigade of Guards. Our sister regiment, the Oxfordshire and Buckinghamshire Light Infantry, is to join the Rifle Brigade and the KRRC, so that there will be three Rifle Regiments. The Somerset Light Infantry and the Duke of Cornwall's Light Infantry are to amalgamate. The KOYLI, the KSLI, and the DLI remain as they are. And we, the PRLI, are to lose our second battalion.'

Everyone had been listening with one ear, sweating in the heat and longing for a long cool drink. Slowly, people sat up, became more alert, and listened. Colonel Rex's last sentence came as a shocking surprise. People darted looks at one another with startled eyes. There was silence, complete silence.

'I don't believe it,' said Burgo.

'I'm afraid, Burgo, it's all too true. We will go to Colchester, where we will be joined by the 1st Battalion. Remember, we are one regiment. We will make it work. I don't envy any of the other regiments that have to amalgamate. There are cuts in every infantry brigade in the army. At least our regiment remains intact.'

Everyone started to ask questions. Colonel Rex put up his hand and said that he now had to go and talk to the serjeants, with the RSM and me. He would re-convene the meeting the following day, when we had all had time to think about it.

That evening at dinner I sat with Francis, Percy and Burgo.

'When I joined the army,' I said, 'it was half a million strong. Now it's going to be 150,000. Are there going to be opportunities for us all in that?'

'Oh, yes. I can see it all,' said Francis. 'A national service army is very expensive. Half the army is engaged in training. Besides, we've never had conscription in peacetime like continental armies. A smaller, regular army is going to be more professional.'

'Maybe, but it's going to be difficult for us,' said Percy. 'The first and second battalions are so different. The second battalion has always been thought to be the better. I've served with both, and it is.'

'Different, not necessarily better,' said Francis 'It depends on the commanding officer There'll be teething problems, but it'll settle down to being a regiment we will all want to be in.'

'I'm not so sure,' said Burgo. 'I've been thinking of joining the Paras.'

'Oh, no, Burgo. You can't do that,' I said.

'It's all very well for you. You're General Jimmy's blue-eyed boy, and you're off to the staff college.'

Yes, I thought, I suppose I am. And then I began to think very hard about the future, and what I really wanted to do. I wondered if I really wanted to be a soldier for the rest of my life.

19

Ten Years On

'Is that you, Captain Miles?'

'Yes, Bradley. How's the general this morning?'

'I'm sorry to tell you that he died in the night. He went very quietly.'

'I'm sorry to hear that, but we were expecting it. He couldn't have gone on for much longer.'

'No, it's what he wanted. I've called the doctor and he says he'll come this morning.'

'Good. I'll come down this evening.'

'Will Mrs Miles and the children be coming with you?'

'Not today.'

'Your rooms will be ready for you.'

'Thank you, Bradley. And, Bradley, I just want to say how wonderful you have been to the general. You and Mrs Bradley couldn't have been kinder or more helpful.'

'Thank you, Captain Miles. We did our best. He was a wonderful man and was so good to us. What train will you be on?'

'I'll take the 6.30 from Waterloo.'

'I'll meet it, and I'll ask Mrs Bradley to have dinner for you.'

'Thank you. See you later.'

I put the phone down and looked out of the window of my office at the plane trees in Berkeley Square and felt an overwhelming sadness for General George. He had been a great part of my life, almost a grandfather to me. When I'd married he had set aside a suite of rooms at Sherborne Court for us, and we made a point of going to stay with him regularly. I realised all that would now come to an end for he had given the house to the National Trust, but that was as nothing to never seeing him again. He had declined rapidly in recent weeks, and his doctor had told me he couldn't last long. Born in 1875 he was in his ninety third year. It's always a shock when it happens.

I picked up the telephone to tell my wife. There were many people I had to tell for I was one of the general's executors.

Bradley met me at the station in the Rolls-Royce the general had bought in the thirties. I wondered what would happen to that and realised it would go with his other personal effects to his cousin and heir in Rhodesia, who would probably sell it. There was some land in Scotland and Cornwall that hadn't gone to the National Trust that he would inherit, too, and probably sell, too, as he didn't intend to leave Rhodesia. As the general had no close family in England, it was left to me to arrange everything. The Bradleys would have a cottage for life on the estate rent free. The general had arranged for them to be well looked after. He had left everything 'All Sir Garnet'.

'The Lord Lieutenant,' said Bradley, as we swung into the short drive in front of the great house with its Palladian facade, 'would like you to ring him, as would the High Sheriff.'

'Yes,' I said, 'there's a lot to do.'

Mrs Bradley had prepared lamb cutlets followed by raspberries and cream, one of the general's favourite summer meals, and Bradley had brought up and decanted a bottle of Chateau La Mission Haut Brion 1953 from the cellar, a wine he knew the general and I loved. I was almost in tears as I sat alone in the dining room, longing for that wonderful, brusque and wise old man to be there.

'I expect,' the Lord Lieutenant said when I rang him after dinner and he'd said how sad and sorry he was to hear the news, 'you'll be arranging a small funeral at Sherborne, and then we can arrange a memorial service at the Cathedral later on?'

'The general made his wishes quite clear, Sir,' I said. 'He wanted no memorial service. He instructed us to hold a funeral service at Sherborne, bury him immediately with his ancestors, and then have a great party at Sherborne Court.'

'Sherborne is such a small church.'

'His wishes are quite clear about this.'

'He was a great man in the county, a great land owner and benefactor. Many will want to come and pay their respects. Don't you think you could see your way to having a memorial service later on? He deserves one.'

'The general was explicit about it. He said all his contemporaries were dead and no one would come. I argued with him, at the time, but he wouldn't change his mind.'

'Oh well, he was always a difficult fellow with a mind of his own.'

I had a similar conversation with the High Sheriff, for the general had been High Sheriff before he had been a deputy lieutenant, and managed to quieten him. The bishop did not telephone.

The next day I saw the vicar, fixed a date three weeks ahead for the funeral, talked to the undertaker, rang the regimental secretary and the secretary of Brooks's, put a notice in *The Times* and *The Daily Telegraph*, and awaited the day.

The church was full. The service was simple. The Lord Lieutenant gave an address, as did General Jimmy. The vicar spoke movingly. Two buglers from the new regiment sounded the Last Post and Reveille. We crowded into the graveyard and watched the burial. I looked round. Those there were mainly from the county. There were a quite a few from the regiment. General George had retired in the 1930s, and there could be few alive who would have served with him in one of the battalions. He was never colonel of the regiment. He had attended regimental dinners and luncheons for a time, but none recently. Those he knew were mainly commissioned before the Second World War. It will be interesting, I thought, to see who does come. As I had been finding my feet and making my way in my new life in advertising, I had not always been able to attend regimental luncheons, dinners, and re-unions, so I had some catching up to do. We walked to Sherborne Court, where a great party had been arranged.

'You fixed that beautifully, darling Miles,' said Sonia, looking magnificent in black, which she wore much of the time since Ivan had died. 'I always think simple is best.'

'That's what he wanted.'

'I adored him. He had such a sad life, first darling Evelyn, his wife, dying so young, then darling Kitty.'

'He never showed it.'

'No, he was a real soldier.'

'Yes,' said Guy Surtees, 'he certainly was.'

'He was indeed, Colonel,' said Sonia. 'Or is it general? Oh dear, I can't keep up with all your promotions.'

'Brigadier, Lady Cathay, and I've left the army.'

'So, you knew George Fisher?'

'I never served with him, but he encouraged us young officers before the war, would invite us for the shooting, and he helped me ride in the Grand Military.'

'Oh, how exciting. Do you still ride?'

'No, but I go racing a lot. I saw you at Ascot, but not close enough to say hello.'

'Oh Guy, may I call you Guy? Do call me Sonia. We must go racing together.'

Sonia, I thought, was about to make another conquest and I left them, as I'd spotted Rex Topham.

'Good morning, General Rex,' I said.

'Ah, Miles. That was a fine funeral. He was a great man. He should have gone further. I remember him from when I was first commissioned. He was a general, of course, but he had a word for all us subalterns. Now, we miss you. I hear you've been made a director of your firm, and so I should expect. American, isn't it?'

'Yes, and I've been fortunate,' I said.

'Everyone needs a little luck. Look at me, a major general

commanding one of the few divisions we have left. They must be mad.'

'Oh no, General. I remember you in Kenya and Aden.'

'Yes, we had fun there, didn't we? I hope you're happy with the decision you made, Miles?'

'It was the right decision, though I do miss it all occasionally.'

I remembered how, after I had left the army, I had started by sharing a tiny office with four others in the advertising agency I had joined, learning the grammar and the trade. Occasionally, I would sit up and wonder what on earth I had done. I would then re-think the logic of my decision. I missed the outdoor military life, and the camaraderie, but I knew I had had the best of it and it had been time to move on.

Rex was now talking to General Jimmy, and I found myself with Percy Smythe and Francis Bowerman.

'I didn't know you knew General George,' I said. 'How good to see you here.'

'We met him at regimental functions after the war,' said Francis. 'We're both at the War Office now, and discussed it, and thought it would be a good thing to come.'

They were both colonels, jostling for position, and clearly treated it as a regimental occasion at which they should be seen.

'I could never understand why you left the army,' said Francis. 'You were on the fast track. Why, now you would be commanding one of the battalions.'

'Maybe,' I said, 'but which regiment?'

'Well, admittedly, the Prince Regent's had to go, like all the rest in the last Defence Review. You know. We have a smaller army now, but you could be commanding one of the battalions of the new regiment, The Light Infantry.'

'Do you remember when we were on the troopship in the Red Sea, after Rex had told us about the Defence Review, and we were at dinner discussing it? Well, I suddenly woke up to what was happening. The empire was going. The army was getting smaller. It was a new world. I had become a soldier to follow my father. Suddenly, I realised the world he had lived in had gone. Everything had changed. Did I want to be a general, if that were possible, in this new army? I felt I had been brought up and trained for another world.'

'That's going a bit far,' said Francis.

'No, I can see Miles's point,' said Percy. 'Things have changed, and still are.'

'You're all looking very serious,' said Tom Warburton who joined us, looking remarkably agile and fit. You wouldn't know he had lost an arm in Korea, for his prosthetic arm was so good. Tom had retired after commanding the depot, and had become the regimental secretary. He knew everything and everyone. He had been commissioned before the war, had known General George well, and General George had liked him.

'I see Guy is chatting up Sonia,' he said. 'You'd better watch out, Miles, or you'll have Guy for a new father-in-law.'

'I couldn't be happier. Guy Surtees is a lovely man, and the best colonel we had. He'd have made a superb general. What happened?'

'Probably he wasn't enthusiastic enough, didn't show he was eager for it, and the openings became fewer,' said Tom. 'The difference between Guy and Rex is that Rex makes things happen, and Guy allowed people to make things happen.'

'After Aden,' said Percy, 'Why didn't Rex get a bar to his DSO?'

'Didn't you hear about that?' said Tom, 'He told the Governor how to deal with the Yemeni. And he told the Air Vice-Marshal a little too openly what a shambles his headquarters was. What did they call it?'

'The Kremlin,' I said.

'Yes, the Kremlin. Of course he should have got a bar to his DSO. He was too outspoken.'

'Rather like General George in the twenties?' I said.

'Not quite,' said Tom. 'General George was saying things to the high command, who didn't want to hear. He wanted to start modernising the army. The Army Council, strapped for money and with their heads in the sand, didn't see the need, because the immediate task was policing the Empire. It was political, too: the ten year rule. You know, the policy that there would be no war in Europe for the next ten years. In Aden, the governor and the air vice-marshal were doing their best, with their hands tied behind their backs. Look at Aden now.'

'Gone,' I said, 'as Rex predicted. And Kenya. Who would have thought that within five years of the battalion leaving the colony it would be given independence under Jomo Kenyatta?'

'Maybe we got Kenyatta wrong,' said Percy. 'The Mau Mau used him as their titular head but now we can see that he wasn't their leader, from the way he ignores them and the actions he's taken. What a statesman he's become.'

'Do you think,' I said, 'we did much to help defeat the Mau Mau?'

'The presence of the British army was vital, but it was the loyal Kikuyu and the pseudo gangs that won the day,' said Percy.

'And didn't independence become inevitable,' I said, 'after the Gold Coast and Tanganyika were given theirs?'

'Probably,' said Tom. 'It started with the nationalists and dissidents seeing through the white man myth during the war. The Japanese conquests in the Far East and the loss of India encouraged them. Once de-colonisation started it did happen with rather a rush.'

'No, it started with the First World War when Europe committed suicide,' said Percy.

'Maybe,' said Tom, 'then Hitler wounded the empire mortally.'

'Maybe it would have happened anyway,' said Francis. 'Colonialism is out of date in the West. I think we could have done more to prepare the colonies for independence.'

'Suez didn't help,' said Percy.

'The Americans didn't help,' said Tom. 'They dislike the idea of empire. They may be our friends, we may have a trans Atlantic pact with them, a special relationship, we may stand together in the face of communism, but they undermine the Empire wherever they can.'

'Do you realise that they've built a commercial empire round the world?' I said.

'Yes,' said Tom, 'it's their world now. It's taken us a long time to realise that.'

'I suppose we do,' said Francis, 'but don't you think our future lies in Europe, in the European Economic Community?'

'Yes,' said Percy. 'Surely our future trading relationships lie increasingly in Europe? The loss of Empire means we'll have to take a greater role in Europe.'

'Not while de Gaulle is alive,' said Tom.

We all laughed.

'Communism is the real threat,' said Tom.

'Do you think,' I said, 'there'll be a nuclear war?'

'It's possible,' said Tom.

'Very possible, I'd say,' said Francis. 'If the Russians attacked in Europe I don't see how we could hold them without recourse to nuclear weapons.'

'That's really gloomy,' said Tom.

'So, Miles,' said Francis, 'how are you doing in the rat race?'

'Rat race?' I said.

'Yes, isn't it all ridiculously competitive in advertising?'

'My company is growing. Every year we employ more people and our billings — sales to you — grow. I work in an expanding world. You're in a shrinking world, Francis. You're in the rat race.'

Someone touched me on the shoulder. I turned. It was George Bulman. He was a brigadier now.

'Miles, I knew I'd find you. What a splendid funeral you've arranged for the dear old general. I almost feel his presence, though I knew him only a little.'

'He was a wonderful man, and he was wonderful to me.'

'I never asked you what he thought of your leaving the army?'

'He approved. In fact, it was he who first gave me the idea.'

'That surprises me.'

'He put it all in perspective for me, what was going on in the world. Remember, he was a Victorian and won his first DSO in the Boer War, at the turn of the century. In the First War he was a major general. He was at Versailles. He watched the Second War from the side lines. He'd seen the fall of empire and the rise of the United States. He once told me, 'if you can't beat 'em, join 'em'. I always remembered that and, after Aden, when Rex had told us that the army was contracting, I decided I had probably seen the best of it and it was time I found a new world. And I didn't want to face the chance of another D.P.Brown.'

'That wound I got in Korea was fortunate in one way. Because of it, I missed Germany and the ogre D.P.Brown.'

'No, you wouldn't have enjoyed Germany much. In fact, it was a wonderful place to be but he had it in for most of the senior officers and anyone with any real ability. We subalterns got off quite lightly, except for poor Jasper.'

'That was a tragedy, Jasper being killed in Kenya. He was the most impressive of the young officers.'

'Do you think he could have pushed Parker Brown?'

'Not in a month of Sundays. Parker Brown jumped.'

'Burgo doesn't think so. He still says Jasper pushed him.'

'Still the same old Burgo. What's he doing now? I've lost track of him.'

'Don't you remember, he went to the Parachute Regiment? Then he moved on to the SAS, and now commands the Jungle Warfare School in Malaysia. He's on leave at the moment and he's here somewhere.'

'Did he transfer to the paras?'

'No. He likes to have a foot in both camps, and plays the two regiments off against each other.'

'Well, he never changes his spots. Talking of the paras, whatever became of Trench Foot?'

'When he came out of prison he disappeared off the face of the earth. Wise of him, I'd say. I think he changed his spots and went abroad. No one has ever seen him in England, as far as I know.'

'And Julia?'

'She divorced him. She's still being accommodating to Adam, so he tells me. She's become a rather good journalist.'

'Do you ever see anything of Adam? I thought his first book, about an imaginary regiment in Kenya, was very readable.'

'Yes, it was a best seller for a week. I do see him, but not as much as I did now his publisher has banned him from living in London. He's become a remittance man on twenty pounds a week, tucked away in Sandwich where he writes a book a year.'

'He must be making money.'

'Yes, and he spends it. He's surprisingly generous when he has it.'

Tom Warburton passed by.

'I don't see Ben Wildbore and Juno here,' he said.

'No,' I said, 'he wanted to come, but he couldn't get away at the last moment. You know he manages a firm of stockbrokers in the city and they find him indispensable. They particularly like his wizardry arranging their lunches.'

'It's wonderful,' said Tom, ' how you all seem to fall on your feet when you leave the army. Look at Algy Stanhope and Olivia over there, talking to Dermot Boyle. Algy, whom D.P. Brown did his best to ruin, is now a captain of industry. And Dermot, another D.P. Brown did his best to do down, has just told me that he's doubled the acreage that his father handed over to him. Both DSOs, and two of the most distinguished officers of their generations.'

'Not everyone does so well, but they were both going to do something with their lives,' I said. 'Algy brushed off the fracas with Parker Brown and forgot about it. Not so Dermot. His undoing still rankles. I was talking to Olivia, once, and she told me that Algy had never got over the time commanding the battalion at Anzio when he was 28. It was such an intense and consuming experience for him that nothing has matched it, and he's been bored ever since.'

Tom moved on and Cecily, his wife, took his place.

'What have you two been gossiping about,' she said, 'old times, I expect. Oh, Miles, we'd love to see more of you and Phyllida and the children.'

'We're all thriving. You must talk to Phyllida.'

'I have, and she's lovelier than ever. You are a lucky man.'

'I know I am.'

'She's been telling me how wonderful you have been to General George.'

'He loved Phyllida, took to her immediately. In fact, he told me to hurry up and marry her before someone else snapped her up. In the last year, when he began to get confused, he started to call her Kitty.'

'What did she do?'

'She played along with it. She was very good to him. I think, in the end, he thought our children were his grandchildren.'

'That must have been awkward?'

'Not at all. Sonia thought it hilarious.'

'But Phyllida?'

'Phyllida is the most equable person. She took it in her stride just as long as I didn't call her Kitty.'

'Understandable. Why, there's Burgo!'

A very bronzed Burgo joined us.

'Cecily, you're looking as lovely as ever,' he said.

'And you look as fit as ever,' said Cecily.

'I've been talking to Sonia Cathay, and she looks as lovely as ever, too. How do you do it?'

'Hard work and lots of lovers. Are you married yet, Burgo?'

'No time for marriage, Cecily. I'm a real professional soldier, unlike Miles the renegade.'

'I expect you two have a lot to talk about and I want to catch up with Guy Surtees.'

'Does Olivia have lots of lovers?' said Burgo.

'She said that to tease.'

'I think Sonia might.'

'Quite possibly.'

'Well, you organised the service rather well. Not lost your touch.'

'General George organised it all years ago, when he made me his executor and handed the house over to the National Trust. All I've had to do is carry out his wishes.'

'I'm enjoying being in England. This is my second funeral. I went to help bury Tom Body.'

'I didn't realise he had died.'

'Once retired, he drank himself to death.'

'He was a lovely man.'

'Well, yes. How many times had he been busted? Twice, at least, from Serjeant to Private. Married three times, as the wives couldn't take the drinking.'

'But what a soldier. Do you remember the time in Korea when he found an abandoned Sherman tank, got it to go, and then Guy Surtees made him put it back where he found it? The expletives were remarkable, even for Tom. Have you seen anything of the Whettingsteels?'

'Big Steel was there at Tom's funeral. He's retired now. You'll remember that Little Steel came to the paras with me and then the SAS. He's done very well, an officer now.'

'What happened to Pete Quartermain?'

'He's dead, too.'

'I am out of touch. Rather young, wasn't he?'

'Those soldiers had tough lives, especially when they were young, much tougher than us. And, believe it or not, they drank more than us. While we drank a fair amount all the time, they would go on benders. Pete left his money — quite a bundle, too — to the regimental charity. Tom Warburton is the one to ask about that. Now, how's my godson?'

'Young George is doing well. He goes to prep school in September. He very much enjoyed the stamps you sent him from Malaysia. He's building a Commonwealth collection. Is all going well for you there?'

'All Sir Garnet.'

'I haven't heard that for years. I don't suppose anyone uses it any longer. Sad to think how it's all changed. Do you still doubt D. P. Brown threw himself off the ship?'

'Who knows for sure? Jasper was the chief suspect. It's a pity you didn't get a dying confession from him.'

'Can't you give him the benefit of the doubt and let him rest in peace?'

'I agree, D. P. Brown *probably* threw himself off the ship, but there's *still* an inkling of doubt.'

'You haven't changed much, Burgo.'

'You have, Miles. Tell me. Do you regret the army?'

'What, leaving it?' I said.

'No, I mean being in it.'

'Good heavens, no. How could you ask that? They were marvellous times. It was a wonderful education.'

EAST AFRICA, THE HORN OF AFRICA
AND THE PERSIAN GULF 1950s

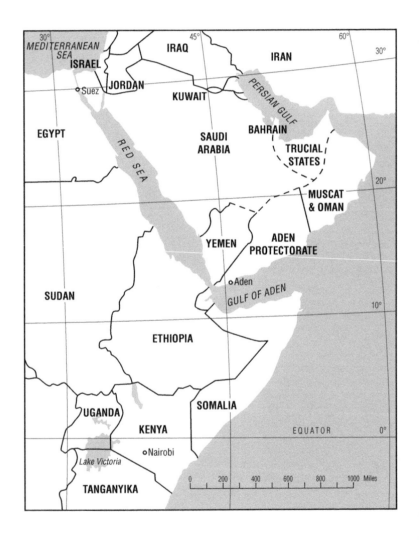

Central Kenya
1950s

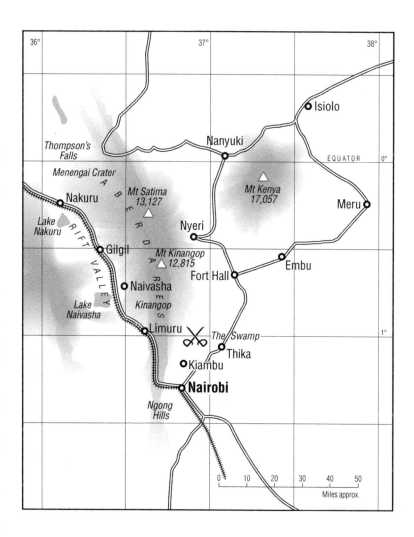

36°   37°   38°

Isiolo

Thompson's
Falls

Nanyuki

EQUATOR   0°

Menengai Crater

Nakuru

Mt Satima
13,127

Mt Kenya
17,057

Meru

Lake
Nakuru

Nyeri

RIFT

Gilgil

Mt Kinangop
12,815

Embu

VALLEY

Fort Hall

Naivasha

Lake
Naivasha

Kinangop

1°

Limuru

The Swamp

Thika

Kiambu

Nairobi

Ngong
Hills

0   10   20   30   40   50

Miles approx.

ADEN PROTECTORATE AND YEMEN
1958

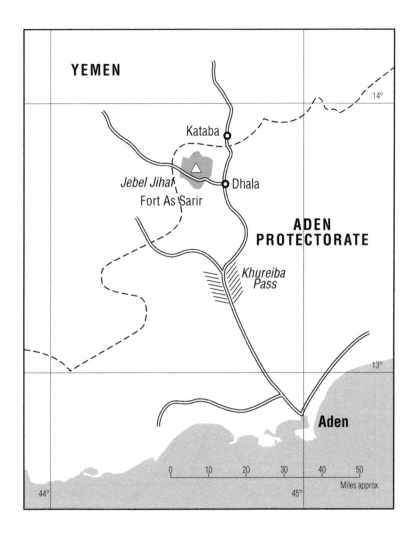

Dhala, Jebel Jihaf
and Yemen Border

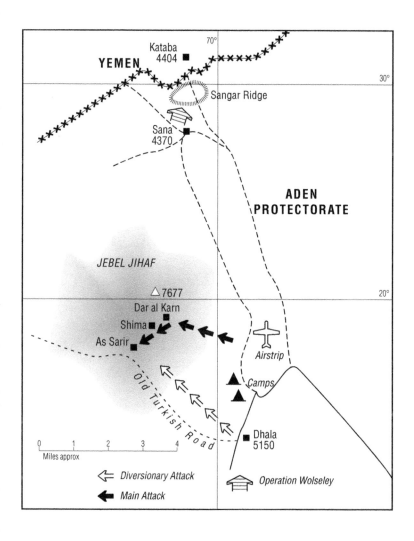

Main Characters

**Characters who appeared in *On Fire* are marked (OF)
and those in *Silken Dalliance* (SD)**

Bill Ambrose	settler
Colonel Banon	Head of Police Bahrain, formerly PRLI
Colonel Battiscombe	Chief Justice Bahrain, formerly PRLI
Bill Bates	Corporal, Commanding Officer's Driver.
Kitty Belcher	daughter of General Fisher, god daughter of Sonia Cathay, unofficially engaged to Miles Player in Hong Kong, married to Horace Belcher (OF) and died from injuries in car accident. (SD)
Nancy Bergman	(Ingrid) widow and settler.
Michael Bishop	settler and politician
Mark Black	Police Officer.
Phyllida Blessington	only child of the Cathays (OF, SD)
Tom Body	Colour Serjeant. MM. Officers' Mess Serjeant. (OF) (SD)
Francis Bowerman	Captain, Adjutant (SD)
Mr and Mrs Bradley	long time retainers of General Fisher (OF, SD)
Dennis Parker Brown	Lieutenant Colonel OBE. Former Commanding Officer (SD)
James Browne	(General Jimmy) Lieutenant General KCB, KBE, DSO. Vice Chief of the General Staff (VCIGS). Colonel of the regiment.

George Bulman	Major MC. Wounded in Korea (OF). Second in Command.
Ivan Cathay	Viscount, formerly Ivan Blessington GCMG,GBE. Past governor of Hong Kong. Now active on fringes of government. (OF, SD)
Sonia Cathay	Viscountess, wife of Ivan, mother of Phyllida, godmother of Kitty Belcher (nee Fisher), cousin of Miles Player (OF, SD)
Charlie Chance	NS 2nd Lieut (SD).
Chang	Driver and factotum to the Cathays
Sam Cheke	Corporal, Officers' Mess Barman (SD)
Corporal Chisholm	Officers' Mess Corporal.
Edward Dering	NS 2nd Lieutenant
Doughty	cab driver. Driver to Miles Player in Korea
Jim Fairford	District Officer
Reggie Ferndale	Serjeant Kenya Regiment
George Fisher	Baronet, Major General CB, CMG, DSO. Father of Kitty Belcher. Served in regiment in Boer War and Great War. Owner of Sherborne Court (OF,SD)
Adam Hare	Lieutenant, MMG Platoon (SD)
Elizabeth Hay-Smith	wife of Tony
Mary Hay-Smith	daughter, works at Government House
Tony Hay-Smith	settler and retired officer
Christopher Hetherington	settler
Tony Henderson	Major DSO. Commands Y Company
Burgo Howard	Captain MC. In Korea (OF) and Germany (SD)
Warahiu Itote	(General China) Mau Mau general

Dedan Kimathi	Mau Mau general
'Teapot' Kettle	Orderly Room Quartermaster Serjeant (ORQMS)
Jasper Knox	Lieutenant. Scion of a regimental family. (SD)
Verity Knox	mother of Jasper
Dermot Lisle	Captain DSO MC. Fought in WW2 Commanded a company in Korea (OF). Diddled by DP Brown (SD) Resigned. Farmer
Anna Littlejohn	Wife of Fred
Fred Littlejohn	Settler. Came to Kenya in 1930s.
Stanley Mathenge	Mau Mau general
Captain Mellor	Field Intelligence Officer (FIO)
Stan Norman	Corporal. Orderly Room.
Tom Nugent	Lieutenant Colonel DSO MC. Military Attache (MA) to CIGS
Peter Petitpierre	Lieutenant at regimental depot
Mrs Pooley	Chatelaine to Ben Wildbore at Harrington Gardens
Alex Poppleton	Lieutenant at regimental depot
Peter Quartermain	Captain. Quartermaster. In Korea (OF)
Algy Stanhope	Lieut Colonel DSO MC commanded battalion in WW2 Age 28. 2IC in Germany (SD) where diddled by DP Brown. Retired. Captain of industry.
Olivia Stanhope	Algy's wife (SD)
Percy Smythe	Major MBE. Commands W Company. Adjutant in Korea (OF)
Becky Summerson	daughter of settler, air hostess
Guy Surtees	Brigadier, DSO, OBE. Commanding Officer in Korea (OF) and Germany (SD)
Tanganyika	Mau Mau general

Rex Topham	DSO. Lieutenant Colonel. Company commander in Korea (OF). Now commanding officer.
Jack Trench	Major. Company commander in Korea (OF) and Germany (SD)
Julia Trench	wife of Jack
Jim Tudor	Private. Orderly Room.
Harry Unton	NS 2nd Lieutenant
David Vane	Captain, adjutant regimental depot
Jeremy Veny	NS 2nd Lieutenant
Tom Warburton	Major, commandant regimental depot. Lost arm in Korea. (OF).
Cecily Warburton	wife of Tom
Jeremy Watts	District Commisioner
Juno White	daughter of senior colonial official
Ben Wildbore	Major, company commander. President Mess Committee (PMC) In Korea (OF) and Germany (SD)
'Big Steel' Whettingsteel	Serjeant Major S company. In Korea (OF) and Germany (SD)
'Little Steel' Whettingsteel	Serjeant MG platoon. In Korea (OF) and Germany (SD)